The Hidden Mirror of La Porete

The Hidden Mirror of La Porete

Susan Shooter

hb

Hurlestone Books

HURLESTONE BOOKS

A CIP catalogue record for this book is available from the British Library
ISBN-978-1-0684339-0-0 (paperback)   978-1-0684339-1-7 (e-book)

Cover design by Ken Dawson www.ccoverdesigns.co.uk
Hurlestone Books Logo by Kayleigh Shooter www.kdscalligraphy.co.uk

DEDICATION

For the women who taught me about Marguerite

CONTENTS

PART ONE   Porete

PART TWO   Béguine Clergesse

PART 3   The Phoenix Who Is Alone

For most of history, Anonymous was a woman.
Virginia Woolf.

PART ONE

Porete

Perfect freeness possesses no why.

The Mirror of Simple Souls, Chapter 134.

Abbaye Saint-Jean

Eve of the Virgin's Nativity 1304

I AM GLAD that when they lead me out into the Grande Place tomorrow, Jacquot won't be there.

Along the deserted banks of the Ointiel, where the elder fronds have turned the colour of rubies, my brother will search for me. At the mill he'll find no one at home but the goats. And when he sees the smoke rising dark above the city spires, he'll undoubtedly think the new provost has lit the great bonfire too hastily.

'For God's sake, Margi,' he'll say next time we meet, 'why couldn't you keep your mouth shut?'

Oh my dearest Jacquot. Why are you churchmen so slow to grasp it? Love has no discretion.

1

Forêt de Mormal, 1291

THE STAG raised his head. His obsidian eye stared back at me and my heart thundered. It seemed I still had the desire to live.

Drifting deep into the greenwood, where the rivers rise like arteries to feed the land that nurtured me, the Ointiel, the Aunelle, the Écaillon, nothing had stirred me. Not the finches chit-chatting in the canopy, not the last shock of bluebells cushioning my feet, nor the heavy scents of fungus and bark. Since the night the count's men bombarded Anzin, not even the reek of decay in the infirmary nor the rattling jaw of death come to gobble up the casualties of war had been able to penetrate me.

Except, if I am to be truthful with myself, on the day the messenger arrived in Rue del Saulch.

I was in my old chamber packing my coffer for the nunnery and gazing out of the window, seeing but not seeing the hens as they flapped irritably in the courtyard dust, hearing but not hearing the bumble bee as she fussed around the eglantine which, every June, sends an explosion of pink across the southern façade. An almighty squawk broke out. But it wasn't the dark stallion kicking up a shower of stones that roused me. It was the horseman's brown mantle trailing over the horse's rump, or rather the emblem emblazoned upon it. I let my casket drop into the coffer and crammed my unruly hair under a coif.

Caught mid-snooze on the kitchen settle, wimple skewwhiff, Ysabeau was making a valiant attempt to serve the sergeant ale without slopping any on the table. The grime of many highways was chased into the man's skin and beard but the instant he saw me, he leapt up from the bench and fell on one knee.

'Lady Marguerite, I am Berenger. For a long time squire to Sir Alixandre de Seraing.' His fingers searched beneath the red cross pattée at his chest. 'Before he departed for Acre, I made him a promise. I vowed I would place this in no other hands but yours.'

I knew instantly what had befallen Alixandre; it was from him I'd learnt that a Templar's promise to a dying man is sacred.

'So the rumours are true?' Jacquot's voice came from the top of the hall steps behind me. 'The port has fallen?'

'Three hundred brothers slain.'

'Then our last stronghold is gone.'

As Brother Berenger handed me the fold of vellum, stained red on one side, I wasn't thinking about the Holy Land. I was thinking how he held the parchment on his palms as though it were the finger bone of a saint. Alixandre had held it in the exact same manner when I gave it to him at Saint-Séverin. Of a sudden I felt as if I were high up in the smutty rafters looking down on some other woman standing by the kitchen hearth, watching her, not myself, take the note and slip it into the belt of her grey beguine robe. I knew, without doubt, she didn't want to learn what dead remnant of love remained inside the missive.

Back in my chamber, I placed the letter in my writing casket alongside Michel's coverlet. The gold stitching shimmered in the sunlight and pain like white fire seared through me, opening a shaft of clarity in my mind. I knew where I needed to be and it wasn't enclosed with a gaggle of chanting nuns.

I waited for nightfall and crept down to the stables.

Burying my face in Miéla's honey-coloured coat, in her biscuitty smell, my nerves calmed. Her first job as a filly had been to bear me away on a journey into the unknown and that had turned out better than expected, hadn't it?

'I'll deal with Master Jacques.' The voice made me jump. Ysabeau had always taken my brother's part and yet here she was, come to help me load supplies. 'Ever were you wilful. But find a company to travel with. The Virgin save us, Count Jan ain't done with his war yet.'

I suppose Jacquot was trying his best. The Abbess of Fontenelle being a good customer of his and fearful for my state of mind, he'd arranged for me to recuperate in her cloisters. But I'd come instead to Mormal and when I caught sight of the regal beast grazing in the clearing, his antlers branching out under a crown of foliage, for one delicious moment the fog lifted from my soul.

THE HIDDEN MIRROR OF LA PORETE

Quieting Miéla, who had humbly accepted her role as sumpter horse, I crept, quietly I thought, to the edge of the greensward. In one fluid movement the buck curled into the air and bounded away, leaving behind a void in the columbines. Despair returned to press down on me like a tombstone and snuff out the last vestige of my desire.

I FIRST DISCOVERED the hermitage by the tranquil pool on my return journey from Lady Marie's wedding and, as I hoped, it had remained unoccupied by wise woman or sage. Allowing my old palfrey to reacquaint herself with the rich grasses and sweet dandelions, I collected bracken for my mattress and swept the earthen floor of the hut. My writing casket looked forlorn at the centre of the rickety table; I stroked the phoenix carved into the ivory lid, her beak now smooth where it was once so sharp, and wandered off to find a wedge-shaped stone.

In the Forêt de Mormal the days merged into one another. My quills became the scattered tail feathers without which a bird will struggle to fly. Only when I stalked the clearing did a sting pass through me like the hunter's lust for his next quarry. I desperately wanted my heart to race as it had on the first day but the stag refused to show himself.

At night phantoms slipped into my dreams. Hellish visions like I'd not suffered since my maidenhood. A knight with tarnished breastplate knelt at my feet. I berated myself, hadn't Alixandre loved the Lord Our God more than I ever could?

A ghostly child lay by my side and touched his cold finger to my cheek. Had I loved Michel more than I should have?

When a charred skeleton trailing blood red hair rose from the ashes of my little corner hearth, my bones shivered. 'Why didn't I go to the nuns?' I wailed and begged of the One who rules Time to return me to the moment before the messenger arrived.

ON THE FIRST WINTRY MORN at the hermitage, I arranged dry wood on the embers and sat by my rickety table with my casket. In the light of the strengthening flames the ivory phoenix appeared to flap her wings and I heard her say, 'It's time.'

The stained little wallet of vellum unfolded in my fingers. On the verso was a hastily scrawled message.

Many miles I journeyed across the Middle Sea, only to prove Sir Hugh right. They say Christ still walks the Holy Land. It is but a chimera. Ever is He sold for a piece of silver or a hectare of land. The Kingdom of Heaven is nowhere to be found in these cities full of hypocrisy and greed.

I looked to the skies above Jerusalem and beheld no angels. All I see now is your trusting face. Forgive me, my Marguerite. I, like Judas, have betrayed love.

Alixandre, Nicosia, Feast of St Michael, AD 1290.

My intention, when I stepped out into the ravening air, was to draw water for my chores. I leaned over the pool. The stripped beech and oaks mocked at me, their reflection in the icy water evoking the colonnades of Saint-Séverin where I'd first succumbed to love and its consequences. As I turned away with my full pot, I caught sight of my face in the brutal mirror and had to look deeper.

It seemed as though I had gone back many years and stood on the edge of the pit; a tiny parcel was being lowered, one white slash of silk against the velvet black of Flemish soil and in my vision I put out a hand, I put out a foot. How willingly I would have stepped into the pit back then, for my heart's only desire was to be with my boy, to share his cradle of earth. But it was not to be. Because her gentle hands had steadied me. But now, oh now, those loving hands were gone.

Beside the hermitage on a December morning in the Forêt de Mormal, when I looked into the waters that fed the tangled roots of the forest floor, when the freezing ripples nudged at my naked toes, my fingers let go of the pitcher. One step. And another. Ice daggers pierced my ankles until the sharp points pushed through to the numbness at my heart, reminding me, life remained quick within me. But I, Marguerite, wanted to escape life. Not that it was my intention to harm myself. I simply wanted Grief and her long, drawn-out suffocation, to get on with it.

Calmed by the chill pressing against my flesh, I turned deftly onto my back. The last I would feel of this world would be the roots of my hair prickling, the last I would see, the full setting moon trapped on the inside of my eyelids. But my breathing accelerated. Life was determined not to surrender me. So I pushed down hard. The pool drew her lacy mantle over my brow, my nostrils, and my lips. Her icicle fingers opened me up and her waters gushed in.

A voice rose from the depths. A woman's voice, I swear.

Up through the surface of the mirror pool I rose, my feet searching for a foothold, the stones carving their enduring shapes into my soles. The green weeds entwined in my hair dragged on me but my hands flung out, grabbing at the sky like a newborn. Waves of light. Surges of joy. Whether it was the cold or whether it was the laughter shaking me, I didn't know. I still do not know. Tearing off my sopping dress, I pressed myself against the rough skin of the ancient black elder, thinking myself crazed as I shook and shook and shook till I wept. No phantoms attended my bedside that night.

THE ONE, who had seemed such a long way off, came closer to me than the breadth of a baby's hair.

'What do you want?' I queried of the Far-Near One.

The darkness smiled at me.

'Who are You?'

The One replied, 'I am.'

'Where are You?'

'I am in all places.'

'You are at the bottom of the freezing pool?'

'I am.'

'You are at the heart of the burning fire?'

'I am.'

'Then, who am I?'

'You are love.'

This response from the Far-Near One astonished me. 'I am love? How can that be?'

'I am Love. And now you and I are one, so you, also, are love.'

'I lack understanding…'

'I am all Understanding.'

'I am all wretchedness.'

'I am all Goodness. And dearest Soul, all I have is yours. Whatever you want of me, I will give it.' And the darkness closed its mouth.

DAYLIGHT beamed through the crack in the shutters. The wings of the ivory phoenix stood out like honed diamonds and as I stroked her beak, I heard the One say, 'It's time.'

On the table an unblemished parchment waited for me to unfold a new universe on her skin but this new universe seemed too vast to contain in ink. I didn't know where to find the words.

How long did I sit in my ignorance?

Until Love made Her presence known and overwhelmed me with Her Peace. I dipped in the inkwell.

I have no comfort, no hope, save in the Goodness of God.

Eros' arrows had left behind more than one splinter to fester in my eye and Love had dissolved them all. Now I saw myself so clearly. Yes, I'd failed to hold onto all my loves, but now I'd been shown. We cannot hold onto love. Because it is Love Who holds onto us. Like a true Mother, She pursues us even into the Hells of our own choosing, so committed is She to our freeness.

Then I saw our Holy Mother Church, her laws and penances keeping us trapped in the nursery. Rather than nurture our spirits, she suckles us on shame. And what clever merchantry! Indulgences and pardons hawked as remedies for our pains. She knows there will always be profit to earn from broken souls, for Grief resides in every human heart.

Love, God's love, brokers no bargains. Love is gratis.

MANY MOONS after my encounter with the Far-Near One, I was on my way to market in the town of Maroilles. I caught sight of the stag nuzzling the snow. He raised his head. He observed me and I observed him. Then he lowered his antlers and continued to feed on the green turf hidden beneath winter's cloak until his hunger was satisfied. I continued on my way through the forest, my heart full, and I knew it would soon be time to return home.

2

Valenciennes, 1296

NO MATTER the hour I arrived, my brother was undoubtedly going to gripe, 'For God's sake, Margi. Do you think of no one but yourself?' and immediately scoop me up in his arms and swing me round. So when the spires of Valenciennes poked up above the southern orchards like the crown of a pagan god, I took the longer, western fork in the road. I wanted to catch a glimpse of the miller's boy, running, jumping, bursting with life.

Miéla stooped her honey-coloured neck to chase windfalls beneath the patchwork of leaves. I chivvied my old girl on. The creaking and splashing of the great waterwheels of Anzin were calling me.

A rabbit flashed his scut and vanished into the horde of vicious nettles which had overrun the bank of the Escaut and my hands tightened on the reins. A scorched skeleton held up by a single timber, the mill cottage had not been rebuilt. Veins of bindweed twisted through the bones as if they would strangle the last breath out of Carmelle's home. Yet in the shadow of Château-le-Comte on the opposite bank of the river, the count's watermills continued to grind away. I turned eastward.

On the cobbles, Miéla's hooves rang out too merry a tune for the heavy silence in the Grande Place of Valenciennes. Not a bleat nor a squawk came from the livestock pens. At one of the four stalls huddled around the belfry a reed-thin maid stood in a begging stance.

'That's the price,' the trader spat out with his gob of willow, 'take it or leave it.' She left it.

Out beyond Porte Cardon and into Rue del Saulch, we rode past the merchants' houses with their tiled roofs and walls of quarry stone. Each of their fine gatehouses was locked and barred and by the time I reached the last willow tree, I felt as if I would arrive home only to discover a stranger asleep in my own bed.

The peephole in the wicket snapped open. An eyeball glared out. The peephole snapped shut. A door creaked. One pincer-like hand shot out of the gap and gripped my wrist. The ghostly figure pulling me through into the courtyard resembled my brother but this man's hair swung like the tail of a wild horse down his back; arcs of dirt were embedded beneath the fingernails of the hand dragging me across the layers of leaf mould to the porch. 'Jacquot?' I kept saying. 'Jacquot?'

Once through the main doors and into the screens passage, the doppelganger stood with his back to the secured bars, arms tightly folded across his chest. It had been fanciful to expect, at our age, he would swing me round like he used to. But no word of welcome? Undoubtedly he hadn't forgiven me for snubbing one of his best customers.

Reaching my arms as far around him as I could, I burrowed my cheek against his ribs and got a full nose of his baggy surcoat. How, I wondered, could it have escaped Ysabeau's laundry regime for months? Although I still wore my simple grey with a plain linen coif, I was, for once, the better turned out. Jacquot was reluctant to surrender but eventually his body subsided like a candle placed too close to the hearth and it was a relief when he eventually pushed me away by the shoulders.

'God's blood, Margi, you look twenty years younger.'

'I feel twenty years younger.' I didn't say he looked twenty years older, merely touched his unshaven cheek and asked, 'Are you well?'

'Well? I suppose I am. And you've not lost your talent for arriving in time to sup.' A spark of the old Jacquot, but instead of leading me into the hall, he strode off down the steps to the kitchen, straight to the stew pot, gave it a stir and sniffed the ladle.

'Where's Jehan?' I asked.

'I sent him and Rogier home. Things took a turn for the worst after you left.' I'd anticipated the reproach I heard in his voice. But I caught another emotion which fitted my brother as poorly as his surcoat. Bitterness, I thought. As he cut hunks from a dark loaf and doled out the grey liquid into two bowls, he kept his back turned to me.

'Where's Ysabeau?' I dropped my pack on her settle. Listening for the woman who had fussed over us since we were infants, I expected to hear her quick footsteps above our heads in the solar, or crossing the floorboards of the gallery; or her broom sweeping round the firepit in the centre of the hall. 'Isn't Ysabeau joining us?'

'Ysabeau?' He sat opposite me at table, staring into the bland steam rising from his gruel. 'Ysabeau is no longer with us.'

'Don't be ridiculous. After all these years?' A pang of guilt. Doubtless they'd quarrelled about her disloyalty over my departure. But dismissing Ysabeau would have been to lose his right arm.

'Ysabeau is no longer…*with* us.'

I listened again to the mansion echoing with her silent presence. She'd seen over sixty summers, yet the news took its time to sink its teeth into my flesh. Napery had been overlooked. So as Ysabeau taught me on the day my five-year-old fingers got caught in the apple press, I mopped my eyes with my skirts.

'Blue and white streamers on the Virgin's Day,' I sobbed, 'covering the whole yard.'

'She said it was for the Queen of Heaven.' Jacquot's face screwed up behind his fist. 'But it was all for my sake.'

'What happened to her?'

'Nasty fall. In the workshop. Never came right again. I wanted to send for you, but nobody knew where you were.'

I thought of how Ysabeau's moon face always beamed when she boasted of her 'gentle Master Jacques' and laid my hand across his skinned knuckles. 'She adored you,' I said, and would have added she was the closest he came to having a mother if he hadn't snatched up his spoon as if he were presiding over a council meeting and wanted to move on to the next item.

'Eat,' he commanded.

I felt again a sense of usurpation. During my years away from Valenciennes, darkness had crept in and made its home inside my brother. It was as if we'd swapped places.

DESPITE the November clouds now darkening beyond the casement window, the mirror of polished silver spilled a liquid sheen over the dresser; Papa had spared no expense when he furnished the bedchamber in readiness for his new bride and their expected child. Resisting the urge to check for an interloper beneath the fine Worstead counterpane, I unpacked my ivory casket, my book of legends, and Michel's coverlet. As I leafed through the sheaf of parchments I'd produced in the hermitage, my eye was caught by my old coffer sitting in the same spot as on the day I struck out for Mormal. It seemed as good a place as any to stow my writings until I knew what to do with them.

Jacquot clattered in with a bundle of logs and a live coal. Crouching beside the fireplace like a skinny frog, his knee poked through his frayed hose. *I'm the foremost mercer in Valenciennes,* he once fashioned himself, *nay, in all Hainault.* I wondered if his business had failed.

Keeping an eye on the kindling he said, 'How was your journey from…wherever it is you've been?'

I let the barb pass through me. 'Quiet. I came in by the Western road.'

He looked up. 'So you've seen Anzin?'

'I saw Anzin. And I rode through the marketplace. First day after All Souls and every awning closed. Why is food so scarce?'

'The King of France enforced a trade embargo.'

'Philippe le Bel? What has he to do with Valenciennes?'

The twigs in the hearth crackled and spat. Jacquot lay on a heavier log and fanned the flames. 'Won't take long. I chose the best wood myself. Well,' he gave me a sidelong glance, 'I have to do everything myself now.' The fresh smoke made him cough. 'Anyway, the truce—you might remember it from before you left? Didn't last five minutes but Count Jan's men were attacking anyone who tried to leave the city. So we stormed Château-le-Comte. Again. Can you believe it? Threw his army out this time.' As suddenly as his enthusiasm had flared, it fizzled out. Doubtless he was remembering the aftermath of the first attack.

'Tell me about Philippe le Bel.'

'Long story.'

'I'll try and follow,' I said with faux patience, harking back to the day he tried to instruct me in the intricacies of our civic charter. Jacquot's customary response to my boredom whenever he wanted to tell me about the terms of La Paix, or about his efforts with the other échevins to implement them, or about what happened at the latest meeting of the guildsmen, or about who was up for election as provost and so on, would be to pull a gormless face and roll his eyes back in his head. But his eyes stayed put.

Brushing dirt from his hands he sat back on his heels. 'Count Jan is a vassal of the Holy Roman Emperor…Oh. You know that?' His eyes rolled a fraction. 'So…we had no choice but to seek protection from the king. Philippe directed us to,' he snorted, '"put our trust" in the Count of Flanders as our lord.'

'Guy de Dampierre?'

'Cunning as a serpent, that French king.' The fire now roaring, Jacquot lurched over to the window seat. 'Life was back to normal. Until Lord Guy squabbled with him.' He told some tale with many twists and turns involving taxation, Edward of England, and one of Lord Guy's daughters. 'Count Jan saw his chance and straightway sent his army down here. So, the Lion of Flanders—'

'I met Lord Robert once. At Lady Marie's wedding.'

A full roll of his eyes. 'Well, the Lion chased his weaselly cousin off without breaking a sweat and, not to waste the effort he'd put into mustering his troops, he went off and sacked two towns. Philippe was livid. And now Valenciennes has become the creaking rope in their tug-o-war.'

The sky had sunk into darkness. As I reached above him to close the shutters, I wondered whether this might be the right moment to enquire about Nicholas but the gatehouse doors began to rattle like thunder.

'THE KING has sent the Provost of Paris to treat.' The voice from the hall boomed through the kitchen doorway, followed by the powerful chest of Amand de le Sauch.

Trailing in his shadow came Simon du Gardin, hardly changed from the days he, Amand, and my brother served on the échevinage. Slim, beard meticulously trimmed, garments of luxurious scarlet wool, Simon was a walking proclamation of his wares. 'The échevins turned him and his kinsman away from Porte Cambrisienne.'

'They got wind of the party,' said Amand. 'Ordered all the city gates barred. God damn them all to the bowels of Hell.'

'So,' I said, 'that's why the sentries closed Porte Cardon behind me when it was barely noon?'

Amand's leonine head swung round towards Ysabeau's settle. 'Sister Marguerite. I didn't see you there.' Momentarily the smile which, in his youth, charmed all the little birds from their nests softened his mouth. 'How delightful to meet you again.' Glancing guardedly at Jacquot, he sat at the table.

'Come into the light, Margi,' Jacquot said. 'And make yourself useful. Fetch some ale.'

Pausing for a moment on the first step down to the buttery, I moved my taper in an arc through the soggy air. Light fell on the apple press. Dear Ysabeau. On so many occasions when the Crow-man banished me into the darkness of the basement to contemplate my sins, a plate of honey cakes always miraculously appeared on the stone wheel. Raised voices in the kitchen stayed my fresh deluge of tears.

15

'Do they not want the embargo lifted?' Jacquot said. 'The poorest will starve now there's naught left in the fields to glean.'

'Lord Robert is the best captain of men,' said Simon. 'And the échevins wish to keep faith with Lord Guy because he'd be sure to let our charter stand.'

'La Paix?' Amand said. 'There'll be no peace unless we listen to Philippe le Bel's terms. Cretins. They might well have condemned us all to the drop.'

I poured the ale and we sipped. Simon and Amand winced. Ysabeau really should've schooled her precious young master in the art of brewing.

'Ssh,' someone hissed, and four bodies tensed. Jacquot lit a lamp from the wax stump on the table. Simon followed him out.

I rooted out and lit new candles. Amand, I noted, didn't appear dishevelled like Jacquot but there was a downturn to the mouth which used to laugh all the time. And oh, how he used to tease! I remembered the bright winter days in Aulnoy Woods, lying on the springy turf outside The Robber's Den, gazing up through the boughs, begging the boys to let me inside the tangled thicket to play.

Amand glanced at the hall door. 'You've marked the change in Jacques?'

'Ysabeau's death was always going to hit him hard,' I said.

A pregnant pause. 'Aye. She was so proud the day he stood up in the Grande Place and addressed the town.'

'Jacquot did what?'

Amand relieved himself of his mug. 'Many were afeared of setting themselves against the Count of Hainault and siding with Flanders. But your brother spoke of our liberty and if we were to risk our lives, we should die for something important. Like defending our laws and privileges. "We only have to die once," he said, "just as many have done before us, and will do after us."'

'I wish I'd been there.'

'You should've been.' For a moment I thought Amand was upbraiding me. But no, there on his lips was a teasing smile. 'To restrain him.' We laughed and I felt for the first time since arriving home a sense of connection, like your foot slipping comfortably into your favourite boot.

'We shared our grief,' Amand said quietly. 'Wept together into our cups. But when—'

'I didn't know you were so fond of Ysabeau.'

'Stalwart woman, your steward. But not long after her, my Coustance succumbed.'

'Oh Amand. I'm so sorry.'

'She never was the same. You know. After the flood.' He reached for his mug and stared into the dregs. 'Nobody saw her climb the tower. They say she lost her footing.' His eyes turned to me, liquid and earnest. 'Do you think, Sister, she is with Manon now? Or will she be like the Preachers say. Will she be in…'

I thought of how I had lost my footing in Mormal and put a hand on his arm. 'Coustance and Manon are safe. They're at peace. I'm certain of it.' Voices echoing in the hall disrupted the moment.

In the hall the odour of burnt herbs and hardwood the firepit used to send out to every room in the house was tinged with mildew. Simon lit the few nubs of candle remaining on the chandeliers and in the waxing light, two strangers took form.

'Lord Aubert de Hangest,' Jacquot announced, 'and his kinsman Guillaume, Provost of Paris.'

'Master Jacques.' Lord Aubert's bagpipe drone suited his bunched-up face. He flicked back his extravagant riding cloak. 'We heard you are an erstwhile échevin and held in esteem by the Valenciennois. We'd like to know, what is your view of treating with King Philippe?'

'I've every hope His Grace will guide us into the way of peace.'

'And Count Jan d'Avesnes? You support his claim?'

'If supporting the Count of Hainault in his title ends this war, freeing Valenciennes to go about her business *without molestation*, I'm for it.' Jacquot stared unflinchingly into Aubert's haughty eyes.

'Hmm.' The Provost of Paris put me in mind of a falcon, soaring high above everyone, ready to plummet at the least sign of prey foolish enough to make itself visible. 'The current council, all twelve échevins, would, it seems, maintain allegiance to the Count of Flanders.'

'If the king would have us treat with Guy de Dampierre, so be it. Gentlemen, begging your pardon, but whoever becomes our suzerain, naught will change for the commons. What is vital is that peace returns. People lie exhausted. The pestilence wiped out many. Anzin must be rebuilt. That's what should concern the Freemen of this city.' The earlier Jacquot, the grey, encumbered Jacquot, had disappeared.

'We mark your words,' Aubert said. 'You may be called upon to assist the people in deciding.' The royal envoys refused the refreshment offered. As soon as they were out of the door, my brother retired, climbing the stairs with his back now stooping. I didn't yet know what deadweight he was carrying, but I sensed it wasn't only the loss of his steward.

The twin aches of his misery and the absence of Ysabeau would keep me awake into the night. Pulling a shawl out of the coffer, my parchments scattered in every direction and I scooped them up from the grubby tiles. As I awaited the dawn light, my soul returned to the Forêt de Mormal.

3

Valenciennes, 1297

WHEN JACQUOT ABANDONED ME at table with the carcase of the scrawny fowl he'd kept against the Resurrection Feast, I guessed where he was headed.

Any stranger could have tracked him along the riverside path. The blackthorn already gushed white in the hedgerows, making him a moving target. Although he had cut his hair and generally cleaned up, he had begun to dress as Papa always did, in unalloyed black. I pursued him to the twin oaks, nurturing hope in my heart that after all the shouting was done, my marvellous tidings would bring him much-needed cheer.

When I reached the bend in the Ointiel, he was already perched on the lowest bough of our oak trees. I'd made my first climb up the conjoined trunks at the age of six, Jacquot taunting me all the way up. Now, as I eased myself into our bower where he sat like a starved chick in a deserted nest, he didn't acknowledge my presence.

'Still aggrieved about the election?' I asked.

No response.

'Is it because Jakemon le Père was deposed?'

Silence.

'Because Jean le Vilain bagged a seat on the échevinage, then?'

'Jean le Vilain always was a snake. Incited Jakemon and all the échevins for years and laid low when he realised, before any of us, the wind was blowing a southerly.'

My brother had endured months of being hurled on the rocks of political expediency by all parties, yet his words betrayed not one flicker of emotion. He needed a jolt back into life and telling him about what had happened a few weeks ago in Aulnoy Woods would do it, I reckoned. First, though, I decided I'd no longer beat my boards around the bush and broach the subject he had so stubbornly been avoiding. 'Jacquot, are you troubled about Nicolas?'

'Why?' From behind Jacquot's huge eyes, a wild man stared at me. 'What have you heard?'

'When I called to see Maîtresse Cécile at the Infirmary, she told me the curé will return to Saint Elizabeth's at Ascensiontide.' Cécile also told me she had no idea why the old Bishop of Cambrai had packed Curé Nicolas off on a long retreat. I waited for Jacquot to tell me but he jumped down.

Squatting on the riverbank his fingers searched around, selecting stones, rejecting others. I landed beside him as he launched his first flat pebble at the Ointiel. Four skips. He inhaled as though savouring the perfume of a rose. 'When I die I want to be buried here. It's my favourite spot.'

'Mine too. Remember Ysabeau's lamp?' To avoid feeling nauseous I bent over slowly and reached up inside the cleft between the trunks. From the secret ledge where we used to hide our childhood treasures, and evidence of our mischief, I pulled out a blue ceramic shard. 'Still here after all these years. How many of our big quarrels have the oaks witnessed?'

'Most. Except the one about me wanting to join the Templars.' Hand on his hip, he adopted a high, squeaky voice. '*Soldiering? You?*'

Laughing together at last, I rested my head against his arm as he studied his next skimmer. 'Margi, I think we're about to quarrel again.'

My heart somersaulted. Had Amand let something slip? Perhaps my news wouldn't come as a shock after all. As the pebble skimmed and sank before reaching the opposite bank, I sifted my words, trying out the right tone in my mind's ear. 'I know you were angry I stayed away so long and spent my time writing. But—'

'For God's sake, Margi. This isn't about you and your *ridiculous* poetry. This is about my vocation.' He lobbed a stone and it plopped into the river.

'Vocation?'

'I admit it. You were right about my lack of suitability for a military order, but I never lost the desire to serve God.' Calmly he launched another stone. What came next would crush the breath out of me. 'A Charterhouse is to be established. Right here, at Marlis. When the priory is built, I intend to take Holy Orders.'

'Brother, you have lost your wits. The Carthusians?' I tried to envisage him switching his funereal garments for a white habit and couldn't imagine him enduring the roughness of a hair shirt on his cosseted skin. 'You don't need to cut yourself off from the world to serve God.'

'Oh, the arrogance of it! You go away for…how many years? Then you return and demand we all stay the same. Well we don't. And I haven't.'

'That's not what I meant.'

'You meant, and doubtless you've written in your *book*, that you understand God and nobody else does.'

'I did not. I do not. But walling yourself into a cell? As if the Creator of the Universe is not here and now—didn't you once say something similar?'

'*Aaargh.* I thought you'd changed. You've been so…so gentle since you came home.'

'Jacquot, you can't use God's will as an excuse to do what you desire to do and pretend it's holy.'

'What *I* desire? What *I* desire is—' He turned away and faced the ploughed strips of Lower Mead. 'You're the clever one. What is it I desire, *Sister*?'

I should have felt the hurt in his voice, felt it deep in my bones which were formed from the same essence as his own. But his anguish was veiled from me by a fear I didn't know I harboured inside myself, the fear of another fall into nothingness, and I responded too hastily. 'You desire to know, despite everything, you are loved.' I touched his jagged elbow. 'The cloister might seem attractive but I beg you, do not be seduced.'

'Seduced?' he bellowed in my face, 'like that knight seduced you?' He pushed my hand away. 'I meet the prior of the new Charterhouse tomorrow.' Hurling his last stone into the furrows, he stormed off.

On Ascension Day he refused to attend the Mass at Saint Elizabeth's.

WITH ONE HAND Jacquot lifted the window bar and opened a shutter. He placed a bowl of frothy milk beside my bed.

'Ah! Maman's seraph.'

I followed his gaze to the embroidered coverlet which lay across my pillow. It wasn't the first time I'd clutched it to my face in the blackest hours of night and drenched it with my tears. And it wasn't the first time I'd spent those sleepless hours imagining Papa in the days when (according to Ysabeau) he still wore peacock blue.

So often I'd imagined him in a room, in a tavern, in Paris, with two fey creatures damp and squirming on the bed, the boy yowling for the breast, the girl grasping onto a slim finger of life. He ransacks his wife's coffer, knowing it was in there—hadn't Eglantine begged him for offcuts from

King Louis' new altar cloth? Hadn't he watched her nimble fingers work the stitches as her belly spread like the waxing moon? He pulls out the coverlet, holds it to the light and with a skilled eye admires the design; the angel flying in the azure sky, his celestial body enfolded by four red wings, the two upper wings embroidered in thread of gold. He discovers the cloth fits snugly around the unexpected arrival.

Six years it took him to explain to us the circumstances of our birth. Doubtless he'd needed the time to weave together his words for when he called us into the solar one June afternoon, when perfume from the Eglantine rose flooded the room, he recited Our Story in full verse. A lyrical flourish to alleviate the pain perhaps. Or to veil it. He sat in the window-seat, back rigid against the slicing sun, whilst on the settle Jacquot and I held hands.

Once upon a time, rumour of Papa's quality thread reached the royal court of France. He was charged with procuring cloth of gold for the dedication of King Louis' new chapel and our hearts beat like an angel's wings to hear about a certain young seamstress he met at the Palais de la Cité. Some months later, when King Louis walked barefoot through the streets of Paris bearing Christ's Crown of Thorns to Sainte-Chapelle, the Northern mercer and his bride attended the Mass in the Chapelle-Haute. Maman 'gazed up at the shimmering light, as if gemstones rained down left and right,' but 'so dizzied was she by the heat, Papa had insisted they retreat.' All humanity was met in the Cour du Palais, and all humanity ignored the young couple. Except for two fishwives. They took one look at the woman's swollen belly, stuck out their elbows and beat a path to a quiet spot on the riverbank. Fittingly for Jacquot, he landed into the world on Papa's velvet mantle. Then one of the wives cried, 'Another comes in haste.' She counselled Papa to fetch the priest 'with a look of sorrow', and told him, 'Ne mother ne daughter will be quick on the morrow.'

Before he finished his recitation, Papa rose and turned towards the window. Doubtless he was remembering Eglantine's beautiful face as her lifeblood drained into the river with the fish guts. 'On the banks of the rushing Seine,' he said, 'everything ceased, except the spring rain.' The fishwife was proved right about Maman.

The tale over, I ran out of the solar and lay on the bed that had been destined for Eglantine, in the home built especially for her beyond the reeking streets of Valenciennes. Bijou sprawled himself at my feet, his gentle greyhound breath warming my toes; Jacquot stretched out beside me and whispered, 'What's wrong Margi?' But I didn't need to explain why my tummy ached so. He'd heard how my birth had caused our mother's death. Wasn't that the reason Papa had turned his face from me?

Jacquot stroked my hair and a vibration worked its way through my ribs. '*Ce fut en mai, de douz tens gai…*' He'd learnt the ditty about unrequited love from the minstrels at Lendit Fair, too jolly for the occasion, but it was the only song he knew. Entwined in the grief we shared from the moment 'the fishwife cut our cords with her gutting knife,' we fell asleep with Maman's golden seraph in our hands.

Nearly fifty years later I said to the brother whose hair was now turning grey, 'Actually, it's my seraph.' I stroked the well-worn cloth, barely a foot in square, to which we'd ascribed miraculous powers as children.

Jacquot clicked his tongue and opened the second shutter. 'Ought to have known not to start that old argument.' He had always begrudged me the talisman which Papa adjudicated should be mine. But I begrudged Jacquot the much costlier gift he inherited from Eglantine: her eyes. Tall, dark, elegant Jacques. It's no marvel we are never taken for twins. My eyes, with their ambivalent colour of melting ice, either startle people or fascinate them. I've always felt Mother Nature stitched me together out of scraps but I'm no exquisite creation like Maman's coverlet. I have the appearance of an afterthought.

Holding out the dampened cloth I said, 'No argument.' I would explain to him later how, many years ago, I'd unpicked Maman's design and restitched it for my own little one. 'Take it with you. Into the monastery. It'll keep you safe.'

He laughed and sat on my coffer. 'I survived six years of war and pestilence without amulets. But if ever it looks like my life's in trouble, I'll call on your generous gift.'

Sipping the honeyed posset, my nausea passed and was replaced by a ringing sense of relief. If, on Easter Day, Jacquot hadn't jumped in first and confessed his intention to take Carthusian orders, I'd have confessed to him what had happened one Lenten day in The Robber's Den.

'Rogier arrives from Quérénaing today,' he announced.

'And Jehan?'

'Apparently Jehan has joined the Friars Minor. Rogier will attend you whilst I'm abroad.'

'I'm feeling much improved.'

'Good. Because you need to make your decision. Are you certain you won't go back and live in Mahaut's house?'

'I'll not live at the beguinage.' Although I felt the gentle pull of my sisters at Saint Elizabeth's, the Lady in Mormal had taught me I should remain unconstrained. 'Do you have to go all the way to Saint-Denis?'

'Lendit is the best fair to sell my stock. Your procrastination will not put a halt to my plans.' Leaning back out of the window he called, 'I'll be right down,' and disappeared before I could protest at his misinterpretation of my lassitude.

My dread of our permanent separation notwithstanding, my own plans were like barge sails devoid of a following wind. 'Write,' Lady Love had instructed me in the hermitage. On what I should do with my writings, She'd been less than forthcoming. And then for one exhilarating moment, I'd conceived the idea that the new life I'd returned to in Valenciennes was a new life growing inside of me. From Good Friday till Low Sunday I'd been plagued by nausea. Now, though, I'd learnt the truth of it. My condition was no more than the turning of a woman's seasons with erratic gushes of blood and drenching sweat. For me, there was no more mothering to be done. Not ever.

With an inner emptiness full of tears yet to be shed, I folded Michel's coverlet into my casket. A piece of grubby vellum drew my eye. I scanned the poem I'd written for Alixandre a quarter of a century before.

My soul remains in Saint-Séverin;
She haunts the stones of Place Maubert...

Like old friends on a major feast day, reminiscences barged in and drew up their chairs. I pictured Sir Alixandre in midnight blue, the gold cross sparkling on his chest; Sir Hugh shouting and stamping his feet like an intemperate child; Raoul sitting rigid in his high-backed chair; a voice saying, *Have I missed something?*

Dear Godfrey. I found myself laughing.

Godfrey!

I pulled on my overdress and darted downstairs. 'Make space for me in the wagon.'

Jacquot turned from his conversation with his groom and said, 'You truly are feeling better. But you should cover your hair.'

ROGIER STEERED the horses beneath the golden foliage of Aulnoy Woods. Inevitably we came to the tangled thicket where, one crisp day in

March, I'd found Amand sitting in the exact spot where I used to lie as an abandoned little sister. He raised his head.

When he saw me on the track, he leapt up and I thought he would bolt like the stag in Mormal. But he tarried. 'Marguerite,' he said, 'I came here to—well, I come here sometimes to find peace.' No longer was he the cocksure lad I once pined for as a maid and I wondered if, as he glanced at The Robber's Den and the mass of denuded branches, was he considering how I'd also changed? He looked at me, I at him. No words were exchanged. We both knew what we would do.

It was warm inside, upon our cloaks, with only the rustle of musky leaves and the flutter of birdwings disturbing the stillness. We looked each other square in the eyes. Our latter-day desires did not sweep us into oblivion. Shame and need absented themselves as love between man and woman was generously given and received. Afterwards he lay with his head between my now softening breasts and wept for his Coustance and Manon, I for my Michel.

Amand was an honourable man. He would have wed me, and I him. But now I knew there was to be no child of flesh and blood to bring into the world. I squeezed the bag in my lap and a new excitement quickened in my belly. With my back to Valenciennes, the wagon jolted on past the thicket, and my eyes were fixed on the road to Paris.

4

Paris, 1297

THE CHANTING of black friars spilled over the priory wall and into my path. Tripping on a heap of memories, I thought perhaps it was a mistake, returning after all these years to the royal city. I glanced over my shoulder at the bulging gatehouse of Porte Saint-Jacques where Rogier had set me down from the wagon and instead of continuing the short walk to Godfrey's house, my feet were drawn back to the Orléans road.

At the first milestone, where meadows and vineyards reached out toward the warmth of the southern sun, I rested my bones and lost myself to the last day I'd spent in Paris.

On the Feast of Saint Michael 1270, no one cared about the fumes of the Seine stinking to highest heaven. For weeks the city, in truth all of France, had rested uneasily. The king had left his sacred lands and it seemed no marvel to his subjects that floods had given way to infernal weather and meagre harvests. On every corner Mendicants had been preaching Armageddon was nigh. No doubt craving the advocacy of the archangel who would soon weigh their souls in the balance, pilgrims choked the dust-laden streets. As the crowds followed the gilded Cross to Sainte-Chapelle, I escaped in the opposite direction, into the scorched fields and cool orchards beyond the ramparts.

I remember I didn't turn for home until late afternoon. The moon rising was a perfect pearl in the unblemished cerulean sky. As I dawdled back along this same road, reviewing my plans for my future life as a widow, I paused to hitch up my skirtful of windfalls. The rider came out of nowhere. Waving my arms around like a tightrope walker, my apples bouncing along the track, I staggered backwards into the field of scythed barley. But the horseman galloped on and I cursed like a *routier* as the black destrier and his golden-haired knight merged with the city walls.

When I emptied my skirt onto the window ledge of the solar, dusk was penetrating the old mansion in the Clos Bruneau. The pearmains rolled alongside a flagon of Beaune—a gift sent by Sir Hugh to honour the Archangel's Feast. The wine's bouquet of wild raspberries was offset by the metallic tang in the air. Rain at last. Paris would rejoice.

Exchanging my soiled linen dress for the dove-grey silk I'd worn on my first day as mistress of the house, I suffered a pang of melancholy. But as I went to fasten the shutters, the restorative aroma of the apples lifted my spirits. I'd be back in Valenciennes in time for the harvest markets.

Of a sudden the walls of the house began to quake. A student, I imagined, returning drunk to the wrong door. When I opened the wicket gate, lightning forked over the street and oscillating silver-and-black was no revelling student. 'Lady Marguerite, may I offer my heartfelt condolences. I came as soon as I heard.'

'But you're in Tunis.' Instantly I suffered the stupidity of my words.

'I arrived back this afternoon. I was despatched on Saint Bartholomew, the day our blessèd king passed over into the next life.'

Dreadful tidings of King Louis, yet I didn't react. I was battling to stifle the memory of the last time I'd seen Sir Alixandre at the early Mass on Corpus Christi. The first crack of thunder quickened me and the mud-starched cloak on his back came to my attention. 'How discourteous of me. Pray, come take refreshment.'

In the solar he dropped on the fauld-stool. I didn't mark it at the time but in my mind's eye I see it now, he'd taken the trouble to wash the travel stains from his tanned skin and change into courtly attire. Relieving him of his cloak which smelt of unidentifiable grime I said, 'It was you.'

'My lady?'

'On the Orléans road. Riding as if Satan and his hosts were hunting you down. You made me drop all my apples.'

'But...you were alone. And in peasant's garb.' I remember baulking at the note of chastisement in his voice. I'd so enjoyed wandering far and wide without a chaperone, there being no man to chide me for it. 'So you were expecting me?'

I stared at his thick mane. The dark auburn had turned golden under the sun of a far-off land. 'How could I know it was you?' As I held out a cup of wine, his hand brushed mine; I tried not to stare at the long sturdy fingers which a few months earlier had slid my poem inside his surcoat. I wondered, was he also thinking of the moment when in the middle of the Mass I blurted out my undying love for him? No marvel I blushed. I forced myself to sit on the couch.

He sniffed the wine, took a draft, wet his lips with his tongue. 'Your husband had impeccable taste. In every wise.' The stare he gave me was the one Hugh must have meant when he'd complained to me of Alixandre's insolence. 'I heard from Godfrey in what circumstances Sir Raoul left you. I'm so sorry, Marguerite.' By no means did it escape my notice that he'd dropped my title. A shiver of excitement ran through me, the kind of excitement I was barely acquainted with, for not one person in Paris, except Sir Hugh, knew the ignominious terms of my marriage contract.

'Master Stephanus made my introduction to the foremost illuminator in Valenciennes, so I'll have work when I arrive back—'

'Wait. Wait.' He signalled me to slow down my gabbling. 'You're leaving Paris?'

'Tomorrow.'

'This is news to me.' I thought he sounded disappointed but with hindsight, I suspect relief. 'And you, Marguerite? A scrivener?'

'A seemly craft for a widow. Recently I had the fortune of acquainting myself with *Being and Existence* by Dionysius the Areopagite. Remember the disputes between your cousin and Canon Vincent?'

He reached inside his surcoat. 'I remember this.' He unwrapped a piece of vellum. And there it was, the verse I'd illustrated with a red ship like Noah's ark, floating away on emerald green waves. 'You captured some truth about me in a way none other could. How I long to fight for God and regain Jerusalem, yet I'm forged by what I left behind.'

'More wine?' I turned my back to him and poured. I knew little of love but I knew I was radiating desire and as I stretched up to finish barring the shutter, I fiddled with the catch, putting off the moment of seeing, or rather being seen by his obsidian eyes. When at last I turned, Alixandre stood inches away, gazing down at me. I felt myself falling as if into a bottomless sea.

Every scene of every Romance I'd ever read in the countess' library fell into place; my knight lifted me as if I weighed no more than a feather; he carried me to the couch; he knelt at my feet and eased off my slippers; cupping each heel in turn, he rested his forehead on my ankles, on the scratches made by the barley stubble. 'Am I forgiven?'

Aye, I nodded.

Moving behind me, he worked methodically; the grey silk was soon slipping from my shoulders and down my back. He gasped. Glancing round I saw the shock in his eyes.

'Did Sir Raoul do this?'

'Of course not.'

His powerful arm encircled me from behind and he drew my body towards him. 'Your father?'

'Papa only ever threatened a beating. He never carried it out. Alixandre, it doesn't matter.' I wanted his lips on my skin again, for our story to continue.

'Oh my little Marguerite.' He stooped and pressed his mouth to each groove in my back, his hand working its way round to my breast. And then it began. A sensation flooding my whole body until it settled, almost unendurable, around my loins. I was ready, and had been for so long, to receive this man who had gone so far away from me and was now so close.

'MARGUERITE.' His voice called me too soon out of my satiated slumber.

'Hmm?'

'Lady Marguerite.'

'*Sir* Alixandre.' Doubtless I looked an imbecile, grinning through my haze of contentment.

Silhouetted in the lilac sheen of daybreak, my lover stood at the window. He surveyed the Rue du Clos Bruneau, feet paddling in rainwater, his back striated with the muscles of a fighting man. 'This morning you depart for Valenciennes.'

'Mmm,' I murmured. 'But I—'

'But *I* cannot accompany you.'

'I can wait a day or two. A week even...'

'What I mean is, I've a different road to travel.'

'Where are you going?'

'I came to deliver a message. Now I must return.'

It should have been obvious the war in Outremer was not over just because King Louis had perished, but hours of pleasure had made fog of my mind. I sat up on the couch and removed a heavy clump of hair from my eyes. 'Return where?'

'First I must go to the Temple.'

'Another errand?'

'My lady, I know not how to say what I must say.'

'My lord, you look so serious.'

'I'm pledged to join the Order.'

'The Order of the Poor Fellow-Soldiers of Christ?' I laughed at what I thought must be a jest. 'Alixandre, Templars are vowed to celibacy. They can't even kiss an aunt.'

'Indeed. Tomorrow I make my vigil. After my profession, I leave for Genoa to take ship before winter sets in.' He sat on the couch and tucked a wet foot beneath him, his thigh pressing against mine. My ears still hummed with the gentle words he had used, coaxing me, teaching me, leading his 'precious little pearl' to abandon herself. I hadn't known where the boundary of my skin ended and Alixandre's began. 'Say something, Marguerite.'

I'd cried out as we blazed through the hours of night, but in the cold morning, I found no voice to speak with.

'I know you are free from Raoul, but I have this vocation.' 'So you're saying…' I reached for a piece of clothing. 'What exactly are you saying?' Even with my chemise pulled sideways across my torso, I felt more naked than when he'd stripped every stitch off my body and gazed at me with the look of a starved wolf.

'The Templars' critics are mistaken. The brothers struggle with all their might to win back the Holy City. What I'm saying is, I must return and fight. I love you, Marguerite, but you do understand? I must do God's will.'

'*Deus vult*,' I murmured. As clear as abbey bells, I heard two voices setting up a conflict within me. The voice I knew well wanted to scream, *What about me?* As yet I was hardly acquainted with the second voice and didn't comprehend her counsel at all.

'Truly,' he said, 'I had no reason to believe you were still a maid. You gave yourself to me so…fully.' His mouth curled into a smile. 'Come, my little Marguerite. I can stay yet a while. Let us play some more.'

Still I wonder, did he imagine I'd let him open me up again so I'd fall back into the infinite ocean where I'd already lost my bearings? I confess, the greater part of me, my familiar voice, yearned to shout, *Aye, I'll dive once more into the deeps with you, my love, and I do not care if I drown.* But my newfound voice was gathering strength. The moment he reached out and removed my chemise, that is the moment she claimed me. 'Go. Now.' I said the words with a confidence I'd not known before.

In a single, co-ordinated movement, Alixandre flung on his clothes and rushed out of the solar. The poem he'd so cherished the night before lay bleeding red ink into the soaked floorboards.

THE HIDDEN MIRROR OF LA PORETE

It would be a long time before I fully trusted my inner voice over and against my long-held convictions and now, a quarter of a century later, she had brought me back to Paris, to the place of beginnings and of endings.

ROOM PILED upon room, the house in Rue Saint-Jacques towered above me. Wasn't this madness, wasn't this presumption, to call on a man I hadn't seen in over two decades? I contemplated turning back to the city gates but when the valet didn't shut the door in my face, I took it as a good sign.

Sunlight blared through the vertical windows of the solar which overlooked the street. Specks of dust scintillated in the air which smelt like curdling milk, taking me back to every illuminator's atelier I'd worked in. I tried to count the manuscripts stacked on the vast oaken sideboard, on the two chests butted up end-to-end along one wall, and on the table, manuscripts worth a king's ransom. My fingers tapped nervously on the chair arms and the fancy occurred to me, had I been born male, I might have ended up living in a scriptorium, trapped like a bleary-eyed moth in a cocoon of parchment.

'Lady Marguerite.' The dark gardecorps would have conferred on Godfrey de Fontaines the austerity of a Regent Master at the University of Paris if it hadn't been for his wilful fringe. Now almost white, his hair still refused to be tamed under the fold of an academic cap. When the young Godfrey first arrived at Raoul's table he had won me to him straightway, making no attempt to moderate his Northern manner amongst rarefied company. His gift for humour was effortless; I once saw him, with a single quip, extinguish the aggression in a room full of choleric men.

'What a marvel to behold you again,' he said as he took my hand. 'The years have made no mark on you.'

'And you, Master, are as gallant as ever.'

'Your message was a delightful surprise. And your treatise.' He kissed my hand and the anxieties I'd had about my reception melted away. 'Come, let us talk as we sup. I sent the boy out for a good wine of Beaune to help us along.' He led me to table where the valet cleared a space and served up dishes that could have graced the high table of Salle-le-Comte.

Godfrey sniffed at his cup. 'Those were rare days *à la porée*. You did realise there were two Northern whelps who were utterly devoted to you?'

Like the maid I still was the last time we met, I blushed.

'Alixandre and I had a nickname for you. La Porete. You grasped metaphysics better than any at Raoul's soirees, even Canon Vincent, God rest his soul. Now, I must know,' he attacked the poached pike on his trencher and tore off a clean wedge of pink flesh, 'how did you arrive at your conclusions about the divine will in relation to human will?'

'By stripping away self-deception. I took a long, hard look at myself in the mirror and began to see it clearly. When I think to do God's will, it's mostly myself I am satisfying.'

'Interesting.' He sucked the grease from his fingers and cleaned them on his napkin. 'I must warn you, your Mirror needs some polishing. Your expression is ofttimes imprecise. Why did you not write it in Latin?'

'What's wrong with good plain French?'

'Hmm.' He picked over his fish bones. Offering me the plate of candied ginger, he selected one of the curved discs for himself. 'I must say, I found your mockery of Reason utterly exasperating. Without Reason, we would be like unto the dumb beasts. Reason enables us to know God.' The whole disc disappeared into his mouth.

'God is a living Being, not a thought.'

'Granted,' he mumbled.

'And like unto the beasts, we breathe the same air as them. We inhabit the same universe.'

'Granted.'

'So…what if God is as present to Nature as He is to humanity?'

He swallowed hard. 'You stray uncomfortably close to the pagans there. Dangerous.' His expression was stern but he patted me on the wrist. 'To talk like this in private is safe. My students say things far more outlandish. Fulsome idiots, some of them.' He frowned and helped himself to a second sweetmeat. 'Your work reminds me of another beguine. Have you come across Hadewijch?'

Like the skylarks that nest beside the River Scheldt, my heart soared. 'I read her verse when I lived in Ghent.'

'Ghent? What were you doing in Flanders?'

'After Raoul died and I returned from Paris, Countess Marguerite resumed her position as my benefactress. She sent me there for a spell.'

Godfrey gestured we should sit in the comfortable chairs by the window. Silently he sipped his wine until the valet had cleared the boards and closed the door behind him.

'You know my cousin was butchered at Acre?' The bluntness of his statement disturbed me far less than witnessing Godfrey clench his scholar's fists.

'I heard.'

'On the eve of his vigil, after he left you, Alixandre was in a frightful panic after he left you. I tried my damnedest to persuade him against his Templar folly. Your timely freedom from Sir Raoul was my leading argument.' He relaxed back in his chair. 'He did reconsider.'

'He did?'

Godfrey grinned. 'Understandably.' So he knew what happened on the night of Michaelmas 1270 after my reckless stroll beyond the city wall. At least, the gist of it. 'He went back to find you. Strange what sticks in the memory. I was rather alarmed when I met him later that day—I thought he had blood on his fingers. Turned out to be red ink. Evidently you'd already flown the nest. So we went to the Pot d'Étain and drank ourselves senseless. Last time I saw him.' His eyes glistened with wetness but he leaned forwards and said with directness, 'Why did Marguerite Noire send you to Ghent?'

Though the loss of my boy still hurt, I reasoned Michel's kinsman deserved to hear the truth. 'I was carrying Alixandre's son.'

'A son?' Godfrey scanned the room as though he expected a child's head might bob up from behind the furniture. 'He must be a grown man by now. Why did you not say?'

'My little Michel did not stay with us for long.'

As if a fresh injury pressed on an old wound, Godfrey groaned. 'I still miss Alixandre like I'd miss my right hand. He was more a brother to me than a cousin. But his son? That would've been...' He took out a kerchief and mopped his cheeks. 'I understand now why the strokes of your pen reveal the biting agony of loss. Yet miraculously, you impart hope.' He drained his goblet. 'My dear Marguerite—I feel I may call you Marguerite, since we're almost kin—I mentioned Hadewijch for a reason. Are you aware they hounded her from her beguinage? She ended her days in hiding. Escaped the inquisitors, but her writings—'

'Godfrey, I write only of the truth I find.'

He threw up his hands and slapped them on his thighs. 'Precisely why I'm frit. I can protect my students. Teach them how to protect themselves. But a beguine? Writing in French? You must come under the authority of a confessor. A priest who will vouch for you lest they call you *pseudo-mulier*.'

Of course I didn't wish to be known as a 'false woman' but a wave of resistance rose in me. I didn't wish to submit to his entreaty. Then again, neither did I wish to reject the care of a man I so greatly respected. 'I'll consider it. And, as you suggest, clarify my arguments.'

'Good. Good. I wouldn't bear it if you came to harm. You must not show your work to any who would misconstrue it. Some of your notions are subtle. Quite subtle indeed.'

'May I call on you with my revisions?'

'I'd be troubled if you did not.' He poured out the last of the wine.

With the taste of wild raspberries on my tongue and the ring of Godfrey's warning in my ears I stepped back out into Rue Saint-Jacques.

Surrounded by a sea of students, black and churning, I might have been transported to my first morning in Paris when it had so surprised me to hear Latin spoken with the cadences of normal conversation. Soon I would come upon the Couvent des Mathurins and wondered whether *The Wheel of Fortune* still adorned the west end of their chapel. Souls ascending. Souls descending.

5

Paris, 1264

MY BACK WAS TO THE WALL on the day of my nuptials. From where I was standing, I couldn't see the freshly painted *Wheel of Fortune* in the chapel of the Mathurins. In truth I couldn't see a thing.

As we made our way from the porch at the west end up to the altar for the blessing, the sun tore through the high windows and the dove-grey of my gown dissolved into a rainbow blur. I sensed rather than saw the ascetic little priest make the sign of the cross, heard the low rumble of the 'Amen', and felt Raoul's gnarly fingers elevate the hand which no longer belonged to Papa but to him.

Papa believed The Wheel of Fortune had turned massively in his favour, just when he had thought all was lost. That a man of noble lineage would assent to take his immodest daughter to wife came as a blinding shock to us both after our catastrophic first encounter. My usually impious father attended daily Mass for a whole month after the betrothal and believed the Countess of Flanders and Hainault should be declared a living saint.

Said encounter with my husband-to-be happened at the white palace in Valenciennes. Countess Marguerite had summoned me to the haute salle and as I approached her sovereign figure drenched in golden light from the magnificent rose window, I feared I must have erred in some way. Then I saw Papa standing below the dais and immediately concluded I was to be dismissed from court. Making my courtesy, I searched my conscience. What was it I'd done, or more likely said, wrong? When I raised my head I noticed the knight standing beside the countess. He wasn't one of the regular courtiers who strutted around like prized stallions. This man's demeanour put me in mind of a manuscript some careless monk had left in the musty corner of a scriptorium.

The countess ordered me to give account of my recent studies. I glanced at Papa and for one blessèd moment of ignorance, hope fluttered her pathetic wings beneath my flat chest. I wondered whether he'd secured the knight as my tutor. Such a romancer I was, imagining a man highborn might school the daughter of a tradesman.

'*Li Roman d'Alixandre*, my lady.'

'Come girl.' She clinked one hand of emeralds against the other and aimed her jet black eyebrows at me. 'You spend every waking hour in my librarium.'

'Book Fourteen of *De Civitate Dei*,' I said. Papa gave me a blank stare. 'Saint Augustine's *City of God*.' Did I roll my eyes? Undoubtedly. I wanted the intrusion to be over soonest so I could get back to said book.

'As you promised, my lady, she is something of a scholar.' The drab knight turned to me. 'Demoiselle, what make you of Saint Augustine?'

I had, during six years as the countess' protégée, been trained by the sarcasm and riding crop of Lady Aveline to lower my eyes on such occasions. As I did so, Raoul's right boot captured my attention. His big toe had almost worn through the leather. 'I'm at the part,' I said, 'where he asks, what human being can live the life they desire when their living be not their own to control?'

Papa sucked in his breath but, without missing a beat, Raoul responded, 'Does the Saint not give counsel, demoiselle, if what you desire be beyond your power, you should direct your wish instead to that which you can achieve?'

Courtliness demanded I remain silently and demurely smiling at his erudite rejoinder. But the words escaped too quickly from my mind for my mouth to catch them. 'And settle for less than eternity?'

Next day I was sent home from court to prepare.

Jacquot shunned me. Steadfastly he maintained I'd planned my '*escape to Paris*'. I longed for him to sing me to sleep, to chase away the phantom with the shrivelled face that slipped into my bed every night and leered across the pillow at me. Even in the moment Papa slapped Miéla's rump and sent me off from Rue del Saulch with the words, 'This is God's Will, Marguerite,' I was throwing a desperate glance over my shoulder into the screens passage. A black hole, carved in the shape of my twin, yawned back at me. Ysabeau's sobs pursued me through the gatehouse and down Rue del

Saulch.

On the morning my marriage was to be finalised in the eyes of God, my nerves were stretched thin on the tenterhooks of many sleepless nights. Standing alone on the gallery of Raoul's Parisian home I peered down into the long, low hall. Windows of slatted animal horn doused the room in melancholy and doused me with the uncanny sense this was the place my bridegroom's ghostly ancestors congregated to mourn their heirless line. 'Here she comes,' they were whispering to each other. 'She's a bit puny.'

A single dash of colour stood out in the hall. Half-concealed by the trestles set out for the feast and two high-backed chairs at their head, hung a tapestry with a pattern at once intricate and bizarre. Raoul's souvenir from his exploits in Outremer, I supposed.

At the doorway to the outer steps, three men stood chatting. My footsteps echoing on the timbered staircase made their heads turn. One was the gaunt secular cleric, Canon Vincent. Another, young Sir Hugh in a tunic and cap of extraordinary butter-coloured silk, lute strapped to his back. The third brought me to confusion. Sir Raoul, in surcoat of blue wool and new boots, was indeed wrinkled as I'd remembered, his lank hair resting on his shoulders, dreary, but I thought how finely drawn his brow and cheekbones. His long nose gave him a morose look, yet overall his bearing was stately. I'd never guessed Reality could be such a robber, to cheat me of my outrage.

As if enticing a falcon to his wrist, Raoul extended a hand. 'Come, demoiselle Marguerite.' His tone was deep but gentle. 'Rue Saint-Jacques isn't far. We will walk to church.' There was nothing I could think to do but take the proffered arm and as we moved towards the stone steps, I saw he was limping.

AFTER OUR WEDDING NIGHT, it would seem to me that the turning of The Wheel of Fortune and the vicissitudes of God's Will were as indistinguishable as they were inscrutable: Cruel and yet surprising.

Following the ceremony at the Mathurins chapel, a handful of black-clad scholars made up our wedding party. Sir Hugh, one canary amongst an unkindness of ravens, took the place beside me at table. Something about him reminded me of Jacquot. His dark eyes, I thought at the time. As Hugh babbled on about fripperies, the wont of a man with weighty things to conceal, it took effort to push my absent brother to the back of my mind. I marvelled, nonetheless, at how many words he managed to utter without seeming to draw breath. 'Canon Vincent considers it his duty to guide our feet into the narrow way. He's reading for his Master's at Robert de Sorbon's college. Shame Robert absents himself today. He never used to miss Raoul's soirees until Louis made him Royal Confessor. I'd wager his knees are now perpetually red raw. My lady, you must have a thousand-and-one questions about our most excellent city?'

In the time it took me to remember I was the 'lady' being addressed, Raoul leapt in. 'Dear boy, Lady Marguerite has had scant opportunity to orient herself.'

'My lord, I do have a question.' I ventured a glance at my husband, remembered the duty I would in a few hours' time be required to perform, and immediately turned back to the charmed expression on Hugh's pretty face. '*À la porée*. Why such a lowly appellation for this house?' Twice I'd passed beneath the painted shield hanging above the studded gates and was itching to know why a nobleman's house bore the symbol of a common leek.

'A little *jeu de mots*. In memory of the great Gilbert de la Porrée. He wrote his most important treatise when residing within these walls.'

Canon Vincent, who for all his elite education had never grasped the more a man knows, the more perfectly he knows that he knows nothing at all, butted in. '*Being and Substance*. The Dominican Aquinas has immersed himself in the same matter.' Vincent laughed at his own witticism. 'I possess two of Gilbert's commentaries on Boethius. Though it was his treatise on the Trinity landed him in trouble.'

My curiosity raised her feline head. 'In what manner did Gilbert transgress?'

The canon looked me up and down with the sneer often cultivated by the children of Reason. 'He argued…one single God is pure and not three Persons…albeit the three Persons be of one God.'

'Ah,' I said, 'he examined the simplicity of the Divine.' Given my new status, Vincent's sallow-rimmed eyes remained on me longer than was decent. I continued to plough my furrow. 'What happened to Gilbert?'

'Naught.' Raoul smiled, revealing the gap in his hind teeth. 'He was merely required to amend some of his propositions. They do not burn bishops at the stake.' The men laughed. 'Vincent, dear friend, do bring Gilbert's commentaries for Lady Marguerite. She reads Latin.' The flock of scholars turned their beady eyes on me. 'And Greek.'

Grinning from ear to ear, Hugh reached for his lute. 'A song by Moniot d'Arras. *Ce fut en mai de douz tens gai…*' My need for Jacquot exploded in my chest. I fixed my face with a Lady Aveline smile.

The impassioned discussions which followed Hugh's musical interlude diverted me. The argument over whether we can have Free Will if God in His omniscience knows our actions in advance has stuck in my mind. But all too soon bars of shadow seeped across the hall floor and silently I implored the Virgin that these men, in love with the sound of their own voices, might jabber on so late my deflowering would be out of the question.

Then Rufin came to light the chandeliers.

When he had arrived at my home in Valenciennes to chaperone me to Paris, I guessed Rufin had a military tale to tell. The colour of the scar running from his jaw to his ear matched his deep red hair. It turned out he was not only valet, but also steward, cook, and groom to Raoul and now executioner was to be added to his duties. After securing the shutters, he eased a candle off its pricket. 'My lady,' he said with a low bow and tarried at the foot of the staircase.

The slash of white linen turned down over the madder-red counterpane screamed at me across the dim bedchamber. As my fingers stumbled over the lacings of my gown, as my body climbed the mountainous bed, as my mind flitted to the expectant ancestors who must have created their dynasty beneath these hangings of rich damask, I demanded of my invisible mother, *How much will it hurt?*

It wasn't long before uneven footsteps plodded across the gallery. I trapped the counterpane under my chin.

Raoul was fully clothed. I looked away and bit down on my tongue. How humiliating, having to watch an old man undress. But Raoul didn't undress. He limped to the bed. 'My wedding gift for you, my lady. *The Consolation of Philosophy* by Boethius. I had Master Stephanus illuminate the title page especially for you.' With a bow of reverence he placed the silk-bound volume on the bed. 'It tells of Lady Philosophy who comes to the author in his condemned cell. She teaches him that none can ever be truly secure until he has been forsaken by Fortune. I hope, after studying its precepts, you'll share your considerations with me.'

As I put out a hand for the book, the counterpane escaped my clamp.

'May I ask of you one thing?' he said. 'How did you regard our company today?'

'Oh, er…fascinating. Conversation at Salle-le-Comte was never as stimulating. Unless I was alone with the countess in her apartment. And at home, Papa always sent me to bed after supper when we had guests and he wished to discuss trade. Except when—' I was gabbling like Sir Hugh.

'Except?'

'Except…' I'd been about to say when potential suitors were at table. 'Except on special occasions.'

'Feast days are always special occasions *à la porée*. Now, my lady, I bid you a good night.'

As I watched my husband bow elegantly and lope away, I thanked the Queen of Heaven for answering my prayers favourably. At sixteen, what did I know about the earthly workings of men?

EVERY NIGHT, I listened for uneven steps on the gallery. Every night the footsteps passed by the solar and continued past my door.

Michaelmas came, a balmy evening for the penultimate day of September and I lay atop the counterpane. The door clicked open and the muscles in my abdomen tightened like the winch of a drawbridge.

Raoul set a dish of honey cakes beside the bed. 'I have a favour to ask of you, my lady. Would you deem it an imposition if I asked you for more?'

My tongue cleaved to the back of my throat.

'Of *Li Roman*.' Earlier, Hugh had prevailed upon me to recite from *Li Roman de la Rose* and it seemed my husband lusted after naught but verse!

'Might I sit by you and hold the lamp while you read?'

'The countess wouldn't approve.'

'The countess?'

'She banned lamps from her library.'

'Ah! Worry not. You've witnessed how Stephanus works with only the best vellum. It would take a conflagration to burn. But I promise I'll be vigilant.' He lounged across the empty side of the bed. 'Pray, begin from the first stanza.'

'*Here is written the Romancing of the Rose,*
wherein you'll find the arts of love enclosed—'

'Marguerite, your voice, as Sir Hugh quite eloquently marked at supper, is indeed enchanting. You are not to recite in company again. It would be unfitting.' He smiled and a queasiness stirred in my belly. I couldn't tell whether I'd pleased him or caused offense. 'Continue.'

'*Many do say that visions,*
Are merely lies and fictions.
But such dreams can be received,
Which do not lie or deceive
And one day are shown as truth.'

It became Raoul's custom at the end of a feast day to recline alongside me, quizzing me on the philosophical points the men had discussed at table. Often we welcomed in the dawn together. Once he asked me, what did I think constituted the distinction between *Essence* and *Existence*?

'I see it like this, my lord. I, Marguerite, in my essence, am taking up space in this chamber. Therefore, I exist here and the same applies to you. If, however, I were not in this room, that does not entail I have no essential being. I might be someplace else, even though I seem not to exist in your world. Thus, *Essence* and *Existence* may coincide, but they are not one and the same thing.' I pecked at a cake.

'Well done. You grasped Vincent's argument. Perhaps you should write down what you just said. So you don't forget it.' He leaned back on the bolster, the upper half of his face in shadow. 'Now, some verse.'

As I gave half my attention to reciting, the other half wandered to why my husband made no carnal demands on me, whereas Hugh had wooed me all evening and sung to me of love inflaming him so nobly, he would *'beg and plead, My lady, show mercy!'* He often left me feeling giddy in the head. Did Raoul want me or not? Was he jealous, like the Lover in *Li Roman* who walled his Rose into a tower? There was no other woman in his life; he rarely went out alone. His passions were philosophy and the arts. I marvelled that my fleeting hope at our first encounter in Salle-le-Comte was being fulfilled. *À la porée* my education blossomed.

A LESSON I learned early in my marriage was Raoul's habit of reading silently at breakfast, preferably without being disturbed. The morning after my phantom-free wedding night, I'd awoken well-rested with the sound of a tinny bell ringing in my ears and men's voices chanting prayers for the Hour of Terce. I found Raoul already at table in the solar. As I polished off a generous helping of herrings and soft bread, he didn't glance up once from his page. His silence smothered my newborn optimism.

'My lord,' I said, 'what is that plain stone church directly behind the bedchamber?'

'Saint Jean de Jérusalem.'

'Wherefore Jerusalem?'

'It's the Commandery of the Knights Hospitaler.'

'Ah, they care for sick pilgrims in the Holy Land.'

'Indeed, though they also fight like the Templars these days. Now. This afternoon I wish to acquaint you—'

'Sir Hugh's father died in Outremer, did he not?'

'He did.'

'What happened to him?'

'Eustache fell at the Battle of Fariskur. Now as I was—'

'How awful. Where's Fariskur?'

'Egypt.'

'Were you at Fariskur?'

'I was. Now Marguerite,' his voice had raised a tone and his foot tapped beneath the table, a sign with Papa I should soonest hold my tongue. I couldn't risk being abandoned by Lady Fortune—or was it the Blessèd Virgin? I kept quiet.

A much harder lesson was to come with winter's chill.

On Advent Sunday Raoul burst into the solar. 'A messenger came. A royal messenger. I'm to present you at court. On Christ's Nativity. We'll worship in the Chapelle-Haute, hear the Angel's Mass. Afterwards we'll feast in the Salle du Roi and then, with the king's acknowledgement, you will truly be my lady.'

It grieves me now that I didn't respond to his childlike excitement. But as he spoke, my heart had constricted, imagining how Papa and Maman spent their last happy moments together in Sainte-Chapelle. Too late I responded, 'What a great honour.'

On the Eve of the Nativity the mother of our kitchen boy was brought in to attend me. Marote's agile fingers laced my under-gown of scarlet samite which accentuated my slender waist and augmented my woefully tiny breasts; the curved neckline, edged with pearls, sat low across my shoulders. When Marote slipped the matching cotehardie over the top and I moved in the light of the brazier, I gleamed blood-red. After fixing the mantle lined with fox, she made a courtesy. 'My lady.' The awe in her lampblack eyes told me that despite my diminutive stature, I looked imposing. For a fleeting moment I wondered about her son Ernoul; he wasn't dark like Marote; he had copper hair and freckles. My attention slipped away, back to Papa, how he had excelled himself with my court robes and how he'd never had the chance to dress his Eglantine like this.

As my neat little kid slippers searched out each tread of the staircase, Raoul was watching me intently. Seated in his high-backed chair, robed in dark velvet, lordship emanated from him. He took my hand, a rare delight transforming his face, and only now did I observe his eyes were the blue of a peacock's throat.

Of King Louis? I recall little, the presentation was over so fast. Nodding from his throne, he faded into a pale mist beside the dusky majesty of

Marguerite de Provence. This was the queen who led the Christian hosts in Outremer while amassing her king's ransom. She raised me from my curtsy and turned my hand over, studying my palm. 'Lady Marguerite, you have such small, elegant fingers. Exactly like your mother's. Eglantine was the most accomplished needlewoman I ever had.' The hangings of blue, gold, and red around the dais seemed to dazzle brighter. Here was a woman who had known Maman. No longer was my mother a mere character in an old story I'd heard. Inside me I felt something connect, like a key opening up the door of a chamber I hadn't known existed.

'Thank you, Your Grace.'

'We pray the Christ-child's blessings on you and Sir Raoul. May your union be fruitful.' Raoul twitched at my elbow so I made my bow.

The fayre must have been sumptuous. I remember now only the pleasure chasing down my spine whenever Raoul's hand brushed mine at the serving dish and how it struck me at the time, if I'd been a more worldly woman, I might have known how wise it was of a man, how seductive, to wait till desire was ignited before making me his own. How naïve.

Many hours later as I slid between warmed sheets, I wondered why Marote couldn't be *á la porée* all the time. I'd been so used to Ysabeau's assistance at home, though I couldn't say I missed Lady Aveline's attentions.

Coals hissed in the brazier and a pang of nerves threw me into a panic. How should I behave? What would Raoul expect? Romances and the chansons of troubadours had been my sole primers on the art of lovemaking. On practicalities, they'd been silent. I leapt out of bed, stripped off my nightgown and cap, lunged back beneath the covers and, shivering with anticipation and a smidgen of fear, waited for the sound of uneven footsteps.

'WAKEY, WAKEY, Sleepy Head.' Raoul pinned back the shutters letting the frosted morning into the bedchamber. I sat up and rubbed my gritty eyes. 'Did you forget we're expecting guests? Oh—' The sheets had fallen, exposing my torso, naked but for a few strands of frizzy hair glued to my skin with slaver.

'What's wrong?'

'Naught. Naught is—'

'I suppose I do look quite hideous.'

'No. Not in the least.' Selecting the heaviest fur from my coffers, he held it out to me at arm's length and waited until I'd covered myself. He sat at the foot of the bed, shedding around him the distinctive scent of dying blossoms. 'Marguerite, I was immeasurably proud to present you to the king. But why do you think His Grace would grant me, a landless nobleman, *entrée* into his presence?'

'Because you took the Cross and accompanied him to Outremer?'

'And, like him, I was taken prisoner.' He glanced away. 'When the Mathurin brothers arranged my ransom, I was in a dreadful state. Doubtless why the Saracen dogs were eager to let me go—claim my riches while I yet breathed.' He laughed, but I didn't feel like laughing. 'What I have to tell you is…My injury means that…'

'That you limp?'

'Aye. That.' He coughed, but the hoarseness remained in his throat. 'You're a clever girl. No need to dot the 'I's for you.' He reached out as though he desired to touch me and I hadn't realised till that moment how desperately I wanted him to touch me, but he let his hand fall. 'Otherwise, things would have been very different.' He stared into the brazier where the embers had died to white ash. 'But I think it to your advantage.'

'Raoul, no. I don't think—'

'Dear little Marguerite. I saw your face on Advent Sunday. You thought the king's acknowledgment of you as my lady would mean I would feel entitled to force myself on you.'

I recalled my weak response on that occasion and how Raoul had limped as quickly as he could out of the solar. 'No. It wasn't because of you—'

'Say naught.' He stood and unable, or unwilling, to look at me, he moved to the door. 'Our company arrives at noon to celebrate Saint Stephen. I'll tell them you're indisposed.'

Though I wanted to beg him to come back to me, I heard myself say, 'No, my lord, I'll be ready.'

'As you wish.'

The resignation in those three words was the *coup de grâce*. Once more Reality had triumphed, though this time I was no fanciful child robbed of her pet monster. I was a woman cheated of having her desires fulfilled. Dear Raoul, however, had been cheated of more. Far more than a king's ransom. Before the tinny bell of the Commandery rang for the Hour of Terce, my bearskin was drenched and for the first time in my life, I was aware of weeping not only for my own loss.

Next day I hunted Rufin down to the solar. 'Window-seat.' I pointed at the cushioned ledge until he sat. 'You've served Sir Raoul since you were his squire. Loyally. Tell me, why doesn't Marote live here? That would be customary.'

'She did. When we came home from Egypt. Then Ernoul arrived. My lord did try. But the cries of a little one, his laughter. Him singing his little tunes around the house is what really did for Sir Raoul. Brought him to the edge of the black pit like naught else.'

'Black pit?'

'I tried to tell you at the beginning, my lady. You remember, when we had to bivouac in the chapel at Senlis?'

'I remember.' At the time, when I'd still thought of him as my gaoler rather than a chaperone, I'd imagined Rufin was trying to impress me with his master's exploits in the Holy Land. I'd cut him off dead and turned my back to him.

'Before you came to Paris, he got so bad. Then you started your night talkings and it's a miracle. He's well again. No black pit. No more physic. That's down to you, my lady.'

THE BEGINNING of the end came the day I was working on one of my compositions in the solar. Raoul and I looked up simultaneously from our pages.

'Sounds like a storm brewing over Paris,' I said.

The roar moved closer.

Raoul cocked his head. 'They're singing.'

'Singing what?'

'Old campaigning song. The city gathers to see the king and princes off to Saint-Denis. They're to take the Cross.'

'Why? When His Grace met with such disaster last time?'

'He once made a vow. To wrest Jerusalem from the infidel.' Raoul stared into the distance, face even paler than usual. 'Old age looms. And The Day of Judgment.'

Pulling on a shawl I stood by the window and listened to the passionate voices:

'My lords, know whoe'er would not repair
To the land where our God did die and rise,
Whoe'er will not take the Cross of Outremer,
He will never enter Paradise.'

Louis' proposed campaign to the Holy Land polarised the royal city. A whole year before troops were due to leave for Aigues-Mortes, violence erupted in the streets and by the Feast of Saint Bartholomew 1269, the

Provost had packed the Petit Châtelet full of belligerent students till the walls were bursting. The violence, however, was about to seep into our home.

Hugh arrived *à la porée* and shared with us his anti-war song.

'My lady fair waits with empty bed.
No man alive with sense in his head
Lets reason compel him to see Outremer.
God is gone. He is not there.'

'Blasphemer!' Canon Vincent leapt to his feet. 'You defame Holy War?'

'We've enemies aplenty in the English,' Hugh said. 'Why court trouble in the Levant?'

As if we were in the scene of a morality play, in strode an upright character in surcoat of midnight blue. The knight, whose custom at Raoul's soirees had so far been to sit back by the hearth and observe the philosophical debates, wore a cross of gold on one side of his chest. I tried not to stare.

'A Christian man of Virtue!' Vincent crowed. 'You took the Cross.'

Alixandre advanced till his nose was within an inch of Hugh's and in his rousing baritone which filled the hall he began Thibaut's campaigning song.

'My lords, know whoe'er would not repair
To the land where our God did die and rise…'

Hugh, without taking his eye off his adversary and keeping his hand on the poignard at his belt, bellowed his own composition back in his face. I admit, the musical joust unleashed a rush of excitement in me as on and on it went, verse after verse, until Hugh was stamping his feet and yelling, *'God is gone. He is not there…'*

Raoul banged his fist on the boards, making the glassware jangle. 'This is not the Pot d'Étain.' My husband had the look of a weathered tree, sapped of life. Hugh stopped yelling.

The spell of silence was broken by Godfrey's arrival. 'Have I missed something?' he asked and everybody laughed.

'Thank the Virgin you didn't bring the Provost with you, Coz,' Alixandre said.

After the soirée on Saint Bartholomew, Raoul didn't leave the house, not even for Mass. As we no longer celebrated feast days, an end came to our 'night talkings', though he did visit my bed once more. On Christ's Nativity.

'What do you think the scripture means,' he asked me, *'to be taken up into the third heaven?'*

'God can be revealed to us at any one moment of any one day, perhaps?'

'We can see God's perfection in this life?'

'Aye, my lord, though it must be the cause of great disruption.'

'Disruption?'

'The apostle left behind all he once deemed of value to do God's Will.'

'Marguerite, I…' His fingertips brushed my face with such a tiny drop of the tenderness I thirsted after. I drew the bearskin over him and rested my cheek on his head, surprised to find his hair was soft like a child's. As he slowly circled the ruby liquid in his glass, I waited for him to finish his sentence. 'How different things might have been,' is all he said. He drained his cup and dozed off. On the last day, when he lay struggling for breath on the same spot, I would think back to how I allowed this moment to miscarry its promise of intimacy. I should have asked him, what was it he wanted to tell me?

I COULDN'T have explained at the time of Raoul's death why the little Mathurin priest infuriated me so. Father Albert arrived *à la porée*, hands flapping like an untethered canvas in an unexpected storm. 'I fear I come too late to hear Sir Raoul's confession.' After the morning I'd had, Raoul's confession was my least concern.

I'd returned from early Mass for Corpus Christi to find the solar deserted. Open on the table beside Raoul's untouched herrings sat my copy of *The Consolation of Philosophy*. He'd left his marker underlining some lines in Chapter Two.

> *Dull-witted is his mind, alas,*
> *Sunk in steep depths below,*
> *Abandoning its native light*
> *It purposes to go*
> *Into the darkness of despond —*

The far end of the gallery seemed to me, that day, more than ever a void sucking in every speck of light. I'd never once ventured into Raoul's private chamber but where else could he be? I knocked. No answer. I opened the door.

Air slugged with male sweat rushed out at me and would have driven me back onto the gallery but for the wafer of daylight creeping in beneath a warped purlin. I finger-tipped my way to the shutters. Sunshine cleansed the air. The room looked, I imagined, like a Spartan military camp: a bare couch stood next to a clothes coffer, contents turned out on the floor; a standard iron chandelier hung with looping wax stalactites occupied the corner; an empty phial lay on the floor and beside it, a bloodied poignard.

A groan came from behind me.

'Raoul!' He was hunched on the oaken chest, arms dangling, and my head emptied of all common sense. I tore at the cuff of his fine lawn undershirt where it was crusted over and instantly a crimson stream gushed down the back of his hand. In a panic, I wrapped his uninjured arm round my neck. Two steps and we crashed down, sending the chandelier thundering across the boards. 'Raoul, wake up. You're not going to die. Not like this.'

'My lord.' By some miracle, Rufin appeared in the doorway.

'Thank the Virgin you came back. But what about Marote?'

'Fine little daughter we have.' He smiled so widely his scar almost vanished, then took Raoul's weight.

The bedchamber was cluttered with linens and brocades. What a novel thrill it had been earlier that morning, choosing my gown with Alixandre in mind, alighting on turquoise for our tryst, to temper the equivocal colour of my eyes. I felt the burn of guilt and pulled my clothes from under Raoul's body.

'I knew this'd happen,' Rufin muttered several times as he tended Raoul's wound, arranging the damaged arm beneath the covers and the other on top. He glanced at my skirts. 'I'll stay by him, my lady.'

It was a relief to go to the solar and peel off my stained gown without having to look at myself in the mirror. Forcing myself to forget Alixandre was now on his way to Aigues-Mortes and I might never see him again, I returned to my husband's side.

Raoul let out a long rasping breath and Rufin leapt up. 'I'll fetch the priest.'

As I lit a fresh candle on the chandelier, a movement in the enclosure outside caught my eye. Red pennants with a white cross pattée flapped in the light breeze. Horses' hooves stamped impatiently. I slapped the shutters to, dropped the bar and settled at the foot of the bed where, one cold morning, a lonely old man had sat to tell a lonely young maid his dreadful secret. Now, as he was slipping away from me, I took the hand which had lifted mine at the chapel of the Mathurins, had held the lamp for me as I read him poetry into the night, and had once touched my face so tenderly.

I wondered about the 'black pit' and the nights he spent alone in his barren room burning down candle after candle. And what about that physic he took to dull his pain. Why had I not thought to go to him, bring some cheer into his darkness? What a selfish, foolish little girl I'd been. But it was now too late.

By the time the priest arrived with Sir Hugh in tow, the clamour of the excited young men of Paris down in the yard was penetrating the shutters. Father Albert took out a silver pyx from his scrip and as he pressed his thumb into the oil, the orders shouted out by the Knights of Saint Jean seemed to muffle. The instant he anointed Raoul's forehead with the sign of the cross, the aroma of holy oil broke through the scent of death. The rasping breaths slowed.

Pressing his still warm hand between mine, I hoped my husband might look on me one last time, perhaps touch my face, speak a word of explanation, a word of farewell. But Reality was to cheat me once again. Raoul drank in one last sip of life and was gone. Dear, complicated Raoul.

A shrill trumpet blast rose from the Commandery.

'Do not trouble yourself for his soul, my lady,' Father Albert said. 'When Sir Raoul took the Cross, like all these brave Christian men today, he earned entry into Paradise.'

For God's sake, why then did you make such a ridiculous fuss about his confession? And what about the consequences of Raoul 'taking the Cross', driving him to an act which, according to you, would herd him with the goats into Hell? That's what I wanted to shout at Father Albert but dared not.

A thunderous roar went up from the knights, '*Deus vult*,' God wills it. The fear of Hell swirling in the pit of my belly evaporated in the scorching heat of my anger. I stood upright and faced the priest. 'My husband risked his life to release the Holy Land from bondage...' Once I'd started, I couldn't hold back and caught sight of Rufin behind the priest nodding along. 'For that cause he was clapped in chains. He returned home to an even worse kind of bondage. Sir Raoul lost all that matters to a man of honour. Finally he lost—'

'My lady is understandably distressed.' Hugh grasped my elbow. 'Pray allow me to conduct you to your chamber.'

I took back possession of my arm. 'This *is* my chamber.'

Hugh and Father Albert stared at each other. Clearly they knew of Raoul's wound, of his fortune paid out in ransom, and I read their look perfectly: *Wasn't this a marriage of convenience? Didn't he marry her for her father's money?* It gave me huge satisfaction, knowing there were things about Raoul's life these men were unacquainted with. I blew out the candle and flung open the shutters. The sun draped a warm shroud over Raoul's body at the centre of the bed where we had shared our singular version of married love. Yes, this was the complete surprise Fortune sprung on me: I loved my husband.

Both the men I loved sought to do God's Will and I lost them both on the same day. If only they hadn't been to Outremer, things would have been so different and I came within a hair's breadth of yelling that out of the window. But the earth was quaking under a thousand marching feet.

6

From Paris to Valenciennes, 1297

'**M**IND yer feet!' The hawker flung out his spindly arms.

Lost in memories of my noble Parisian days, I'd been slow to walk the few hundred yards from Godfrey's house to the Couvent des Mathurins. Eyes irresistibly drawn to the dismal little porch at the top of the chapel steps where I'd made my vow of obedience before God, I'd hoofed over the hawker's threadbare cloth. Several of his pewter tokens now lay in the dust of Rue Saint-Jacques.

'Oh, I'm terribly…' I began, but the hawker had already rolled up his shop and was merging with the stream of people heading for the church. I let myself be borne along.

On the top step stood an emaciated Franciscan. As the grey friar's congregation swelled, so did his voice. 'Scripture instructs us, after the Holy Ghost descended upon the apostles, they shared all their possessions…'

A few yards back from the crowd, his slender hands hugging his elbows, stood a tall beghard. He wore a brown habit like our sermoniser but like all men of his ilk, a tunic sat over the top, cinched in with a leather belt. I wondered whether the beghards emulated John the Baptiser in other ways; living on a diet of locusts and wild honey, I imagined, must make the winter months tricky.

The Franciscan friar stretched to his full height and pointed an index finger skywards. 'It is not poverty brings us closest to God. Nay! What brings us closest to the Divine is *o-be-di-ence*.' With well-paced drama he descended to the parvis and prostrated himself in cruciform submission on the flagstones, motionless as a corpse. Now it was the hawker's voice swelling, 'Come get your likeness of The Obedient Virgin. She'll heal you with one touch.'

Throughout the sermon, the flint-like profile of the willowy beghard had remained impassive. 'You disagreed with the friar's premise,' he said without turning round, but I knew his words were aimed at me.

'On what do you base your judgment?' I said.

'I sensed your spirit resisting. Yet…how extraordinary.' He stroked his sandy beard, trimmed to the shape of his pointed chin. 'You are in tune with God's will.'

'You're a man of discernment?'

'I'm told I have the gift.' He broke his pose. 'You're from the North. And judging by your attire, I'd say you are one of our beguine sisters. What brings you to Paris?'

'An old friend. And purchase of the finest stationery in the land.'

His feline eyes stared down at me. I stared back.

The yard was emptying of pilgrims. The friar pushed himself upright, brushed the dirt from his palms and strolled off. The hawker rolled up his empty cloth and scurried across Rue Saint-Jacques in the direction of Le Lion d'Argent.

'Stationery?' The beghard turned back to me. 'For what purpose?'

'I think you a mite forward.'

He held up his milk-white palm. 'Forgive me.' He bowed lightly. 'Guiard. From Cressonessart. Also visiting friends.'

'Marguerite. From Valenciennes. Though some have been known to call me *La Porete*.' Using my nickname made me smile.

'A thing of hardly any worth, yet you have the skill of letters?'

'A small leek has infinite worth if you're starving.'

Guiard laughed with his whole body—his most attractive feature, I've always thought, his facility in moving from deep reflection to spontaneous mirth. I walked on towards the church of Saint-Séverin trying to mind my feet as he interrogated me about my education. 'Do you know the Gospels?'

'I do. And with Meester Jens in Ghent I worked on the Apocalypse.'

His eyes lit up. 'What are you copying now?'

'Copying?'

'You said you're a scrivener.'

'I did not.'

'But the stationery?'

'For my treatise.'

'A woman? Writing a treatise?' He sounded not shocked but charmed.

'And your theme?'

'The soul who truly knows God is simple. All she must do is return her will back to God, whence it came as pure gift, then she becomes one with the Divine. And since she is filled with the Divine Will, there is no need for *o-be-di-ence.*'

'Marguerite…*Porete*, will you take refreshment with me?' His red-gold hair glinted in the sun. It's possible I accepted Guiard's invitation because he shed around him the colour of autumn.

We crossed to the Pot d'Étain. 'I see you wear clerical habit, Guiard.'

'I took minor orders. But now I find myself increasingly at odds with the practices of Holy Church. Makes me dangerous to know.' Guiard's least attractive feature, I've always thought, his grandiosity.

The sepia air in the tavern was thick with chatter. My belly fluttered as we moved deeper inside, past the firepit where dripping hissed from the half-boar on the spit. The buzz of conversation shrank to a muffled hum as we took a table by the rear door. Outside in the yard a scullery maid sieved mash, shaking the golden liquid into a fresh vat.

Guiard spoke *sotto voce.* 'Do you ever feel you are alone in the world? That no one thinks as you do?'

'Ofttimes. Though I look for the like-minded.'

'Have you found such souls?'

'I've found many who are lost in the desires of a good will, but very few who live the life of freeness.'

Guiard waited while the landlord served our ale. 'What do you think about the miracle of the Host?'

'Which miracle?'

'Here. In Paris. You don't know the story?'

I shook my head.

'A Jew from the Place de Grève tried to cut up a consecrated Host. He failed. So he boiled it in a stew pot. They say the water transformed into Christ's blood. The Jew met his end at the stake.'

'How appalling.'

'What? Trying to destroy Christ?' He tilted his head and smiled as if daring me to gainsay him. I glanced around the tavern. The maid in the yard tasted her brew and nodded, satisfied. Inside, the chatting and bursts of laughter merged into a pregnant hush; a hooded man lollopped over his table as if inebriated, but his intense eyes stared up at me. 'Fear not.' Guiard leaned in close. 'I'm well-known here. When the doors are barred, we discuss the things of God late into the night. Many a monk has seen the light and, abandoning his cell, is forced to abide in the shadows.'

The frisson of excitement returned to my belly. 'The Host is a piece of bread, manufactured by human hands. God is in it, but…God is in all places to be found.'

Guiard looked like the tomcat Ysabeau once shut by accident in the dairy shed. 'Tell me more about your treatise.'

JACQUOT had sold all his cloth at Lendit Fair and now resembled the brother I knew at the age of twenty-one who had insisted he was ready to pledge his life to the Templars— or 'be damned for all eternity.' After my meetings in Paris, I, too, was feeling confident I was on the right track and found it easier to put aside my fantasies of what might have been.

Of course, as the wagon jolted home through Aulnoy Woods, my mind strayed to The Robber's Den. In a quiet moment Amand had shared with me his deep concerns about Jacquot, that after Curé Nicolas left the parish, he'd been in danger of losing his footing. Amand had known my brother's secret, and kept it, since they were youths, and had protected him in the city against wagging tongues when Jacquot passed up Coustance's hand in marriage. Amand insisted loudly, and often, that, for his sake, his best friend had made the costly and noble sacrifice of the most enchanting girl in Valenciennes.

As the oaks thinned out and the ripe barley strips of Lower Mead gleamed in welcome, Jacquot struck up a lively motet. It had been a long time since I'd heard the voice our Dominican tutor once likened to 'an angel kissing the air.' I seldom found myself in such harmony with the Crow-man.

'I'll sing a new song, fine and beautiful,
Of a Virgin, a Maiden, a Mother and—'

I knelt up on the wagon bed behind Jacquot to see what had curtailed his praise. My jaw tightened. I'd been led to believe Notre-Dame de Macourt was to be a modestly sized Charterhouse but the gateway of chalkstone confronting us was of breath-taking proportions. Beyond the arch stood the ribs of the church nave which would swallow in the chapel of the beguinage threefold. To one side a cloistered row of neat stone houses, two storeys high, was already complete. My heart felt sick, for at the middle of the quadrangle stood our entwined oaks. They were going to be obliterated from my life.

'They're about to hang the gates.' Jacquot took the reins from Rogier and steered aside onto the track towards the hamlet of Marlis. 'You'll not see inside again.'

'Won't they make an exception for a twin?'

'No females allowed. Ever.' He jerked the reins as if a cony had darted across his path. 'What's *he* doing here?'

I followed the line of his vision to the mason's lodge. On a block of quarry stone, beside a stallion worthy of a king riding into battle, stood the newly elected échevin, Jean le Vilain. Jacquot moved the wagon on slowly. As we approached, Jean bowed with mock reverence. 'I've been showing the Ma*sh*ter here the land I've donated to the priory,' Jean said. 'I hear you convin*sh*ed Prior Pierron not to e*csh*tend up to the mill? Shame.'

Jacquot's jaw tightened. 'The prior *and* Count Jan were in accord. Pascal and Antoine are not to be turned out of their home. Isn't that right, Master Maçon?'

The mason looked down and fiddled with the document in his shovel-sized hands.

'Pa*sh*cal should've drowned that cretin at birth.'

Jean le Vilain's words fell on me like sparks to dry tinder. 'I'm sure if Antoine had been born to Mistress Yolent,' I said, 'you'd think differently.'

'Truly, *Lady* Marguerite? Or should it be—' Jean was doubtless reluctant to pronounce the word 'Sister'. Without taking his ferrety little eyes from me he mounted the destrier, his red silk mantle swishing against the saddle. 'Or should it be *plain* Marguerite?' He kicked his spurs into the horse's flanks and sped off.

'For God's sake, Margi. I despise the man but that wasn't pretty.'

'I was with Blanche, may she rest in peace, the day she believed the floods had taken her Antoine.' Feeling the want of a woman's company, I jumped down from the wagon. 'I'll make my own way back,' I said and strode off down the mill path in search of Agnès.

7

Valenciennes, 1298

THE DAY BEFORE JACQUOT ABANDONED ME, we met on the stone footbridge.

'Let's do it.'

'For God's sake, Margi. We were considerably younger the last time we risked it. And remember what happened then?'

I remembered clearly the last time we'd played the Dangling Game. Earlier that afternoon I'd ridden in from Paris, just in time to watch Ysabeau laying out Papa in his winding sheet. In the night, every time I closed my eyes, I saw the waxen skin stretched over Papa's cheekbones, the dark 'O' of his mouth. I went into Jacquot's bed in the solar. For once, his singing didn't sooth me and after living cooped up *à la porée* with an ever more reclusive husband, my emotions threatened to break out of my ribcage. I tugged at Jacquot's shirt. 'Let's go to the river.' Placing my feet firmly on the parapet of the bridge, face down to the Ointiel, Jacquot holding onto my wrists, I leaned over the rushing waters as far as I dared. Suddenly his head ducked low. Spectral in the dawn mists, an owl on her way home to Hamon's barn had screeched past his ear.

'You still managed to snatch me up,' I said. 'Come on. There are no owls in broad daylight. Let's do it. Just once more.'

This time he caught me up easily and set me safely down.

Facing upstream, where the elder blossoms were pushing out their creamy scent and catkins their strands of glorious yellow, he leaned over the parapet and gave the Charterhouse a lingering look.

'Impressive towers,' I shouted in his ear, loud enough to make it tingle.

'Notre-Dame de Macourt looks like the pasty sister of Château-le-Comte.'

'And how's your hovel?' Around the merchant class of the city, 'hovel' was the name Master Jean le Vilain had given my new home.

The idea of where I might spend my future years without Jacquot was born in me the day we returned from Lendit Fair. When I'd arrived at the mill cottage out of breath, Agnès went to fetch ale. Resting on the mounting block by the leat, I thought back to the moment I'd first sat there and made my proposition to Blanche and Pascal about their daughter. I'd recently returned from Ghent and had come across the scrawny seven-year-old with the straggly blond hair picking elderberries on the river path. My heart, and my sore womb, had gone out to her. Blanche and Pascal invited me to a meal of fresh goat's cheese, washed down with Pascal's best brew, and I managed to hide my pain as the two of them exchanged discreet little glances, silently sharing their delight at their child's good fortune.

Under my tutelage their daughter had proved a born scholar. She learnt to interpret a Latin text as easily as she could read a mood in the adults around her. It was Agnès who brought Katarine to Saint Elizabeth's beguinage.

It must have been after the Mass for the Dead—I remember the old chapel was illuminated with scores of votives. Cécile de Nimy, prioress at the time, floated across the flagstones looking as though she could rise above all things. 'Prioress!' I called out and without awaiting her acknowledgement, 'I wish to don the sack.'

'Lady Marguerite,' she said, 'you've worked a marvel with our girls in Sister Mahaut's absence. They recited the psalm so beautifully at the Mass. But aren't you also tutoring your protégée?'

'There are more hours in the day than Latin grammar can fill.'

'And didn't I see you on All Hallows' Eve,' she raised an eyebrow, 'knee-deep in the river with Sister Florie, beating linen?'

The doorlatch clicked.

As Agnès drew near, the sight of her plump, pink cheeks gave me the warm glow of self-satisfaction. Then I noticed she was biting her bottom lip. It had been her regular expression when she first lived with me until, perhaps a year in, she accepted there would always be plenty of food for us both to eat.

Behind her, someone was hanging back in the shadows. The woman's hood was drawn down to her chin.

Cécile turned back to me. 'Increasingly you're living the evangelical life, my lady.' She patted Agnès' golden braids. 'Pray take the time to consider where your priorities lie.' She floated to the back of chapel and as she led the woman out, the hood slipped to reveal the luxuriant auburn tresses of the blacksmith's wife. From her forehead to her jaw ran a groove, the width of an auger, filled with the dark gel of blood.

'What happened to Katarine?'

'Master Durant,' Agnès said, 'that's what happened to Katarine. I found her wandering in a daze beside the Ointiel.' She grasped my hand and didn't let go till we reached the stone bridge. 'I'm never going to marry.'

'Master Durant had a moment of madness, 'tis all.'

Agnès nodded but her body remained taut.

'Come on,' I said. 'Let's play the Dangling Game.'

'The river moon is a fish,' she shouted as she hung facedown over the water. 'Nay…it is a lamp. Nay…it is Sister Florie's bottom.' We giggled so much I almost dropped her.

'Let's go finish the coverlet for your new brother.'

'Might be a sister this time.' Agnès kicked off her clogs and ran. 'Can't catch me.' I did catch her, for the very last time. And the babe turned out to be another brother, Antoine, who would one day become the reason Agnès left the beguinage and returned to live with Pascal.

And he was the reason my 'hovel' now stood beside the mill cottage. Jacquot had traded with Hamon for the land and employed Master Maçon to build my home with the quarry-stone left over from the priory.

'My *hovel* is perfect,' I said. Jacquot stared down into the rushing river and our distorted reflections made us appear, for once in our lives, like twins. 'If the white palace of Salle-le-Comte were offered me in exchange, I'd refuse it.'

'And Agnès?'

'Ecstatic to be back at Saint Elizabeth's. Settled into Mahaut's house as if she never left. Believes me crazed for taking on Antoine. But Jacquot, he's always so enthusiastic when we do the most mundane of chores. "Magrite, Magrite, we knee bread?"' I hooked my brother's arm and we walked along the river, veering onto the new pathway which now bypassed the monstrous monastery. 'Every black friar proclaims the Day of Judgment will come with the new century. Doubtless the man who tried to force his *droit-de-seigneur* over us has harkened to them. Everyone in Valenciennes claims Count Jan d'Avesnes endowed the Charterhouse as penance for his war.'

'Naught wrong with making amends. A man can change,' he said and added, 'can't he?' as if he needed to convince himself. 'After a decade of strife, here on our doorstep we'll have a haven of peace.'

'*You* will. Not *we*.'

'Stop it.'

'Stop what?'

'You know. Your defiant mule look.'

Despite myself, I smiled. The priory bell clanged. Unfamiliar. Jarring. 'Count Jan's wicked conscience has despoiled *our* Ointiel. *Our* oaks are gone.'

'Though you cannot see them, that does not mean they do not exist. Didn't I hear you say something similar once?' I've never invented a name for the Jacquot smirk. 'They'll remain within the cloister garth,' he said, 'not far from my cell. A sign of God's calling, Margi.'

I imagined him in his little house, all alone, and thought of the intense friendships he had forged with Amand and Nicolas. A stab of guilt. How often had Jacquot exposed his need of me and I'd refused to respond? Like on the Nativity feast, only a month after I'd joined Saint Elizabeth's. When he waited for Ysabeau to stoke the fire. When he waited for her to bring us spiced wine. When he waited till she disappeared into the kitchen for her snooze. When he yelled at me.

'You went and did it. Without consulting me.'

'Why would I consult you?'

'I'm head of this family.'

'If you want someone to lord it over, find yourself a wife.'

'The very state of you. Sister of the foremost mercer in Valenciennes, nay, in all of Hainault. Small wonder they call it *donning the sack*.' He looked me up and down as if I'd emerged from the midden heap and sniffed the aromatic wine of Alsace in his goblet. 'Hence your long absence. You couldn't have me talking you out of joining the fanatics.'

'You hold Mahaut for a fanatic?'

'Mahaut?' He eyeballed me. 'Not in the slightest. But last week, a sparrow hopped into my workshop and, Lo! Sister Florie insisted it was a sign from God. God tells the beguine to do this, God tells her to do that. Fanatics.'

'Ah, they feel they must pledge their whole lives to serve God rather than be damned for all eternity?'

'Not the same.'

'So it was the beards and flowing mantles attracted you to the Templars?'

He drained his cup and glared into it as if he thought somebody else must have drunk it dry. 'I wouldn't have known about your initiation ceremony if it hadn't been for the new curé.' He went to the dresser for more wine. 'So, now you're a beguine, will you join my stitchers?'

'I teach in school. I scribe for the prioress, and I'm busy with—'

'For God's sake, Margi. Don't make me say it.' Maman's eyes were turned on me but I hardened myself. I refused to let him beg anything of me.

Now here we were, the day before his own initiation into the Charterhouse, before he was to don the serge and I had to ask, 'Are you ready for the solitude, Jacquot?'

He stared at the priory turrets. 'Beyond ready.'

The afternoon warmed as we continued along the new path to the mill yard. 'So,' he said, 'how have your readings been received at the beguinage?'

'Agnès and Souveraine Jeanne are enthusiastic. Sister Florie pretends to be.'

'Well, on my final visit to Salle-le-Comte last week, I came across Lady Germaine. Rather, Lady Germaine came across me.' He stopped and, with a look of self-congratulation, held me by the shoulders. 'Countess Philippine wants you to read for her household.'

Something elusive slid through my stomach, like a handful of eels somersaulting and returning to their burrow. 'I don't think I'm ready.'

'Nonsense. These ladies are steeped in courtly love. Isn't that what you write about?' Allowing himself to remain ignorant of my work has always been his most effective strategy for provoking me. I determined not to take the rise.

'Godfrey was adamant I should clarify my thoughts before sharing them.'

'Remember what Papa used to say? "Inspect not the teeth of a given horse."'

'Perhaps he should have inspected my marriage settlement more closely.'

He let ancient history pass. 'What should I tell Lady Germaine?' His eyes shone like Bijou's used to when he brought me a mangled bone to share. As with my old hound, I ignored my reluctance and welcomed the gift.

'Tell her to send me word of when to come.'

The path through Lower Mead ran out. At the one table in the one room of my hovel, we ate our last supper together. Doubtless we will never play the Dangling Game again.

ONE DOZEN EYES tracked me across the Countess of Hainault's solar. Not for the first time in my life. At ten years old, wearing one of Papa's unique designs which would attract much business from ladies at court, my hands had trembled. Nearly forty years on, I suffered no anxieties about my appearance. I remained in grey, albeit my gown was cut from the finest wool as Jacquot had insisted. He wrung this last promise out of me before he descended the path to the priory. It was a peculiar moment, watching him go, wondering, was this how he'd felt on our tenth birthday when I left home for the white palace? As though his heart was leaving his body so that he could hardly breathe, fretting over how I'd fare living amongst strangers?

My anxiety about how my brother might be faring without quality thread on his back disappeared as soon as I took in the familiarity of Salle-le-Comte. In the countess' private apartment where the wide casements opened out over the Escaut, the figure of Saint Catherine still stood out from the mural, holding the spiked wheel on which an Emperor tried to break her. The clutch of ladies stitching at the broidery frame was also familiar, except the faces behind the goggling eyes had changed. The eyes swivelled to the left. The door to the bedchamber had opened.

Countess Philippine was as small as her predecessor was tall. The barbette, tied like a tourniquet under her plump chin, drained her complexion; her gown of matching gold brocade couldn't hide the toll twelve childbeds had taken on her body. Buttressed on the arm of the statuesque Germaine, lips pressed into a courtly smile, Philippine's puffy eyes scouted the room. The instant they fell on me she flashed a warm and genuine smile. The smile transformed into a grimace as she eased herself into her cushioned settle.

A second lady-in-waiting took her seat beside the countess. A linen chin-band drew back her powdered cheeks, accentuating the pinched nose of Lady Catelon. As if it had happened only yesterday, the insult she had once paid my mother blazed through my innards. I'd wanted to keep a veil drawn over the years I'd lived under the guardianship of Marguerite Noire, but throughout my audience with Countess Philippine, flashes of memory stole through. Particularly memories of Catelon and our mutual friend, Yolent.

Yolent was the girl who had to wear her grandmother's clothes to court. In my first few months at the palace she took an interest in me, demanding to know all about me, probing me about Our Story: Did I know, worship in the upper sanctuary of Saint-Chapelle was reserved for the royal household? Was Eglantine really a servant if she wore gold thread in her hair? And was I aware, Isabelle of Hainault, grandmother of King Louis, had died after giving birth to twins? *In Paris*. Strange coincidence, don't you think?

In the summer months when Marguerite Noire went on her summer progress to Flanders, I was sent home to Rue del Saulch whilst the girls of noble houses accompanied her, including my special friend. On the day we all returned to Salle-le-Comte, I could hardly contain my excitement at being reunited with Yolent. In this same solar, the girls stood in a circle in front of Saint Catherine: Catelon, Heloys, two girls whose names I don't now remember, and Yolent.

Heloys set her fair eyes on me. 'How wretched we feel for little Marguerite, having no noble lineage.'

'Oh, the fault lies not with her,' Catelon chimed in. 'Who would ask to be born of a common seamstress? Yolent, dear,' she gripped my confidante by the arm, 'what delightful days we spent with your esteemed kinsmen in Bruges. Nobility in all four quarters.'

Heloys nudged Yolent. 'Didn't you ask the countess about Marguerite's mother?'

As a player well-rehearsed, Yolent delivered her lines. 'Eglantine was an orphan. The queen took pity on her. She found her a position in the royal household.'

Catelon said, 'I wager Marguerite believes she lives here amongst us because she has royal blood in her veins. She's not even a noble bastard.'

Yolent shrunk into Catelon's shadow, though not before I noted my former friend's new gown of lilac silk; it was the very same Heloys was wearing the day they left for Flanders. Heloys smiled her sweetest smile. 'A velvet gown, no matter how fine, a lady does not make.' She pointed at the floor and hissed at me. 'Bow, draper's daughter.'

'Mercer's daughter,' I said, mulishly. As the circle of young ladies tightened round me like a shield wall, fire ignited my inner defences and they went up like a city built of wattle and thatch. But I didn't bow. It's no marvel I retreated into the library and erected for myself a fortress of impregnable words.

I didn't meet Yolent alone again until the day of my betrothal when I ran for sanctuary into the *librarium*. Sprawled across the desk, her elbow resting on a manuscript, my former friend was seated in the 'Bishop's Throne'— she and I had given the enormous library chair its sobriquet the first time we squeezed together onto its scarlet cushion, foreheads touching over *Li Chanson de Roncevaux*; it was on the 'Bishop's Throne' we had shared our girlish confidences.

Afraid her tears might crud the ink, I pulled it from under her. *La Vie de Sainte Agnès*. As I clutched to my chest the 'Life' of the martyred virgin, my mind worked through more sainted women whose example I might follow to avoid marriage. Queen Elizabeth of Hungary who threatened to cut off her own nose. Not a good plan, I realised. No man would ever want me without a nose, and although wriggling out of the contract with Raoul seemed impossible, I was still entertaining a forlorn hope for Amand.

As if the countess' library were my own personal demesne, I demanded of Yolent, 'What are *you* doing here?'

A face harrowed by the spikes of misery turned to me. 'You shouldn't be here either. It's time for Prayers.' Burying herself beneath her skinny forearms she resumed her wailing; the cuffs of the lilac silk gown reached halfway to her elbows.

'What's amiss?'

'Feign not concern, Marguerite.'

I ran through a quick resumé of our history. She was right. I had absolutely no concern for Yolent. In fact I wanted to hit her across the head with the Life of the virgin saint, but as I turned to leave, she wiped the slaver from her cheeks and said, 'I've been promised in marriage to…to…'

'An old man?'

'He's not old. But he's a…' she shrieked the word, 'tradesman.'

Fuelled by anger and bitterness, my words shot out. 'Fortune smiles on you. You're not being forced to marry your grandsire.' For one lengthy moment we glared at each other, our faces a mirror of tragedy. I forget which one of us sniggered first, but soon we were laughing like two imbeciles. Breathless, I wedged myself on the 'Bishop's Throne'.

'Who, pray, is the lowly bridegroom?'

'You may know him,' she said, with a touch of pridefulness. 'His father is rich and his grandfather was once Provost of the city. Master Jean le Vilain.'

'I know Jean.' I didn't mention that as children, Jean would follow me round as a lamb a ewe; but I only ever wanted to be with Jacquot, and Jacquot only ever wanted to be with Amand. Deeming it a kindness to the girl who received naught but hand-me-downs, neither did I mention Papa had refused Jean's suit for my hand in favour of Sir Raoul. I shelved the *Vie de Sainte Agnès*.

A VOICE trilling like a linnet called me from my childhood memories and back into Countess Philippine's presence. 'Sister Marguerite,' she chirped, 'I believe you were well-acquainted with my husband's grandmother,

Marguerite Noire as they called her?'

Awkwardness buzzed around the solar.

Philippine assumed her official voice, clipped and high-pitched. 'Any displeasance has been allayed for many years now. And it is good to welcome back a former courtier to Salle-le-Comte. Now,' she returned to trilling, 'I've heard favourable report. How remarkable we have a woman writing here in Valenciennes! A beguine, like Hadewijch. Would you read for us, Sister Marguerite?' She signalled to Lady Germaine who glid like a swan around the room, plucking up a fauld-stool, setting it down by the fireplace for me.

'My lady, I'm working on a song in which Truth praises the Soul who belongs only to God.'

'Something new?' Philippine clasped her dimpled hands together. 'Oh, please do share.' The childlike joy in the aging woman moved me; it evoked trifling pleasures, such as splashing barefoot through muddy puddles or feeding Pascal's naughty goats, all incongruous with a lifetime spent at court. I fumbled in my scrip till I had a hold of my folio, and of my emotions.

'*O Emerald Soul,*' I read, '*exquisite gem,*
True diamond, queen, and empress,
From fine nobility you give your best,
Asking naught from Love of her treasure,
Except to will Her divine pleasure.
O deepest spring and close-sealed fount,
Wherein the sun doth hide subtly still,
You cast your rays by divine skill.
This we know, says Truth, by insight,
Her shimmering grace sets the Soul alight.'

The silence must have lasted seconds but it felt like an hour before the countess applauded enthusiastically. Her ladies followed her lead. Except for Catelon. Catelon was bending forwards, scrabbling on the floor, pretending she'd dropped her needle.

'*Shimmering grace sets the Soul…*Truly inspired.' Philippine frowned. 'But how…wherefore would the sun hide in a sealed fount?'

'Even in the darkest of places, my lady, there exists a mote of Love's light.'

As her eyes flitted round the room, toques and wimples dipped and the goggling eyes concentrated on the broderie frame. I wondered how dark Philippine's life had been with the warmongering count, a man who'd sired several children outside the marriage bed.

'Marguerite, will you return and share with us the Soul's response to Truth?'

'With pleasure, my lady.'

A new kind of Dangling Game was about to begin, but there would be no Jacquot to snatch me up.

8

Valenciennes, 1302

THE KINGFISHER PLUNGED into the deep channel of the river. Flashes of her iridescence captured the full attention of Blanche's boy whose eyes were the same intense colour as the hen-bird's crest. Though his body retained the shape and softness of a child's, Antoine was now a man and as our Halcyon rose with her plump catch, he stepped up onto the balls of his feet; as she turned in the air, he turned in the air, two simple souls at one.

We were on our way to the friary, our first visit to Brother Olivier since Antoine's latest attack of the grippe. Pascal had been terrified it was the sweating sickness returned to the city. I knew it was not. One rainy day in the spring, Amand's distraught sons had sent for me and I arrived in time to hold his fevered hand as he passed into the next life. Antoine's signs were different and on this balmy afternoon, he was once more bouncing up and down.

'We see Frey Oliber?' he said.

'And we'll chop vegetables for the pot.'

'An' knee bread?'

'Aye. Soft white bread.'

'For the Prire.' As he stared long and hard at the kingfisher, Antoine's blissful expression transformed into puzzlement. Perched in the hazel bush, mercilessly she bashed her minnow on a bough. Then the shout which made us jump a mile. Agnès came at us, waving wildly. With no comprehension he was too heavy to swing, Antoine leapt into her arms. Kissing the top of his head, she pushed him firmly away. 'Lady Germaine send—' She grimaced. '*Pfoo*...sends for you.' Leaning forwards, she braced her palms on her knees. 'Bring your manuscript.'

'It's Wednesday. The countess isn't expecting me.'

'You haven't heard about Courtrai?'

I shrugged.

'The Lord of Beaumont fell.'

ONCE MORE on entering Philippine's presence, I was overtaken by a sense of *déjà-vu*.

Thirty years before, when Marguerite Noire visited me in Ghent, I was the woman lying catatonic on a bed. Countess Marguerite had dropped her bag on the same floor where I'd given birth and sat herself beside my fast-diminishing body. 'Come back to us, dear girl,' she begged me. When I remained silent, she hutched up closer. 'Listen, Marguerite. My firstborn, my Baldwin, perished before he saw two summers. But my next child needed me.'

'My Michel needs me,' I whimpered. 'He's all alone in the darkness.'

'Oh no,' she said, 'he's in the lightest of places.'

'But he wasn't...'

'Baptised?' She drew in a long breath and exhaled. 'Do you recall the day Brother Thomas Aquinas preached at Saint-Paul's in Valenciennes? One clever young maiden in my entourage was deeply troubled to hear him claim that if a soul is destined for perdition, no amount of praying for them will change that end, but pray for them we must. Well, it seemed to this maiden so pointless, so cruel to pray for a soul going anywise to Hell. "We do this," I told her, "to show mercy." The maiden answered me, "But my lady—'

'"How is it possible for a human creature to act more mercifully than God?"'

'Exactly that.'

'You remained silent for such a long time I was sure I'd incurred your wrath.'

'Divine mercy, Marguerite. At the tender age of eleven, you schooled a countess about divine mercy.' Reaching inside her bag, she brought out a casket the colour of heavy cream. On the lid was carved a phoenix rising from the flames. She placed it in my lap, against the womb which still bled, and left me to discover for myself the sheets of vellum folded inside, sitting between penknife, whetstone, and inkpot, all held in place by dainty leather straps.

A further torrent of tears failed to extinguish the fire Michel had raised in me, the flame kindled the moment his father's lips had brushed my skin and I begged to know of God, *Why did I not die instead of my little one?*

Days passed before I forced out a single letter onto a pristine page. Eventually, a second. A word formed. A sentence. The ink transformed into a mountain stream. I laboured till dusk blinded me and rose at cockerel crow to begin again. My dearest Mahaut appeared in my room carrying a bowl of broth and a worried look. 'You must keep up your strength,' she said. But I couldn't stop, I didn't stop. Not until my benefactress called me back to Valenciennes.

During the course of our first conversation back at court, she asked me if I knew why she had been nicknamed Marguerite *Noire.* I had to admit that I did. The rumours about her birth were well-known. It was said, when her father ruled as the first Latin Emperor of Constantinople, his empress, Marie de Champagne, was bedded by a Moor. The story was hard to disbelieve—at my first sight of Countess Marguerite I'd thought her eyebrows looked as if someone had drawn a piece of charcoal across her forehead. And of course there was the dark scandal of her two marriages, the first illegal, the second potentially bigamous, leading to the poisonous feud between her Avesnes and her Dampierre sons. 'Let them think what they will about me,' she said, 'but truly, I am Marguerite Noire.' She drank down her goblet of wine in one. 'Bouchard d'Avesnes was my guardian. He tutored me, sang me courtly love songs. He was a handsome warrior and I, a lovesick little orphan. When I was ten years old, I was given to him in marriage. Bouchard was thirty-four. At thirteen I bled and soon discovered what his love meant.' Her rings clinked against the Venetian glass. 'Yes, I *am* Marguerite Noire. There are places a woman must go…'

Now, decades later, when Lady Germaine admitted me into the same private chamber where Philippine was laid out on the bed like a bird with crushed wings, I wondered about Bouchard and Marguerite. Were they looking down with pity on the mother of their great-grandson, crippled with grief that her firstborn lay dead in the soil of a Flanders field? Did Marguerite Noire regret her dynastic wars?

'*Mon petit Jean, mon petit,*' Philippine droned as she stared out at me through dead fish eyes. When I read words to her about God's inexhaustible mercy, she made a sudden grab for my hand. '*Mon petit.* He was always so afraid of the dark when he was a child.'

'My lady,' I said, 'when my son died, a very wise woman told me not to fear. Michel is in the lightest of places.'

Philippine held onto me and I remained with her until she slept.

UP CLOSE, Jan D'Avesnes II, Count of Hainault and Holland was more powerfully the image of his grandmother. The first time I'd set eyes on him at a distance was two decades ago in Abbaye Saint-Jean.

It was shortly after the old countess died and he came into his title. The crown of spires was concealed by dense fog, the pavement slippery underfoot, and the voices of Valenciennes spoke in muffled tones. How would the son conduct himself, we asked, after the father had been cut off from his inheritance? At the abbey, herded like sheep into the fold, our bleatings echoed around the clerestory. Bodies well-seasoned with winter penned me in on all sides but I was determined to get a sight of the guildsmen. I wheedled, pushed and finagled my way to the front.

Amand had taken up his position at the west door; the honour of greeting our new suzerain fell to him. Taller and narrower than Amand, Jacquot stood at his shoulder and I congratulated myself that the hem of his mantle was perfectly level.

I'd spent four days fitting and stitching and with only two hours to go, one sleeve still looked too bulky.

'For God's sake, Margi, it must hang properly.'

'Who are you trying to impress? The count?'

'Don't be ridiculous. I want the fellows at the guild to see I'm serious. Trustworthy. Sober.'

'Sober?' I laughed. 'With all the ale you swill?' I snipped off a knot and pulled out a long thread. 'And why, as our liege lord, does the count need to swear allegiance?'

'Not allegiance.' Jacquot rested a hand on his hip, gesticulating with the other as he lectured me. 'Count Jan must swear the oath to abide by the terms of La Paix. Acknowledge freemen direct this city. You do know, don't you, that it's due solely to our charter the échevinage has been able to establish, through our own judiciary, such stability as—'

'Hold still.'

'Margi, are you listening? Margi?'

'Hold still, I said.'

'When Amand had me over to dine on Candlemas—'

'Ooh. Dining with the new Provost of Valenciennes. You *are* rising in the world.'

'You know he's always been my best friend.'

'Aye. It was always the two of you in The Robber's Den, hiding from me and Jean le Vilain.'

'Stop bellyaching. Anywise, Amand says Papa was kept on the margins of city affairs by failing to get himself elected onto the échevinage.'

'It hardly encumbered his trade. He left you very well off.'

'Things never stay the same, Margi. Competition heats up.'

'So, you're taking part in a contest?'

'Must you always mock?'

In the abbey, many of the congregated flock eyed Jacquot up and down, nudging each other, whispering, admiring, I thought, the grey and white lining of Muscovy vair so striking against black silk. Hush swelled through the nave. Drumbeats thundered. The procession entered. First the glittering train of clergy, followed by the standard-bearers and their noble lords. I sucked in my breath. Swarthy, taller than any who had entered so far, the count held himself as one of the lions rampant on the Hainault banner. Marguerite Noire's true heir.

Now, on the Feast of the Epiphany, twenty years or more after his accession, a place had been reserved for me at the high table of Jan d'Avesnes II. The air in the salle haute tingled with the scent of evergreens. Candles from two dozen chandeliers supplemented the thin January sunshine and the series of murals, depicting a fair king on a stag hunt, glistened in the flickering light. The hearth behind the high table was filled with a blazing tree trunk. As a girl, when my place had been at the opposite end of the hall where a draught was always blowing under the doors of the antechamber, I used to think the attendants in their gold and black livery sprang like salamanders from the gigantic fireplace. But now, seated on the dais, I learned the door to the kitchen was obscured by a huge dresser.

Philippine had insisted on my presence at the banquet. This was to be her first court appearance since the Battle of the Golden Spurs as the Flemings were styling their humiliating victory over Philippe le Bel and his allies. One of the five hundred pairs of knights' spurs now hanging from the ceiling of a church in Courtrai had been ripped from her son's armour by a band of weavers who had bludgeoned to death the flower of French nobility. From her seat on my right, the countess whispered to me, 'You give me such heart.'

Surreptitiously I studied the count who was seated on her other side. His resemblance to his grandmother aided me in tempering my anger toward the man who had been the cause, however indirectly, of my breakdown; if it hadn't been for his attack on Anzin, I'd never have fled to Mormal. As I was pondering the relationship between fate and destiny, Philippine, though her voice wobbled, made herself heard to all who were seated above the salt. 'Sister Marguerite, do tell us about Paris. You dwelt there at the time of Robert de Sorbon. I believe you were acquainted with him?' 'Sir Raoul ofttimes entertained scholars at our board.'

'Intriguing.' Count Jan leaned in. 'Did you chance upon the great Thomas Aquinas?'

'Nay, my lord, though I heard him sermonise here in Valenciennes.'

'Ah,' said Dom Alard, Abbot of Hasnon, who was sitting at the count's right hand, 'when the Dominican Chapter convened at Saint-Paul's. 1259.' Reaching out his bejewelled talons, he selected a pear from the mountain of fruits and sniffed at it. 'Made quite the stir. So many folk packed into the church, the walls fell in.'

'His philosophies, my dear Abbot, have acquired a certain orthodoxy. Some say he is destined for sainthood. Last year's heretic, this year's authority. Think of Saint Francis.' The count guffawed.

Dom Alard let the ripple of polite laughter subside. 'I gleaned a story about Doctor Thomas. The year before he died, he neither spoke nor penned a word. When his scribe begged him to get back to work, the doctor replied, "I cannot, Reginald. All I have written seems to me as straw."'

'Perhaps,' I said, 'he realised at the last that whatever we say of God is more like lying than telling the truth.' A row of eyes popped out at me. The abbot's. The count's. Philippine's.

The countess was first to recover some composure. 'Abbot, Sister Marguerite is instructing me in divine things. She has so much inspiring to say.'

'Perchance Sister Marguerite would deign to share with us some of her *instruction*?'

Not yet on her mettle for the bearpit that is courtly discourse, Philippine trilled, 'Oh Marguerite, you *must* read the piece for us about the Mother of Virtues. Most pertinent.'

'We might suffer our guests to sup in peace.' The count had clearly marked that the abbot's sarcasm had passed his countess by.

'It would be an honour,' I said also wishing to deter Philippine, 'but you recall, my lady, the piece is a dialogue.'

She raised her chin towards her husband. 'My lord, I am rehearsed. We read it together only this morning. Should you approve, I will recite Love's words.'

'As you wish, my dear,' the count yielded easily.

The countess rose and extended her hand, giving me no option but to take the folio from my pouch and hold it out between us. Philippine's rapid breaths spread the sweet aroma of almonds as she began:

'*I am Love, and I will tell you what Reason would ask, were she still alive. Reason would ask: Who is my mother? And who is the mother of the other Virtues? Are they not also mothers? And I would have replied, Aye, all the Virtues are mothers.*'

'*Who then, asks this Soul, is Mother of the Virtues themselves?*'

'*Humility is the Mother of the Virtues.*'

'*And this Humility, who is Mother of such a great lineage, whence comes She?*'

Philippine glanced at the abbot. '*The one who knows the answer cannot put it into words.*'

I kept my eyes on the page. '*How true. For it would be lies if I said aught of it. Humility is daughter of Divine Majesty. She is very close to the Far-Near One who, divesting the Soul of all her works, frees her from all servitude. For whoever serves, is not free; whoever desires, wills; whoever wills, begs. And whoever must beg, well, they lack divine sufficiency.*'

'*Those loyal to Love, however, are always surprised and disarmed by Her.*' Philippine's voice quivered and I feared she might weep before the whole court. '*They would endure torments for eternity on Love's behalf. Any soul who doubts this is the truth has never loved nobly.*' She applauded and, to my relief, so did the count.

Barely had we taken our places and the hum of renewed conversation was pierced by Dom Alard's voice. 'Why did Love speak on Reason's half? Were you suggesting, Sister, that Reason is dead?'

'Only at this point in the dialogue, Father. Reason bobs back up again later. She's hard to do away with, I've found.'

Everybody at the high table laughed spontaneously, except the abbot.

Philippine dabbed her napkin across her forehead. 'Marguerite, I believe you once encountered Saint Louis.'

Before I could begin my tale of the day I lived through the sweetest moment of my marriage, and the bitterest, the count jumped in. 'King Philippe should browbeat Pope Boniface into more canonisations of his dead relatives. Divert the burghers of Paris from noticing how hard he taxes them for his war chest.'

'His Grace *will* avenge Courtrai.' As the abbot spoke dispassionately of the massacre in the Flemish mud, Philippine gripped the edge of the table. 'The Count of Flanders had best keep watchful.'

'Poor old Uncle Guy,' crowed the count. 'He'll be back in a French dungeon anon.'

Setting her back squarely to the men, the countess muttered, '*Mon petit Jean, mon petit*.' Her hand grasped my wrist. 'Marguerite,' as she held my gaze, her dark-rimmed eyes were perfectly steady. 'It behoves me to search for a "mote of light" in the blackest of places. I wish you to prepare for me a copy of your *Mirror of Simple Souls*.'

'It will be done, my lady.'

As she stood and bade her husband good night, I marvelled at the woman's dignity and at how, walking so deeply through the valley of the shadow of death, she had ignited a spark of life in my own breast. Lady Love was undoubtedly working Her will, without our knowing.

Intending to take my leave, I was halfway to standing when the count leaned across his wife's vacated seat. 'I believe you knew my grandmother and my Dampierre cousins?' He raised a hand in a gesture of peace. 'Fear not. We all make allies where we must.' He smiled wryly and I sat down again. 'A fine diplomat, your brother. Shame he took Carthusian Orders. If he were a secular, a Dominican even, I could have used his skills.'

'My lord, Jacques seeks the contemplative life after so many years of needless conflict.'

The count studied the defiant mule who had taken over my face. 'You'd make a formidable abbess. You've never considered the veil?'

'I do not come from noble stables.'

'Of course, but more notably from...what was it? *The great lineage of Humility?* His laugh was friendly and, despite myself, I warmed to this man in whom were combined the sturdy features and humorous grace of Marguerite Noire. If only he hadn't repeated her mistakes and made Valenciennes pay for them.

'Should Humility not be Mistress of the Virtues?'

'For womenfolk perhaps. For men, our virtue lies in our courage on the battlefield.'

'What of the courage to confront the inner foe? Is that not a virtue for any, no matter their sex?'

Confusion flickered across his eyes. Without doubt I'd pierced his armour of courtly propriety and I wondered if my blow had struck at his sense of worth, or at what he had more artfully concealed—his grief for his firstborn son. I hadn't the opportunity to discern which because Dom Alard rapped his knuckles on the table.

'Perchance Sister Marguerite would care to school the Pope?'

The count retrieved his charming smile. 'Dear Abbot, I do believe our guest would have the Holy Father tied in knots.' He laughed softly. 'Sister

Marguerite, do you ever see your brother?'

'Twice a year. At Eastertide and on the Virgin's Day.'

'When you next meet, be sure to extend to him our...*humble* regards.'

'By your leave, my lord.'

The count commanded an escort. As I followed the young page across the hall to the antechamber, ghosts passed through me; my ten-year-old self who once knelt before the whole court at her presentation and the sixteen-year-old maiden reeling from shock at her betrothal. A buzz of energy dispersed the uncomfortable memories. I'd received my first commission. My mind began to organise the title page for Philippine, thinking I'd use best vellum, perhaps illuminate the letter 'M'... A prickling at the back of my neck alerted me, someone's eyes were tracking me across the tiles. My attention was drawn to the west wall of the salle haute.

Sitting beneath the painted monarch aiming his spear at his quarry, I recognised Lady Catelon. One seat down from her sat a guildsman. He was leaning over to whisper in the ear of a gentlewoman whose brilliant white wimple obscured the last panel of the mural. From memory I knew the panel showed the image of the royal hunter poised with his knife, ready to sever the tongue of the felled hart. The gentlewoman in the wimple stared at me as if she knew me, but I couldn't place her. Then the guildsman beside her straightened up in his seat. Master Jean le Vilain.

I knew life had forced Mistress le Vilain to drink of many bitter cups which undoubtedly is why Yolent turned her ravaged face from me.

9

Valenciennes, Feast of the Virgin's Nativity 1304

WHEN JACQUOT ASKS ME why I couldn't keep my mouth shut, I'll tell him I could have said all manner of things to the Italian. Like what an ass he made himself look when he asserted, 'Women do not write books,' and at the very same moment threw my manuscript on his desk. But I held my tongue. For a while.

It's fortunate I'm not a tall woman, or even medium-sized, else the afternoon sun pouring through the lancet windows of the abbey parlour would've blinded me. That said, the violet episcopal silks were enough to startle a goat. So I fixed my eyes on the stonework behind the bishop's head. Carved beneath the corbel, a pair of conjoined heads faced in opposite directions from each other, the male staring prayerfully up into heaven, the female gazing down on Lord Guido with an expression of eternal forbearance.

Alb cut from softest white lawn, satin-stitched apparels at the wrists, immaculately shaven tonsure smooth as jet-stone, Guido da Collemezzo sat down behind the desk. Planting an elbow on either side of my manuscript, his fingers assembled into a steeple beneath his chin. The amethyst in the episcopal ring sparkled. 'You've been extremely busy, Sister Marguerite.' The steeple pointed to the stack of vellum. 'What intendment do these articles have?'

'My intention is to assure people of God's boundless love.'

One of his sleek eyebrows arched. 'I'm informed you've been teaching our noble ladies appalling errors.' Lord Guido raised himself to his full six feet, blocking my view of the forbearing lady. 'You know the punishment for a heretic?'

He-*rrr*-etic.

My thoughts scattered like a flock of alarmed sheep. Who'll milk Pascal's herd when the drink claims him, take Antoine to visit Brother Olivier, or read to the countess if I'm dead?

The amethyst flashed at the edge of my vision, directing me towards the fauld-stool. As I sank onto the leather seat, my eyes drew level with my manuscript. Given the chance, I felt sure I could convince a servant of God about the truths in its pages and it looked as if he was going to give me the chance; the amethyst flashed again, dismissing the dark sentinel behind my back. They might call the men who enter Saint Dominic's Order of Preachers 'black friars' for their outer capuce, but as a child I always thought of them as crows and this crow picked over the scene, missing not a single detail. He glared at me as though I were responsible for his exclusion from my interrogation.

The bishop waited silently until the latch dropped.

'The count's death unexpected. Countess Philippine distraught. Chaos in the city, only days before the Blessèd Virgin's Feast. Then I am receiving this denouncement.' He sat back down. 'Your *Mirror of Simple Souls* gives grave offenses.'

'I intend no offense, my lord. And I have the support of a renowned scholar.'

He leaned across the desk. 'Oh? Which scholar?'

'Master Godfrey de Fontaines.'

'Godfrey de Fontaines?' I'd taken a wrong step. The bishop had flushed the colour of a bruised peach. 'A man who rates his own cleverness above episcopal authority?' He waved a dismissive hand in the vague direction of Paris. 'It's clear to me that in this season of instability, malice motivated these accusations. What opportunism. What ambitiousness. What vanity. Ubiquitous sins.' Glancing out of the window, across the abbey precinct, his eyes came to rest on the imposing belltower. 'Dom Alard, Abbot of Hasnon, petitions for a charge of heresy.'

It had never been my intention to make an ass of the abbot at the Epiphany Feast. He'd managed that all on his own. Men like him rarely understand anything of which Reason is not the mistress, but that was an opinion I kept to myself. 'My lord, you haven't said in what this *heresy* consists.'

The bishop lifted a corner of my manuscript. 'You are stating, in your scheme, Nature may be given *all She desires*. Thereby you sanction debauchery. It is incontestable that debauchery leads to anarchy.'

'With respect, this is a misunderstanding of my text. The vanity and the ambition you spoke of? They find their origin not in our physical nature. Sin is caused solely by human will.'

'Try not my patience, Sister. Free will is an article of doctrine you are having no authority, indeed no capacity, to speak on. You are not a scholar. You certainly are not a Preacher. You are a woman.' He glared at me.

'So you are saying my *Mirror* should be condemned, not because it contains falsehood, but because of vexatious accusation, and because of my sex.'

'Interesting.' The sneer of the cunning lawyer. 'You decry Reason yet you utilise Her particularly well when it suits you.'

'Reason is a good servant of the Virtues but should never be their master.'

'Enough,' he barked. 'I cannot suffer your erroneous teachings to infect others, or for you to go unpunished. Understand?'

Again my thoughts ran loose: I've heard of them pulling down a heretic's home to cast out evil from the place. At the very least, it'll be a flogging. Or will they— The bishop brought his fist down so hard onto my *Mirror*, the desk and I jumped in unison. He roared, 'Do you understand?'

I have no memory of kissing the amethyst he brandished beneath my nose or of what the Dominican said as he marched me to the abbey penitentiary. I remember only the reek that hit me in the back of the throat when he pushed me through the door.

I AM BROKEN. My most precious belongings lie scattered on my bed in the home I must leave.

They made me wait until the Virgin's procession was done, until all of Valenciennes and its environs were gathered. It was well past noon when Simon du Gardin arrived at the penitentiary. I had straw in my hair and stank like hog's urine and beneath his cap of scarlet Simon couldn't look me in the eye. Not until the constable shoved me in the back to force me over the cobbles of the Grande Place did our new provost find his tongue. 'No need for that,' Simon growled, 'Sister Marguerite is no scapegrace.'

Our glum little procession wended its way past the belfry; higher than the abbatial tower, the familiar banners of azure and white rolled down like dragon's tongues from the turrets. Aromas of pork fat and apple tarts drifting across the square from the temporary cookshops unleashed memories of the dead. Provost Amand leading the Virgin's raft as it was borne through the streets on the shoulders of cartwrights, tanners, farriers. Ysabeau lifting young Master Jacques to see the holy cord which the Queen of Heaven once held around our city, saving us from the pestilence 'and all works of the Devil since.' Dear little Manon squealing with delight as Mahaut, blinking like a frog, surfaced from the duck-apple tub.

The faggots at the centre of the market place were piled high, ready to be lit at dusk, but the spectators had their backs to the great bonfire. This year, their attention was fixed on the stone pillory.

A sullen hush hung over the sea of heads. The silence was all wrong for the Virgin's Day and shockingly harder to bear than the jeering I'd prepared myself for. A fractious child wailed. One face stood out in the crowd, and another; the old fishwife who has always kept back the finest Flemish oysters for me; Bertolot's apprentice Landry, Master Illuminator himself now, whose russet hair is turning to snow. On every jaw, anger. In every eye, pity. Oh, the pity. I couldn't bear it so I studied the firewood on the pyre. Tiers, laid stick upon stick, one, two, three, four; kindling neatly tucked between, exactly as I prepare a new fire in the hearth when the embers expire because my mind has wandered from the world.

Willow twigs crackled in the brazier.

In the night, on the stone cold floor of the penitentiary, as I'd raked over the coals of how I'd come to this pass, a ball of grief had been gathering in my deepest parts. It rolled upwards now, biting and clawing its way out into the silent but disquieted city as I counted my manuscripts. Three were stacked on the pyre. So they'd been to the beguinage and confiscated Souveraine Jeanne's copy.

Dom Alard's voice broke in. 'Hearken to Lord Guido's judgment.' It seems the Bishop of Cambrai had delegated the honour of overseeing my mortification to the abbot, who was now holding up Philippine's manuscript. The letter 'M', Landry's handiwork, shimmered. 'Persist with your false doctrine, woman, and your flesh will burn also.' Murmurs in the crowd. Did I hear a laugh? 'And then your soul will suffer eternal punishment in the fires of Hell.' As if the abbot's threat needed underlining, the constable took a torch from the brazier and drew a wide arc in front of my face.

The kindling was alight and the abbot threw the sheaf of parchment on the pyre. Sparks flew. Despite the gentle September sun on my back, when he bowed in prayer the pale dome of his scalp made me shiver; I couldn't help but picture in the mounting fire the tortured face of Katarine, the woman who fought back. Her head, like a delicate swan's egg, had been sheared of its auburn glory. And now the flames licked around my manuscripts as they had licked around Katarine's feet.

I had thought myself stronger. But as the acrid smoke scorched my throat I couldn't stop myself from reaching out as I had once reached out for my child. And the same as before, a gentle hand stayed my arm. Through my grubby sleeve, Simon's hand felt warm but I trembled as the parchment slowly curled up blackened corners. 'Steady.'

Flakes of ash and charred skin lifted on the breeze. If the wind gets up, I thought, they'll carry as far as the Escaut and float away into Flanders, on and on till they reach the opening where the River Scheldt flows into the ocean. *Scheldt.* The name the Flemings have for our Escaut. I once stood by the Scheldt where it meets the North Sea; the bleak expanse of grey merged with the bleakness in my heart, and I'd thought at that moment of our own Ointiel, our bright and lively, laughing Ointiel, sliding through the ripe barley strips of Lower Mead, under the stone footbridge, on towards the spires, to Pont Néron where it empties itself into the Escaut. I stood on the drab grey sands of the North, my breasts leaking milk. If only I'd stayed…
If only I'd stayed beside our river, he would have lived, mon petit. He would have grown up, safe, amongst the gillivers, the elders, and the kingfishers. He would have learnt to climb the twin oaks.

Simon released my arm. 'Go home, Sister Marguerite.'

Home? How will I go home, now all was again lost? Transfixed, I stood by the glowing ashes. I heard no voice. The townsfolk continued to stand by, mute, contemplating perhaps their role as accomplices in an act of violence, willing or unwilling.

A body pushed to the front of the crowd. My cold, deadened fingers responded to the touch of his skin. The hand holding mine possessed the emergent strength of a boy on the cusp of manhood, when limbs are clumsy and voice undecided in its register. The youth guided me away from the smouldering debris at the foot of the pillory and like the Red Sea for Moses, the crowd parted. He led me through the walls of silence, across the dry land of the square to the Halle aux Drapes.

Two women stood by the guildhall, laughing. One wore a starched wimple; the other, with pinched nose, gripped her arm. They turned their backs on me. Without relinquishing my hand, the boy spoke in a bold voice. 'Sister Marguerite, you carried me through the flames and saved my life.

You have my eternal gratitude.' Right behind his shoulder, the miller of Anzin nodded in approval as his guided me into two waiting arms.

'Let's go home,' said Agnès. In the Grande Place the pipes and tabor struck up a dour tune.

AS I FUMBLE with my linen in the dearest hovel I can no longer call my home, the threshold darkens.

'What's this hogwash I'm hearing from our Agnès?' Pascal's eyes, ordinarily big like a cow's, are bursting out of his head.

'I won't let you and Antoine suffer.'

'Suffer?'

'Bishop Guido—'

'Bishop Guido can go hang hisself; no Italian will stint me from being a proper Christian. *Proper*, I tell you.'

I slump down on my bed. I think I may have damaged my casket. 'Folk will shun you.'

'Are you meaning the folk as already shun my Antoine? Well, they're not worth a piss in a poor man's—Begging your pardon, my lady. Anywise, my Antoine ain't here.'

'Oh no. He's not sick again?'

Pascal straightens himself up as far as his old labouring back will let him. 'My Antoine is at the friary. The prior's made him the kitchener's new assistant. If he settles, they'll make him a lay brother, *proper* like.'

While I weep into my skirts Pascal gazes out across the yard. I pull myself together. 'Won't you be lonely?'

'He'll be home with Agnès on feast days. And *you*, my lady, *you* be going nowhere.' He strides off to the barn before I can put up an argument.

PART TWO

Béguine Clergesse

When it happens that white and black are together,
one sees better these two colours,
one against the other,
than each by itself.

The Mirror of Simple Souls, Chapter 60.

Susan Shooter

Marguerite's Wax Tablet

Susan Shooter

UP AND DOWN the furrows of Lower Mead we chased wagtails till we collapsed in the tall grasses. You rumpled your skirts between your thighs, fashioned for me a nest. 'Wouldst hear a tale, *ma petite*?'
You rested your chin on my coif and I breathed you in, my dearest Nan. Fresh perspiration laced with lavender and wise understanding.
'Ne'er lived there a truer maid, ne fairer, than Halcyon. Loved her King Ceyx with all her heart, she did. But their great love vexed that jealous old Zeus good and proper, it did. So when Ceyx set out across the Middle Sea to consult the Oracle of Apollo, the Father God whipped up a mighty storm. Hurled the waves into a frenzy, he did.' Ah, what joy it was, to be pitched from knee to knee in your beleaguered ship.
Eventually the tempest calmed and you sighed.

'ALAS FOR LORD CEYX. Drowned, he was. Alas, for poor Halcyon. Struck dumb, she was. No other love did she desire. None greater could there be. So off she sped to the ocean. Down she plunged, down, down, down.' Knowing my little heart was breaking, you clutched me tighter. 'Fret not, *ma petite*. The lesser gods showed mercy, they did. Up from the deeps rose a dazzling bird, up, up, up above the waves. Turned our Halcyon into a beautiful kingfisher, they had.'
You pressed your damp cheek to mine. 'Behold,' you said. 'Do you see her?' And what a marvel. The hen-bird was hovering over our Ointiel, her breast all aflame, then in a flash of colour, she flew out of sight.
My child's heart didn't understand why your tears were streaming down into my neck-hole. I thought it a sad enough story, but didn't the kingfisher live on?

Susan Shooter

10

Marlis-en-Valenciennes,
8th September 1308

MARGUERITE LEAPS UP from her stone block beside the mill leat with a sprightliness she hasn't known for years. When a lozenge of purple light appeared over the Ointiel where it babbles through the hamlet of Marlis, when the choir monks behind the walls of Notre-Dame de Macourt began to chant the Hour of Prime, she heard Jacquot's voice. The nightingale has finally shown up to prove how much sweeter is his song than robin or throstle.

In the distance the drums start up. Moving her naked feet to the rhythm across the yard, she pauses by the barn to argue with Pascal, says he really should go to the revels and not mind her, wins the argument as she did last year, and the year before, and dances into her cottage.

She cusses, not at her carelessness with the last decent candle which is now a warm pool on the table, but at the wax tablet still lying open beside it. She slaps the top plate shut.

Throwing her overdress of finest wool on herself and some dry sticks on the embers, she catches up her largest pot from the hearthstone. By the door she stops to brush a cobweb from the armoire. It may be her imagination but this year the spiders seem more prolific than usual.

Crouching on the sandy flats where she and Jacquot used to fish for purple-backs, she watches her neighbour. He's already made it to the other side of the plank bridge, his arms curled around a huge jar. The ripe barley in Upper Mead shimmers around him as if the sun, in his haste to illuminate the Virgin's birthday, has dropped a sheet of gold leaf on his workshop floor. Pascal is aiming for Marlis Cross, less than a league hence, where the minstrels are drumming pilgrims into town with the tempo of an estampie.

The drumming cuts out and Marguerite shades her eyes.

The stone cross has been engulfed by a roiling mass of bodies. They separate down the middle to let two riders pass through. Who on God's good earth turns their back on Valenciennes today, on bonfires, duck apples, and roasted hog? Who else, that is.

The new tune the minstrels play sounds more like a dirge than a dance but it doesn't dampen Marguerite's spirits. No one important comes this way as a rule but she feels a pang of excitement as the two horsemen veer off the main track. They can only be looking for Hamon's Mill. And about time too. It was Eastertide when she wrote to Bishop Jean.

SHE FIRST MET Lord Jean at Lady Marie's wedding shortly after he received preferment to the See of Châlons-sur-Marne. It was a beautiful summer's day as she traversed the marbled hall of his ancestral home in Châteauvillain and she thought how, in lilac, ivory and green, the bride was the manifestation of a woodland sprite.

'Dear Sister Marguerite,' Marie linked her arm. 'I promised myself, since I couldn't have my grandmama at my nuptials, I'd have you.' The first time she had seen Marie de Dampierre, she was peeking out from behind Marguerite Noire's skirts like a timid squirrel but it wasn't long before the child was squeezed beside her in the 'Bishop's Throne', confidently naming the creatures in her grandmother's bestiaries.

'My felicitations on your marriage to Lord Simon.'

'It's so joyous the second time around. I can't tell you how much I appreciated your letters from Paris when I was betrothed to Wilhelm. The old goat, as Grandmama used to call him. Now. You see the Bishop of Châlons over there?' Marie pointed at a clutch of wedding guests and groaned. 'That one. Being bored to tears by Robert and his triumphs in Sicily.' Her brother, the Lion of Flanders, could have been dressed in rags and his military prowess would still roar back at you. He was engaged in animated conversation with an equally imposing man. 'I'm keen for my new brother-in-law to meet you,' Marie continued. 'He's a lover of the arts, especially poetry.'

'What would he think to a woman poet?'

'Oh, Lord Jean has a deep appreciation for the fairer sex.' Her eyes flashed mischief. 'Fret not. I've instructed Sister Nycaise to take good care of my favourite teacher. She'll come to escort you to your bed ere night falls.' As Marie steered Lord Robert away to the dais, Lord Jean looked utterly relieved. He turned to greet the newcomer.

'Lady Marie speaks very highly of you, Sister.' The bishop's voice was the throaty coo of a woodpigeon. Around his shoulders he wore a mozetta of indigo silk; a cincture of the same stuff held in his paunch. Most dazzling was the sapphire in his pectoral cross, the size of a plover's egg; it matched his piercing eyes which, even when he wasn't laughing, creased at the corners. 'She warned me of your sharp wit.'

'She's rather canny herself.'

'I must forewarn Simon. My brother is a dullard, though I fear he is ignorant of the fact.' Lord Jean guided Marguerite to a seat beside him at one end of the high table. 'Are all beguines literate?'

'Most of us.'

'What's the point of women reading?'

'We study devotional texts.'

'Hmm. Exemplary. The Count of Flanders there,' he gestured along the table to where Guy de Dampierre was seated beside Marie, his eldest daughter, 'he holds your male colleagues for heretics. Chased all the beghards out of Bruges. A touch zealous, I feel. But less of that. I'm told you compose verse.'

'With meagre talent.'

'No need to act coy with me.' He grinned raffishly. 'Ah, I used to love recitals in Paris. *Li Roman de la Rose*. What do you make of de Meun's addition to Loris' text?'

'I think it does not subtract from the original. Rather it multiplies its charm. Though opinion is divided.'

His laugh began as a low rumble in his belly and came out shaking at his shoulders. He leaned forwards to inspect the sweetmeats in the serving dish. As the fragrance of the rose otto oiled into his fringe entered Marguerite's nostrils, a warm flush spread through her veins. 'After the formalities,' he said in a hushed voice, 'you and I must retire to the solar. Share some verses.'

If only to herself, she had to confess her pang of disappointment when Sister Nycaise appeared later in the evening at the door of the solar. Lord Jean, like a child being robbed of his comforter, held onto Marguerite's hand and wouldn't let go till she promised to visit him at his palace in Châlons. At the time she didn't follow up his offer but on her most recent visit to Godfrey de Fontaines in Paris, she bumped into the bishop quite by chance in the Cour du Palais. After all these years he hadn't forgotten her, or his invitation.

THE TWO HORSEMEN clatter across the plank bridge. Marguerite rests the full waterpot on her hipbone and pushes a wilful strand of hair under her coif. The first rider halts at her stone seat and uses it to dismount from his palfrey. His brigandine is polished to a sheen. Undoubtedly he's a captain of men is her immediate thought, but he's lowborn; he holds his head proudly, and you might even call him fair if it wasn't for the nose that's been broken a time or two, but it's the sardonic twist to his mouth. Before he opens it she can tell the sergeant was reared in the back alleyways of Outre-Petit-Pont.

At the gateway to Lower Mead there's a commotion. A third mounted gen-d'armes reins in by the barn; behind him, a wagon and pair. And now the goats are a-blathering and she's thinking how Chou-Chou and Canard will lead her a merry dance come milking time. Heavy boots crunch on the gravel. The third guard stretches out his skinny legs in their mottled brown chausses; he looks as though he could move fast and without warning and her eyes flit to her open door.

'Are you Marguerite,' the sergeant's voice is like metal grinding on stone, 'known as *Porete*?'

'I am. And you must have come from the lord bishop.' As the words leave her tongue and become separate little entities from her thoughts, as her eyes fix on the fleur-de-lys embossed at the Parisian's chest, it strikes her, an escort of four royal guards is excessive even for Lord Jean de Châteauvillain. And the sergeant looks bewildered, as though she's given him the answer not only to a question he didn't ask, but to a question she wasn't even supposed to know.

He brushes the back of his left hand across his lips. 'By order of Philippe de Marigny, Lord Bishop of Cambrai…'

Water slops out of her pot making an inkblot down the light grey wool. She looks past the leathern torso, beyond the river. Upper Mead has turned the colour of scraped parchment. There are a few stragglers near the stone cross but no one else is coming this way, although why that would be of any help, she doesn't know. And now the sergeant is saying, 'under guard… something… something… Paris…' The pot slides away from her hip and makes the sound of a well-loosed arrow striking quarry.

Unable to sink into the parched earth, the water butts up cool against her toes. Paris? The slow drumbeats from the city throb in her ears. Her breath feels cut off. For the first time this year the northeasterly blows across the yard, making the reeds shiver and Marguerite inhales the friendly breeze. As she picks up her pot and straightens up, her eyes come in line with the fleur-de-lys. Though she fears the worst, she has to hear it.

'What am I charged with?'

The Frenchman stares at her and a jab of anger at his silent insolence focuses her mind.

'I'll be packing my coffer.'

'No coffer,' he grunts. 'One small bundle.'

The guard who rode in with the sergeant from Marlis Cross jumps from his courser; the poor beast scrabbles its hooves on the grizzled turf. 'Hébert was right.' The giant guard is also a Parisian. 'We don't need no wagon. I could pick her up with one hand.' The men laugh.

By the barn the reins jangle. 'Hébert reckons we should strap her to one of the hacks.' The driver has the accent of a Picard. He scratches his balding head as if he has lice.

'Changed my mind, I have,' says the spidery Hébert, 'now I've seen her. Reckon we tie her to a rope and make her run all the way. Put her on her back at night, that will.' Hébert's southern drawl brushes up against Marguerite's skin, sending a quiver across a web of memories, threatening to disturb something grievous at its hub and immediately her mind flicks to her wax tablet. Driving herself towards her hut, for one absurd moment, she thanks God that the Parisian sergeant is at her heels—his odour of saddle-sweat and tavern common room is as effective to keep her upright as any physic Agnès can concoct.

Inside she rests her forehead against the limewashed stone which muffles the sound of the rushing stream, the creaking waterwheel, and three men arguing who'll take first turn with the Northern slut.

The Frankish sergeant stands at her armoire, his barn-door back to her. He picks out the book with the red velvet cover. 'I pray you,' she says, 'do not...' Now he's seized a bundle of her parchments, he's touching her poems and she lets out a groan. The man may as well prod her flesh with his martial fingers.

'Bishop's orders,' he says without turning round.

Dark spots dance in front of her eyes. The same vision, flakes of burnt skin falling as filthy snow on a landscape of silent heads, dragged her out of bed in the middle of the night. She grabbed her stylus and tried to write away her sleeplessness but ending up more alarmed, she went to her thinking place, to her stone where this intruder stood with his foot up just now as if she no longer had any rights to it. Her body creases in two and reaching out for something solid, finds the bedframe. She wants to know, she needs to know why, after all these years, Jacquot was singing this morning with the voice that has always chased away her worst nightmares. But this afternoon she won't be there to ask him.

Mellow sunshine spills through her window yet her fingers have frozen around the top edge of her counterpane. The nap of the cloth, shiny from wear, feels more like silk than wool she's always thought. Her father always said they do things differently in England. The scrape of a boot on the beaten earth summons her back to the present but the sergeant's barn-door shoulders are still turned away from her. He's taking a long time over her manuscripts. Perhaps he can read. For God's sake, why is she thinking about *him*? She grabs her ivory casket from the coffer, places it in the centre of the blue Worstead, folds a clean coif over the lid, picks out two pairs of warm hose, fumbles, drops them on the rush mat, retrieves them, wipes a clout across her soles, and pulls on her kidskin boots. No need to change. She's already wearing her best dress in honour of the Virgin. Mutely, almost hysterically, she laughs at her pridefulness and unhooks her mantle of boiled wool, the one with the vair lining; she'll be glad of it if there's a frost before she comes home. The corners of the counterpane won't tie properly. *Why won't they tie properly?*

The sergeant turns round with her small library tucked beneath his armpit. For pity's sake, she prays, take care of them. Immediately the man holds the stack of manuscripts out in front of him. How odd. It's as if he heard her silent petition. Then she forgets about him. The last time a Bishop of Cambrai sent men for her she didn't have to battle her way to the door against this miasma of black billows which are threatening to knock her sideways. Bolstering her shoulder against the jamb, she tells herself to run. But where to? Pascal will be in the Grande Place by now, hailing Our Lady of the Holy Cord with his finest ale; the great bonfire will have fizzled out before he staggers home. And under no circumstances would Prior Pierron admit a woman into the Charterhouse. Besides, she's seen too many summers to outpace four well-fed men. Glancing back at the ashes whitening in the hearth, she can't stop her jaw from quivering.

The sergeant doesn't look her in the eye as he gives the order, 'Wagon.'

The Languedocian, Hébert, swaggers out of Pascal's cottage, cheeks bulging. He throws aside a cheese rind and rubs his palms together. She'll be damned if she'll let him lay a finger on her. Launching herself over the threshold she climbs onto the wagon-bed, trips on a lump of ironmongery hidden beneath winter livery, and lands on a pile of horse blankets. That'll spare her a nasty bruise.

The Picard flicks the reins and the wheels fall into the ruts of the track through Lower Mead. The goats are bleating after her like spoilt children. Why, she wonders, is there a sharp tug at her breast. And why Paris?

THE SWAYING of the wagon blends into a rhythm with the sound of hooves thumping on the track and question in her head. *Why Paris?* The new Bishop of Cambrai must be there. *Why Paris?* Lord Philippe de Marigny is one of the king's right hand men. *So, why Paris?*

By the time the mounted guards catch up, the giant and Hébert on the left, the Parisian sergeant on her right, the spires of Valenciennes have melded into a blur.

'Four gens-d'armes?' the giant scoffs. 'Those are some dread eyes she's got, but how dangerous can she be?'

'You heard the Provost,' says Hébert. '"She ha*sh* important friend*sh* in Valen*sh*iennes. And in Pari*sh*." Pompous little cretin. He was full of *sh-sh*-shit. Who's heard of a woman writing a book?'

'Roused the malice in him.' The sergeant draws his hood over his chestnut mane. 'Didn't like having her whisked away from under his nose.' He spurs his palfrey forward.

'Perhaps the little woman has hidden depths.' Hébert's bulbous eyes, the colour of pondweed, latch onto her. 'And if she does, her dirty little secrets will be winkled out by Guillaume de Paris.'

On all fours, Marguerite crawls to the back of the wagon and retches onto the moving ground. Through her damp lashes, the Virgin's statue above the gatehouse of Notre-Dame de Macourt is no more than a chalky smudge. When Jacquot last came out through those gates to meet her on Easter Day, he spent the afternoon fretting about Guillaume de Paris. Even a cloistered monk has heard the name of the Inquisitor of Heretical Depravity for the Kingdom of France.

The laughter of the Ointiel has gone silent. The drums are silent. All she hears is the kaw of a crow flying high.

11

The Road to Noyon,
September 1308

'WHY HAVE YOU STOPPED?' Moreau's words drop like wet clouts onto the sludge.

'Must be past noon by my reck'ning.' Étienne leans forward and pats the rump of one of the hacks. 'We're not even half way.'

'All the more reason to press on.'

They must be close to where the Beyne flows into the Somme. The ground has turned treacherous. While Moreau deliberates, Marguerite catches Hébert rolling his eyes. When the sergeant finally accepts they'll not reach Noyon by curfew, walls of mist have closed in around them. Étienne will have to rely on memory to divine his way to the hulking ramparts of Ham.

Beneath the wicker shelter spanning the rear end of Les Deux Lions, she fidgets from one buttock to the other. Ruminating on who denounced her was a distraction from the wagon tossing her around like a sack of turnips, but this hard bench makes her hips burn in deep places. She passes the scalding bowl of broth round her cupped hands until sensation returns to her fingers.

As she wipes a cuff across her damp lip, her eye is drawn to the opposite end of the yard. Someone is lurking in the shadows. The sergeant flinches and withdraws inside the stable. He must have caught her watching him. The man has hardly uttered a word since Sunday morning when they passed by The Robber's Den. Rising on her knees in the wagon bed she had pleaded with him. 'We must go back. I've left something important behind.' He glanced over his shoulder, said, 'There's no going back,' brushed a hand across his lips, and cantered off deep into the woods which camouflage the village of Aulnoy. On the two occasions he was obliged to give her direction, he stared straight past her ear as if *he* were the one feeling intimidated.

His little troop of three stands around the brazier in the tavern yard, stamping their feet against the chill. 'Foul rain on the morrow,' Étienne says.

'Another filthy day, another filthy mood.' Foulques, the Parisian giant, drains his tankard and passes it to Hébert.

'Reckon it's the weather vexing him like the Devil, do you?' As Hébert creeps past her on his way to the common room, she studies her supper; there's no need to tangle with a man who'd bleed a woman's spirit dry as soon as look at her.

Moreau steps out of the stable and strides to the brazier, self-control drawn over his face like a steel visor, but in the slits of his eyes Marguerite reads panic. Accepting a mug from Hébert, he drains it in one, and hands it back. 'Your turn for first watch. I'll be off to my bunk.' The sergeant passes by the wattle shelter without casting her a glance.

His deputy steps forward, all eyes. 'Allow me to assist you to your quarters, your ladyship.'

To avoid his touch, the scaly dirt of his skin, she all but runs inside the lean-to. The stink of goat is preferable to Hébert's. Before he can wedge his boot in the gap, she slumps down behind the ramshackle door.

There's some milling around outside. The boardwalk creaks. No doubt Hébert stretching himself out.

A muffled voice. 'His mind's not on the job.'

'Started when he clapped eyes on her, it did.'

'Nah. He were acting queer at the château. Found him on the battlements, staring out into the night.'

'That's Moreau for you. Moody cock-stick, he is. But when he came out of her lair and walked across the mill yard, well, dithering all over the shant, he was. The Chief is smitten with the little witch.'

'Looks younger than the Provo*sh*t made out.' Whooping and laughter. Somebody must have made a crude gesture.

'No messing with her, though. Under the bishop's protection.'

'We all know what that means.' More whooping.

THE TWIN TOWERS are the first glimpse you get of Noyon when turning south onto the old Roman road. Marguerite's hood is pulled so far over her head she has to imagine the cathedral where Charlemagne was crowned King of the Franks. The damaged north tower is doubtless still pressing like a decayed tooth stump against the relatively unblemished south tower.

The rain hasn't stopped pelting them since Ham. Down inside the tent of her cloak her head feels like it's clamped into one of her old headdresses, the one which made her temples throb till all she wanted to do was tear it off and have a good scratch. If only she had a task to do, anything to keep her from thinking about Jacquot waiting in vain for her beside the Ointiel and the Dominican awaiting her arrival in Paris.

The pelting stops and she peels back the folds of fur and boiled wool. Breathing in deeply, the taste of rotting vegetation does nothing to stop her head pounding, nor the wheel finding a pothole. She fishes inside her bundle and flipping open the bent clasp of the ivory casket she manoeuvres her hand around.

Pressing Michel's coverlet to her face she tastes the odours of iron and gall steeped into the fabric. The seraph's wings sparkle in the dull air as she bites off a tiny knot on the underside. Working gently at the edge of the azure couching until eventually she pulls the loose strand through, the next stitch gives more easily, the next more easily still. She winds the lengthening thread around her little finger until suddenly she's aware of a presence alongside the wagon. The sergeant dawdles there awhile and she can't help speculating on what's consuming the man. A debt? Possibly. A lover? Most unlikely. The wagon swings her sharply to the right.

Above Noyon, a rainbow cuts a precise arc as if it were holding the stormy heavens at bay from the tangle of scaffolds and spires below. She wonders how many more years it will take the masons to finish the rebuilding work after the day one tiny spark, leaping from thatch to thatch, incinerated half the city. Moreau moves Gäelle up beyond the wagon and Marguerite returns to her unpicking, but it's not long before the golden mare gravitates once again towards the sidebar. As if mesmerised, the sergeant watches her fingers unravelling the thread, up and down, round and round. When he touches the back of his left hand to his lips, he's close enough for her to observe the skin is purplish and puckered. She'd wager he's been to Outremer and her stomach turns over with the kind of curiosity which can get a cat killed. She knows she must keep her wits about her and with determination, returns to her industry.

The rose-tinted walls of a convent slip by. The wagon zigzags past cottages which shoot up like mushrooms from the loamy earth, and on towards the cliff face of Noyon's ramparts.

Étienne reins in sharply and Moreau pulls up short, cursing. He strokes Gaëlle's neck. 'There, there girl.' Gaëlle reminds her of Miéla, good-natured. And if there's one thing she'll grant the man, he loves his palfrey.

Étienne waits for two peasant women to pass. 'Did alright in the end,' crows the woman with skin the texture of hessian. 'Sold all me cheeses.' The younger woman raises her skirt to her thighs and leaps over a puddle of filth.

'Got aught for me, missy?' shouts Hébert.

'Me basket's empty, but me bed ain't.' The women shriek bawdily. Hébert trots on towards the turrets of Porte de Wez, shedding his smell of drenched dog. As the wagon wheels rock on the apron of mud funnelling traffic through the archway, Moreau holds back.

The vaulted ceiling of the gatehouse echoes with the clang of steel-on-steel; in episcopal livery, quartered red and blue, two lads are exercising with poleaxes. Thankfully, Étienne is soon driving out from the stench of latrine onto the paved streets. Moreau, still behind the wagon, lurches forward in his saddle and she thinks one of the youths has landed him a clumsy blow. But as he clutches onto Gaëlle's mane with his scarred hand, he's pushing the other fist into his lower abdomen. The moment they're out into the soft light of Noyon, his eyes flit to Hébert, then to Foulques. The two guards ride on, oblivious to their chief's distress. Marguerite drops her gaze. She won't let the sergeant catch her studying him a second time.

THE COVERED ALLEYWAY alongside the Augustinian house steams with damp horse. Étienne holds the wagon stationary by the open gate. Beyond it, the neatly cut lawn of the cloister garth glistens with wet sunshine.

'You overstep yourself, monk.' The sergeant stands nose-to-nose with a hawkish canon of Notre-Dame de Noyon. 'My orders are from the Bishop of Cambrai—'

'Couldn't care if your orders are from the king himself,' the canon hosteller shouts back, 'she is *not* going in our penitentiary.' He sucks in his cheeks and folds his arms across his chest, making the hefty keyring at his belt jangle.

A touch of colour has penetrated Moreau's face. 'Fetch me your superior.'

As if by magic, a second canon appears in the gateway. His black habit strains around his middle and he has the face of a bulldog. A smiling bulldog. 'What is all the tumult?'

'I've told him, Prior,' the hosteller sounds smug, 'our penitentiary is occupied. We cannot allow our wayward novice to be exposed to a female. Not even,' he jabs a blunt finger in Marguerite's direction, 'one as old as that.'

'And I've told *him*,' Moreau jabs a finger in the hosteller's direction, 'my orders, from Lord Philippe de Marigny, are to conduct this woman, under guard, to Paris.'

The prior gives her a long stare, long enough for her to feel needled. What is his disposition towards her? She cannot read the man. He glances at her mantle. Lacing his knuckles together beneath his chin, he leans forward and contemplates his sandals. 'Brother Claude, billet the prisoner in our new guest cell.'

'But Prior,' Brother Claude looks scandalised, 'the guest room is for noble visitors to the episcopal palace.'

'It is our only cell which locks with a key, is it not?' The prior glares at the hosteller's belt. 'I advise you to remember your vow of obedience.'

Claude ruffles his shoulders like a fighting cock and snatches up the traces of the nearest horse. He leads them to the end of the alleyway, the prior walking alongside Moreau.

'Prison quarters will be hard to come by in Paris. I trust Bishop Philippe's brother, the Lord Chamberlain, has his eye on the matter?'

'I'm to take the prisoner to the Dominican priory and discharge my duties to Brother Guillaume de Paris.'

'What? Guillaume Humbert?' Despite her heart pounding as it does whenever she hears or even thinks the Inquisitor's name, Marguerite notices the prior's voice has risen an octave. 'The man is in dis*grace*. He went too far. God be praised the Holy Father has taken matters back under his jurisdiction. The Templar brothers are answerable to him only. And, of course,' he signs himself with the cross, 'to Our Lord Jesus Christ.'

As they pass by the arcade which leads to the treasure chamber, she wonders what sin the figures beneath the sandstone capitals might represent—two devils holding onto the arms of a screaming child. Brother Claude halts at an ornate archway and Moreau indicates, with an irritable twitch of his hand, she should get down. He follows her through the shaded yard and up a stone staircase, the prior still dogging his heels.

'Were you ever in the Holy Land, Sergeant?'

'Nay. But I was in Tunis with Saint Louis.'

She knew it. She glances round at Moreau. He can't have been more than a boy.

Casually, the prior asks, 'And were you involved in the arrests last year?'

The sergeant shrugs his shoulders, curling his lip as if to say, *Of course, and what of it?* 'You? A veteran of Outremer?' The canon's eyes seem to turn black with anger. 'You stood by whilst the Soldiers of Christ were shackled? Old men. Faithful men. Taken to their torture. Even the Grand Master himself. Shame. Shame on you.' She decides it isn't anger in the prior's eyes. It's fear. Even the divinely ordained are not safe from the reach of the Frankish king and his Confessor.

They've reached the landing and the hosteller shoves her through a doorway. A blaze of sunlight greets her with the aroma of fresh-cut herbs. The room she finds herself in has a southerly aspect, reminding her of her bedchamber at the house in Rue del Saulch, except these windows are mullioned and glazed with expensive Venetian glass. She hears Moreau say, 'I am bound, like Claude, to obey my orders, Father,' and imagines the Parisian scorn on his face. The robust door clunks snugly in its frame.

Scarlet soaks the vast bed. The kneeler of the prie-dieu standing beside the sculpted mantelpiece is padded with velvet and in the corner is an exquisitely painted privy screen. She strokes the elmwood desk, its carved fishtails and ocean swirls, and her grateful hips sink into the cushion on the wide chair, smiling how odd it is that she truly is sitting in a bishop's throne. The key makes a decisive click, confiscating from her the sense of blessedness this apartment is designed to inspire in its occupant and like a dog with a bone, her mind scurries back to the question of who betrayed her.

THE LAST TIME she visited Paris was the day Saint Louis' skull was translated from the Basilica of Saint-Denis to Sainte-Chapelle. Guiard de Cressonessart had promised to meet her after the golden reliquary had been settled in its resting place. He was to bring with him her old manuscript.

By the time she arrived at the Court du Palais the crowd was decanting through Porte Saint-Michel into Rue de la Barillerie; she had to push against the flow. In the courtyard, her attention was drawn to the Chapelle-Haute. The silken bishops of the realm were descending from on high and she imagined the sound might be similar to an army of serpents sliding through dry grass. Amidst the violet haze, one tall bishop caught her eye. His body tilted forwards like the Titan who was condemned for all eternity to bearing the weight of the world on his back. Was it really Lord Jean? As if a cloud had uncovered the sun, his countenance lit up and the boy-man from the solar of Châteauvillain broke from the episcopal ranks.

'The Little Poetess! How fitting our paths should cross in this merry month of May, when *"Earth her poverty disregards…And now drunk with dew she doth awake, new attire desires to take."'* If Lord Jean had heard of the Northern beguine and her condemned book, he showed no awareness of it. 'What brings you to Paris, Sister?'

'Godfrey de Fontaines.'

'Is the Regent Master composing verse now?' He gave a laugh, not the subterranean rumble she remembered but a laugh like she used to hear at court, so well-honed that, unlike some words, it can have no more than one meaning. 'Lady Marie, God rest her beautiful soul, was such an admirer of yours. Pray, Marguerite, what are you working on?'

'A fable, my lord. About God as our courtly lover.'

Desire flashed in his eyes and his clammy palms closed around her hand. 'I would dearly love for you to read me your fable.' He glanced at the bishops who were now snaking up the Grands Degrés, Philippe le Bel's new ceremonial staircase. From memory, Marguerite estimated the steps would take them straight into the Galerie des Merciers; Raoul had once led her through it and into the Chambre du Roi. 'His Grace, however, requires my presence. Some trouble fomenting in Jewry apparently. But you, Sister Marguerite, you owe me a visit. Come to Châlons. Honey cakes will be served.' She kissed the gemstone in his ring and Lord Jean shambled away as if the universe had dropped back onto his shoulders.

She walked in the opposite direction towards the Chapelle-Basse. A rusty head of hair stood out from the thinning crowd. 'Whatever has befallen you?' she said. Guiard was all aglow.

'I feel altogether light-headed.' His attention was momentarily drawn away to the Dominican walking by. The friar, in the pied habit of his Order, joined the tail-end of the bishops' train.

'Somebody you know?'

'Used to. How high he now flies.' Guiard frowned as the black friar began his ascent of the Grand Degrés. 'Let's find somewhere we can talk.'

Their footsteps echoed round the nave of Saint-Pierre-des-Arcis but didn't seem to disturb the solitary woman kneeling on the flagstones. Guiard, she noticed, carried no scrip. He glanced over his shoulder and pushed her into a side arcade. 'It happened,' he whispered urgently. 'All the years I've searched out my mission and now, it has been revealed to me.' He held his splayed hands up to the ribbed vaulting as if he were skeining yarn. 'I am the Angel of Philadelphia.'

'Do you mean…the Angel of the Church in Philadelphia? As in the *Book of Revelation*?'

'Porete, I knew you'd grasp it.'

'Guiard, who told you this?'

He spoke as if instructing a child. 'I was in the lower chapel. I was pondering the prophecy: the Sixth Seal has been opened. And I heard…Nay, I *saw* the flourish of an angel's wing. And lo, a voice said to me, "You are the Angel of the Sixth Seal. Protect my adherents."'

Staring into the face of a fanatic, it was a struggle for her not to reach up and slap it. 'You do realise the apocalypse is allegorical? And furthermore it's—'

'Holy Church has erred, Marguerite. The time of Antichrist is upon us. Those who should support Christ's adherents remain silent. And *I* have been chosen for this office. It will be perilous, following the path allotted to me, but I knew one day I might have to suffer. Even unto martyrdom.'

Her defiant mule kicked. 'Guiard, you shouldn't seek martyrdom. Remember Saint Paul to the Corinthians? "*If I give my body to be burned, but have not love—*"'

'Christ has appointed me to speak on behalf of his servants bringing the Church back to task. Prophets like you. The True Church is suffocated by men who do not see. It's in your treatise. "*They are called kings, but in a land where everyone is one-eyed*".'

'Guiard,' her skin had flushed cold, 'where is my manuscript?'

'With a friend in Saint-Denis. I'll journey north with you. We can collect it on the way.'

12

Noyon, September 1308

NEITHER FEATHER MATTRESS nor starched linen sheets have enticed sleep, not even knowing her penknife was stashed beneath the downy pillow. Every time she crossed the threshold of oblivion, dread dragged her back into wakefulness, dread that the solid oak door of the episcopal suite would open.

In the darkness her mind like some nocturnal creature has crept back to her riverside home, sniffed around the cold hearth, scratched under the table where the clay indents perfectly match the soles of her feet, and espied, next to the slick of candle fat, the boxwood casing of her wax tablet. She can only imagine that, in the moment, the shock of having a foreigner ransacking her possessions blinded her to the item she would most need.

The myriad bells of Noyon shatter the silence. Hooded figures will be gliding through unlit cloisters to fill dark sanctuaries now. Sleep-stretched eyes turned to the East where day is yet to break.

Within minutes, prayerful voices are rising and falling in the cathedral, rising and falling. Before the Hour of Prime subsides, a sliver of mauve daylight creeps around the shutters of the apartment and Marguerite is out of bed, having a thorough wash at the dresser. The dawn light is sufficient for her needs.

The previous evening, the hosteller brought her a substantial supper but no lamp and hunting through her casket, she found neither candle stump nor flint. Fortune, however, struck. Beneath an old parchment she discovered what she'd forgotten stowing there: three clean folios of vellum. Thank the Virgin she didn't start her commission straightaway, else

Countess Philippine's new copy of *The Mirror* would now be sitting in the sergeant's saddlebag with her exemplar and Guillaume de Paris won't baulk at winkling out the identity of her patroness.

Ear to the door, she listens. Not a sound.

Over the top of the writing board, which stands at a steep angle to the desk, she positions Michel's coverlet, and takes out the one piece of scraped parchment. She cuts a nib with her penknife.

Noyon, AD 1308, Thursday after the Virgin's Nativity. To Jacques, choir monk and priest, from his loving sister Marguerite.

It grieves me sorely I was stayed from seeing you on

Booted feet on the stairs. Moving like a cutpurse, she pulls the coverlet down over the letter, throws her quill in the casket, hides the casket behind the privy screen, and is sitting on the edge of the bed, heart banging against her ribs, before the key turns. From the corner of her eye, she pinpoints the glint of steel on the desk.

The door flings open as easily as a wicker hurdle in a pig-run. Through the Venetian glass the rising sun catches Moreau full in the face. He looks like he had a wash by dunking his head in the horse trough and as he leans heavily against the doorposts, she's reminded of an illumination she once saw in the Hebrew scriptures—Samson standing between the two pillars in the Temple of Gaza. Master Stephanus had captured so well the expression of a man who knew that, as he pushed, the falling masonry would crush him to death alongside God's enemies. Nevertheless, he would go on pushing.

'Good morning, Sergeant.'

Barely perceptible, Moreau's index finger hinges upwards. Wondering if he's made up with Brother Claude and is assisting the hosteller in his duties, she nods at the loaf under his arm. 'Is that for me?'

He squints as if he's having trouble focusing, staggers across the room, and lays the bread on the desk. Michel's coverlet flutters, Marguerite's pulse flutters, but the sergeant doesn't seem aware of her letter. With one fist leaning heavily on planed elm, he stands rigid, staring at the side wall as if he's admiring the pattern of gold chequers on the red ochre plaster. Doubtless he's concentrating on holding back the contents of his stomach. He sways. He lurches to the door. His head jerks to one side. In a slow, deliberate movement, he turns back.

'We leave on the morrow at first light. Wagon needs repair.' He scowls.

Aye, she thinks, why *are* you explaining the delay to your prisoner? As she observes him, her fingertips stroke up and down the pad of her thumb in the way her father used to test a piece of cloth for its quality. It's an unconscious habit of hers which Alixandre found charming. Moreau's eyelids close for a moment longer than a blink. When they open, at last she catches his bloodshot eye.

'What do you want, Moreau?'

The noise he makes in his throat sounds as though he's coughing and swallowing at the same time. Taking a step onto both feet he fails to balance himself, and now he's not Samson but the prophet Jonah thrown overboard into the Middle Sea, desperate to catch hold onto anything that will save himself from drowning. His finger ends find the grooved lintel above the fireplace. 'I want…' He makes the gargling sound. 'What I want is…' Inch by inch, his bulk sinks down until he's sitting on the padded kneeler of the prie-dieu. 'I shouldn't be here.'

When a needy soul enters in through your door, Mahaut often told her, *discretion flies out of the window*. Crossing over to him, she cups his elbow in her palm as if to hoist him up. Of course, she couldn't lift him, but the gesture encourages him to stand. Returning to the ornate bedhead, she sits on the bed, pats the counterpane, and waits. He stares at her, mouth gaping.

'Despite what your deputy thinks, I'm no witch.'

In an awkward movement, he finds a pathway to the bed and sits a good yard away from her. She lets him be, but she remains alert; if there's a hornet in the room she wants to know when it moves, and where to.

'What Hébert thinks is—Look, I've not come here to—' He glances away and she can't help smiling. Is she flattered, she wonders, or amused at his embarrassment? Neither. Undoubtedly it's the peculiarity of this moment that's touching her.

Though his limbs are tight parcels of muscle, flesh bulges from under the collar of his undershirt. Splashes of last night's gravy are dried into his tunic. With a swift glance at her, he gazes at his feet and she wonders if he's reliving the moment she caught him off-guard at Les Deux Lions.

'Women don't scare me.'

'I imagine not.' What she *can* imagine is he's paid some and forced quite a few, but what she can't easily imagine is the sergeant making love with a woman. Of course, she's yet to discover what—or who—has brought the royal guardsman to his knees.

'Something happened.' He presses the heel of his hand into the crevice below his brow. 'In Valenciennes.'

The silence stretches out and she dabs her forehead with her wrist. It's turning into one of those golden September days which will not yield summer to autumn without a fight. She's about to ask what happened in Valenciennes when he says, 'We arrived late at the city gates. The provost offered us rare hospitality—a night bivouacking in Château-le-Comte. What a shite-hole.'

Inarguable. Since the war the fortress has only been used by *routiers* who are paid by the count to guard his watermills. Right now, however, she doesn't want to revisit the mills at Anzin.

'At daybreak, we crossed the Escaut. Porte d'Anzin was thronged, it being the Virgin's Feast and all. I don't know what made me look back. The curtain wall was stained with pitch. No great marvel. But then,' he looks as if he might well throw up, 'some manner of unnatural vision. I saw myself. High up on the tower. Staring down into a black scarp. I knew, at the bottom of the scarp, was the mouth of Hell waiting to swallow me down into its bowels. But I don't understand why I thought you might…What in Christ's name has all this to do with you?'

'Go back,' she says.

He glances at the door.

'No. I mean go back to the beginning.'

The Parisian shoulder-shrug.

'Go back, then, to Porte de Wez. What made you lurch so?'

'You saw that?' He touches his scarred hand to his lips, combs the fingers through hair silvering at the temples. 'I heard his voice.'

'Whose voice?'

'Hervi's.'

So. A man. Tentatively she says, 'Hervi?'

'I heard him in my sleep at first. Then at Ham. "You promised me." And this morning he really started on at me, on and on, "You promised me. You promised—" This is some sort of devilry.' He tries to stand and falls back down on the bed, closer to Marguerite.

She knows she'll have to work gently, ease away the crusted layers of concealment, let her heart search out the deep wound in him. 'So, it all begins with Hervi. Who is Hervi?'

'My brother.'

'Ah, your brother. Tell me about Hervi.'

'He was brave. And he was strong, though his eyes were the softest blue like our mother's.' He stares into an invisible distance. 'I'd not seen thirteen winters but he persuaded Papa to let us take the Cross. To benefit Maman's soul. And we were promised vengeance on the Mussulmen who stole the Lord God's lands. We'd see the Holy City, they said. *Pfff.* Never set eyes on Jerusalem. Like a whipped dog I was, cowering behind the siege engines. All around, the stench of human flesh frying like a hog's on Saint-Denis.' Making a fist with his left hand, he stretches out the puckered skin. 'Boiling pitch. Hervi dressed it. But the worst was the horses. Their squealing.' In a burst of frustration he says, 'Why am I telling you all this?'

'Do you want to tell me?'

Chastened perhaps by her gentle words, he bows his head. 'Real war was nothing like playing soldiers in the yard behind the Pot d'Étain.'

'The Pot d'Étain?'

'Our father's tavern. Outre-Petit-Pont.'

She thinks about her meetings at the tavern in Rue Saint-Jacques with Guiard, the proximity to Clos Bruneau and the train of her thought circles back to the house *à la porée.* Doubtless Moreau and Hervi were two of the young men mustering at the Saint-Jean Commandery on the day Raoul died and—

'We call the south side of the Seine Outre-Petit-Pont.'

'Oh…yes…I know. But do go on. You used to play…'

'Leaping off barrels. Thrashing paddles around like those pups tip-tapping yesterday. Never spotted the scimitar.' His voice goes high. 'Hervi threw himself in the way. Dropped on me, screaming. I heaved him off. Scooped up his tripes, warm, stinking…tried to push them back. Wouldn't go in. Just wouldn't go in. And I yelled…' Struggling to breathe, Moreau digs a fist beneath his ribs. '"Don't you dare," I yelled at him.'

She reaches for her pitcher and he drinks greedily, small beer dribbling down the sides of his neat beard.

'We were sitting in blood, vomit, shit. Always the horses squealing, *squealing.* Hervi looked up from my lap, me begging him to stay, his eyes telling me he could not. He'd saved my life more than once. Him barely more than a lad himself. He made me promise. And I did. I promised I'd bring him home to Pari…' Leaning forwards, his tears flow in a bent course down his nose and drip in a slimy ribbon on the floor tiles. Then he swings round so fast it makes her jerk back into the bedpost. 'You know how Saint Louis' war ended?'

'He died in Tunis. His brother treated with the Sultan.'

'Aye. And I marched back to France with a king's bones. *Fucking bones.*

Left my Hervi behind. But I promised him.'

Imagining the boy wandering through the disease-ridden camp, starving, alone, she feels the weight of Moreau's despair like a millstone dragging them both into the ocean's depths. She stretches her fingers around the top of his clenched fist and fixes him with her eyes. A flux of febrile energy saturates her body and in its heat, her heart clarifies like butter.

'What do you want, Moreau?'

'I won't bow to any priest, won't beg for absolution if that's what you mean. They abandoned us on the field. But…' The drowning sound again. 'But I abandoned him. I, Moreau, walked away and abandoned my Hervi. I want…' The next wave of grief topples him. His head comes to rest on the counterpane beside her and she watches him as he weeps for the brother who many a long year has been buried alive in his soul.

The whole time he is suffering, she desires to hold onto him. The Lord knows she needs someone to hold onto, someone to hold onto her, for the warmth of another's humanity to meld with her own. But she must not. What she must do is enter into nothingness once more, go back to the nothingness which existed before she was, when all that existed was God Himself. God will do His will without her interfering.

∞∞∞∞∞

OH, MY DEAREST Mahaut. I don't want to go back there. I don't want to go back to the last time I saw you, when I believed you had abandoned me. But it was I who did the abandoning.

Oh my Mahaut. I remember the first time I saw you in Jacquot's workshop. No matter you wore the grey uniform of the beguine, you shed around you the colours of a benevolent autumn afternoon such as this one and I couldn't take my eyes off you. When Sister Florie told the tale of Old Wateniers le Vilain losing his breeches and you flung back your head and brayed like a donkey, and when the seriousness returned to your heart-shaped face, you leaned forward to oversee your young charges like a cat to lick her kittens. What natural authority you possessed. You'd make anyone feel safe in a storm, I thought, and a mighty storm was approaching.

'So you're with child?' You happened to be in the vicinity when I rushed into the back yard of the Mouton Blanc.

I raised my head from the barrel into which I'd just vomited to meet the calm stare of eyes like amber gemstones. 'I can't be,' I said, my voice hoarse. 'With child.'

'How late are your courses?'

'A week or so.' Panic had packed a lot of days into those two words 'or so'.

You whisked me away from the Mouton Blanc to your house at the beguinage, one of the new stone buildings which had sprung up alongside the Ointiel whilst I'd been living in Paris; with the older daub huts they made a horseshoe shape around the courtyard. You sat me down in your parlour with a cup of your liquorice tea to sluice my raw throat. I felt I was sitting inside a giant apothecary's chest with its limewashed walls and bunches of divers herbs drying in the rafters.

'So, Lady Marguerite,' you said, drawing up a stool. 'Talk to me.' You enclosed one of my hands between yours. I snatched it back. I wanted to run to the seclusion of my own chamber, a habit I'd acquired *à la porée*, but within moments I was bailing out my distress to you, you bossy woman!

'We need to decide what you're going to do.'

I stared at you.

'About the baby.'

I hadn't allowed myself to consider the consequences of my one night with Alixandre, as if mere thought had the power to effect reality.

'Few in Valenciennes will count the months between Sir Raoul's death and the conception of your child. But can you trust those who will?'

'Jacquot will be livid. But I don't think…No, he wouldn't betray me. And Ysabeau will do whatever Master Jacques tells her.'

'Ah, your indomitable steward.' You smiled as one indulging an infant.

I smiled. Ysabeau had warned me already about *those women who sit in the workshop as if they own it. Those grey gowns ain't habits. Those beguines ain't nuns.*

'So there's no danger you'll be shunned. Will you send Sir Alixandre word?'

'A Templar can hardly be responsible for a child.'

'Such things happen.' You gave me the look you often gave me in the early days, *How sad you've been so sheltered from the world*. 'Let not your heart be troubled. You're not alone.'

And you never did leave me alone though, wretch that I am, I would accuse you of it.

SUCH A MANIPULATIVE creature I was back then. We crossed swords more and more towards the end, especially when you became Souveraine. On the Eve of Saint Bartholomew before the real storm broke, I knew you'd be coming to join my Greek class. So I chose the passage about Christ's visit to the family in Bethany.

From the lectern I surveyed my eager clutch of beguines sitting on the refectory benches in a higgledy-piggledy circle. The grey wave of bodies was unusually still and although it was a humid August evening, their faces were a line of pegged out linen which had been through too many washes. Momentarily I felt saddened by Agnès' absence and hesitated to ask the question I'd prepared.

You beat me to it. 'What do we think Our Lord meant when he said, *"Mary chose the better part"*?'

'Her sister Martha fussed too much,' said Jeanne. Even as a girl, Jeanne de Bavay always got straight to the point.

'It's *so* unfair,' whined Colete. 'Mary sat listening while Martha did all the work.'

'So,' you persisted, 'why did Christ praise Mary?'

Florie lurched forwards. Dramatically she pulled herself upright to prove she hadn't nodded off.

'Souveraine,' I said, feigning humility, 'are you suggesting the noblest occupation of the Christian woman is to sit quietly in contemplation of the Lord and forget supper?' A ripple of amusement passed along the benches.

'Should it not be?'

I read challenge in your eyes, I swear, which disappeared the moment you turned to look at the other beguines. 'Our Lord's brother, James,' I countered, 'wrote in his epistle, faith without works is dead.'

'Indeed. But this passage from John's Gospel teaches the contrary.' With the authority invested in you as the Souveraine of Saint Elizabeth's, you turned to Jeanne. 'Sister, ring the bell for Compline.' The lesson came to an abrupt end.

After prayers I returned, raging, to the home you and I had once shared. There was no longer any Agnès sleeping by the kitchen hearth. I stood alone in the empty shell of the bedchamber we'd shared for years. The strewn herbs smelt of dead leaves and the touch of the bedsheets felt cold and unfriendly as I railed at you for abandoning our little haven to take up residence in the Souveraine's quarters. Seeking out the old comb you left behind on the dresser, I prodded it into the callouses on my palms. Red hairs were still wrapped around the ivory tines and I wrenched them away.

Immediately I gathered the clump back up, tears scalding my eyes, and twisted it back around the tines, carefully poking in every strand. There'd be plenty of opportunity for us to talk after the Mass on Sunday, wouldn't there?

I DON'T WANT TO go back to the Sunday after Saint Bartholomew, 1290, the date branded into my memory by Greek Fire. I don't want to. But I must.

You and I were due to dine with Jacquot and Nicolas and I was doubly glad of your company—I hadn't seen my brother since the spring when he'd insisted I meet him one afternoon at Pont Néron.

'Why are we meeting here?' I'd said when he arrived at the bridge, late, and I was already irritable enough before he squashed my cheeks between his palms. He twisted my head like a weathercock to face the setting sun.

'What do you see?'

I tried, and failed, to slap his hands away. 'Porte d'Anzin.'

'And?'

'Scaffolding. Pulleys. The glowing red hair of Master Maçon.'

'He's building a brace of towers. By order of the Great Council.'

'I heard the two bells ring on Sunday. This was the result?'

'The whole city turned out. Where were you?'

I sidled away from him and leaned over the parapet. 'Busy.'

'Did Mahaut tell you about the Brochons boy?'

Unwilling to admit to Jacquot I'd been seeing less and less of you, I shrugged and stared into the iron-grey Escaut at the point where it gulps in the translucent green Ointiel. Beneath the surface lay a boulder the shape of a giant duck egg, undoubtedly deposited there by the flood. It would have been knobblier back then, I thought. Not like people. People seemed to grow knobblier with the passing of time…and…if the boulder had lodged farther upstream, would the river have taken a different course? One stone, one stick…one flap of a fishtail, can change the direction of—

'Boo!'

I jumped back from the parapet.

'The Brochons lad,' Jacquot continued doggedly, 'went to pick an early crop from their strip in Anzin. The castle guards seized him. Said he was stealing from the count and…For God's sake, Margi, are you listening?'

'Aye.'

'Well, they beat him black and blue.'

'How dreadful,' I said without emotion. 'But fortified towers? That's an overt threat to Château-le-Comte.'

'Count Jan was already strengthening his garrison in Lent. Don't you think that's threatening? The wooden palisades by Anzin won't hold against war machinery.'

'Then battle seems inevitable,' I muttered.

Jacquot was watching me closely as I tried to force some answers out of the stubborn duck egg, some wisdom about you, my dearest Mahaut. Why, when the watchman sounded the bells, had you decided attendance at the Council was more pressing than dining on the oysters from Damme I'd procured especially for you?

Jacquot nudged my elbow. 'Is this about Agnès?'

'I helped Agnès leave. She was so torn. But Pascal needs her.'

'Souveraine Mahaut, then?'

The question unwedged a stubborn blockage in me. Words poured out. 'She is everything to me. I used to be everything to her. Or so I thought. When she took over as Souveraine, she promised we'd have time together every Sunday. But our moments become rare. You must have marked the change in her?' I gave him no opportunity to answer. 'I used to rely on her. She knew how to guide me, always had the right words. But now—'

'But *now,* she's responsible for more than you.'

'Community meetings are long recitations of our good deeds. Each virtuous act, one more rung on the ladder to heaven. Every beguine vies to be the most industrious. Well, no one can compete with *Souveraine* Mahaut—'

'So, you're taking part in a contest?'

Oh, how I wanted to knock the smirk off his face. One of his arms reached around my shoulders like a giant tentacle. I fought him off.

'Margi, are you jealous?'

'Jealous?' I screeched. We looked round in embarrassment. A guildsman and his wife crossed to the other side of the bridge. Jacquot leaned in close.

'When Nicolas asked you to take on the leadership of the beguinage you didn't want to. Neither, apparently, did you want Mahaut to.'

'It was I who suggested Mahaut to your panicking curé.'

'And she was the perfect choice. People need her. You, Margi, are being self-indulgent. There are infinitely more important issues afoot than your petty resentments.'

'Petty?' I spat the word out.

'Perhaps Mahaut *has* changed. And *you* must change.' He pointed in the direction of Anzin and the grey crenelations of Château-le-Comte. 'A storm is coming.'

I marched away from him and from the one argument in our lives when I knew Jacquot was entirely on the side of right. Which is why I'd avoided him for two months.

AND SO, on the Sunday after Saint Bartholomew, I'd thought I'd have my chance to get you, Souveraine Mahaut, alone and interrogate you why, during the Greek lesson you'd championed dreamy, philosophical Mary over industrious Martha. It didn't make sense.

But after the Mass you approached me in chapel.

'I fear I cannot join you and Master Jacques today.'

My heart plummeted like a stone. But, imagining my tone was conciliatory, I said, 'Why don't I fetch oysters from market tomorrow? I've a flagon of fine Rhenish. Come share with me what troubles you over a cup.'

You sounded exasperated. You'd discerned my wheedling. 'Marguerite, I'm afraid you are the one who needs to—' you glanced at Sister Jeanne sweeping the flagstones by the porch. 'Pray extend my apologies to Master Jacques.' Your retreating footsteps in the bare sanctuary echoed through my chest.

In Rue del Saulch the willows wept. In the shade of Jacquot's stables, chickens sank their belly feathers under the baking dirt. In the hall, three tombstones of light lay across the rushes; the aromas of tansy and rosemary took me back to when I used to hide beneath the trestles and peer out from behind the day cloths at the beleaguered Ysabeau. Today, the boards were littered with a score of mugs. Two flagons weighted down the edges of a parchment—a plan of Valenciennes with principle buildings inked in red.

'Lady Marguerite!' Ysabeau was never reconciled with my loss of title, and as I considered our steward standing on the kitchen step, I wondered, when did her shoulders begin to crook over like that? 'Jehan and Rogier are with Master Jacques. There's no dinner.'

'He must have forgotten us. Me.'

Ysabeau shambled to the table. 'Provost Regnier and the échevins were here.' She glanced at the screens passage and lowered her voice to a whisper. 'Planning an attack on Château-le-Comte. They've all gone to Tour Saint-Gilles.'

My finger traced the iron-gall contours of the city, stopping at the miniature red tower by the Porte d'Anzin. Tour Saint-Gilles stood in the direct line of fire from the fortress.

'The Virgin will protect him, won't She?' Ysabeau, who had always been so strong and capable, looked like one of the exhausted little hens in the yard. For the first time in my life, I hugged the woman who had always favoured my brother.

Twilight was advancing over the western spur of Valenciennes when I reached the Grande Place. The edges of the belfry were blurring. The air tasted of metal and scorched dust. Men's voices jabbered. There were bursts of running feet. I hurried on towards Notre-Dame-la-Grande.

The parvis in front of the cathedral was deserted except for a figure I'd have recognised anywhere. You, thrusting forwards with purpose, scrip slung across your shoulder. My fear for Jacquot smelted with a mass of less defined emotions.

'Souveraine.'

'Not now.' You tried to walk on but I blocked your path. 'I must get to the miller's wife.'

'All I want to say is, can't we return to how it used to be? If we were living alongside each other again, things would be easier and—'

'There we have it. You wish life to be easy. Think of others, Sister Marguerite, not only yourself.' You took in a long breath, puffed it out. Were you annoyed at yourself for stumbling into my ambush?

'I've followed your example. I teach. I work in the laundry and the fields. I spin and I mend. Yet you defended Mary for taking the *better* part.'

'We should stop this right now,' you said firmly. 'I must go to Carmelle.'

If only I had stopped. 'Always doing such good, aren't you?'

'I was there when *you* needed me.' Oh, my Mahaut. There was gentleness in your voice. I've sieved your words through my heart a thousand times and know the truth of it. You spoke gently to me, like the same woman who, years ago, had laid my pink-purple, warm-wet babe across my swollen breasts.

'Busy, busy, busy Mahaut,' I taunted. 'You are losing yourself.' Oh how utterly I failed to see, losing you was what *I* feared. But you, my dearest love, could see it.

'Look in the mirror, Marguerite. Sometimes, ofttimes, God's will is hard. But therein lies freedom.'

'Is it God's will you should be so indispensable?'

How long had it been since I'd seen that now twitching jaw wide open in laughter, or heard the sound of your braying? 'Sister,' you said, 'I think you should leave the beguinage.'

'Leave?' I was stunned, yet my rejoinder sprang straightway to my lips. 'Because I find no consolation in heaping up my good deeds on the altar every night?'

'So why do them?'

'Because it's what you want of me.' The moment the words left my mouth, I knew this was a deceit.

'What is it *you* want?'

I knew I wanted to reach out, but I could not reach out. I dared not expose my weakness. Instead, I chose to cloke my need of you by exposing *your* weakness. What I thought was your weakness. Your beautiful weakness. 'Are outward deeds any more effective than silent penance for achieving heaven?'

'Marguerite, I've no answers for you right now.' I could see thoughts busily at work behind your creased forehead. There was so much more you had to say to me. 'We'll talk another day.' Dropping your head you pushed past me and disappeared into the night. Inch by inch my body folded onto the cathedral steps.

Two bells clanged. I leapt up.

The smell of pitch clogged the air as I rounded the last corner. Higher than the hoardings of Porte d'Anzin, the curved Tour Saint-Gilles rose sheer and dark against the blood-streaked horizon. The western face of the tower lit up. Above the Escaut a blazing clod arced from the battlements of Château-le-Comte towards the city but the projectile would fall short of the palisades. My legs froze. I'd come in search of Jacquot, to help him, with no idea of how, but I knew undoubtedly you'd already be with the miller's wife. As I raced down the track to Anzin, the river hissed at me.

A moan came from the back of the dim room where an upright timber supported the thatched loft. Beside it Carmelle, her mantle of pale hair splayed over her shoulders, squatted over a blanched linen sheet.

'That's it. Breathe,' you encouraged from behind her. 'Push now.'

Carmelle pulled on the post and roared like a tigress.

Overhead, a spitting sound. A crackle.

You spoke calmly. 'Now breathe deeply.' The sweat fell from your forehead like great teardrops. When thick strands of hair slipped onto your face, I leapt beside you and scooped back the tresses, now peppered with white, which I used to comb at bedtime till they shone like burnished copper.

'One more push and we'll have you out.'

The flames gorging on thatch growled and spat but Carmelle, letting loose her life force, drowned them out.

'Good girl. He's here.' You pressed the greasy, bloodied child to Carmelle's breast and the new mother looked down into her son's eyes. She cooed at him. She wept tears of joy.

You don't know how smoke was circling in a halo around your head as you looked at me. Then you looked down at the sheet where a black lake had submerged the linen. Taking the sticky bundle from Carmelle, you thrust it at me. 'Take him out.' You held onto Carmelle by the waist. 'Go!'

I gazed down at the tiny scrap of life and saw again the face of my Michel, his hair slick and dark, his fragile chest pulsating. Then I heard you say to Carmelle the same words you said to me when they held me down, when they untangled my own little one from my arms. 'I'm here. I have you.' But this time, though the flames roared all around us, although Carmelle was keening, there was no grief in your wise face, no distress in your eyes about the decision you'd made. Only peace.

I drew Carmelle's son to my chest and took two steps away. The centre roof beam crashed down, sending an explosion of sparks across the hearth.

'Sister, do as you are told for once and get him out.' When you drew Carmelle between your thighs, you were holding her as you'd held me in my agony, speaking into my ear, rocking me as if you were rocking a little one to sleep.

I didn't want to go. I did not want to leave you. A tiny hand on mine, the weightless touch of pristine skin, was the spur that propelled me to the door. A thundering boom. More timbers had collapsed into the cottage. Without you, I ran alongside the Escaut and the waters seethed orange and black and I believed the maw of Hell had opened up at the foot of Château-le-Comte. I fully expected devils to reach out, seize my selfish, wicked soul and drag it down into the eternal fires.

The infant mewled. His tiny fists reached out and opened like stars against the night sky.

∞∞∞∞

THE BELLS OF NOYON are ringing the Ninth Hour when Sergeant Moreau raises his matted head from the counterpane. His eyes open a slit and he shudders as though he might be coming down with a chill. Marguerite offers him a dampened episcopal towel and he applies it to his face. Mumbling some words which sound like 'Thank you', he's out of the door. There's a long pause before she hears the key turn.

Sitting at the desk, stroking the ivory phoenix, the intensity of the fire in her heart burns out. She takes up her quill.

You must have been beside yourself, imagining I'd abandoned you. Yet how impatient I remain to hear of your profession, Father Jacques. I picture you now, all in white.

I expect you will have received the tidings I am arrested again.

As afternoon turns to dusk, Brother Claude pushes a tray round her door. She takes a little of the carp, some fennel, a heel of Moreau's loaf and feels better for it.

Under the crisp bedlinen she watches night spill its ink into the corners of the apartment until it blots out the last margin of light beneath the shutters. Footsteps scuff on the staircase. Her fingers close around her penknife.

The lock clicks and a man's silhouette moves in from the landing and crosses to the fireplace. 'I can't be with the men tonight.'

Her hand relaxes.

She guesses the sound is the sergeant's back sliding down the golden chequers and when it stops, he has come to rest on the floor.

'The bed has ample space for two bishops,' she says and catches a flash of his teeth. No doubt he's also imagining a pair of plump prelates tucked up together. 'Come on,' she says. 'I won't bite.'

A metallic clunk on the tiles. As Moreau stretches out beside her, she moves to let his heavy head rest in the curve of her neck. Surprisingly, his hair smells sweet, of frankincense, taking her back to the Resurrection Feast when she last embraced Jacquot and for the first time since she dropped her best pot by the Ointiel, every muscle in her body unwinds.

13

Senlis to Saint-Denis, September 1308

S HE SHOULD FEEL BLESSED. The last time she spent the night in Senlis she had to sleep on bare flagstones. Every inn and guesthouse was packed to the rafters with pilgrims because King Louis was visiting the Priory of Saint Maurice for the dedication of the chapel. Rufin, brandishing his shoulders and his scar, procured them a tiny square of pavement for their bedrolls. Tonight, however, she gets to sleep in a bed. Louis' grandson, Philippe le Bel, has packed the dungeons of the Château Royal.

Volleys of rain pursued the wagon through Porte Rieul earlier this afternoon. The constable, accommodating to the prisoner of royal guards, turned over his own lodgings on the top floor of the gatehouse. The room, smelling damp rather than odorous, felt capacious although as she groped her way to the bunk, she twice stubbed her toe. She tested the bedlinen between her finger and thumb. The fabric felt stiffened with the Lord knows what but she reminded herself of what Hébert had said when he shooed her up the stairs, *If I had my way, you'd be in with the Templar scum.* She had no trouble imagining what might happen to the soul of even the most devout of the *milites Christi* after months underground.

The storm has lifted. Early evening light reaches through the arrow loops revealing divers items of discarded ironmongery on the floorboards. The hearth looks as though it hasn't been cleared out since last winter and there's a three-legged stool with one fractured leg. The weapons rack is empty except for a pike-axe which must be the constable's pride and joy. Its blade shines.

The latch clinks. A candle flame flutters in the draft. Moreau's face looks even more wrecked than when they left Compiègne this morning. He's been avoiding her eye again which seems to vex Hébert. The deputy has acquired the habit of glaring at her, then at the sergeant, then back at her, presumably to intercept some subtle exchange. He must know where his chief spent Thursday night and has undoubtedly drawn a false conclusion. It was the one night Marguerite has slept soundly till the lull before dawn and awoke to find Moreau gone.

At the niche in the wall the sergeant tilts the candle and fixes the base into the wax. Pulling the stool between his legs, he finds his balance on it. 'Can't stay long. The men…' He risks a glance at her. 'I want to know why. When you have so much…' He shuffles around on the stool. 'What did you do?'

'To warrant arrest?'

'To attract the inquisitor's attention.'

'I wrote a book—'

'Aye. That I know. But I don't understand. What's so offensive in this book?'

'Truths, Sergeant, which one-eyed Reason struggles to comprehend.' Hmm, she thinks as he fidgets on the contrary stool, it was inevitable you'd start questioning your purpose, Moreau, though I'd wager you're not ready to confront all your demons. Not yet. 'Did you enquire after my treatise because you wonder if it's right to obey the orders you've been given?'

His expression of alarm is one she's seen on the faces of other men who can imagine only the chaos they believe her teaching would create, yet they are blind to the trail of chaos they leave in their own wake. 'A soldier who refuses to obey orders is no soldier.'

'You said you will not bow before a priest?'

'I saw them on the battlefield. Rats scurrying behind the lines. Letting us wage the war they preached.'

'Yet you became a soldier? And remain one.'

Planting his feet on the boards, he leans forwards precariously. 'I serve the king.'

'Why?'

'Because…because…' The answer doesn't seem as obvious to his tongue as it did to his face. 'His Grace is grandson of Saint Louis and son of Philippe, third of the name.'

'What if you, Moreau, were to learn you are the son of a much higher authority?'

'There's no greater prince than Philippe le Bel of France.'

'Tell me, on the battlefield, would a prince respond to a challenge from a mere bondsman?'

'By no means.'

'Why, then, do you offer obeisance to one who calls himself servant of the King of Heaven?'

He stares at his feet. She expects he'll get up directly and leave. In the bowels of the gatehouse the sergeant-at-arms shouts a command. The winch begins to crank. Moreau stands and points in the direction of the rattling chains as if the regular guards of Senlis need his aid to raise the portcullis. Three strides and he's melting back into the shadows. 'Why,' he says, 'did you write your book if you knew what the consequences would be?' He disappears onto the torchlit landing and she can only stare after him, dumbfounded.

It's true, she's always asked impossible questions and writing down her answers has brought her into trouble. But it's only a half-truth. Finding her own answers has also brought her out of the dark places where her soul was imprisoned for far too long. If only she had her wax tablet to unburden herself right now.

A breeze through the loopholes sends bronze ripples across the axe blade, making her shiver. But she must be grateful for the constable's charity. Aiming for the niche in the wall, she treads a careful path through the mess to bring Moreau's light closer.

HER HEART is hurling itself around her chest. She's convinced there was a movement, over by the hatch where the loft is cloaked by nightfall. Then again, she's been jittery all day until they arrived here in Saint-Denis.

If only the storms lashing them as soon as they left Senlis hadn't diverted them to Luzarches. If only they hadn't had to spend last night in the Château d'en Haut.

Earlier this afternoon, when the wagon pulled into the rear yard of La Tête Noire, her palpitations calmed. The taverner helped her down, greeting her as though she were a visiting dignitary. She doesn't know Alain but she's seen him before. You'd not forget such a man. Passing through the door of the common room, his shoulders touching both jambs, his raven curls squashed against the lintel, Alain led her to a comfortable seat by the hearth. He bowed with every offering he brought to table: cup, napkin, soft white bread. Now and then he would turn towards the rear lobby, his ursine face creasing with delight, but she could make nothing out beyond the wisps of steam escaping through the scullery door.

She was still drying off her soggy hem by the firepit when Foulques came to bundle her into the lobby. Just inside the scullery, the maid stood wiping her hands on her apron and it was easy to see why Alain couldn't keep his eyes off her, with her huge eyes the colour of cornflowers floating in a tub of milk. The guard drove Marguerite on and up the ladder. As she emerged through the hatch into the aroma of a good brew, she thought immediately of Pascal. She thought of him again as she admired the cross timbers of the roof; the trees they were fashioned from must have been twice the height of the oak he felled to replace Hamon's mill-shaft after the flood.

Between the middle post and the vats along the far wall she discovered a nest of empty sacks, neatly laid out and topped with bedlinen. Immediately she dropped down and dozed off, exhausted after her stay in the dungeons of the Château d'En-haut. The Templar priest had howled all night like a wounded animal.

A few minutes ago she awoke to the sounds of Saint-Denis settling back from the day's labour. In the street, a mother was calling home a wayward child, her voice intimate in the thinning air. Around the corner in Place Panetière dogs barked; she imagined them scrapping with beggars for leftovers from market-day as she'd seen them do the last time she stopped off in this city, when she waited till nightfall with Guiard for the friend who didn't show.

Stretching out on her comfortable bed, through a gap in the roof she enjoyed the dance of the dusky clouds twirling round till they folded into darkness. Curfew sounded and her heart was still perfectly at rest until— she screws up her eyes and yes, there's definitely a pale hand groping towards her. Spine braced against a post, she pulls her knees into her chest.

'Good evening, Hébert. I've been wondering, where is it you call home? Would it perchance be Quillan?' That stopped him in his tracks, she from Hainault being familiar with the accent of an insignificant town in the Languedoc.

'I'll be asking the questions,' he grunts. 'We want to know what you've done to our chief. He'd normally follow bishop's orders to the letter. Bewitched him, have you?'

She listens hard for Étienne and Foulques but hears only Hébert's agitated breathing, gets a whiff of his distinctive odour. 'If you hold me for a witch, are you wise to come so close?'

A glint of metal. A clank on the floorboards. Out of the darkness the whites of his eyes emerge and her hand scrabbles to reach her casket. His arm scythes forwards and an iron grip locks around her ankle. He yanks, she topples backwards, her head smacks against the post, she flails around, he drags her towards him, forces up her skirt with his knee and pins it down to the bedding in the precise spot that immobilises her. His hip slams into her groin and she cries out. Her cry turns to a yelp; his knuckles are digging into the soft flesh of her inner thigh, his iron fingers searching her out. She fixes her gaze on the ridge beam and holds her breath, trying to think of nothing, preparing for the stab of pain that's coming.

'Be there a problem?' The woman's voice is clear and sparkling as a mountain stream. It's a voice she hasn't heard before, and she thinks she might be hallucinating when a dull orange glow spreads around her assailant. He rolls off of her and covers his manhood with his hands.

'Mind how you go with that, missy. This witch'll burn soon enough.' Hébert leers down at Marguerite and pulling her dress over her legs, she crawls away on shaking arms. The deputy lets his hands drop. 'Come to join us have you, A-dé-lie?'

The scullery maid laughs derisively. She steps from the ladder into the loft and sets her lamp down on the nearest vat. 'If you're having trouble wi' your braies, I can call the stable boy. He'll give you a hand.'

Speedily he arranges himself. 'Think you're clever?' As he edges towards Adélie, the women stare at his clenched fists. 'Master Alain needs to show you who's boss.'

'You go tell him. I'll be coming to watch the fun.'

Hébert hisses in Adélie's face before scuttling down the ladder. She spies on the lobby. Bringing the lamp closer she says, 'Did he do you mischief, my lady? You be white as a sheet.'

'Nay. I'm unharmed. But you were a marvel. I owe you my deepest—' The words catch in Marguerite's throat. Involuntarily she rubs at her ankle.

'But he did hurt you. Let me.' She kneels and massages the bruised foot. 'I guessed that one's game, volunteering for the watch when the sergeant went out. Not the volunteering type. 'Specially not the last night on the road.' She laughs a knowing laugh. 'You are La Porete, aren't you?'

'Some know me by the name.'

'I've longed to see you again.'

'We've met?'

'Two year since. You sat on the basilica steps, wi' the beggars. Nursed a hungry babe in your lap. Popped a sweetmeat in his mouth.'

'I remember. His poor mother was battered and bruised.'

'Her man died. Left her no land, no craft. Pleaded wi' the abbot's steward not to turn her out of her home. He kicked her in the chops.'

'What befell her?'

'She's here, kneeling before you. Everything changed for me that day. My lady, I owe you my life.'

She tucks Adélie's escaped tresses under her cap. The faded scar sits above fine lines on her skin, the little grooves like stretchmarks she's often observed on the faces of the young whose spirits have been strained too far, too soon. 'I recall naught I did on your half.'

'It weren't what you did, but what you said.' She shuffles around uncomfortably on her knees and Marguerite pats the bedding. The maid eyes the vair lining of her cloak. 'My lady?'

'I'm no lady. But my story can wait. I want to hear about you.'

Adélie sits on the sacking. 'I always prayed to the Virgin. Every morning, on my knees in Her chapel. But that day, I could not. I'd naught left in my paps for *mon petit* Christofle. I sat by the stoup, couldn't even raise a palm to beg. Then, your lovely voice drifts over. Saying how noble it is to give alms. Not for what you get back, mind. And a thing I didn't grasp, not right away. Felt it, here,' she puts a hand to her heart. 'You said we are *all* wretched.'

Marguerite wants to explain what people mostly misunderstand about her sayings, but the maid rushes on. 'Suddenly, I forgot everything as happened to me and wanted to hear more. "There's no need to beg for mercy," you said, "mercy has already been granted." Friars, priests, the Virgin Herself never told me the like. You looked out across the market place. "It's a fool thinks he can pile up profit in heaven like a merchant stuffs his purse with coin." Alain repeats your words to himself every time he sees Abbot Gilles. Resents abbey rights over our fairs.' She sniffs. 'Abbot Gilles resents Alain's ale.'

'It's a fine brew.'

'Best in Saint-Denis. Anywise, no gossip passes by La Tête Noire. Alain came out looking for us. Took us in. That man demanded naught in return. Not even…you know, what a man might expect. But as soon I was on my feet, I worked for him. And a miracle happened.'

'A miracle?'

'I felt free as a bird.' She jumps to her knees and glances at the hatch. 'Begging your pardon. I'm supposed to be bringing *you* aid. You can't be going to Paris, my lady. I mean, *La Porete*. But that's what we reckon. Every dungeon, even the cellars of big houses are filled wi' Templar brothers. And we know,' her voice dips, 'they've been *made* to confess. You must stay free.'

'Dearest girl, I confess openly what I believe. What use finding the road into the land of Peace and keeping it to yourself?'

'Share it wi' folk as need it. We'll hide you where the king's men won't find you.'

Marguerite hates refusing a gift given by so generous a heart, but she must. 'You reminded me just now, captivity consists not in iron bars and fetters.' An image of the priest in Luzarches flashes through her mind, his ruined body, the blackened stumps of his toes but she couldn't bear it if she put these people in danger. Gently she presses her palm to Adélie's disappointed face. 'There *is* something. Although I'm asking much.'

'Ask it.'

'I need a letter delivering. To Valenciennes.'

'I'd gladly take it myself. But Alain journeys north soon.'

Coarse laughter blares up from the common room and Marguerite wonders whether she's as brave as her words sounded. Standing, she puts her weight on her good foot and embraces Adélie.

'I'm so afeared of what might befall you, my lady.'

'Who can foretell what's to come? We happen on surprises. The most surprising when we think all hope is lost. You know this already.' She rummages in her bundle. 'Let me light my candle and I'll have the letter finished by morning.'

'No need. I trimmed the lamp especially for you. I'd best go. The drinking has barely started.'

When the hatch closes, the silence wraps a cocoon around Marguerite. She allows herself to enjoy the peace for a while.

She props up the lid of the vat.

One petition I make, dear brother: I pray you will protect the phoenix from the crows. And fret not. The sergeant of the guards is a good man. And I've found friends I never knew I had, such as the bearer of this letter.

Trusting we will see each other again very soon beside our Ointiel. By the Day of the Lord's Resurrection, I'm sure to have returned from Paris.

Paris. The place which birthed her body, and her wild free voice. The place she once thought would be the end of her but all turned out very different from the way she expected.

14

Paris, September 1308

A BUZZARD mews above the deserted Plain of Saint-Denis. With dappled grace he soars high against the iron-cold sky, then plummets. Coming to rest on the *croix penchée*, his unmoving eye watches them splash through rivulets of stormwater. He takes off, dragging his legs until they flatten beneath him and flies back across the Plain. He circles over the lone rider who stands out, a tiny speck, against the sombre horizon.

At La Tête Noire Moreau seemed to have gone missing. Étienne fetched Marguerite down into the lobby where the dawn had yet to penetrate, ordered her to 'Stand there,' and disappeared. Listening to the clink of harness, a sudden rush of doubt assailed her. Less than a fortnight ago these men invaded her home—it felt like a lifetime—and today they were going to hand her over to another set of gaolers. Perhaps she should have agreed to Adélie's plan. But when the maid poked her lovely face out of the scullery, she knew she'd made the right decision.

Adélie scanned the lobby. On her way out to the well she took her hand and gave it a lingering squeeze; Marguerite felt the slender weight of metal pressing into her palm and she glanced up. 'Adieu,' the maid whispered and was off before Hébert stumbled past, looking as though he'd spent the night on the common room floor.

Out in the yard, Gäelle whickered. So the sergeant hadn't deserted. One day, though, one day.

Flopping on the bench beside Étienne, Foulques' corners spilled out like wool from an overstuffed sack. Marguerite arranged herself in the wagon so she would be facing back towards Saint-Denis.

Moreau is still only halfway across the Plain when they ford the gushing Ménilmontant. Hébert trots alongside Foulques and says, loud enough for her to hear, 'Chief seems good and ready to hand her over.'

Foulques glances round, his eyes slashes in over-proofed dough. 'Ne word 'bout being in her bed. Ne word 'bout anything much.'

'Should've had her bound all the way, like I said. And gagged.' Hébert canters ahead of the wagon. Foulques nods off. Still not daring to examine Adélie's coins, she manoeuvres them inside her sleeve and ties one of her embroidery threads around her cuff.

As Moreau makes up the last hundred yards, the leaden clouds expel their burden.

THE TERRIFYING OGRE waiting eagerly to gobble up little twins. That's what she and Jacquot thought of Paris when they went to Lendit Fair. Papa forbade them to leave the canvas city which sprung up like magic every year on the Plain, but the dark haze hanging in the sky beyond the *croix penchée* drew her child's macabre fascination. Later, as a desperate young bride entering through the mouth of Porte Saint-Denis, where today waterlogged Parisians are going about their Tuesday morning business, she had felt sure the ogre would swallow her down into its bowels. Before Étienne steers into the tunnel of houses overhanging the Grande Rue Saint-Denis, she inhales deeply.

By the time the wagon is spewed out into the open air of Rue de la Sellerie, the rain has stopped. Towering above her, the rust-stained walls of Louis VI's fortress and its assortment of towers are sharpened with a steely clarity and a blade of dread slides down into her marrow. For one short moment, she finds relief in remembering they're taking her to the Dominican friary, not to the deep oubliettes of the Grand Châtelet. Then the punch to the face you're never prepared for, no matter you know it's coming: the faecal smells of the tripe houses. If only Rufin were here to pass her the lavender posey he always kept for her against this moment. She's grateful when the needle spire of Sainte-Chapelle appears above the cluster of palace buildings to reorient her.

Moreau stretches his shoulders out as if he's putting on the city like a familiar garment.

'Good to be home, Chief?' says Hébert.

'You bet,' says Moreau, 'and I know how you love a bet. If fortune smiles on us, our orders will keep us here.' Hébert glares at him, then at Marguerite.

THE HIDDEN MIRROR OF LA PORETE

On the Grand Pont, braying livestock presses around the wagon. The houses on both sides of the bridge have been rebuilt taller than ever since the great floods; she wonders if Paris will one day scrape the sky. The tiled roofs spill torrents the colour of midden water onto the canvas awnings which belly onto the heads of the moneychangers huddled beneath. When the horses step onto the Île de la Cité and the throng yields, Moreau leads the wagon away from Marché-Palu making heart sink. The marketplace will, of course, be a quagmire, but there's no wonder Hébert is grinning; they will have to cross the parvis of Notre-Dame.

A single merchant is betting on an upturn in the weather, spreading out multi-coloured bolts of cloth on his stall in Rue de la Draperie. As they turn at the end of the street, the north tower of the cathedral rears like a mountainside. She glances at the file of Judean kings embellishing the stone façade, robed like the Capetians in blue, red, violet.

Turning away, she flinches. Hébert has crept up on her and is thrusting his gargoyle face in hers. He nods dramatically towards the *échelle de justice*. She doesn't need to look. She can picture the ladder rising from the pavement up to the pillory, as high as the polychrome monarchs, and her heart turns over. With terror. Or is it with fury? The exquisite rose window of Notre-Dame was created to honour God. How can men use it as the crowning glory over their cruel theatre of absolution?

'Can't wait to see you on your knees,' Hébert sneers over her, 'begging Thévenot for mercy.' *Thévenot.* The butcher of Paris. She can't keep herself from thinking of Katarine, clawing at her executioner before he tied her to the stake. 'Tonight, after some good *French* wine, when you are all alone in your prison cell, Moreau will forget you ever existed. Wager my last denier on it, I will.' He tries to make his little bay gelding rear on its hind legs and Marguerite laughs an involuntary gasp at the caper.

So that was Hébert's Parthian shot? Hébert knows nothing. He doesn't know his chief as well as he thinks he does. And he certainly doesn't know about Godfrey.

CONCEALING DEEPER, more ancient foundations, the green waters of the Seine swirl around the feet of the Petit Pont. Although pale timbers bend like a ribcage over the southern arm of the river, the customs desk at the end of the new bridge is still no more than a lean-to. Lazy sentinels wave the royal guards through.

Moreau veers to the right and Marguerite's heart sinks again.

'Not going down Saint-Jacques?' Hébert asks.

'We've to approach the friary from the side entrance.'

'Didn't know it had a side entrance.'

'Well, Hébert, what would you know about holy houses?' The guards laugh, too heartily for men at their ease.

At the end of Rue de la Harpe is the small gateway into Couvent Saint-Jacques. Moreau dismounts. Hébert disengages his boot from his stirrup and the sergeant growls, 'I'll manage,' and grabs her bundle. On his way round to the back of the wagon, he drops the bundle and fumbles picking it up.

Putting out a hand to assist her, she leans on him and their eyes meet for the first time since the guardroom in Senlis. His face is wearing the same expression as at Noyon, the one before he spilled the burden of his broken promise. The memory of their shared intensity latches onto her and tightens around her heart, but she won't let herself, or Moreau, become enmeshed. She pushes his arm away and is glad to be rescued from the moment by the tall Dominican striding across the lawn at them.

'I expected you by yesterday.' Every syllable is lean and clean.

Moreau bristles. 'Well, Prior, we're here now.' The instant he drops her belongings on the pavement, the sergeant is off.

The effect of the black cappa and capuce covering the friar's white tunic and scapula is to accentuate the razor-sharp features of a man who doubtless gained his preferment through guile. His neat tonsure, a three-quarter halo, incorporates two tones of grey. The prior gives her cloak a protracted stare. 'Follow me.'

The weather cannot make up its mind. In the courtyard of the black friars you'd think it was midsummer. Abundant foliage still adorns the lone hazelnut tree at the centre and she leans against the slender trunk. She glances back at the sergeant. He may look like the soldier who left Paris a few weeks ago, but beneath his carapace of duty she perceives he'll never be the same man again. 'God's speed, Moreau,' she murmurs and swallows down the lump in her throat.

The southern boundary of the enclosure is formed by a section of the city's fortifications. Immediately she recognises the tower where the prior stands waiting; she often wandered past its semi-circular foundations when, newly widowed, she used to escape to the southern meadows. Pausing on the threshold of the old guardroom, she takes a long breath of still, clear air. Inside, the air tastes of soil and poorly rendered tallow.

'This is our penitentiary. You are to be detained here until I have further instruction. This house observes the Great Monastic Fast. You, however, will be brought a regular diet. If you have resources, you may negotiate items with our hosteller.'

'Items?'

'While you are lodged within these walls, Brother Laurent has oversight of practicalities. Understand?' Without waiting for her answer, he's on his way out.

Noonday spills through the broad slit several feet up on the priory side, perhaps originally the threshold of an upper doorway. Following the curve of the outer wall where the light paints the patchwork of stone a creamy colour, she thinks the cell might feel homely, if she could forget this is the penitentiary and sometime soon she will have to face Guillaume de Paris. Even the thought of his name drains her energy, and now they share a dwelling-place. Couvent Saint-Jacques is his territory. He has the freedom to move wherever he pleases, whenever he pleases, whereas she—The bolt on the outside of the door slots emphatically into its cradle.

Ever so slowly she lowers herself onto the edge of the pallet. As her fingers trace across the cotton ticking of the palliasse, the coins at her wrist bunch together in a smooth drop of comfort. She pulls the thread. Dear God! *Adélie*. This is none of Philippe le Bel's debased currency. In her lap are three silver gros. And how on God's good earth did Alain come by a *chaise d'or*? No more than the width of her thumb across, as the *chaise* nestles in her palm, the sceptre of the embossed king shimmers. She once saw golden coins like this in Raoul's hand. It must be worth two Parisian pounds. Doubtless more.

Working her silverpoint across the stitching at the bottom of her shift she unpicks the thread and slides the coins into the sheath of the hem. She has no needle and it's going to hurt her heart to pluck out a line of the gold thread from the topmost wing of Michel's seraph. But when it's done she wiggles the stiff wire inside the old needle-holes and gradually they widen. She laces the layers securely back together. Against her mud-starred linen the golden seam shouts out, but beneath her overdress, it's invisible to the world. The world! Who but the prior and the hosteller will see her in this penitentiary? The inquisitor. She kicks her toe against the comforting weight of metal and reminds herself, Alain will soon be on his way north and in his purse, the little parchment folio tied with an azure thread, sealed with wax from Moreau's candle.

She will have to negotiate more candles from the hosteller. And a tinderbox. But there is yet light to write by. She must get a letter to Godfrey.

Reaching beneath the clean linen in her bundle, her hand is stopped by a solid object that isn't her casket. Passing her fingers over the smooth surface of the board, she pushes her fingertips into the conversions her father etched for her years and years ago. Ells to feet; feet to nails; Flemish ells to English ells. Her hands fumble as she pulls out the tablet and it takes her several attempts to undo the leather strap. Canvas hinges hold the covers and the three boxwood frames together and when they flip around, she holds one of the green wax plates to her nose. She savours the greasy aroma. The iron stylus is exactly where it belongs; whoever took the tablet from her cottage carefully replaced it through the top loops. The story she scrawled in the night before the guards came for her is still legible.

UP AND DOWN *the furrows of Lower Mead...*

She won't read it right now. She needs to allow herself a rest from dark memories, to enjoy this moment of grace. Folding the frames back together, her eye is caught by scratches on the verso of the third plate. Three words, not in her own hand. The script is broad and uneven as if made by a child learning his letters.

For your mercy.

15

Couvent Saint-Jacques, 29th September 1308

WHEN SHE FIRST LIVED beside Hamon's mill, the chanting of the Charterhouse monks used to irk her. Jacquot's voice was missing and every Hour of every day reminded her of his absence. Eventually the harmony of male voices wooed her and brought her the sensation she can only describe as an old wound being caressed by a lover.

She needs intimate beauty this morning and can't wait for the friars to fill the chapel with their prayers. Balanced on the knife edge between sleep and wakefulness, she rose in the solid blackness of night. Striding up and down on the beaten earth, she stubbed her foot on the desk leg, right in the gap between her little toe and the fourth toe. She threw herself on the bed, wept furious tears until, subdued, her eyelids closed like untethered blinds. It can't have been more than minutes before her dreamworld threw up Nan's face. Not Nan's coaxing face as she stretched out her hand to little Margi tottering around on chubby legs. But Nan's face thin with terror, her neck bent sideways on the floor like a snared dove. Chased back into consciousness, Marguerite listened to the click-clicking of bats who live under the old hoardings and the foxes keening in the meadows until the cock crowed.

The cantor opens the liturgy for Lauds, invoking God to hurry up and save him. The friars respond, '*Domine, ad adiuvandum me festina.*' Aye, Lord, make haste to help me.

The Psalms work their healing, '*His love endures forever...*' and she loses herself in the Peace which dissolves all the contradictions in her head, allowing her to escape the seesaw of fate on which fear sits opposite hope: the fear that history will repeat itself against the hope that events never turn out the same way twice.

'*Give thanks to the Lord for He is good…*'

The Hour of Lauds ends. How tranquil the colours of a Michaelmas dawn are Outre-Petit-Pont. She'd forgotten it. The early autumn sunrise spreads a lilac-pink sheen over her and for one splendid moment she's back in the solar *à la porée* lying dishevelled on the couch. The friars bustling noisily out of chapel bring her back to the cold Spartan furnishings of the Dominican penitentiary and freeze out her memory of a short-lived bliss.

At the shelf she replenishes her mug from the smaller pitcher and drops the jagged crust from yesterday's loaf into the tolerable priory brew. Cursing how everything in this world is man-sized, she clambers onto the stool and sips around the edge of her bread.

A cart rattles up to her door. Old Smiler is the first of her two daily visitors. Tilting forwards like a tree shaped by prevailing winds, the lay brother pads in on fatigued leather; the scapular over his fraying habit is more grey patch than black serge. On the first day she believed him deaf because when she greeted him, he didn't respond. Yet he isn't blind and when she smiled at him, his face remained impassive like a rock washed by relentless tides. Perhaps he's merely unsociable. After he's filled her water jar and exchanged her night-pot for an empty he pads out.

Shortly after the Hour of Sext the hosteller will deliver a warm meal and her daily rations. Brother Laurent will grunt when he enters, look neither to left nor right, grunt when he departs. Today she intends to distract him from his duties.

As she's forcing down her soggy pap, the sound of a man clearing his throat intrudes on the plans in her head. He speaks in Latin, breathlessly, as though someone has stopped him on his way from one weighty task to another. '…the beguine…supporter…legal…'

The voice responding sounds sympathetic. 'All this…Templars…'

The first speaker clears his throat and takes his leave. When his footsteps have receded across the courtyard a third voice speaks in French. 'Well, *he's* fortunate.'

'…Guillaume?'

'…back in favour…'

Tutting, she drags her stool to the corner beneath the window and climbs up, one cheek against the crumbly stonework.

'…he survive?'

The sympathetic friar turns scornful. 'King Philippe is loyal to his Confessor.'

The stool wobbles. The man with congested airways must have been Guillaume de Paris.

'No one has ever held both offices together. It was Philippe manoeuvred his appointment as inquisitor.'

'You can't know that,' the third friar says.

'Well, when you were off chasing heretics in the Languedoc, His Grace sent for old Prior Hugo.' He reverts to Latin for the versicle, '*May he rest in Peace.*'

'*And rise in Glory.*'

'I was acting as his secretary. Copied his letter of recommendation to the nuncio.'

'Ah! I get it. Pretext for the arrests. Guided by his confessor, Philippe le Bel must follow his conscience?'

'I heard the Holy Father was apoplectic.'

'I heard some poor souls confessed to,' he lowers his voice, 'the sin of Sodom.'

'Ecclesiastes 1:9, Brother. *There is naught new under the sun.*'

The long silence is penetrated only by the creaking of Old Smiler's cart as it retreats. Marguerite is about to climb down when the third friar says, 'So why do we have to put up with this beguine in our penitentiary?' Her fingertips dig into the worn slab of her window ledge and find a groove to hang onto.

'Written a treatise. Thinks she understands the Trinity.' He guffaws.

'What possesses these women? No conception of what it requires to comprehend the greatness of God. The years of study. Shouldn't think Brother Guillaume will let her off lightly now he's reinstated.'

'Don't be so sure. Friends in high places.'

'Said who?'

'Said the kitchener. Reckons she knows people at the Palais.'

A low whistle. 'Then our inquisitor will have to tread carefully. Wouldn't want to blot his exemplar a second time.' Their footsteps move away. 'I'd wager her Latin is woeful.'

'My dear Brother Feliz, she wrote it in *French*.'

The footsteps halt. 'Virgin preserve us. Heresy spreads faster than the pestilence.'

'Every day I give thanks I joined the Order of Preachers. I had such a yearning in my youth to take the Cross and join the Templars.'

MARGUERITE SITS on her stool, counting off the number of blocks the royal stonemason used to build her section of city wall.

One. You hold no jurisdiction over me. Fact.

Two. Valenciennes belongs to Hainault in the Holy Roman Empire. Fact.

Three. The Lord Bishop of—

A pair of sandals crunch over the gravel. It can't be the hosteller. Noontide prayers haven't begun yet. The bolt is screwing back. So, now she will see Guillaume de Paris, get the measure of the man. Her hands twitch in her lap. She sits on them. One. You hold no jurisdiction over—She lets out a long breath of relief. It's Brother Laurent. Perhaps he comes early on major feast days.

He places her usual provisions on the shelf. From his trug he pulls out two plump apples, a flask of wine, and a ripe cheese which smells like it came from Maroilles. Briefly she's transported to the hermitage where people from the neighbouring villages and towns used to bring her gifts of food in return for her prayers.

'Blessèd be Saint Michael,' she says. 'Thank you.'

'Not from our cellarer.'

'Oh? Who sent them?'

No answer. Laurent stacks a bundle of candles next to the wine.

'I need to ask you—'

'The morrow.' He waves his podgy hand at her and leaves.

She scoffs at herself. What hope does she have of persuading a hostile Dominican to deliver her letter? But she can't wait much longer to contact Godfrey. He surely hasn't heard about her predicament or he would have sent word; she might even have been on her way home by now and like a coin flipping over in her breast, hope lands face up.

But to draft her letter, she must erase the story of Nan's last day from her tablet. Fear sinks her.

MICHAELMAS draws to a close in a lilac-pink blush. Buffing the rusty patina of a pearmain on her sleeve, the mystery of who her benefactor might be still occupies her thoughts. Does Countess Philippine's daughter still reside at the Palais? She doesn't think so; not since the Battle of the Golden

Spurs when her French husband, the Count of Artois, perished alongside her own brother.

She divides the apple with her penknife. A perfume with the delicacy of a rose-petal is released, accompanied by the memory of the knight who once knocked her off the road and galloped past these walls. She holds a translucent slice to her lips in a smile. The skin of the fruit is rough on her tongue, the flesh crisp between her teeth— A crescendo of coughing fills the courtyard and she's still forcing down chewed apple from her craw when the door swings open.

The black friar striding in can't be the visitor she's been dreading. She imagines the Inquisitor of France is a crueller looking version of the prior. This man is unexceptional. Neither tall nor short. Neither self-indulgently fat nor ascetically lean, neither swarthy nor fair. Smooth cheeks. He doesn't look as though he could hurt a flea. But when he takes up position in the curve of the cell where the sunlight lingers, her heart is pulled by a cold undertow.

'Marguerite, known as *Porete*.' He gives her the ecclesiastical glare which demands deference; without doubt he expects her to stand in his presence. Thank the Virgin she's seated not on the bed but on the tall stool so her eyes are on a level with his. 'I am Guillaume Humbert, Inquisitor of Heretical Depravity for the Kingdom of France.' He draws his hands from up his sleeves, elegant hands which look as though they might swoop through the air like a swan's wings. She slips her rough hands inside her sleeves, pinches herself on the forearms, reminds herself this is the man responsible for the damage done to the priest in Luzarches.

He twitches a finger. The young, undernourished lay brother skulking by the door closes it and creeps into the shadows.

'You have been committed to me on suspicion of heresy. On the morrow you will answer to the allegations against you.' The inquisitor gives a swift little nod as if checking off an item from a list. 'When we have gathered the information and put you to the question,' nod, 'we proceed to trial to determine whether you are *de facto* guilty.' Nod.

Marguerite decides he's not a crow. He's a magpie, pecking around for precious things, never one to miss a trick.

Sighing lightly, he glances round the cell and crosses to the shelf. With a marble white index finger he traces a slow, precise line down the perspiring curve of her wine flask. Returning to where the evening shadow hasn't yet encroached, he's one step closer to her. The brownish circlet of his tonsure tilts forwards. 'As Papal Inquisitor, appointed by apostolic authority, you understand I have the power to convict you and turn you over to the secular arm for punishment as laid down by the law?'

She reins in every muscle and produces a steady voice. 'I understand the burdens of your office.'

His half-smile acknowledges the response as prudent. 'Then I require you to take the oath that you will answer truthfully about the things which have been reported to me.' He points at the clerk who slithers to the desk, lays down an oblong of parchment, slithers back to his corner.

Her eyes fix on the city wall. 'You hold no jurisdiction over me.'

'Marguerite of Valenciennes, I am Inquisitor of Heretical Depravity for the—'

'Kingdom of France. I know. But Valenciennes belongs to Hainault in the Holy Roman—'

'Empire. I know. But Valenciennes is in the See of *Cambrai*. Lord Bishop Philippe de Marigny, after taking counsel with the Inquisitor of Lorraine, deferred your case to me.' He slides his hands behind his scapular. 'In two days, I will return with witnesses to hear you take the oath. Then we proceed.' He waves at his clerk and pursues him out.

The bolt screws home.

Grabbing the slip of parchment, she narrows her eyes to read, slams it back down. A draught of wine. She needs a draught of wine.

Warmth flows through her as she sits in the last dregs of sunset and forces herself to think of what she'll say tomorrow. Or…will he come back in two days' time? The man contradicted himself. She recalls the movements of the refined hands of which he seemed so proud. After mentioning Marigny, he hid them. Were they shaking? *Brother Guillaume will have to tread carefully.* That's what the friar said this morning. If the Inquisitor of Heretical Depravity is on thin legal ground, if his tenure of high office is insecure, there's cause for hope.

As night absorbs the edges of the penitentiary, she fetches one of her new candles. In the orb of golden light she copies out her letter to Godfrey on a fresh piece of vellum.

Warming the flat end of her stylus in the flame so she can smooth out the words from the wax plates, she counts herself blessed to have the Master's friendship. Poor Nan had no one to speak for her. She was alone in the world.

THE DAY Saint Louis walked bear-foot into Sainte-Chapelle with the Crown of Thorns was the day a woman from the Languedoc chanced to arrive in Paris. Béatrice from Quillan walked into a tavern in Rue de la Draperie and found a broken man with two motherless babes. In a trice the infants were assuaging the throb in the woman's breasts. By all accounts, Marguerite's appetite for life was voracious. Her father, not a particularly pious man, recognised Divine Providence when She showed up. Béatrice told the Northern mercer her story about her child perishing. Would she consider a trip farther north, to Hainault? He'd pay handsomely.

With her rich tones of the far south, Béatrice (a name which would be difficult for the small girl to pronounce) was the angel of flesh and blood who loved Marguerite into life. So when her Nan vanished without trace, little Margi was inconsolable.

It wasn't until the day of Papa's funeral she learnt the secret about Nan's departure. She and Jacquot were sitting in their oak bower and Jacquot asked her forgiveness about the Crow-man, but she'd forgiven Jacquot his duplicity a long time ago.

'Brother Rémy only suffered my presence in your lessons,' she said, 'because the countess insisted on it. You were the Crow-man's true mission.'

'Aye,' he said, 'he was grooming me.' He dropped a toe to the first foothold.

Marguerite pulled on his elbow. 'Papa told me, when the Templar mania seized you, he'd already talked you out of joining the Preachers. He refused to say why. What's the big secret?'

He slid back onto his perch. 'Papa made me promise not to tell you.'

'Well, he's gone now.'

'You won't like it.'

'For God's sake. Get on with it.'

'The night of your betrothal, I overheard Papa and Ysabeau reminiscing. About Paris. About Béatrice.'

'Did he find out where Nan went?'

'He knew all along where she went. Béatrice, your Nan, was a Credente. An Albigensian.'

'Don't be absurd,' she laughed.

Jacquot's face remained serious. 'Papa said the real reason she fled north was to evade the Inquisitors in the Languedoc. She was forced to leave her infant son behind. The moment she arrived in Valenciennes, Ysabeau said, people whispered about her. Béatrice was taken for examination but she held out for months. Refused to swear the inquisitorial oath. A trick she learnt from others of her sect.'

'Trick?'

'Legally they can't put you to the question without it. Stymies the process. Anyway, in the end it was Brother Rémy's testimony did for her.'

'The Crow-man? What did he know of Nan? She'd disappeared before he arrived in Rue del Saulch.' A grizzly notion entered her head. 'You're not going to tell me they— No. Not my beautiful Nan…'

'Papa whisked you off to Ghent that summer, didn't he?'

'He would never have let Brother Rémy back in the house. Remember the rage he flew into the day he beat me?' The wheals the tutor made on her back were still bleeding at bedtime despite Ysabeau's special unguent of egg-white and lard. It was the one night in her life Papa stayed with her and nursed her through till morning.

'Margi, you don't understand, do you? It wasn't only my voice they were after. We were being watched.'

Marguerite thought back to the day she watched Jacquot trailing his new tutor into the solar for his first lesson. She hid behind Ysabeau's skirts, singing to herself in Occitan, '*Es la paouro Joanna que 'n es anado al paradis, al cèl ambé sas cabros.*' Crow-man turned his head to listen. If only she'd stayed silent. But singing Nan's hymns evoked her presence like lavender petals carried on the breeze. 'Crows don't like goats,' she murmured. 'They prefer sheep.'

The risen sun pierced through the oak leaves but now she knew she was the one who'd betrayed their milk-mother, she needed a dark corner to hide in. She shinned down the trunk and ran alongside the river till she fell in the tall grasses. Jacquot was right behind her. He scooped her up. 'You were a child, Margi. We were both sad little children.'

Over his shoulder, a flash of colour caught her eye. 'Halcyon!'

'What?' He followed her gaze. Above the Ointiel the kingfisher was flying to her nest with her catch.

'She knew, Jacquot, she knew. That last day, Nan told me the story of Halcyon who dived down into the ocean out of grief for her love. She gave me a piggy-back ride home, kissed me, and sent me up to play with you. Nan knew they were coming for her.'

16

Couvent Saint-Jacques, October 1308

BEFORE THEY BURNT KATARINE ALIVE, the outraged men of Valenciennes shut her in the cattle pen nearest the belfry. They jeered at her devastatingly pale and shivering beauty.

Today, Marguerite feels like a heifer brought to market. She thanks the Virgin she was already dressed before the three clerics burst in and made her stand in the middle of the penitentiary. The notary, nose and lips pinched together lest he breathe in the miasma of heresy, shooed her from the stool and set out his writing paraphernalia on the desk. He smoothed out the pleats of his well-cut robe and now sits glowering at her, stylus poised an inch from his stippled face. Although the Inquisitor of France didn't bother giving the notary's name, he puffed out his shoulders when he introduced Brother Jacob. The Franciscan friar, whose eyes look like Pascal's on the morning after the Virgin's Day, folded his flabby hands and rested them over his belly.

She hooks her fingers together beneath her breasts and eyeballs the inquisitor.

'Marguerite, known as *Porete*,' Brother Guillaume's tone is honeyed, 'you have acknowledged me as Inquisitor of Heretical Depravity for the Kingdom of France.' He nods at the notary who scratches something on his tablet. 'Now, the oath you are required to swear before we proceed with our examination.'

The notary holds at arm's length the slip of parchment the clerk left with her two days ago. Marguerite's eyes remain fixed on Guillaume. The notary shakes the slip.

'You must swear the oath,' the inquisitor says, 'so we can commence proceedings.'

'I'll not swear this oath.'

He sighs and shakes his head. He puts her in mind of the jongleur in the *marché aux herbes*, who was so thrilled his audience had turned out despite heavy rain, he gave a spectacular performance. 'Then we cannot proceed. Which means we cannot hear your deposition. Which means we cannot decide on your case.'

She turns her eyes on the shelf and lets the aroma of the half-eaten block of Maroilles seep into her; she conjures strength from another time, another place, where she lived in peace with the birds of the air, the greenwood trees, the stag—The inquisitor leans into her sightline. 'You are aware, relapse into heresy is a very serious charge?' With heavy sarcasm he adds, 'Of *course* you are. We both know Bishop Guido's judgment. Now. Take the oath.'

'Who brought the present charges?'

The greyfriar and the notary make tutting noises as though they deem her a froward child who's asking for a good wallop.

'When you've sworn the oath,' Guillaume says, 'we'll come to the detail.'

She wants detail. She wants answers. She needs to see Godfrey.

'And you are foolish if you are waiting for a man of standing to come to your defence.'

Can he read her mind? She hopes he can't detect what self-control it's taking to stop her body shaking.

'I'll give you one further chance to show you are of good will. You can swear the oath when you appear *in curia*. But understand this. If you remain obdurate, you risk the penalty of excommunication from the Community of the Faithful. Although,' he smirks at Brother Jacob, 'I believe she has scant reverence for the Lord's household.' He turns back to Marguerite. '"Holy Church the Little." Isn't that what you call us?' Guillaume aims a finger in her face. 'I adjure you, as a woman who purports to love God, reassess your attitude toward the One True Holy and Apostolic Church. Accept the Lord's will. Submit to my inquisition. It can all be over very quickly.'

Keep your peace. Keep your peace.

'I'll send for you.' One last glare from the inquisitor and he's off. The notary gathers his effects and flounces out after him.

'Arrogant crone.' Brother Jacob lurches through the door and the bolt screws into its cradle.

Her head wants to burst. What has happened to God's household? Where are the followers of the saint who renounced all to Lady Poverty and stripped himself of his privileges. All these friars have lost their way.

No. That's not quite right. There are Franciscans and Franciscans. For example, the friar whose eyes held a tenderness she's rarely seen in any man…

'SISTERS, CAN I help you ?' The God-like voice echoed through the church of the Friars Minor.

Pausing mid-hop between the pillars of blue-stone, the women gawped at the magnificent drops of stained glass in the sanctuary, wondering, had the voice come down from heaven?

'My apologies for the stench,' continued the voice. Four pairs of eyes travelled down to where a finely sculpted head popped up from behind the altar. As the greyfriar descended the chancel steps and navigated a delicate path through the carnage, his tonsure gleamed like gossamer. 'I believe the raging river brought in the contents of the latrines and left them behind.'

'We seek a small boy, Father,' Mahaut said. 'Lost since yesterday.'

For a fortnight Valenciennes had been capped prettily with snow and it must have seemed like the freeze would go on forever. When their turn came to feed the livestock the previous morning, Marguerite didn't immediately register that the yard no longer crunched underfoot.

Mahaut caught her by the arm.

'What?'

'Sssh.' Her head tilted. In the amber rings of her eyes Marguerite viewed a complete world. A streak of white meadow, the sharp line of the horizon beneath the dark sweep of a bird on the wing. She lost herself in the flawlessness, looking, looking, wondering, had she entered the woman's very soul?

Mahaut shook her. 'The Ointiel!' She skidded away to sound the alarm bell and within minutes beguines were sliding across the yard, herding oxen into Rue del Saulch, tethering goats to the willows. Above the shrieking, bleating, and lowing, Mahaut roared, 'Into the refectory! Now!' Jeanne barely made it through the door as billows like smoke clouds broke over the riverbanks, spluttering debris into the enclosure.

'It's coming in,' Colete squealed, 'We're going to drown.' All the young beguines were now squealing.

Mahaut's voice rose over the din. 'We are not going to drown. Push the tables against the back wall.'

A score of grey bodies heaved and shoved. Hauling one another up, they clung to each other as the river knocked the trestles skewwhiff and the boards juddered underfoot. Helplessly they watched Hamon's mill shaft undermine the chapel and the collapsed timbers barging their way into the city.

Someone asked, 'Where is Souveraine Ermengarde?'

DESPITE THE LOUD BANGING, Mahaut snored on.

It seemed to Marguerite only seconds ago they'd stripped off their sopping clothes, collapsed into bed, too exhausted to clear the detritus that once was their parlour. She picked her way downstairs into the biting air of the kitchen which smelt of rotting vegetation and lemon verbena. Opening the main door a slit, peering back at her out of the grey dawn was a pair of teal-blue eyes, enormous in a white face. 'It's all my fault,' Agnès wailed.

In the heart of the city, a new lake had appeared. One edge of the water lapped against the walls of Abbaye Saint-Jean; the shallow end reached as far as the *marché aux herbes*. A market trader in a skiff swished his oars across the dark green surface. Then a flash of white. They stood mesmerised, Mahaut, Agnès and Marguerite, as the undercurrent of the Ointiel conveyed a pair of swans, dazzling and serene, towards the Escaut. *Slap-slap-slap.* Across the shallow pool of what used to be a string of grain stores on the quayside, four swan feet cut a fissure. Up they rose, two sleek arrow necks aiming for Le Roleur, the hill where the gibbet remained untouched by disaster.

Pont Néron had been reduced to three black spikes poking out of a whirlpool. The wall, which once upon a time the day before ran out to meet it, was half demolished and the three of them clambered up for a better view of the apocalyptic scene. Agnès spotted Blanche, skirts hoisted, slipping and sliding through the shallows, and rushed to her aid. 'If Antoine was here alone,' Mahaut whispered to Marguerite, 'there's little hope of finding him.'

'Not a body saw him.' Blanche's breath rose like steam and she anchored a clump of dripping hair beneath her cap.

'It's all my fault,' cried Agnès. 'I should've tied him to the loft post when

Hamon said what was coming.'

'None of that, my girl. Papa yelled 'cause he were frit.'

'What would Antoine be doing out here?' Marguerite asked.

'Scavenging,' said mother and daughter in unison.

'Folk like giving him titbits. They take to him even though he's...' Blanche's chin trembled.

'Different?' Mahaut suggested. Blanche closed her eyes and nodded.

The trader paddled his skiff towards them. 'What you after?'

'Small boy.' Mahaut shouted. 'Antoine.'

'I know Antoine. Strange whelp. Upside-down eyes.'

'That's him.' Blanche waded out into the icy lake. 'You saw him?'

He shook his head. 'We all ran for it when the waters rushed at us from the Grande Place. A wave high as Le Roleur washed back from the Escaut. The friary stopped the force. Miracle it's still standing.'

Blanche rocked the side of the skiff. 'But you never saw Antoine?'

'Try the Halle aux Drapes. They're taking the...the ones they find to the Halle aux Drapes.'

The reek inside the guildhall knocked them sideways. The floor was soaked the colour of tar and between the timber posts lay a dozen corpses, each draped in a length of pale cloth. Two were shorter than the rest. Agnès held Blanche back by the arms. At the edge of each cloth was stamped a pair of angel's wings, Jacquot's mark of trade, and Marguerite scanned the hall. Doubtless he's out searching, she thought. Mahaut lifted a corner of linen. The head of the boy beneath it was so mangled, he was later claimed by his mother who recognised her own stitching on his tunic. Mahaut shook her head at Blanche. Marguerite reached for the next shroud and gasped.

'My Antoine.' Blanche broke free.

'No,' she said. 'Not Antoine.'

The nose was compacted, her lips and eyelids violet, but they knew the child. Poor Amand. Poor, poor Coustance. Marguerite covered the sleeping face of their darling girl, knowing now where Jacquot must be. In the weeks following the great flood, Mahaut would break down and weep whenever she thought of Manon lying with her little hand curled to her chest like a tiny white chick, but today there was a child yet to be saved. 'What did the man say, about the wave?'

'It rushed back from the Escaut,' said Agnès, 'and was stopped—'

'By the friary.'

'SO MANY GO ASTRAY in the storms of life.' The Franciscan splayed a hand at his thigh. 'Is this fellow so high, with a golden head and the sweetest smile?' Unable to get words out, Blanche clutched at his sleeve. 'You must be his mother,' he said, 'eyes the same blue. Come. Let's find Brother Olivier.'

Smoke puthered out from the huge kitchen hearth. Nestled in the hissing flames was a blackened cauldron. In one corner, away from the fog, the boy sat on a milking stool. A young Brother Olivier crouched beside him with a bowl of foaming water and when he touched Antoine's toes, he giggled himself breathless.

A trail of mire followed Blanche across the freshly mopped tiles. 'Maman!' The little body wriggled as she crushed Antoine to her breast, his little arms flapped. 'Maman, Maman,' he protested till she released him and he ran on chubby feet to Agnès who lifted him under the armpits and swung him round.

Father Daniel insisted they stay for a warm repast. Blanche insisted they let Pascal know his son was found. Olivier insistently slung a cloth of cheeses and salt pork over Blanche's shoulder. She loudly insisted it was too much and he should take it back.

'He won't hear you, my dear,' Daniel said. 'Brother Olivier is deaf.'

Antoine ran to Olivier and tugged at his cord. The friar hoisted him into the air, let him fall, caught him to his chest, and sent him back to his mother. Blissfully she took one of his hands, Agnès the other, and they returned to tell Pascal how their little one had been found, floating into God's house on a barrel.

Though the pottage tasted like the smoke stinging their eyes, the two beguines wolfed down every scrap, taking turns coming up for breath to answer his questions.

How had the beguinage fared during the freeze? *A man's corpse had been found by the gates, petrified on all fours. Otherwise no casualties.*

And after the flood? *The stone buildings are still standing.*

Had they lost livestock? *A few mangled hens.*

Next time Marguerite looked up to suck the orange slop from her fingers, Daniel was studying her as if he were comparing her features to a picture in his memory. 'And how is Ermengarde?' he asked.

Mahaut's eyes flickered. 'You know our Souveraine?'

'Ermengarde is my sister.'

'Your hospitality is kind, Father.' Mahaut rose from table. 'But I must check on a woman near Porte Cardon. Her confinement draws close.'

When Marguerite didn't jump up at the pretext to leave, Mahaut threw her a puzzled look. At the time, she interpreted her reluctance to depart as curiosity about Ermengarde, the beguine who had led her down a slippery pathway; with hindsight she knows it was more about the pull she felt from Father Daniel; not the pull of a man you want to know with your body, like Alixandre or Amand, but you want to know them with your soul; their presence will, you sense, open to you some mystery of the universe.

Marguerite was never able to cloke truth from Daniel, often startling herself with her frankness. When he asked her, 'How is my big sister?' she answered, 'Saint Elizabeth's is not a joyful place under our Souveraine.'

'Ermengarde is not a joyful person.' He glanced in the direction of the refectory door which led into the friary. 'Leadership is an exacting vocation and motive such a slippery fellow.'

'Is it forward of me to ask why Ermengarde isn't joyful?'

'Forward? Indeed it is.' As he studied her, his eyes widened, as if he were slowly realising how he knew her face, though they'd never met. 'God has used the floodwaters to bring me more than the angelic Antoine.' Reclining against the wall, he laced his working man's fingers in his lap. 'I betrayed her. Not that I comprehended how I was betraying her. I was a boy with scant knowledge of the world. When Papa asked where Ermengarde was, like any mischievous brother, I told him.'

The clattering of Olivier's utensils blunted the silence.

'Three knots.' He lifted his cord girdle. 'Chastity. Poverty. Obedience. The zeal of the Friars Minor is inspiring, is it not? Especially for one blighted by conscience. I was uncompromising in my spiritual ambitions. Secretly I enjoyed hearing whispers that one day I'd surely be elected prior.' He sighed a world-weary sigh. 'Then one day I was reading the Church Fathers, Tertullian I believe. *Women, you are the Devil's gateway*. I dreamt of Ermengarde. But it wasn't her face glowered at me like Satan's in Hellfire. It was Papa's. I began to preach about Divine Mercy. And when I questioned whether God loves the Devil, said He must do because He loves even me...'

'They banished you to the kitchen?'

'Precisely. Our founder's faith in the infinite mercy of God for every living creature has long been compromised. But I've learned to savour the aroma of every fruit that passes through my hand. I rest my cheek against the warm flank of the cow as I milk and give thanks for the largesse of creation. Ah, it's so refreshing to share with another what's in my heart.' Pursing his lips, he nodded as if he were receiving a new lesson. 'How curious it should be with a woman. I trust I can depend on you to hold my confession sacred?'

'Without fail.'

Marguerite has wondered since whether Daniel knew life at Saint Elizabeth's beguinage had become a grey rockface and her visits to the friary kitchen with Antoine stood out as shining gemstones. He must have known.

One afternoon they found him on his stool in the kitchen doorway, the enormous cauldron at his knees; next to it, a mountain of peapods. They flopped down at his feet and started shelling. Now and again a handful of peas found its way into their mouths and Antoine purred at the sweetness of summer bursting on his tongue.

Without raising his head Daniel asked her, 'Are the squabbles over candles in the new chapel still fraying your temper?'

'I asked the Souveraine to reinstate study-time now the rebuilding work is complete.'

'Her response?'

She shook her head.

'My sister is afeared.'

'Afeared of what?'

'Not what,' he said. 'Whom.' He gave her one of his inimitable, inscrutable looks. 'Sister Marguerite, what does the Beloved of Solomon tell us?'

'*Love is strong as death.*'

'Precisely. And?'

'If one were to give all the wealth of one's house for love, it would be utterly scorned.'

'Precisely. The lovers of the Song are passionate, no?'

'Precisely.' They laughed like playmates and turned serious again in a heartbeat. 'It's cruel of our Creator to give us the capacity to love, then deny us the object of our love.'

'My dear, no matter who is our beloved, or what becomes of them, real love never ends.' He gazed into the depths of the cauldron. 'Love is a bottomless pit.' Picking out a handful of peas he placed them on Marguerite's palm. 'Aye, Love keeps on giving.'

'I loved my son. Fiercely.' She flinched at how fiercely the words shot out and realised the peas in her fist had squished. She glanced over to where Antoine had been quietly shelling, but he'd gone off to harass Olivier.

'You've been in the bottomless pit? Where all seems naught, and naught seems all there is?'

She nodded, biting her lip.

'Be not afeared of the Great Nothingness. It is your friend.'

They kept silence until all the pods were emptied. When she and Antoine reached the friary gate, she turned and asked, 'Of whom is Ermengarde afeared?'

In the setting sun Daniel's tonsure shimmered like a halo. He gave her no answer, and never would.

BOOTS SCRAPE to a halt at the door of the Dominican penitentiary. A man's early morning hawk and spit. Marguerite has the pitcher in her hands and ever so gently she sets it down on the desk, not a drop of ale spilt. The bolt screws back.

Later, when she recalls glimpsing a mane of chestnut hair, silver at the temples, she'll recognise this moment as joyous. But when the guard moves further in, the daylight shows up his leathers which are creased with dirt. The man who is not Moreau gazes at a spot on the curved wall a few inches above her head.

'Marguerite of Valenciennes, by order of the Inquisitor of Heretical Depravity for the Kingdom of France, you are summoned to appear on the Wednesday after Saint Michael,' he glances down at her, 'that's today,' his eyes return to the same spot on the wall, 'in the Church of the Mathurins. You are to accompany us.'

She doesn't move.

His head twitches as if he's coaxing a rick from his neck. 'You are to accompany us. Now.'

Ever so slowly she picks up her cup and takes a sip of ale. She savours it. With the tip of her tongue she removes the wetness from the corner of her mouth. She takes another sip. She savours it. The younger guard extends a hand as if he would make a grab at her.

'Not our orders.' His superior nods at the door.

As the men are on their way out, Old Smiler arrives. From the threshold he watches the guards leave, a sort of frown on his face. Perhaps he doesn't appreciate the grubby masculine odour they've left behind; he always smells of peppermint and the lemon vinegar Ysabeau used for cleaning the most stubborn of stains. Marguerite smiles at him. No reaction.

When he's gone she twists together a blue and a red thread into a braid and ties it around her letter. She secures it with the last few drops from Moreau's candle. Perhaps it was for the best the Parisian sergeant wasn't on escort duty today. How dispiriting that would've been.

IT'S THE HOUR when nocturnal creatures are out hunting and the silence amplifies the most insignificant sound. Though he's sitting on her stool, the inquisitor might be standing right by Marguerite's ear.

'Who has a copy?'

He's asked her the same question three times and the soles of her naked feet are cold, cold as the cold, cold clay rising to meet them. It was foolish of her to leap up in only her shift, but she won't have this man in her room whilst she's lying abed. She reaches for the blanket.

Guillaume can't seem to keep his luminous hands still. She imagines him in his dark cell, perched on the edge of his pallet, clutching at his knees, muttering to himself about the beguine's contumacy, and the idea comes to him: without witnesses, in the treacherous hour before dawn, *I'll bend her to my will.*

'The dowager Countess of Hainault possessed a copy of your first treatise.'

'I haven't seen Countess Philippine since before her husband died.' This is true. It was Lady Germaine who came seeking Marguerite at the mill cottage in the summer. Fleetingly the notion passes through her mind once more, it might be Philippine's daughter sending her food. Another delivery arrived yesterday.

The inquisitor sniffs the air. 'Hmm. Autumn berries and smoked ham.'

How does he do that? Where her thoughts go, his follow.

'Do not assume anyone is above the law.'

As if she could forget the hundreds of soldier monks who have been chained up and tortured, some of them high-born.

'Bishop Guido kept meticulous records. One of the manuscripts burnt in the Grande Place belonged to Philippine of Luxembourg. Another belonged...' his fingers make clawing movements in the air, 'ah, yes... the Souveraine of Saint Elizabeth's.'

'Beguines hearken to me no longer.' This, also, is true. Since the day the Abbot of Hasnon threw her manuscripts on the pyre she has stayed away from the beguinage. Souveraine Jeanne has read the new treatise but doesn't possess a copy. So which manuscript does Guillaume have? He didn't mention the Bishop of Châlons. Or Guiard. Or Friar Jehan. 'Who brought the charges?'

'Take the oath.' Guillaume's tone is suggestive, as if tempting her to whore herself to him and in payment receive the answer she craves. 'Refuse to co-operate and excommunication might persuade you. And…oh yes,' he yawns as he stands, 'we shall be making our enquiries around Marlis-en-Valenciennes. Including the Charterhouse.' He grunts as though he has satisfied some base urge, then he's on his way to join his brothers in the chapel for Lauds.

Terror fills her mouth and rips her mind to shreds. He knows everything. He knows about Philippine. He knows about Jacquot. She tries to stitch her thoughts back together…perhaps if she swears the oath, swears no one other than Godfrey and Bishop Jean has a copy…but he'd sniff out the barefaced lie…and once she's sworn the oath, he has the legal right to put her to the torture.

THE SOUND OF METAL on stone makes her jump. But it's only Old Smiler. When he's gone, she stoops to pick up a leaf his cart brought in. It's yellowing round the edges. The hazel trees on the banks of the Ointiel will be shedding their leaves, the willows in Rue del Saulch turning golden. Alain must have made it to Valenciennes by now.

She splashes fresh water on her face and digs out her winter hose. A breakfast of the succulent ham and bread pushes warmth back into her limbs, new ideas into her head. Perhaps Brother Laurent would arrange a second delivery for her. He has softened towards her. When he learned the identity of the last letter's recipient, he gave a bow on his way out of the penitentiary. Jacquot isn't a mere few yards up the road, though. Taking out her tablet, she drafts some lines and finds herself writing out one of her old verses.

The bolt wrenches back. It must be the prior. One of the minutiae she's observed in eighteen days, such as how King Philippe II's stonemason used one hundred and twenty-three blocks to build her portion of the fortifications, is that every visitor to her cell screws the bolt in and out of its keep. Except Prior Guillot de Saint-Euverce.

Standing in the doorway, the early sun highlights his left side. 'How long have you known Godfrey de Fontaines?'

'Longer than you have.' She sounds belligerent. She needs to calm down. 'Forty years.'

'Your communication with the Regent Master is most informal.'

'You've read my letter?'

'You expected me not to?'

How ridiculous of her to hope for Brother Laurent's discretion.

'You depend on Master Godfrey's support. By what claim on his authority?'

'As someone well-acquainted with my writings and,' she puts down her stylus, 'as a friend.'

The prior moves into the light beside her desk, showering her with the scent of his scrupulosity. He pulls the tablet from under her elbow. '*On pillars set both high and wide, Two mirrors blazed, one on each side*…Hmm. Mirrors. You write often about them. And in common speech. Perchance you should have asked your *friend* to teach you Latin.'

In perfect Latin she says, 'Do you not find, Prior, words spoken in your Mother tongue touch not only your head, but your heart also?'

He takes a step back from her. 'Master Godfrey returned north in the summer. Would you have me forward your letter by courier to Liège?'

She realises her mouth is hanging open. 'That is some largesse.'

'Ah! *Largesse of Pure Charity*?'

'You've read my treatise?'

With a brisk step he crosses to the door. 'The Master was in ill health when he left Paris.'

The bolt shoots into the cradle.

She glances up at the window. The sky is darkening with rainclouds above Rue Saint-Jacques.

17

Couvent Saint-Jacques, November 1308

SHADOWS are flitting like restless souls across the stonework when the priory bell begins to toll for the Dead. Hoping the last stub of candle will stay alive while she makes her remembrances, Marguerite kneels on her folded mantle.

For years she and Pascal have lit their votives together but thankfully he still has Agnès to pray with him. They will remember Blanche and the daughter who perished with her, too fragile to stay in this world. How is it Marguerite can recall Blanche's face exactly as she saw it the first time they met on the mill path? Guileless eyes. The ruddy sunken cheeks of a pregnant woman who often has less than enough to eat. But with Michel it's different. She can't be sure her recollection is a true memory. The face of her perfect boy with infinitely dark eyes might be merely a picture she invents in her head.

The bolt slides back.

Prior Guillot places his lamp on the desk beside the guttering candle. The white serge of his breast glimmers darkly beneath the wings of his cappa. '*Eternal rest grant unto them, O Lord.*'

'*And may light perpetual shine upon them.*'

They cross themselves.

'I understood you hold no reverence for such practices.'

'I wrote that the Freed Soul, unencumbered of all things, needs no Masses nor sermons, no fasts nor prayers. But I also wrote—'

151

'How do you fail to see, your assertions corrupt the faithful?'

'I was about to say, I *also* wrote that what such souls do, they do by practice of good habit.'

'And you deem it a *good habit* to pray for your dead?'

'My prayers can afford them no aid, but—'

'You question the state of Purgatory?'

She sighs and scrambles up off her knees. '*But*…God is the God of mercy.'

'He is also the God of judgment.'

'Prior, is it to dispute over doctrine you come to me at this hour?'

He crosses himself. What a sin he must deem it, debating with a woman. 'I'm here to say, Brother Guillaume returns before Saint Martin. Be assured, if you resist him further, he will carry out his threat. You will be excommunicated from all Christian practice and commerce.'

'I've naught to gain from taking his oath.'

'You've everything to gain. And…if I report to him your faithful observance of All Souls—'

'If I give my deposition, will I be permitted to say all I wish to say without being interrupted by the Disciples of Reason?'

He bends close to her. In the mirror of his eyes is reflected the smoke curling from the spent wick. 'Who are you protecting with your silence, Marguerite? Your fellow beguines?'

'I've told the inquisitor, I no longer belong to Saint Elizabeth's.'

'You wear the grey robe and white coif of the beguine.'

She retrieves her mantle from the earth and throws it around her shoulders. '*A velvet gown, no matter how fine, a lady does not make.*'

He lets out an exasperated breath. 'I fear for you. Do you not understand that?' As if he would rise above her, above this cell, above this situation which is taxing him so, he glides to the door and without glancing back says, 'Swear the oath.'

The bolt slides in. The bell tolls on for the Christian dead.

Sitting at the desk she traces a shaky finger across the sheen on the ceramic lamp bowl. She conjures the image of her mother as it has always inhabited her mind, 'her hair thick and lustrous black with gold thread braided, down her back' and eyes 'deep as the mill pools of Anzin'. She gives thanks for the seraph who saved her life and remembers Nan and the soft, warm breasts which nurtured her. Next, Papa and his endeavours to do his best on her behalf which she didn't understand at the time. And Raoul who still pains her heart.

As always, the inventory of her losses advances inexorably to Michel but this year only Philippe Auguste's walls will hear the sound of her weeping.

THE GRIEF sown in her innermost darkness took longer to gestate than the child she once conceived in her womb, though she can pinpoint as accurately the moment of its quickening.

When she left chapel on the Feast of the Holy Innocents, mud that had been whipped up by carts criss-crossing the courtyard of the beguinage had frozen into rigid welts. She tripped and reflexively reached out. A hand, hard as iron, gripped her above the elbow. 'You look pasty, Sister Marguerite.'

She hadn't noticed Ermengarde's oxen frame amongst the ranks of beguines shivering in the nave; then again, during the Mass her mind had wandered far, far away from Saint Elizabeth's. Not to the Christ Child escaping Herod's assassins. No. She stood with the mothers of Bethlehem, refusing to be comforted as they clutched their dead babies to their breasts.

'Too much festive spirit,' Marguerite lied.

'It doesn't do to indulge.'

She felt sorry for Ermengarde, living alone in one of the old daub huts. When they came to where their paths should have diverged she said, 'It's a day for sewing by the fire. Come join me.'

They settled on kitchen stools with piles of mending, the glow from the central hearth warming her guest's hollowed out cheeks. 'Where's Agnès?'

'With Florie,' Marguerite said, 'feeding the livestock.' She leaned forward and stirred the pot. The stew released aromas of garlic and thyme and would be ready for her girl when she came in, fingers cramped.

'Who would have imagined? A peasant's child reading Latin. Pascal and Blanche cannot possibly appreciate the magnitude of your charity.' Ermengarde had a mighty reputation for devoutness. *You see godliness in Sister Ermengarde's every move,* Colete used to say, regularly, so Marguerite tried her best to represent humility in her smile.

'Oh, they truly are grateful,' she said and thought back to the mill yard when she shared with them her great plans for their daughter. Remembering again how she would never teach Michel his letters, she had to cloak her pain from the holy woman sitting in the kitchen and redirected the conversation. 'Some of the beguines in Ghent undertook rigorous practices during the Lenten fast.'

'And some of us do likewise,' Ermengarde said, 'but not every soul is keen.'

'It must be arduous,' she fawned.

'On bread and water fast, you might faint during Vespers. But the benefits, Sister Marguerite,' she laced her fingers prayerfully, 'when the Day of the Lord's Resurrection dawns and we receive God's special blessing, oh the ecstasy!'

And that was the moment of quickening.

'Can I join you next time?'

Ermengarde smiled and resumed stitching. She sounded tentative as she said, 'Sister Mahaut returns soon from Ghent, I hear.'

Marguerite hadn't shared with anyone the contents of Mahaut's last letter and, with a stab of infantile jealousy, wondered if she'd failed to detect a special friendship between the two of them. The door flung open.

'I could eat a whole goat.' Agnès bustled in with moments to spare before dark blades of rain began pounding the enclosure.

THE DORMANT CREATURE which on Holy Innocents had stirred inside its winter nest began to swell inside her. She fed it. She nurtured it. Every Friday in Lent, she knelt beside Sister Ermengarde on the steps of Abbaye Saint-Jean, gazing at the monstrance held aloft by the priest. The glass case at the centre of the gilded rays contained a phial of deep red fluid. Christ's Blood.

On Holy Friday she contemplated the nails driven into Christ's hands and feet and chanted, '*Mea culpa, mea maxima culpa.*' *The fault was mine.*

She repeated to herself, *He died instead of me. He died instead of me.*

At dawn on the Day of Resurrection, when Curé Nicolas lit the Easter candle from new fire, she walked alongside her new friend into the empty tomb of the nave, sang the Hallelujahs and danced. Death was overcome. Wasn't it?

LATE SUMMER in the barn, Ermengarde stood with the bale-hook atop the first layer of winter fodder. Grappling the straw bundles, grunting with every bend and stretch, her tunic worked its way out of her belt. Marguerite couldn't help herself from staring. Ermengarde followed her gaze to the livid rash beneath her milk-white breast and froze for a moment. Staring right back at her, she tucked in the baggy cloth and said, 'Tied my cilice too tight.'

'You wear a hair shirt?'

'Do you not know, Sister Marguerite,' she lectured as if she were the prioress, 'despite being committed to a life of service, your worldly desires must be chastened? To approach God, Who is Spirit, we must mortify the flesh.'

'I kept the Lenten fast. Rigorously.'

'Aye, we all noticed the great lengths you went to.' She must have marked the shame colouring her protégée's cheeks. 'To enter into true contemplation, you have to submit your whole self.'

As Ermengarde spiked the bale with renewed vigour, Marguerite turned to haul the next one and caught sight of Agnès. Skipping up to the barn door she was about to speak but with a hesitant wave, she turned and ran off.

Mahaut breezed in with the autumn winds.

One day, when Agnès was visiting home and Marguerite was working through a pile of laundry, Mahaut joined her in the kitchen with her sewing box. Never one to beat her boards around any bush she said, 'You're wearing a cilice.'

The sheet she was folding fell into a muddled heap in the basket. How had her secret penance been so obvious? Watch your pride Marguerite, she told herself, watch your pride.

'It's barely a year since you took on the beguine Rule. And when did you last spend time with Master Jacques?'

One uneasy afternoon in April, was the answer. After they'd said their prayers for Maman's soul, Jacquot had sat brooding in his great chair and wouldn't speak to her. 'On our birthday.'

Mahaut stabbed her needle through her mending and threw it aside. 'October begins the morrow. Marguerite, I'm not convinced you are suited to this life. Beguines live near their families so they remain grounded in the world.'

'Except you don't.'

'You know I have no family. And what about your writing?'

'I'm busy. With the school. With Agnès. With—'

'With Ermengarde d'Aubenton?'

'Mahaut! I wouldn't have believed it of you.'

'Believed what?'

'You could turn jealous.'

In bristling silence they completed their chores. Before retiring to her bed in the parlour, Mahaut paused in the doorway. 'Have a care, Marguerite.

The purpose of such exercises is to bring you closer to God, not to make you spiritually proud.'

Words rushed to her tongue. Ugly words. What did Mahaut know about how it feels to have your son die? '*You* do not know—' she began, but Mahaut had closed the door.

HOW INFINITELY more difficult it is to conquer the will of the spirit than it is to conquer the demands of the body. The vicious little demon gnawing away at her innards convinced her of her special vocation, her giftedness. Ermengarde often reminded her of the scripture, *Unto whomsoever much is given, of him shall much be required.*

Hunting down her newest mentor, she found her in the dairy shed, sleeves rolled up. Marguerite checked Agnès was at the henhouse collecting eggs, then sidled in and closed the door.

'It's a while since I took on the cilice,' she said.

'Finding it difficult?' Ermengarde gave a lop-sided grin and sent a wooden dish clattering into the stack of empties.

'It's a challenge, aye. But it's not that. The times of consolation are...'

'Becoming fewer and farther between?'

What a relief. She understood. Marguerite's body relaxed as far as her goatshair singlet would allow.

'Pass me the saltbox.' Ermengarde wiped a forearm across her brow. 'What of the poetry you read to us? And the Greek you teach? Are they not sufficient nourishment for your spirit?'

She shook her head. How utterly useless she was.

Sounding confident like a wise woman of the woods who possesses the vital remedy, Ermengarde said, 'Come to my house. After night prayers when none will see.' She rubbed a good handful of salt into the cheese rind.

In the pitch blackness of the courtyard, as she scurried home from Ermengarde's hut, she tripped on the cobbles, skinning her hands and knees. In the kitchen, she forced herself to walk slowly, without limping. A pair of eyes tracked her to the stairs. 'My turn to sweep the chapel,' she said cheerily. Agnès chewed on her lip.

As if she'd lost all memory of why she had it in her possession, Marguerite contemplated the seven knotted thongs fanned out across the counterpane. The wind blew under the shutters, raising gooseflesh on her shoulders. Revivified, Ermengarde's words came back to her. *True humility demands secret penance.* She pulled her chemise down to her waist. The wooden handle of the scourge stung her palm like the most savage of nettles.

First stroke. Nothing.

Second stroke, harder. As the knots scraped her chafed flesh, she shuddered. A voice screamed in her head, *Stop!* but her belly swirled deliciously like a swarm of butterflies let loose.

The third stroke. Who knew pain could create music? A cascade of hot and cold notes sang through her body.

That night she dreamed of Alixandre. He held her close to his chest and wrapped his voluminous white mantle around her. Casting off the cloak, as gently as he once kissed her old scars, he pressed his lips into her open wounds. Suddenly he was gone, floating away across an emerald ocean to an obscure horizon, and she stood alone on the shore, her toes paddling in a scarlet pool.

She awoke, famished.

The next night, and the next, she practised her secret virtue.

On the fourth night, her dream took her back three years. She saw herself sitting in the barge with Mahaut, waiting to push off for Ghent. Curled up on the berth, shielding her head with her arms she cried, 'Beelzebul and his hosts are upon us.'

'It's a hailstorm,' Mahaut shouted, 'nothing more.' The pounding on the leather roof brought the bargemaster down into the hold. Her new beguine friend smiled behind her hand. Squatting in the corner, dripping rainwater over Marguerite's coffer, the gruff old Fleming resembled the uncomeliest gargoyle.

They left Pont Néron in the after storm glow. Salle-le-Comte floated by, the 'O' of the rose window like a surprised mouth beneath crenelated brows. She sank into duck-down cushions whilst Mahaut produced a basket of the last berries of autumn and fired questions at her about her childhood visit to her own home city.

Had Marguerite been in Sint Baafskathedraal? *Yes.*

Had she eaten oysters fresh from the sea near Damme? *No, but I yearn to set eyes on the ocean.*

Could she take her there? *Oh please, please.*

Marguerite wanted to know why Mahaut had 'donned the sack' and learned she was a widow but none of her reasons why, when she was young enough and wealthy enough to remarry favourably, she had entered the beguinage.

'The countess told me you know Latin,' Marguerite said.

'And Greek.'

'So you've read Aristotle?'

'My lady, I waste no time on pagan philosophy. Although reading the Church Fathers is hardly of more value. They use so many words to say nothing much.'

'Sister!' Marguerite giggled as though she'd shared a bawdy rhyme.

'What? And the countess told me you were a true scholar.' Mahaut laughed amiably and offered more fruits. 'Does it not irk you, we are only supposed to hear what the learned men tell us about God?'

'Alas that women do not speak of divine things.'

She clicked her tongue. 'Women have always spoken of God. And written about Love. You've read Hildegard? No? Beatrijs? Hadewijch?'

Anger flared in Marguerite's breast at her own ignorance and, doubtless like Jacquot, at being bested by a female. She interrogated her companion about the spiritual mothers she never knew existed. Nuns. Beguines. Poetesses. When Ghent reared above the misty Scheldt like towers cut from ice, she wrapped her fox fur around her inconspicuous womb. A ferocious love overcame her for the unborn child she was yet to behold and she began to mistrust Aristotle. How could he think the pleasure of the eye was the beginning of love?

The dream skipped to spring, to the scent of May blossom solidifying in the air and to the edges of Sint Niklaaskerk standing out sharply against an azure sky; to her waddling across the bridge over the Lei to Meester Jens' atelier and the smell of perspiration; to the fine white dust on the smock of the stonemason who bid her good day. The stab of pain. The mason half-carrying, half-walking her back to the beguinage. As Mahaut eased her down onto folds of soft cloth and unpinned her headdress, Marguerite grabbed at her sleeve. 'You said the end of June.'

'Be not afeared.' Mahaut sat behind her. 'See how like the full moon you are.' As she helped her shuffle between her thighs, Marguerite laughed, not knowing it would be the last time she laughed in Ghent.

The dream skipped over the hours that drifted by in the stifling room, the hazy respite interspersed with the agony like a belt tied too tightly so the buckle stuck into her private parts. The agony and Marguerite melded and together they loved the little body into life.

He whimpered. He snuffled. She touched the tight little curl at his forehead, his inheritance from his mother. His eyes looked into hers, deep and plunging as the abyss. He had Alixandre's eyes. As she gazed at Michel and he gazed at her, they were lost together in a world more real than any. With him she belonged. With him, she'd come home. She heard him snuffle.

She *did*.

It seemed only a moment from him lying so snug at her breast. Only a moment till Mahaut snatched him up. As the dawn broke through, the beguine's ghost-face turned to her and Marguerite knew. She knew but didn't believe. She wouldn't believe. Because she'd heard him. *She had heard him.* 'Let me see him. Let me see Michel.'

Mahaut dropped to her knees. Laid across the coffer on a red-stained towel was her little white lamb, his arms raised up, wanting to be nursed, waiting to be loved, and it was she who was to love him. Her legs, still drenched in bloodied waters, wouldn't hold her up. 'Wrap him in his coverlet,' she demanded. 'Give him to me.' She rubbed the tiny limbs which had lain so complete on her flesh. She kissed the berry lips, the sweetest lips. She smoothed his curl. King Louis' gold thread twinkled beneath the tiny chin. 'Come back, *mon petit*. Come back.'

But he didn't come back.

What could exist but her desire for him? So many times he had reached out to touch her and she wanted to catch his tiny hand now, save her little one from falling into the black maw of death. She would follow him. She willed herself to fall. And she fell and fell until at the extremity of all things she saw and reached out and for one blink of an eye she touched Eglantine and she knew, unequivocally, her Maman would have chosen to die one thousand more deaths to ensure that she, child of her flesh, would live. And she knew that she, Marguerite, would choose to die one thousand and one deaths in exchange for the life of her Michel, sacrifice the joy of witnessing her son grow into the boy and into the man, so he could exist on God's good earth. How blessed was Eglantine in her eyes, a thousand times blessed, to have died for her child's sake.

She awoke from the dream, her hand still clutching at the scourge and her heart at one question: Why didn't *I* die instead of him?

'WHAT ARE YOU DOING?' Her words bounced off the walls of the side-chapel.

'What are *you* doing?' The sacristan's jowls slobbered like a bull mastiff. 'A profanity. No woman may approach the altar of the Lord.'

'I heard the bell for Matins, calling me. I couldn't sleep because…' She didn't wish to tell the sacristan the reason she couldn't sleep.

'Go, lest I report you to the abbot. He'll have you flogged.'

'It would be of no benefit,' she murmured. She'd tried Ermengarde's medicine after waking from her nightmare but the fury inside of her remained unsubdued. She scourged and scourged till at last she cried out in shame to God that Michel had died instead of her and in the same instant, the abbey bell had rung. God had answered her distress. She believed without a doubt He was calling her into His Presence.

Tiptoeing out of the house, she'd battled through the squalling rain and found the abbey empty but for one speck of light which flickered in the blackness. Thinking it must be the sanctuary lamp burning beside the reliquary which held Christ's Blood, she decided she should come and offer all of herself in repayment of her unpayable debt.

In the candlelight the gilded monstrance glistened, but the glass case at the centre was empty. In one of his hands the sacristan held a phial. It was also empty. She'd come expecting to find the miracle of God's Grace and found nothing at all.

She ran out into the rain and like the hue and cry, the abbey bell ringing for Lauds pursued her through the streets and the rivulets of filth. *Sinner! Sinner! Sinner!*

Her legs dragged her towards Pont Néron.

THE WHITE-HOT pain seemed no more than the brush of a feather. '*Ma petite,*' said a weeping voice. 'What have you done to yourself?' Unguent-cool hands pressed lightly on the frayed layers of skin, easing the cloth from her back.

'I want him.'

'I know, my sweetest girl.' Mahaut dabbed at her hair. She wrapped her in her downy shawl, drew her onto the bed and once more rocked her back and forth, back and forth.

'I want my little boy.'

'Shush now.'

'I'll never touch his silky skin again.' A wounded animal, Marguerite howled.

Back and forth, back and forth. Mahaut's tears streamed into hers. 'He was so very beautiful.'

'It's so dark for him. And there's no one there...'

'Michel is with Our Father in Heaven.'

'There's no one there.'

'Marguerite, I have you, my love.'

'I see his eyes. Alixandre's eyes.'

'Marguerite, drink this now.'

She recognised the aroma of the cup at her lips. The warm liquid tasting of sweet petals on her tongue coursed bitter down her throat and Mahaut drifted away, away on an ocean of pitch.

LIKE A CHILD with a loaded paintbrush, spring had leapt around the meadows by the time she was well enough to open the shutters for herself. A throstle fluttered past on her way to her nest in the fork of the chestnut tree. In the yard Agnès was feeding the hens. When the girl glanced up at the window, Marguerite stepped back into the obscurity of the chamber.

Mahaut came the doorway. 'It's time.'

A pustule of terror burst open inside her chest.

'You know what you need to do.' Mahaut came and took her hand. 'I'm not judging you, my love.'

She knew this to be true. When grief crashed its billows over her head and swept away the anchor of her childhood faith, it was Mahaut who kept her moored to this world. With Mahaut's strong arms around her and her breast as her pillow, Marguerite had poured out her story; her bizarre life with Raoul; the gaping wound Alixandre had left.

'Have you ever had a love like that?' she asked one night in the bed they now shared.

'Pieter.' Mahaut wrapped one of Marguerite's curls round and round her finger. 'Pieter was one of the wealthiest wool merchants in Ghent. Everyone said we were the perfect match. We lay together long before we were betrothed.' She sighed. 'I fasted hard. Drank every potion Wise Trude concocted for me. No child came. The first time he beat me, he was utterly contrite. Bought me a darling little pony. The second time, I found the fault within myself. Didn't I deserve the rod? Surely some sinfulness in me had closed my womb.

'One day, I heard bawdy chatter in my scullery. The tavern maid had given Pieter a son. Bore him two more before he died. Saint Anthony's Fire, said the physician. Guilty conscience, said Wise Trude.' She laughed and dropped a kiss on my forehead.

'Mahaut?'

'*Ma petite?*'

'Michel would have been a fine boy wouldn't he?'

'The finest. He was your son.'

'I've been numb for such a long time.'

'You mean, your flesh feels like it's drowning and it's holding its breath?'

'I think I know now why Raoul did what he did. Even Hell cannot be as wretched as—'

'Marguerite, Hell is a place in our hearts. And to stop ourselves from having to feel it, from out of our hearts we foist it onto the world.'

'I let Agnès down. She saw me—'

'I've told you. She came to wake me and I made her go to my bed. When Cécile and I brought you home, she was still in the parlour like the good girl she is.'

'Mahaut?'

'Yes, my love?'

'Will you stay here with me forever?'

Every morning Mahaut made Marguerite recite the tasks for the day. Every night as she combed her red hair and the silky mass dropped through her fingers, they sifted through the fine details of how to entice the goats when it was your turn to do the milking, how to teach Plésance to pronounce, '*Expectans expectavi*,' and why it was that Sister Aaliz wept when she was passed over for lighting the candles in chapel. Dropping exhausted at the end of their daily grind into the bed they now shared, Marguerite didn't realise she was learning about love. Because love is not always found in grand gesture or romantic surges of the breast. Not even ofttimes.

As she hid behind the shutters from Agnès on that spring morning, she wanted Mahaut to embrace her, draw her for the hundredth time away from the edge of the abyss. But her dearest friend repeated, 'It's time.'

Marguerite found her protégée at the desk in the parlour. The once familiar twist had reappeared around her mouth. 'Let's start with something simple, shall we?'

The girl's head bobbed up but her eyes didn't meet with hers.

'I'm sorry, Agnès. I let you down.'

'You looked like Katarine, the day I found her on the footbridge.' The anxious little face screwed up. 'Sister Marguerite, I thought you were going to…'

'If you hadn't alerted Mahaut, I wouldn't be here now to tell you all about the nature of the imperfect.'

HERE THEY COME, the humble servants of the Lord, marching in and lining the walls of the penitentiary as if they've come to a bearbaiting. It's no marvel Brother Guillaume stands out in the ranks of such men. The

Franciscan, red-nosed from too many visits to the buttery. The notary constantly smoothing his gardecorps. A Dominican friar Marguerite hasn't seen before, scruffy for a Preacher; the candle he's carrying flickers side-to-side, side-to-side. Perhaps he suffers from the palsy.

Offering her no opportunity to flout his authority, the inquisitor immediately opens his large book and clears his throat. 'On the Thursday after All Souls, *anno Domini* thirteen hundred and eight, Marguerite of Hainault, being summoned to our presence and refusing to appear, knowing fully the consequences thereof, by authority of Lord Guillaume de Baufet, *Parisiensis episcopus*, you are from this day forwards excommunicated from the community of the faithful. Praying you will reflect on your contumacy, the holy sacraments are forbidden to you and all commerce with the Lord's household is cut off.'

The palsied friar needs three attempts to blow out the candle. She's contemplating how she doesn't feel at all deprived of the light of heaven when Brother Jacob rings with gusto the bell he had hidden behind his back, making everyone in the penitentiary jump.

At a nod from the inquisitor the men shout, '*Anathema. Anathema.*' He snaps his book shut and announces, 'The Book of Life is closed to you.'

She should feel mortified but remembers what she wrote in her *Mirror.* That in the witness of a good conscience, the soul who carries Peace with her always sits in the Book of Life.

'You will observe a bread and water fast to hasten your repentance…' While the inquisitor lays down his rules, she fixes her eyes on the deepest part of the curve in the wall. With November's damp a dark patch appeared in the shape of a footprint and it gives her comfort. It reminds her of one of the stories Alixandre told her about the Holy Land, that the Rock of the Ascension bears the footprint of Our Lord Jesus Christ from the time he was taken up into heaven.

'…Should you wish to be saved,' Guillaume goes on, 'you must confess your faults and then you may receive the sacrament from my own hand.'

On his way out, the notary trips over her slop-bucket. She'll laugh about it later. But not now. Right now she's grieving. Not for herself, but for Holy Church. How absurd, how petty this community from which they imagine they can exile her. Holy Church should be so much more noble than this and she shouts at the bolted door, 'HOLY CHURCH SHOULD BE SO MUCH MORE NOBLE THAN THIS,' her voice tapers to a whisper, 'and more gracious.'

What complete asses these churchmen are who believe fasting and penance will undermine her faith. She used to find fasting reinforced rather than broke her spirit. What breaks her in pieces is that it will be impossible to persuade her Dominican gaolers to deliver a letter now she is forbidden to communicate with any Christian soul, not least a Carthusian priest.

18

Couvent Saint-Jacques,
Advent 1308

HER TOE REACHES OUT from under the covers, searching for the rush matting. She stretches her calf gently, gently, and more vigorously till she can hobble to the brazier. The embers are still alive, just, and using a stick as a poker, she lays on her last three coals.

Her body is beginning to warm through when the bolt slides back.

The prior has taken to pausing in the doorway before he enters, allowing her time to compose herself. Marguerite has a theory about Prior Guillot, that the solicitousness he's shown since her excommunication discloses a wish to cancel out Inquisitor Guillaume's malice. He doesn't linger on the threshold this morning, however. Advent Sunday has brought a blanket of freezing fog and laid it over Paris.

He taps her pail with his foot. 'I'll have Brother Laurent bring more coals with your meal.'

She raises her eyebrows. Dry bread hardly constitutes a meal.

'From today you will join our regular Advent fast. A warm meal of fish or fowl, every day except Fridays.' Her stomach responds with a grateful rumble. He takes a ceramic pot from his belt pouch. 'From my own physic chest. Against inflammation.'

Tears prick behind her eyes. 'How generous. Thank you.'

'Please, sit down.'

Gingerly she lowers the spiky corners of her hips onto the bed.

'You are leaving us.'

Immediately her imagination is off the leash and running—I still have the *chaise d'or*, plenty to buy a ride; I'll be in Marlis by Fourth Advent; I'll celebrate the Nativity with Agnès and Pascal. Picturing Antoine dressed in his Gabriel costume makes her smile.

Prior Guillot isn't smiling. 'You won't be transferred until after the Feast.'

Transferred. Her heart hammers in her chest and her breathing accelerates. Oh God, please, don't let it be the Grand Châtelet.

'I'm not privy to your destination. But you must prepare yourself for what may be a less…pleasant environment.' He glances outside the door, double-checks it is properly closed and takes the unprecedented intimacy of sitting on her stool. 'I'll be brief. Brother Guillaume has risen high from humble roots. He is anxious to redeem himself with the Holy Father. Marguerite, do not keep poking a stick in the hornet's nest. Submit to his inquisition.'

'I cannot submit to a process which will not hear me out in full.'

'Truth never can be confined in a legal formula, this I understand.' His eyes wander to the glowing coals. 'I attended some of the early examinations of the Templar brothers. Of course, not all the allegations are false. But my point is this: the Templar Order is under direct papal authority, yet they were not untouchable.'

'Retreat from the Kingdom of Jerusalem. Saint Louis' disastrous campaigns. Acre. Their situation was becoming untenable.'

'Failure to subdue the Saracen is indeed insufferable.' To himself he mutters, 'If only that were all.'

'You mean, King Philippe's desire to rule men's hearts as if he were equal to God?'

The prior stands, clearly uncomfortable hearing her speak his indiscreet thoughts out loud. 'You yourself wrote, the *Enfranchised Soul* becomes the same as God.'

'Pray, do not take the chaff and leave behind the kernel.'

'God is the uncaused cause.'

She glances at the ceramic pot on the desk by the prior's elbow. 'God is absolute Generosity. And being absolute Generosity, God shares with us all He has and all He is. God can do no other because that is His Nature. Since, by this sharing, we have all that God has—and we become what God is— then indeed are we the same as He. Except in one human respect.'

The coals in the brazier snap into life.

'In what respect?'

'We can change our will. God cannot, and *does* not, change His.'

In two strides he's at the door. 'Take the oath.'

The bolt slides in with monotonous inevitability. She considers the man who just listened to her without his usual warning about Eve falling to the clever serpent. Clearly he's interceded on her behalf with the bishop and secured dispensation for hot food. He's taken it upon himself to give her counsel, sent her the brazier and rush matting without her asking or paying for them. Perhaps she can trust him with her letter.

AROMATIC STEAM rising from the bowl on her desk fails to tempt her appetite. In her head Mahaut's voice is telling her, *You must keep up your strength*, but before she can contemplate eating, she needs to relieve herself.

Her slop-bucket is sitting lop-sided; doubtless a clump of leaf mould or mud stuck to the bottom. But it isn't leaf mould or mud. Under the bucket is a wedge of folded paper. Her eyes flit to the door and around the cell. What an idiot. No one can be watching. Smoothing out the creases, it sends more warmth through her than a bellyful of chicken soup to know Moreau still thinks of her.

> Guiard de Cressonessart preached at Saint-
> Séverin in support of you.
> He's in the Grand Châtelet.

'Oh Guiard.' She screws the paper into a ball. 'Why would you do such a thing?' She always considered the man rash. The spectre of the fortress on the north bank of the Seine chases all thoughts of supper from her mind.

SHE'S RUMMAGING frantically in her coffer; Sergeant Moreau is standing at her armoire; he has a book with a red velvet cover in his hands; at the other end of the room stands Marguerite Noire, statuesque, swarthy like a Southern Madonna—Marguerite isn't in her cottage, she's in the great hall of Gravensteen and she's meeting the Countess of Flanders and Hainault for the first time; Papa is right beside the little Margi as she tries a curtsey and trips over her cloak; Papa's sharp intake of breath turns into Marguerite gasping for air. Her eyes open and she finds herself inside the impenetrable night of the Dominican penitentiary.

Her dream must have some meaning but the ephemeral images slip away like water through her fingers. What does she remember of Countess Marguerite in the great hall in Ghent? Her infectious laughter resounding to the rafters. *Oh, my dear little one!* she trilled like the skylarks nesting in the water-meadows alongside the Scheldt. *Scheldt. Scheldt.* She remembers the sound *Scheldt* delighted her six-year-old palate so greatly she kept saying the word over and over until it sounded ridiculous. She remembers Papa's stupefied face when the most noble lady sat next to his daughter on the bare flagstones and read to her from the priceless manuscript she'd stolen from the shelf.

Well, they shouldn't have left her alone.

Her eyes shut out the penitentiary and she's back in her dazzling dreamworld. This time she's in the private apartment at Salle-le-Comte, reading out the poems she composed under Raoul's tutelage. 'I knew it!' says Marguerite Noire. 'I foresaw your giftedness, the day I walked into my antechamber and found you sitting on the floor with my favourite book in your lap. The wonderment in your face! Your father was not so convinced, poor man.' The countess chuckles. 'That was the lightest moment in my life for some long while. It delights me enormously I was the one who taught you your first letter. "M" for Marguerite.' Sergeant Moreau appears at the other end of the apartment and she can hear the mill wheels turning. He's holding the book with the silver monogram, the book Marguerite Noire gave her; in his hand it metamorphoses into her wax tablet.

She wakes but it is still night and she sees nothing clearly.

THE LAST TIME I saw Marguerite Noire she plumped herself down, filling Mahaut's double settle, and pointed at the footstool. 'Read to me!'

'O Virtues, make me holy, Soul cried.
Multiply our works, the Virtues replied.
Soul strove so hard and took no rest,
Desired to show she was of all the best.
Ensnared by the cunning charms of Pride,
Till, scarlet patterns traced in her side,
Soul learnt, at last, Humility requires
She enact God's will, not her own desires.'

The countess pursed her lips at me. 'Lady Marguerite! The Virtues are the bedrock of our faith. Oughtn't we to strive to be virtuous?'

'Not by our own efforts,' I said, 'which in truth is false virtue. I learnt this from our new Souveraine.'

'SOUVERAINE!' The countess choked on the word. 'Did the woman christen herself? She'll be wearing a diadem to Mass next. How the blazes did she contrive her election?' I explained to our noble patroness, many sisters observed in Ermengarde a life of spiritual discipline and were eager to accept her stringent rules, even her confiscations.

As any grandmother on her threshold sharing one of life's secrets with a granddaughter, the countess leaned forward. 'The cloister draws me, my dear.' Her oyster-shell eyelids closed. A tear leaked down her patrician nose and she reached behind her for a fold of her attendant's skirts to dab her cheeks with. 'I'm handing Flanders over to Lord Guy. He must spread his wings. And I'm going to bequeath my residence, Hôtel Comtesse, to Saint Elizabeth's.'

'PRESERVE a space for poor women like Agnès,' she
said, 'who need the freedom to follow a righteous path.
A virtuous path if you will.' She scowled at me and we
laughed. As she nodded off, her hand in mine, I thought
back to the first time we'd laughed together.
'What in the Virgin's name are you doing, girl?' She'd
found me pressed up against the shelves of her library,
arms reaching for as many books as I could touch, nose
squashed against the spine of *La Chanson de Roncevaux*.
'You may read any manuscript in my collection,' she
said, 'but I'll not have you eating them.'
Only two days at court and I'd landed myself in hot
water. How Jacquot would crow if I were sent home.
'My Lady,' I stammered, 'I was just —' then I realised she
was laughing. She made a steeple of her fingers and
pointed them at me.

'RULE ONE. Not a jot or tittle is to be removed from this
room. Rule Two. Bring no lamp in here. Wood and oil
make an excellent pyre. Now, I can see the Dominican
has done well with you.'
I didn't enlighten her that escaping Brother Rémy's
punishments for the slightest error in my work had
indeed made me a good scholar. 'Lady Aveline tells me
you're settling in well,' she said. 'Making friends. Hm?
Hm?'
Happily I replied, 'Even now Yolent and Heloys await
me in the *petit jardin*.'
The countess held me by the shoulders and stooped so
low her brow almost touched mine.
'A word of admonition, little Marguerite. Pray be careful
in whom you trust. Remember this: *Corvus oculum corvi
non eruit.*'

THE HIDDEN MIRROR OF LA PORETE

When Marguerite puts down her stylus, the dawn has broken. She is wide awake.

∞∞∞∞

WHEN SHE STANDS on the threshold of the penitentiary, the air makes her lungs crackle. The grey-washed sky might be the most beautiful sky she ever beheld. Clutching her mantle at the collar, her eyes devour the curly branches of the hazel tree and the drops of golden catkins. The lawn has a sheen like a field of ripe flax; in front of the oblong refectory building, footprints have stamped it the colour of midnight.

The guard she once mistook for Moreau prods her in the back. 'Like this,' he gripes at his protégé. Young Lucas can't seem to do a thing right this morning.

In chapel the Hour of Terce will soon be over. '*Dominus custodit te ab omni malo: custodiat animam tuam Dominus.*' Guard me from all evil, she prays, and please, please bring my soul not into the keeping of the Grand Châtelet. Lucas prods her in the back. One hand on the cudgel at his belt, the guard who isn't Moreau, points to the gates.

A bent figure comes out of the shadows. 'God's speed, Sister Marguerite.' Old Smiler's accent is Parisian. Perhaps he drinks in the Pot d'Étain and he's seen her in there with Guiard. No. She can feel it in her marrow, that's not right. 'You know Moreau, don't you?' He neither confirms nor denies it. As he pushes his trolley away, she curses herself for not pressing him about the sergeant's note. Too late now.

The glassy water in the horse trough reflects a white blur back at her; it's hard to tell which is her face, which her coif, and which is her hair. The subdued hum of men chatting draws her eye to the open gate. Two friars hooded in their black capuces. The Inquisitor of Heretical Depravity for the Kingdom of France and, at his right hand, Prior Guillot are watching Lucas as he excels in his new skill of driving his prisoner forwards. Marguerite steadies herself. Thank the Virgin she didn't put her trust in the black friar on the strength of the few kindnesses he showed her. Guillot de Saint-Euverce was elected Prior of Couvent Saint-Jacques by his peers, one of whom is Guillaume de Paris. When the value of degrading her environment was on the agenda, he was undoubtedly at the table.

Corvus oculum corvi non eruit.

The crow will not put out the eye of another crow.

Her hand tightens round the knot on her bundle. Marguerite Noire's message in the night may have pulled her back from a terrible error, but if she's on her way to join Guiard in the Châtelet, how will she get a letter to Marlis? She limps into Rue de la Harpe where, for one summer, a lifetime ago, she ran free as a peasant girl into the fields. Lucas is standing beside an animal cart.

19

Rue de la Bûcherie,
Epiphanytide & Lent 1309

S HE ALWAYS KNEW that one day Paris would suck her down into its
Hellish bowels. What she didn't anticipate was finding here a taste of
Paradise.

Last night the heavens opened. The Seine, perhaps a hundred yards
away, emptied its guts into the basement of the old saltery which is now her
prison. Shortly after daybreak, a kerfuffle started in the curing room and she
desperately wanted to cross her pen to find out what was happening but
remained stranded on her little island. She recognised the voices of Lucas
and his chief as they herded the men into the pen next to her own—Sir
Ymbert's pen has an iron gate with a lock and the guards don't want any
trouble whilst carrying out their duties. They huffed and cursed as they
dragged what must have been Sir Raimond's corpse up the steps into the
yard.

The Paternosters began. A shiver passed through the infested cellar. The
shiver passed through her bones. On and on the knights chanted their
prayers and Marguerite didn't want them to stop. When the rivers of grief
eventually ran dry, the void left behind filled with the sound of rainwater
dripping into her slop-bucket. *Drip-drip-plink*.

Drip-drip-plink. The sound will drive her witless. *Drip-drip*—More scuffles
in the curing room. 'Stop struggling,' the old guard says. A snap of knuckles
against flesh. 'Bastard.' That's Lucas. It sounds like they're dragging a live
body into Raimond's vacant pen. They unlock Sir Ymbert's gate.

She has no worries about the knights. On her first day in Hades, she didn't venture into the curing room, thinking it can't be all tittle-tattle, the tales of Templar apostasy. On the second day, thirst forced her out. Keeping an eye on the three wicker gates opposite her own and both ears cocked for the two iron gates she would have to pass on her left, she snook to the well in the furthest corner of the room. Before she'd filled her jug, the impenetrable blackness inside the other pens began to shift. Five Lazaruses emerged from their tombs. No meat was left on their bones but she judged that, together, the knights were more than a match for her. When they caught sight of her, however, they cleaved to the opposite side of the curing room.

She tried engaging them in conversation. They wouldn't have it. Every day at feeding time, they deposit a portion of bread on the corner of the table nearest her pen. She's convinced they aren't acting out of gallantry; they're undoubtedly afraid guilt might stick to them like mud if they go anywhere near a *bona fide* heretic. Or female flesh. Or both.

Drip-drip-plink.

She nestles into the blankets on the wooden platform which is nailed over with planks and serves as her bed. So far she's managed to keep them free of grime. A trickle of light sneaks in through the vent above her head. If she craned her neck she could catch a drop of pale winter on her skin but that would mean resting her head against the wall. Creatures inhabit the wall. She pulls up her mantle and breathes in the faint muskiness of the lining.

A broken tile in the curing room tips and falls. Sir Maurice wails, 'No, no, I beg you. No more.' He must think they're coming for him but the visitor's footsteps halt outside Marguerite's gate.

The sallow flame of Gringoire's lamp highlights his anaemic scalp. Always grinning, the merchant's lips make her think of fat earthworms. He was grinning the day Lucas prodded her down the steps from the saltery yard, though why Gringoire believes himself the luckiest man in Paris, she hasn't figured out.

'Come to check you're settled in your new lodgings.' He chortles and scrapes back a strand of hair. 'Expect you find it gloomy down here?'

Momentarily he puts her in mind of the usurer who came to the house in Clos Bruneau the day after Raoul died; he demanded payment, there and then, of all her husband's debts. Like Gringoire, the man wore fine Italian cloth, doubtless funded by his talent for fleecing vulnerable widows. Fortunately Sir Hugh was on hand to ward him off but in the end she had to pay up with what was left of her dowry.

So, it's money on Gringoire's mind, is it? She can't deny she craves his merchandise. 'The winter nights do indeed drag.'

'Perchance I can offer assistance?' He paddles through the slurry to her island. 'Would you like a lamp like this?'

'How much?'

'How much you got?'

Nice try, Gringoire. She lifts her chin. 'I've a little coin.'

He positions the lamp by her foot. 'You'll need a cruse of oil...' His tongue slides along his bottom lip, leaving a dull sheen. 'Say...six silver *gros*?'

More than double the value, and had he known the colour of her little coin, the price would likely have tripled. 'Oh dear,' she murmurs. Gringoire turns out his palms as if he's powerless against the vagaries of market forces and playfully wafting the flame, waits for the customer to capitulate.

She listens to the *drip-drip-plink*.

'Can't chase a bargain whilst I've you lot to mind.' He leans into her. His breath stinks of fish and half-digested onion. 'Still, things might change now the Pope's settling in Avignon.' He glances into the curing room and sighs ruefully and it strikes her: if the Templars are acquitted, they'll leave Gringoire's custody and he'll lose significant revenue from the Crown. 'Saw this Templar business brewing, mind. Fortresses full of gold. Up to all manner of devilry it turns out. No wonder they lost the Holy Land to that Sallydin.'

'The Mamluks.'

'The...what?'

'Acre fell to the Mamluks. Saladin died a long time ago. I learnt about these things at court.'

'You? At Court?' He lets out a shriek.

'I have dined in the Salle du Roi. Guest of Saint Louis.'

As if he would protect his credulity, Gringoire folds his arms high across his chest. 'So now you're causing trouble for his grandson.' The merchant's eyes narrow with suspicion. 'Brother Guillaume said you wrote a wicked book. Not my place to examine the inquisitor,' he snorts, 'but he must have been confused. You're a woman.' He perches on the corner of her bed. 'So, what can you tell me about court?'

She studies the fashionable chaperon he wears in a clump on the back of his neck like a peasant's snood instead of draped around his head. 'Full of men making deals. A marketplace like any other, only with fine raiment and jewels on show.'

'Here's a deal. Give me five *gros* for the lamp and I'll throw in some bed linen.'

Despite her pulse galloping, she purses her lips. 'Four *gros*.'

'You drive a hard bargain. But for the sake of old Saint Louis, agreed.' He jumps to his feet like he has the body of a youth. 'I'll take payment upfront.'

For the first time since Lucas drove her in here, she feels a spark of life in her belly. She wiggles the *chaise d'or* out of her hem and holds it under the shaft of daylight. The enthroned king glistens and Gringoire whistles through patchwork teeth. 'Why didn't you say you are a woman of means?'

'I'm also a woman of my word.' She makes a fist around the coin. He could easily wrest it from her, but she's banking on him believing she has powerful friends with more gold. 'It'll be here when you return with the goods. I'm going nowhere.' She thinks she's spent too much time in Paris.

'Keep it hidden. Don't reckon the Templar boys are capable of robbing you,' he jabs a thumb over his shoulder, 'but you never can be too careful around a Jew.'

'Jew? Aren't they all gone from France?'

Gringoire is already in the curing room.

WITH NO HINT of Parisian scorn, as Gringoire lays out his offerings on the bed, he calls her 'my lady.' He takes up a prayerful pose, awaiting payment.

'There's one more service you can render me, Master Gringoire.'

'I'm yours to command.' That sounded scornful.

'Clean, dry clothes.'

He bows and scurries out.

She weighs the cruse of oil in her hands. Heavier than she expected. With the pad of her finger she strokes the sheets. Smooth. She presses them to her face. Well-used, but laundered. Gringoire must have anticipated her sartorial desires because he's back in no time, laying his next tempting bargains over her arm. The dress is made from fine wool dyed in madder. She hasn't worn red since Ghent. Running a finger and thumb down the seam of the chemise, she nods with satisfaction.

The clothes sounded a reasonable price until Gringoire gave her a poor rate of exchange for her *chaise d'or*. But she forgets him as she makes up her bed. Like a sacristan laying out the corporal on the altar, straightening out the corners, smoothing out creases in the linen till it would be worthy of holding the Blessèd Sacrament, she stares at the pale luxury, its simple order.

No more rain has fallen. The slurry has drained away leaving a puddle in the corner which froze in the night but the desire in her is too strong to hold back. Dirty layers drop from her like spent autumn leaves and with the force of steel, the air slices into her flesh. She sheds a few tears as she scrapes off her boots on the grey dress, the last vestige of her beguine life. Raising the new chemise over her head, it smells of the meadow where the linen was staked out in the sun to bleach; as the cloth slides down, it fondles her skin like the spikelets of long grass.

In the lamplight the gown looks brazen but it fits as if it was made for her. Though her blood is warmed and energy pulses through her limbs, she envelops herself in her mantle and weeps a little more. Then she takes up her stylus and out of the silence carves for herself a sanctuary of words.

BEFORE NOON on a brisk day in February, Marguerite has taken up position in the small lobby at the bottom of the outer steps. She's named the lobby 'The Birdcage' because if anyone were looking down through the grille above her head, they might think she's a pheasant in a trap. In her madder red, she might even be one of the exotic birds in Marguerite Noire's bestiaries.

She plants her feet on the slate slab across which the gate into the outside world opens and shapes her back into the corner where two foundation stones meet. From here, the saltery basement resembles a church crypt with pillars running down the centre aisle and each side. Incense is lacking. The underlying whiff is of animal dung. The pens, built into the wings like side chapels, used to house livestock awaiting slaughter.

Tilting her head upwards, the feel of the cool blue light through the metal grille gives her a sense of freedom, though today she's not here to daydream. The prospect of confronting the men makes her feel sick. But in Gringoire's gaol things have deteriorated so far she must do something about it.

The slide into violence began on Ash Wednesday. She arrived in the curing room promptly at noon to find the table empty. Not one scrap of bread to be had. Gringoire had decided, it being the start of Lent, to cut their rations from one loaf per person, to four loaves between the six of them. Since then, when the Angelus rings, the signal for feeding time, her heart drops into her concave belly. Yesterday an elbow rammed her in the neck and Oshaya almost lost an eye. Gringoire stood in The Birdcage, grinning at the battle for survival.

There's movement in the yard. She straightens up. He's early, but if, as she hopes, it's Gringoire's skinny lad on duty, he'll want to throw their loaves onto the table and run for the gate before the pack of starving wolves gets him.

A shabby boot appears on the top step. Her heart quickening, she springs to her tactical position by the table's edge. And here come the men, shoulders arched forwards, talons out. The youth empties the hessian sack and the instant he leaps away, she launches herself across the table and embraces the warm loaves like a hen gathering chicks beneath her wings. She senses rather than sees the vultures circling round. From one side an arm comes at her.

'Whoa!' When she needs to, she can still make quite a noise.

In the night, when she lay planning her strategy, she wasn't confident they'd do as she commanded but they've all stopped still. Oshaya's unswollen eye is on her. Above unkempt beards the faces of Sir Pons and Sir Ymbert are as white and soiled as their tunics; she can't tell if their skeletal features are any more defined by disgust at her than usual. Sir Bertrand looks as though he would grab at her, but she smiles at him— Bertrand has her sympathy; every day he takes it upon himself to feed old Sir Maurice who gave up the fight two days into their Lenten fast.

'Sires. Oshaya.' Her torso is in an awkward pose but she doesn't shift a finger. 'Would it not be wise to divide the loaves into equal portions? Thereby all of us are assured of receiving sustenance.' The men eye each other. 'We may be forced to live in byres but we have the choice not to behave as swine at the trough.'

Bertrand scratches his beard. It's impossible to tell what used to be the colour of his matted hair. Auburn perhaps. He looks from Marguerite to Oshaya, undoubtedly calculating how much more robust the two newer prisoners are than his brothers-in-arms. 'Cooperation won't work,' he says. 'Bad for business. Gringoire will cut rations again. He did that before when we stopped buying his little extras.' A growl of agreement.

Her shoulder muscles burn. 'If Gringoire is here, we can give him his little entertainment. But we agree to share out all of our bread fairly when he's gone.' Letting go of the loaves she looks from one sullied man to the next. 'We'd have to trust each other.'

'An equal share must be given Brother Maurice.'

The knights and Marguerite turn towards the melodious voice. It's the first time they've heard Oshaya speak. 'Without fail,' she says.

Each man nods his assent.

With a sense of euphoria, more than half a loaf, and no further bruising, she returns to her pen and instantly recoils. The river detritus in the corners has dried out. Not for the first time she wonders how the Templar brothers have endured this hellhole for a year, and whether they are in truth guilty of all they confessed to and fear drenches her heart. If examined about Jacquot, could she hold her tongue?

IT WAS A LONG TIME, too long, before she asked the question. She should've asked it on the day of Papa's funeral, if only her eyes and ears had been open. But next day she was due to return to the suffocating pressures *à la porée*, with Alixandre about to leave for Outremer, and so she was preoccupied by her own temptation to the sin of lust.

The instant the last guildsman and his wife were out of the door, Jacquot tore off his mantle and dragged Papa's great chair beside the firepit. The air lay perfectly still. Slabs of peachy light fell across the floor tiles making a new pattern. The eglantine Papa had planted by the window put out its haunting perfume. Neither Maman's rose, nor the enchanting evensong of the robin in its branches, made a dent on him as he sat like a marbled chieftain on his judgment seat.

'So, will you finally take a wife?'

An irritable grunt.

'Passing over Coustance's hand for Amand's sake was a noble deed. But you're an excellent—'

'Margi. Stop.'

She didn't stop. Like a spur digging into the flank of a skittish warhorse, her ruthless streak drove her on. With what she thought an infinitely reasonable tone she began, 'Perhaps you just haven't yet found the right wom—'

He leapt to his feet. 'Papa's gone. Leave me be.' Pausing only to swipe an arm across the nearest board, smashing crockery across the floor, he charged out.

A few years later, after their argument about her 'donning the sack', there was another missed opportunity when he asked her opinion of the new curé. She'd first spotted Father Nicolas de Gerpinnes at Saint Elizabeth's patronal festival in the November. He stood stiffly in his liturgical robes— edged with golden crowns, the silk chasuble he wore was unmistakably a creation of Jacquot's workshop—but the consecrating razor hadn't eliminated all trace of his yellow curls; they brimmed over his elfin ears and softened his sharp nostrils and cheekbones.

'Awkward,' she'd said. 'Humourless. Good singing voice, though.'

'He makes a wonderful priest, doesn't he? I've invited him to sup with me on Twelfth Night.'

He was suddenly cheery and she'd responded with the stinging contempt only a sister knows how to deliver. 'You'll be able to croon "Festa Januaria" together. In harmony.'

The truth became crystal clear one Feast of Pentecost. When she arrived with Mahaut in Rue del Saulch, Ysabeau showed them to the solar instead of the hall. The steward couldn't look Marguerite in the eye. The scent of extravagance filled the room; knights errant were woven into the tapestries Jacquot had purchased from Bruges and a table had been laid out by the window; silver knives glinted beside pure white napery. Ysabeau didn't stay to dine.

The two of them sat in the double settle by the hearth, the curé with wine goblet in one hand, Jacquot's wrist in the other. They were howling with laughter. Pompous Nicolas. Her melancholic brother.

'The Baulieus, for God's sake!'

'Is it not the mark of their trade?' said Nicolas.

'Three bells and a chariot d'or on field azure?'

'Do they not cast bells, metalworkers?'

'My dearest Nicolas, they've had it emblazoned on a shield above their gatehouse. Some of these échevins are ridiculous—' Jacquot leapt up. 'Margi. And Sister Mahaut. I was telling your curé about the latest fashion. Coats of arms for all our houses. One doesn't need to be highborn now.'

'What's the difference,' Marguerite retorted, 'between a wealthy freeman who thinks he's exceptional and a landed noble who thinks *he* is. Neither has merit in himself.'

Nicolas took the fauld-stool at table. She fancied the cushions in it were already moulded to his shape. 'You believe merit the indicator of fitness to rule?' he said. 'To lead men, oughtn't one to be of good lineage?'

'Our city has had elected representatives for nigh on two centuries. See. I *was* listening.'

'And every count has ratified La Paix since,' Jacquot said, 'but the way this one intimidates the échevinage is ridiculous.'

'Make up your mind. You just called the échevins ridiculous. Now you defend them.'

'You're twisting my words. I defend our liberty to self-rule, but under the jurisdiction of a rightful lord. Then all have protection.'

'Protection?' Her shriek was sparked less by his vacillating argumentation than by the frequent glances he shot at Nicolas for approval. 'Did you spot one man in comtal livery wading through wreckage after the floods? No. Clearing the quaysides? No. And do not mention the rebuilding of the mills at Anzin. The mills belong to the count himself. Then there was the starvation. Fifteen little bodies buried in one grave because their papas couldn't afford mortuary fees.'

'Amand lost Manon too, Margi.'

That shut her up. She hadn't forgotten how, after delivering the devastating news, her brother lay abed for a week, or how Amand would find Coustance wandering by the Ointiel at night, calling out the name of her little girl. She glanced at Mahaut; her eyes were closed.

'God be praised,' said Nicolas in a reassuring tone, 'the weather is back to normal. The harvest promises to be abundant this year.'

'Except people are exhausted,' said Marguerite, still tetchy. 'Where was the count's protection when they needed it?'

'He is a great benefactor. His uncle has endowed Saint Elizabeth's with a stone chapel and a new house for Souveraine Ermengarde.'

'So now, Curé, we, and you, spend our days on our knees, praying to keep Lord Baudouin and Lady Felicitas out of Purgatory.'

Jacquot slapped a hand on the board. 'For God's sake, Margi.' She stared him down, and won.

Rogier brought in the first course, breaking the tense silence.

'What grieves your sister, Master Jacques,' said Mahaut, 'is the rich enjoy great comforts in this life, and still they would steal a march on the next.' Marguerite shot her a grateful smile.

The curé's knife stopped half-way to the game pâté. 'Do you propose we stop praying for the souls of the faithful departed?'

'I propose,' said Marguerite, 'we attend the living and let the dead bury the dead.'

Her brother groaned.

'Dearest Jacquot,' Nicolas began. Mahaut later informed her that when the curé used her own pet name for Jacques, he may as well have bashed her in the face with a shovel. 'Although Sister Marguerite threatens my living,' he laughed mildly, 'I have sympathy with her viewpoint. But returning to Count Jan d'Avesnes. As our liege lord, you believe he should be obeyed?'

'Of course. But if he throws his weight around much more he'll find Valenciennes closed against him. Which terrifies me.'

'Why so?'

'We'll be at the mercy of those who would rule for their own profit, not for its people.'

'So you and your sister are not far from agreement, albeit you see a different enemy at the gate.' Nicolas' hand found its way back to Jacquot's wrist.

Rogier brought in the next platter. As her brother sulked over the creamy monkfish, Marguerite's appetite had been swallowed up by terror. Perhaps if she hadn't lived away from home since the age of ten, the truth wouldn't have been veiled from her for so long that her Jacquot's mortal soul was destined for Hellfire.

20

Rue de la Bûcherie, Eastertide 1309

THE AIR IS SATURATED with sap. In the gardens along the Seine tiny leaves will be groping their way towards the faithful sun. The tender afternoon on Marguerite's face tempts her to linger in The Birdcage but she can't stop speculating about the portion of food on the table. On the one hand, she feels she's interfered enough. On the other, it wasn't Bertrand's elbow in her neck that time.

At Easter Gringoire reinstated the full portion of loaves and allowed local Christians to practise their almsgiving for the holy season. Today, Low Sunday, more provisions arrived. Ymbert and Pons fell on their food, oblivious to all else. Oshaya has gone to take Sir Maurice his share. Inhaling a last lungful of spring, she collects the loaf, the chunk of cheese and the apple and approaches the door beyond the well shaft. It yawns like the entrance to a bear's cave.

'Sir Bertrand?' No answer. 'Sir Bertrand?' she says louder. 'May I enter?' A grunt comes back at her. She takes it for an 'aye'.

Bertrand's pen is a mirror version of her own, except the wall behind his plank-bed is the rockface into which the cellar is built. The lumpy surface, reflecting the basement's muted light, resembles puckered skin. Semi-recumbent, long legs extended, the knight's form is sketchy as though only half of him is present. On his breast the cross of his Order, the colour of dried blood, stands proud.

'May I sit with you awhile?' She sidles up to him. His silence roars back at her and deep in her soul she tastes the desire for oblivion. She's approaching a man who at any moment might leap off the cliff edge he believes he's standing on; the bread in her hand, even the tang of the ripe cheese, seems meagre bait to lure him back from the precipice. She perches beside him and without thinking, starts to sing.

'*The herdsman returns from his daily round,*
Plants his fork into the ground.
His wife is at the foot of the hearth, all in disconsolation...'

No reaction, but she soldiers on to the end.

'*...Who is it in this place died?*
Poor Joanna, who went to Paradise
with her goats by her side.'

'Where did you learn that song?'

'From my milk-mother.'

His eyes open and fix on the void where the rafters must be which hold up Gringoire's emporium. 'You had an Albigensian nurse?'

'By God's Providence. My mother died birthing me.'

'My mother too.' As if his bones were cast from lead he hauls himself up into a more solid form. 'My father was highborn. I, his bastard.'

'How did you become a knight?'

'He paid for my training till I was of age. Visited me every Easter. On the day of my Vigil, he said to me..."Son," he said, "you have made me so proud..."' Noisily Bertrand expels air from his lungs. She wants to touch him but she keeps her hands on the food. 'And you, a lady of breeding. How did you end up in this stinking pit?'

'I wrote a book, and before you say it, yes, I *am* a woman.' She lays out the provisions between them on the sackcloth. 'Well, I shared my book with people I thought I could trust.'

'Ah, you've also tasted the bitter fruit of betrayal?'

'I don't know for sure by whom, but I was denounced to the Bishop of Cambrai.'

'Philippe de Marigny? Met his brother once.'

'You've met the king's chamberlain? Tell me more.'

'Pleasant creature. Eyes of a snake.' He pulls a grotesque face. 'When the royal mint devalued the coinage, mobs rioted in the streets. We gave His Grace refuge in the Temple. He was there, Enguerrand de Marigny, eying up the plate.' Bertrand sweeps a hand in a wide arc. 'Fine return of our hospitality.'

'Ah, such mockery. You're clearly Parisian.' The knight's face is boyish when he smiles. How dishonour ages a man.

'Born on the Île de la Cité. Soon afterwards, my father departed for Tunis.'

The summer Michel was conceived. She wonders, if her little one had lived, would he have wished to follow in his father's footsteps? No doubt they'd have quarrelled, she and her son, over his determination to take Templar vows; he might have rallied Uncle Jacques to his cause and—

'Saint Louis must be looking down at his progeny in horror. There's naught fair about Philippe le *Bel*, but you have to admire his guile. The Grand Master himself didn't see this coming. Every serving brother in France arrested in one dawn swoop. Only two escapes as far as we've heard. The royal guards practised their methods well on the Hebrews.'

'They released Oshaya yesterday. But why was he still in Paris after the expulsions?'

'A convert perhaps? Relapsed? Or accused of relapse. Shouldn't believe all you hear.'

'It's all lies then, what they say?'

'That we deny Christ in our secret initiation and spit on His Cross?' He clenches his insignia. 'The Cross we Templars have fought and died for?'

'So you didn't confess?'

Bertrand looks away. As he speaks, his breaths shortening, she feels panic tightening like a strap around her own chest. 'When they hoist you up, tie on the weights—oh and they make sure you see the weights lined up—when you're stretched out…and you feel your flesh beginning to tear from your…I beg your pardon, my lady.' His hand is trembling as he wipes his forehead. 'Any who says he can resist torture is a braggart or a half-wit. You'll say whatever it is they want to hear simply to make it stop. But when we stood with Jacques de Molay before the cardinals in Notre-Dame, we revoked our confessions. Every last man of us. Why do you think they sent us down here?'

'To break you?'

'And by God's bones, it's working.'

'Is that why I no longer hear you praying?'

Bertrand leans back as if he would disappear into the rockface. 'What did you write in your book? The king is no closer to God than a Templar or a Jew?'

'I wish I'd thought of it.'

'You make sport of me?'

'Not at all, sire. But the longer I dwell in Paris, the more I think like a Parisian.'

Bertrand laughs and starts, as if the sound is new to him. 'I don't know how you've managed to bring laughter in here.' He sniffs at the cheese. Tearing off a chunk of bread, he chews at it with some difficulty.

'No prison can keep out the source of Joy, my lord.' She hands him a cup of water. 'Neither can the grandest palace contain it. Which is why my words frighten men like the Marignys.'

He uses his sleeve as a napkin. 'Meaning?'

'They are braggarts and half-wits who believe they'll find contentment in wealth, land, titles. All are burdens. Even our virtues hold us down until we allow ourselves to be free of them.' She tries to fathom the questions in his eyes and ends up asking herself questions like: Can eyes have the colour of violets in May? What should she do with this growing urge to take Bertrand in her arms and cradle him? Before she caves in to the urge, she returns to the doorway. 'You have my gratitude, Sir Bertrand. You've made me feel human again.'

'My lady, today you have been my salvation.'

As she returns to The Birdcage, Bertrand's baritone pours into the curing room like a soothing balm, '*All in disconsolation…*'

She turns her face into the sun and hears a woman's voice calling from her memory. '*Goats!*'

'GOATS!'

Marguerite jumped from the window of the bedchamber where she'd been enjoying a cat-like stretch in the early sunshine. 'Souveraine?'

'Goats should not be the ones sent to Hell.' Ermengarde was sitting upright in bed. 'They've far more character than sheep,' she said and collapsed back into the pillows. Marguerite knelt beside her on the palliasse where she'd been bivouacking every night for a week and leaned in to catch the slurred whispers. 'The world around me was crumbling…Fire…disappearing into darkness. And I was lost. So lost. But when you sang, I was floating. It was such a peaceful place.' Ermengarde reached for her hand. 'All this time I've lain here unable to speak, praying for forgiveness.'

'Forgiveness?'

'Oh, little Marguerite. How I've envied you. Your wonderful gifts. Agnès' devotion. Your favour with the countess. And…your love for Mahaut. Aye, jealousy has had me in its thrall. I've been so afeared of…' Her voice diminished almost to nothing but Marguerite caught the word 'you' and was taken back to the day she and Antoine podded a mountain of peas at the friary.

She never got the chance to ask Father Daniel again about his sister being afeared—*Not of what, of whom*. Shortly after the podding session, she'd gone off to Lady Marie's wedding at Châteauvillain, a week's hard ride away. After one touch from Lord Jean and realising how ridiculously susceptible she still was to the pull of a man's desire, she returned to Valenciennes, anxious to seek Daniel's wise counsel about the ache which wouldn't leave her chest. When she arrived at the friary, Brother Olivier was alone in the kitchen, utterly distraught. Daniel, quite suddenly, had passed into the next life. Souveraine Ermengarde's reaction to the tidings was immediate and devastating. Seeing her laid out on the floor like a malformed chick pushed from the nest, the coldness in Marguerite's heart towards her thawed. And after what she unearthed when she got her to her bed, she refused to let the other sisters near her: beneath the superficial grazes from her daily rituals, Ermengarde's back and flanks were criss-crossed with tough, silvery-blue ridges like cartwheels make in ice.

'Rest now,' she said.

'I must speak…while I can. Do you remember, in the barn, you asked about the cilice?'

'I remember.'

'Dreadful feelings crashed down on me. Swept me away. You so reminded me—You do remind me of…'

She helped Ermengarde to sip water, dabbed her slack chin. 'You must rest.'

But Ermengarde wasn't going to rest. She propped herself on an elbow. 'You remind me of someone I loved. The only one I loved after Maman died. Papa punished me for loving my Candice…and I punished myself. And you were grieving your little son, but I wanted to punish you too. Punish you hard. And I did. I punished you. And,' she said triumphantly as if the will to punish herself was still hard to resist, 'I enjoyed it.' She fell back, almost spent. 'I enjoyed it because you reminded me of what it was like to be loved. But how tenderly you've cared for me, little Marguerite,' she whimpered, 'after all the wickedness I did to you, all I took from you.' Tears emptied from her eyes, dampening her grizzled hair to the pillow. 'I'm crying like a babe, and precisely like a new-born, I feel so alive.' She laughed. 'It's such a relief.'

Marguerite held her hand. 'Everyone will be relieved you're recovered.'

'No. I meant I'm relieved I no longer have to be Souveraine. Dear

Marguerite, fetch your writing casket. You saw it on my desk. That day in the parlour. I will dictate to you my resignation. And afterwards, please sing to me again about the goats. If you will.'

And she did, until Mahaut came to the door.

'KEEP THE TITLE,' Jacquot said.

Mahaut stopped wiping her fingers on her napkin. 'Why would I do that?'

'The vote was unanimous. And,' Marguerite laughed, 'it'll remind you how high you've risen.'

'Go the whole hog,' said Nicolas, 'insist on Your Grace.' He licked each of his fingers clean of Madeira sauce. Jehan had surpassed himself for the Nativity Feast.

'I fear the new king would not share the title with any,' said Jacquot.

'You foresee French aggression, Master Échevin?' Nicolas gazed at him with the devotion of a puppy dog. Marguerite's heart rejoiced knowing her brother had found love, whilst her guts tightened lest his secret were laid bare to the world.

'Philippe *le Bel*, as they're calling him, hates foreign competition. Like the merchants of Valenciennes. They've no enthusiasm for the policies of open trade established by Marguerite Noire and they do not appreciate me citing the benefits.'

'You were re-elected,' Mahaut reminded him.

'I confess, it surprised me.'

Nicolas rested his hand on Jacquot's. 'Your fellow échevins and guildsmen appreciate the genuine care you have for the fate of the city.'

'Which, Nico, is now at risk. Emperor Rudolph has convinced the count to order that any Valenciennois wishing to foreswear must go to Mons to do so.'

'What?' The curé wiped away the wine that had escaped from his mouth. 'What of the poor? The elderly? How will they have legal redress with their lord?'

They all stared gloomily into their cups.

'There's more,' Jacquot said. He rose from his chair and reached for the flagon. 'No matter. Today we will be jolly and salute Souveraine Mahaut.'

As they drank to the Souveraine Elect, who frowned and swirled the fine Burgundy round in her goblet, Marguerite wondered whether her devotion to Ermengarde while Mahaut was busy deputising had drawn a veil between them. When she'd come to the bedchamber in the Souveraine's quarters and said, 'Let other beguines share some of the burden. You can't do it all yourself,' Marguerite had refused to relinquish her role as Ermengarde's shield wall.

On Christmas night as they lay abed, she knew Mahaut was pretending to be asleep because she wasn't snoring. She elbowed her in the ribs. 'You were quiet at table. Is your move to the Souveraine's quarters troubling you?'

'Of course not,' Mahaut said.

Back-to-back, both feigning sleep, Marguerite imagined her dearest friend was calculating how soon she could get away. Even though it was only a hop, skip, and jump across the courtyard, her departure felt deeply injurious. But as Mahaut knew well, Marguerite's pain was born of a misconception of her motives and her understanding was obscured by her unquenchable desire for love's presence.

21

Rue de la Bûcherie,
Feast of St Bartholomew 1309

IT'S BLAZING HOT outside. She should be basking in the sunlight pouring down her vent but there's an unfamiliar voice echoing in the basement and she can't see who it belongs to. Gringoire has pushed the curing room table against her gate.

She paces up and down, side to side, picks up her tablet, scratches a few words, slaps it back down on the bed, goes back to the gate, strains her ears, catches nothing, repeats the whole dance.

After Notre-Dame has rung for the Hour of Terce, when her nerves are crying out for the mercy of news, the table legs screech across the tiles. Bertrand bounds in like her old dog Bijou when he was let into her bedchamber. 'I've good tidings.'

'Come. Sit. Tell me every little detail.'

He picks up her tablet and casts an eye over it. '*Troubled is Martha, but Peace has Mary. Praised is Martha, more so Mary. Loved is Martha, but much more Mary?*'

'A Martha has been on my mind of late. The love of my life.'

Bertrand drops onto the platform. 'I've heard such things of beguines. But you? Falling to the sin of Sodom?'

She laughs. 'I didn't understand it either. But real love is not a matter of the will. Now tell me.'

An infant wails in the street above them. Traders shout to one another as they unload their carts. Hooves clop away down Rue de la Bûcherie.

'Sir Bertrand, have you ever been so at one with another living soul, they became part of you? But because you were with them every day you neglected to tell them you loved them. And when the parting came, it was an agony beyond words.'

Syllables clipped he says, 'I've not known such a love.'

'Well, I loved Mahaut like that. She was like a mother to me.' For a moment she's back in the stifling chamber in Ghent beguinage where there was no Eglantine to rub her sore back, bathe her neck with rosewater, tell her the pain would soon be over. But Mahaut was there. She was the one with her elbows crooked under her arms. She *was* her mother. 'Bertrand, has there never been one being as dear to you as your own flesh?'

His hand creeps to his chin, curls around his beard, twists it, tugs at it, shapes it. 'You'll hold me for a fool.'

'I will not.'

'Ephraim filled that place for me. Aye, my Ephraim knows me. I know him.'

Here we have it. He's ready to open his heart.

'Fast. Fearless in a fight. He bore me through many a long march.'

'Ah! Your horse.'

'Doubtless my Ephraim is in the royal stables now.'

'There. You see? You speak his name with a sob in your voice. That's love, Bertrand. And who would accuse you of impropriety for loving your horse?'

'Impropriety?' He looks as if he's been struck by a mace he didn't see coming. 'Oh, my lady, I've been on campaign...oh dear, dear, dear.' His body doubles up as if a second blow caught him in the stomach. 'I've been on campaign with soldiers...who haven't seen a woman for weeks.' She catches hold of the picture he must have in his head and now they're both howling.

Their laughter exhausts them into silence.

Bertrand's mood turns sombre. 'Jesting aside, you know we Templars are branded Sodomites? And the penalty for it?'

'Sir Bertrand, you came in here with good tidings.'

'Aye. So I did.' He perks up. 'Master du Bos, envoy of our Archbishop in Sens, informed us just now, a commission has been set up.'

'What sort of commission?'

'On the orders of Pope Clement. Every Templar in every dungeon in France will have his case heard. Here, in Paris. The king won't like it, but we will have our defence.'

She pushes aside thoughts of how papal interference will outrage Philippe's loyal inquisitor and confessor. 'Then you have hope.'

'Hope.' He smiles mischievously. 'Is that not one of the Virtues?'

'One of the Divine Virtues.'

THE CARMELITES. The Bernadins. Saint-Eloi. The booming peal of Notre-Dame de Paris. All ring for the Mass of Saint Bartholomew. If she listens hard she can make out the tinny peal of the Saint-Jean Commandery.

Sitting back on her heels, blowing the dust from her silverpoint, she admires her artwork. In the dark crust of the stone beside where she lays her head at night she has pierced two white eyes staring out of a round face. Two triangular wings reach up to heaven above the head, two reach out in flight, and two conceal the celestial body. Her etching hardly captures the intricacy of Michel's seraph but she refuses to expose his coverlet to this air—over the summer the pen has dried out but her clothing is stiff and smells of dirt. Not the good clean dirt you find by a swift flowing river, but the piles of malodorous tilth which collect in the corners of any underground place.

Putting the finishing touches to her rudimentary icon, she doesn't realise the bells have ceased ringing. The outer gate rattles and bangs shut. She glances into the curing room. It seems murkier than usual for this time of day; the umber shadows tremble. A man clears his throat and she drops her silverpoint.

Guillaume de Paris enters with Gringoire bearing a stool. The inquisitor stops a few feet from her bed. Bobbing up and down with an obsequiousness which makes her pity the man, the gaoler polishes the seat of the stool with his sleeve and sets it behind the black friar's knees.

'Leave,' the Dominican barks without sparing him a glance.

She knows exactly how far Gringoire has retreated. Eight months studying the behaviour of shadows underground has taught her how they gather and disperse, what disturbs and distorts them, the information they offer or conceal such as, whenever Bertrand comes in for a chat, the greyness that curves a foot or so beyond her gatepost. The shape of a knight listening.

Arms folded, Brother Guillaume leans back on the stool and waits, not with the look she remembers from Couvent Saint-Jacques, demanding her deference, but with bored detachment. The inquisitor must have studied the behaviour of shadows in a prisoner's mind, what disturbs the tempo of his pulse, what makes it race or stall. He'll understand her desperation to discover whether he's ferreted out more copies of her treatise, or interrogated the people she loves. Or had Jacquot arrested. This time she won't allow her mind to wander anywhere near the hope she might be set free.

'I've news of great import to you.' Guillaume's smile reminds her of someone, she can't for the minute think of whom. 'Your accomplice is in custody.' She holds her breath, praying he's not going to say the name she most fears to hear. 'Guiard de Cressonessart was—' Her outbreath of relief, that he didn't say 'Father Jacques', must have given him pause.

'A copy of your so-called *Mirror* was discovered in Guiard's possession. Yet you show no remorse?'

'I've done no wrong.'

With the back of an index finger he strokes his brow. 'Guiard languishes in the Grand Châtelet. Have you no shame? Luring a man into mortal danger?'

'I take no responsibility for the actions of another.' She mustn't think of Guiard in some filthy oubliette. There are many thoughts she can't allow herself. Her mind darkens.

'Not your *brother*'s keeper, eh?' He smiles and waits. What for him are seconds must for his victims, with weights dragging on their limbs, seem an eternity. He's waiting now for the perfect moment to drop the next load on Marguerite, pull away every bit of her strength, push her resilience to the point of no return so it can no longer recover its shape, make her light dark and her dark light.

'Let's talk about *your* actions, shall we? Here, *in camera*.' The smile. 'Divers men have supported you. Religious men, and seculars. Men loyal to Holy Church.'

Who does he mean? Bishop Jean? Godfrey? Friar Jehan? He could mean Jacquot of course. A black pall of dread twists around her heart and lungs, like damp serge shrinking, inflaming, suffocating.

'Why force your heretical book on them?'

'It is not heretical. It is proven by scripture.' Her voice sounds far away, dislocated from herself.

'It's not too late to recognise my inquisition. Take the oath. Then I'll be free to disclose information about the charges and discuss your...*alleged* heresies.'

One more load. One more temptation to yield. Oh, how she wants to yield. She needs to know about Jacquot. The wheels of her desire turn; they drive her towards a single destination, *Submit!* She opens her mouth to speak and feels a tearing inside, as if the black pall has ripped free and is no longer a pall but a diaphanous veil, hooked up by the wind of the Spirit, floating away. Her mind clears, her breath comes more easily, she feels becalmed and fully herself.

Guillaume must have perceived, from how much higher she holds her head, her resolve has returned. His shoulder twitches and she remembers where she's seen that smirk before. Latin class. When Jacquot was unable to conjugate the verb and she blurted out the correct forms. The Crow-man wore the same expression when he picked up the switch and shrugged as if what would happen next had absolutely nothing to do with him.

The inquisitor moves to the gate. 'Consider the godly men you've harmed, Marguerite.'

Marguerite. Spoken with silken intimacy. *Marguerite* crawls in between her skin and her bone. Marguerite leans over the slop-bucket and retches.

'MY LADY?'

Vertically, Bertrand fills the gateway. His tunic is grimy. The hollows beneath his cheekbones look as if the flesh was removed by hammer and chisel. Yet he has the stature of a knight who has ridden into battle and confronted a far more fearsome sight than an aging woman with raw eyes. 'I saw you had a visitation.' He holds out a cup and makes sure her fingers have hold of it. 'We keep a measure against such occasions. Not a fine wine, but it's strong.' He gestures to the stool.

'Please,' she croaks.

'Feeling his presence again was a…' Bertrand's torso makes a weird movement, less than a spasm, more than a shudder. 'It was an unpleasant reminder.'

'Brother Guillaume is hard to withstand.' Even without the estrapade, she thinks but doesn't say.

'He looks so harmless, with his baby cheeks. Did he get what he came for?'

'I almost surrendered. Time is running out and I need to know…' She takes a gulp of wine. 'It's my brother, you see. He's not been of strong mind these past years and he's under suspicion.'

'You needn't say more to me than to the Dominican, but if you wish to share your burden, my lady…'

Is it such a bad thing she enjoys hearing him call her 'my lady'? She should own up. 'If Jacquot comes to harm, the blame will all be mine.'

'What does Guillaume know?'

'His whereabouts. But Bertrand, I gave him a copy of my manuscript. I've managed to get one letter to him, warning him to hide it, and I began to write another to tell him he might himself be in danger, but there was none I could entrust it to.'

'Jacquot will guess the inquisitor might suspect him of collusion with his sister.'

'Of course.' She sips the wine. 'But I've been thinking…What if I write, making it look as if I'm angry at my own twin brother? A diatribe, as if I believe he's the one who betrayed me, because he's always been against me—'

'The letter would stand surety for him?'

'Precisely. But I've pondered it. If the letter were successful in its purpose, the inquisitor might force Jacquot to testify against me.'

Bertrand is about to speak and stops himself. Doubtless he's realised what she now realises herself having expressed her anxiety out loud. Jacquot could be made to testify in any case.

'I see you love him dearly.'

She rubs the cool ceramic cup across her eyes. 'Not all the enmity I've been planning to accuse him of is untrue. We fight, like any brother and sister.'

'I grew up knowing none of my kin. Pray, tell me of Jacquot.'

She drinks the rusty dregs from the cup, considers where to start her telling. She won't mention what happened with Brother Rémy, and certainly not the rage Jacquot flew into when she gave him the news she was pregnant by a Templar. She'll begin with his musical gift and his devotion to the Virgin. And she must tell Bertrand the story of when he took punishment in her stead for breaking Ysabeau's lamp.

By the time curfew rings over Paris, she's recounting the one time her brother went into battle.

SHE PUTS DOWN her quill and reads through what she has so far composed.

Paris, AD 1309 Feast of Saint Bartholomew
To Father Jacques from his sister Marguerite

Know that I am in a filthy cell. Was this by your design, dear brother? Long have you been my severest detractor. Dissatisfied with chastising me for taking up my pen again, I can only deduce you had a hand in the calamity which now befalls me. Sorely am I grieved, remembering how once before you were in league with a Dominican. 'Crow-man' as I called him. It was, I know, humiliating for you that day in class. But my sole intention when I marked the panic in your eyes was to come to your aid. In silence you stood right beside our tutor. Far worse, the next day, you turned your smooth back on me and gave him your undivided attention. I imagine you never forgave my besting of you.

You were always destined for the life of a religious. When Papa obstructed you from taking Holy Orders, you resented me taking his side. The Preachers were, of course, always keen to recruit you. And think not I've forgotten your part in exposing my teachings to Bishop Guido's judgment. Indeed you admitted to me your guilt. If I could see you now, and we mayn't see each other for some time, I'd respond with the exact same words I said to you then. Repeat them to yourself, I beg you.

And by what marvel were you singing so exuberantly on the morning of my arrest? Aye, Father Jacques, I heard you. Did you know I heard you? Did you plan it that way? Were you crowing over me like you did as a boy when you'd bested me? Crow-man. It's a sobriquet which now fits you, dear brother.

Tears spill over her chin. She rubs her face into her cloak, his parting gift to her when he left for the Charterhouse. She tried to protest such a garment was for a lady and not for a simple soul like her. He insisted she keep it. A true Valenciennois, her Jacquot.

22

Rue de la Bûcherie,
November 1309

THE THUD rouses her and she supposes someone is knocking on the door of her cottage and she should dress and cover her hair. Low tones of dampened hoofs and men chit-chatting funnel down from the street. It's Monday morning, chez Gringoire. Of course she isn't at home.

There's a fuzziness around all her edges as she rises in increments. Her elbow knocks the wax tablet on the floor. The stylus seems to have a will of its own; her fingers struggle to pick it up.

In the leaden light of the curing room a man's silhouette stands out. As she goes to greet him, a broken tile sucks in her toe and her knee jars. The man rushes forwards, catches her by the forearms. Her palms slide down silken sleeves and fingers like the roots of an ancient olive tree curl around hers.

'How fortunate you're back,' she says. 'For me, not for you.' She releases herself from Oshaya's grasp and rubs her knee.

'It was only a matter of time. Have the knights gone?'

'They're in with Sir Maurice. They spend hours in there, chewing on rumours. Yesterday Gringoire threw them the juicy morsel that Pope Clement favours a full acquittal of their Order. But what about your pardon?'

'Temporary. Please. Wait.' He vanishes into his pen and reappears with a bulky package. 'Please, my lady, take it.' The boiled wool she unfolds is of the highest quality. Vermin have ravaged her mantle and she needs some dry warmth but so does Oshaya. She pushes the cloth back at him. 'I'm already in your debt.'

'I beg you.' He puts a hand to his breast. 'It would give my heart the greatest comfort.' The black curls dropping from his cap bring the taverner of La Tête Noire into her thoughts.

If the Simple Soul possesses a thing, she once wrote, and knows others might have greater need of it, she will never withhold it, even if she were certain nothing would grow on earth any more.

'Your generosity is most welcome.' She bows. 'May I ask, why was your pardon only temporary?'

'I can no longer offer assistance to the king.'

'To do what?'

'When he expelled us from his lands, it had the benefit of cancelling his debts to us. And the debts were heavy. But his men also confiscated every promissory note. They wanted me to help identify creditors, and I did. Till I refused.'

'So that's why you didn't leave France with all your kin?'

His eyes widen. Even in this dim light they dazzle like the blue of the lapis lazuli reserved by illuminators to paint the Virgin's robes. 'All except my brother.'

'Is he safe?'

'In a manner of speaking.' He picks up a loaf and goes to his pen. 'Benjamin is now with the Divine Presence.'

BERTRAND comes into her pen, brandishing her letter. 'Your brother is a knave.'

'Do be careful with that. The air in here is sodden. I told you, I've written no falsehoods. Merely embellished the truth. A little.'

He opens out the folio. *'Ever were you a staunch supporter of Jan d'Avesnes II. When it came to war, you stood with our fellow townsfolk out of loyalty to them. But in the end, you remembered your duty to the count as your rightful suzerain. You cooperated with the royal envoys. You helped draw up the peace treaty deposing our Provost, Jakemon le Père, and stripped all twelve échevins of their livelihoods. You truly were the Count of Hainault's man. And for that matter, King Philippe's.* He betrayed them all.'

'How it tormented his soul to do such deals.'

'Delighted to hear it.'

'Bertrand, it was complicated. The stalemate dragged on throughout winter. For the sake of the destitute, he had to steel himself to negotiate with the lord who had wrought such havoc. He had to beg for the lives of Jakemon and the échevins to be spared. Few saw what it cost him.'

'I yield, I yield! He mightn't be the scapegrace I took him for. But you wrote…yes, here it is, *Think not I've forgotten your part in exposing my teachings to Bishop Guido's judgment. Indeed you admitted to me your…*You altered a word there…*your responsibility.* How can you trust him?'

She draws the blanket of boiled wool more closely around her.

'My apologies. I failed to ask. How fare you this day, my lady?' He sits on what, in her inventory, has become 'Bertrand's stool'. 'The blanket keeps out the damp.'

'It was a good thing Oshaya did. Who would have imagined it, from a Jewish moneylender?' He rests his forearms on his thighs, losing himself in his thoughts, and she would no more disturb him than she would a dreaming child. He laughs.

'Did I miss the jest?'

'Lady Marguerite, I knew exactly what your game was. Yet even I was hoodwinked by your letter. If it comes into Brother Guillaume's hands, he's sure to be deceived. But will Father Jacques discern your stratagem?'

'I'm confident of it. But the letter needs to reach the Charterhouse so he knows what's in it. I can't trust Gringoire. Besides, my coins run out.'

'Isn't there a Temple commandery near Valenciennes?'

'Beaulieu. Not far from Marlis Cross.'

'Hmm. Our hearings begin tomorrow. The word is, it'll all be over by Christ's Nativity.' He lays the folio on her lap. 'Finish the letter. I'll deliver it myself. I would meet this brother of yours.'

When he's gone, she lies down and imagines the moment Bertrand will meet Jacquot for the first time. She pictures the monastery path where she once stood, waiting, watching, believing the portal would never open. That was eight months after the spectacle in the Grande Place and when a figure stepped out of the gate, she rushed forwards. But the monk coming towards her had an ungainly gait and wore white robes without the black cape of the novice.

'*Christus resurrexit.*'

'*Vere resurrexit.*' She glanced past Prior Pierron. 'Where's Jacques?'

His eyelids, hooded like a hundred-year-old tortoise's, opened a sliver. 'Your brother cannot meet with you today.'

'But you promised.' She was all for beating the holy man on his bony chest. 'Two visits, you said. The Virgin's Day. Easter Day. Is it because I failed him last time? Does he know why?'

A hand waved for quiet. 'Brother Jacques is indisposed.'

'He's ill?' In the time it took the prior to contemplate his answer, she had imagined Jacquot struck down by every malady from the pestilence to the sweating sickness which took Amand.

'Sister Marguerite, entering our life has great challenges, particularly for one of his—'

'I *must* see him.' She adopted her haughtiest tone. 'I need to see Jacquot. Now.'

'You must wait.'

'Wait how long?'

'A year.'

She gasped as though he'd slipped a knife between her ribs.

'Possibly a year. The novice master insists he needs absolute peace.'

How could any monk know what her Jacquot needed better than she did?

The prior perceived she was about to lose all control. He was right. She remembers all too horribly the feeling of her feet teetering at the brink of the black pit. He took her arm and shepherded her away and when Pascal saw her stagger into the mill yard, he sent for Agnès.

Two Virgin's Days passed before Jacquot came out of the gates again. Without a glance at the feast she'd laid out for him on her mantle, he stared at her with persecuted eyes. 'It was all my fault.'

'Of course it wasn't your fault.' She inched around to him on her knees. 'Have a honey cake. Ysabeau's recipe. I baked them in honour of our reunion.'

'If I hadn't mentioned Lady Germaine…if I hadn't arranged the audience with the countess…the bishop wouldn't—'

'Be still.' She hadn't meant to speak so severely, but his anguish was a rusty nail grating on her bones. 'None of this was your doing. I do not regret one minute of the time I spent with Countess Philippine.'

'I almost deserted my vocation. I was so desperate to see you.' He made a strenuous effort to sit up straight, faked a smile. 'Things are better now. So here we are.'

'Yes. Here we are. Tell me how things are better. Will you make your profession soon?'

'Soon.'

'It's possible I'll join you in the cloister.' In as manly a voice as she could muster Marguerite grunted, 'Not here, obviously. Don't think I'd get away with it.' That drew a genuine smile. She chose not to tell him it had been Godfrey's counsel to take the veil. She didn't mention Paris at all because she couldn't confess to him the reason for her most recent visit to Rue

Saint-Jacques. She held a cake under his nose.

'You'll be safe with the nuns. Please, Margi, do it this time.' He nibbled at the cake. When the Vespers bell rang, he trudged back down the monastery path and she wondered what miracle would make him sing again. She still doesn't know what did.

'FOR GOD'S SAKE, what does that mean?' How like Jacquot Bertrand sounds when he's vexed. '*The Soul is a servant of herself when she desires God do His will in her, to her honour.*'

Marguerite retrieves her tablet from Bertrand's lap and lays it on her side of the platform. A sallow ripple of lamplight ebbs and flows over the wax. 'Look at you.' She's sounding more and more like Mahaut used to when they lived together. 'You're shivering.' She drapes the lion's share of the boiled wool over his legs. 'If you must know, I've been playing my own inquisitor. Interrogating my motives. How did I start writing again?'

'My lady, I do not comprehend it. Why so reckless? And after what happened, you remained in Valenciennes.'

'I intended to leave. Though I'm glad Pascal bullied me into staying. I kept away from the city, and yet it seemed the city would come to my door.' She feels the angles of Bertrand's body fold in towards her, ready to hear one of her stories. 'Well, on the Virgin's Day after the fire, Jacquot still didn't get to visit. Imagine, if you will, everyone is at the revels. You hear the drums. You smell the hogs roasting. You try to shut it all out, slam the door, sit yourself by the back window, get down to some stitching. Then the door opens. With a sudden joy, you look up. Standing in the doorway, arms akimbo, is someone you've known all your life and your smile fades because it isn't the brother who, for one tiny moment, you'd thought might be back to health.

'"To what do I owe the pleasure of your company, Master le Vilain?" "*Provosht* to you," Jean said. I eyed the fur trim of his silks. It was a warm day. I told him I'd heard of his rise in status. He told me I'd do well to remember the lowliness of mine and asked whether I ever rued the choice I made.'

'Choice?'

'Oh, Jean was sweet on me as a child. Swore he'd marry me when we were of age. Shall I go on?'

'I'm all ears.'

'Well, Jean swaggered over to my stool and looked down at me, a man who normally is obliged to look up at everyone, including his wife. "I'm here," he said, "to make sure you're obeying the bishop." His eyes rested on my armoire—that's where I keep my writings. At the time there was only one precious but blameless manuscript on the shelf. "Well," I said, "now you've seen I've no heretics hiding in the thatch, perhaps Mistress Yolent will be glad to set eyes on you." He came so close to me I could see sweat forming into globs on his lip. He gripped my chin, pinched hard enough it came out in a bruise. "One tiny hint of you defying Lord Guido and you'll be on my pyre," he said. "No mer*shy.*" His eyes strayed behind me to the bed and I thought, *He's going to force himself on me.* I believe Jean thought so too. He walked away.'

'That was it?'

'The strangest thing, Bertrand, I didn't feel afraid. Nonetheless, when a loud knock came on my door next day, I leapt like a startled rabbit. It was only Brother Olivier, the kitchener who took Antoine under his wing. I didn't recognise the friar he'd brought with him. The ascetic cheeks and tonsure were a good disguise. But then he spoke. He said he'd recently arrived from Paris but his accent was more local. "Jehan of the delicious sauces," I said. "My lady who likes extra almonds in her honey cakes." Friar Jehan was once Jacquot's cook.'

Bertrand blows on his fingers.

'Shall we warm ourselves with a stroll around the curing room?'

'Later,' he says, 'I would hear about the friars.'

She tucks the blanket snugly around him. 'Friar Jehan told me how for many years he had yearned to practise the simple life of faith. But after joining the Franciscans, he'd discovered friaries rich with endowments. On the other hand, he also discovered the more disturbing allure practising radical poverty had for him.'

'Some of my Templar brothers urge the use of cilice and scourge.'

'Undoubtedly basking in our humble deeds can be a real temptation. Anywise, in the taverns of Saint-Séverin, Friar Jehan had heard about the Northern beguine and her treatise. His cousin Rogier told him about my visit to Godfrey de Fontaines. He came to his point.'

'He wanted a copy of your *Mirror*?'

'"Holy Church," he said, "must be brought back to the way of Christ and a beghard told me you know this way without falling prey to fanaticism."'

'Guiard?'

'Possibly. Though Guiard verges on the fanatical himself.'

'So you relented?'

'I protested. That I dared not defy the bishop. Bertrand, I must have sounded angry. In truth, it was terror provoked me. Well, Jehan said he was cognisant of the Italian's judgment and pointed out how carefully the bishop had chosen his wording so as not to condemn me in person, only the book. And besides, he said, Lord Guido was leaving Cambrai for Salerno. Still, I told him, he asked too much. But when the door closed behind him and Olivier, it was as if an invisible door opened inside of me.'

'And you had to write.'

'I secured the bolts. When I dipped in the inkpot, pushed my nib down onto the page…Nothing. Bertrand, I'd approached this threshold before. Wanting to speak. Nothing coming out. As if rocks were wedged behind an invisible door. Panic. Grief. Fear. No matter what barred me, I couldn't get inside. I couldn't get to the words, piled high like treasure in a robber's den. I set off on a long, long walk.

'Close to the footbridge over the Ointiel there's a crater made by an uprooted tree. I sat inside it. The sweet smell of fern and wood-rot soothed my temper. Of a sudden, a balding pate bobbed over the edge. "Whoa!" I cried. Pascal, laughing, picked his way through the brambles. "You strode off like Old Beelzebul were after you," he said. I began to tell him about my visitors but he raised a hand. "You've naught to explain to me, Lady Marguerite." I asked him why he never called me simply "Marguerite." "You'll always be Lady Marguerite to me, cos that's who you are—you're a woman and you're noble."'

'Wait. Wait. You are a lady.'

'I'm afeared I've led you astray, dear Bertrand.'

'I'll not believe it.'

'I bore Sir Raoul no child. As a daughter of merchantry, no heir, no title.'

'What a dreadful shame. You having no children, I mean.'

She stares at Bertrand, letting the sting pass through her. 'Well, Pascal tapped his forehead. "I know what you wrote were good and proper, and you frit a body by it." I pointed out he didn't know what I'd written. He said, "I not be knowing my letters like our Agnès but I've watched you for a long while." He gazed out across Lower Mead. "I plough the earth, harrow it—real hard work that, even with the mule—then I cast the seed. But you know the hardest thing the farmer does, my lady?" I guessed at harvesting. He shook his head. "Wait," he said. "You do the work you can do. The Lord God does the rest. Can't hurry Him, no matter how much you mither Him with your prayers. You have to wait. Then comes the harvest."

'How foolish I'd been, Bertrand, wanting to read for anyone who'd listen. I should have waited. I should have trusted my instincts, trusted Godfrey.

'When Pascal and I reached the mill yard, Agnès was at my door with Antoine. He looked so fine in his habit. "We knee this for Magrite," he said and held out an oven-fresh loaf. I fetched wine, smoothed out a napkin, told him the bread was the best I ever tasted. And it was. Do you not find, Bertrand, some manner of pride seems magically to heal wounds?'

'Undoubtedly.'

'When we waved them farewell from the plank bridge, the sky over Valenciennes was a sheet of burnished copper. "I'm mazed," said Pascal, "how the Lord showed us, when he floated into church on that barrel, where the lad should be—never changed his mind 'bout it." I said how he'd loved Brother Olivier from the start. "Antoine?" Pascal said, surprised, "I meant *God* never changed his mind."'

Her oil lamp expires plunging the pen into darkness.

'You know how at dusk the colours transform first to mauve and eventually all turns to grey? I watched the living Ointiel becoming one with the night and suddenly I grasped it. Bertrand, there exists more than one kind of death. I went into my house, lit my candle, didn't even bar the door I was so certain God hadn't changed His mind about where He'd led me. This time I knew, as I dipped in the ink, there was no going back. My spirit of fear had died.

'I was aware of nothing but the One, present in me, present outside of me, without *me* being there, as if all my edges were dissolved into Him. On the pristine vellum there rose up the form of a phoenix, her wings outspread. From then on, I no longer woke up in the middle of the night with the taste of ashes in my mouth.'

Bertrand rests his hand on hers. '*Not for us, my Lord, but to your Name give the glory.*'

'The Templar motto?'

'It's clear to me, as if looking in a mirror, how wide I've missed the mark. My desire to serve God was for my own honour. It's true, my lady.'

'My lady?'

'Ah! You remind me of a detail. You wrote in your letter to Jacquot about being with child when you returned home from Paris.'

'Bertrand, do you have the will to hear another story?'

23

Rue de la Bûcherie, December 1309

WAS THAT THE SCREECH of a barn owl? she wonders when the gate scrapes over the tiles. Lying on her back, in a waking dream, she has been treading through frosted bracken, welcoming the spectacle of winter in the Forêt de Mormal. Did she really used to walk barefoot to draw her water from the icy lake? That's how she remembers it. Once, her legs sunk so deep into a snowdrift she—

'Why do you always refuse to stand when I enter?'

Is the voice of the angry man inside her head? She twists her neck round. Two white fists are clenched around folds of black cloth.

Pale mushrooms explode from Brother Guillaume's mouth as he speaks. 'No matter. Upright, kneeling, prostrate, you may receive my offering.' His face looms over her, gargantuan. Doubtless, in comparison, her own face resembles the faces of the starved children she sewed into their shrouds at Saint Elizabeth's Infirmary.

'In the spirit of this holy season,' his tone is softened, redolent of cloistered alcoves, but something has happened to the smooth examiner of the summer. The bags under his eyes look like half-healed bruises. 'I come to offer you the mercy of Christ's Church. Seek absolution, Marguerite. Take the host from my hand.'

'It would bring me little benefit.'

'Again you blaspheme.'

'Blaspheme?' Anger pokes fire into her bones. 'When did I blaspheme?'

'Your treatise is replete with error.'

'You approach it with a closed mind.'

'I am Master of Canon Law—'

'Precisely. Godfrey de Fontaines, however—'

'Ah, the illustrious Regent Master.' The inquisitor licks his lips like that tomcat when Ysabeau let him out of the dairy shed. 'Godfrey de Fontaines is no longer with us, God rest his soul.'

Her tormentor must be disappointed she shows no sign of shock. She knew the news was coming. Last night before the big freeze petrified her fingers, like Nan and Marguerite Noire before him, Godfrey appeared on her wax tablet, one of Love's couriers.

'Now, Marguerite of Valenciennes, will you confess and be shriven of your sins?'

She remains silent. In Godfrey's last letter he wrote: *Your Mirror now reveals what is divine living. You illuminate a practice which surpasses all human practices.* He had confidence in her words.

'Pride. Such an ugly sin. I've given you ample opportunity to repent and receive the Blessèd Sacrament. My generosity must end. I will now progress with my investigation despite the obstinacies of you and of your accomplice.'

Making a huge effort, she raises herself to sitting. 'So Guiard has not sworn the oath?'

The black friar is gone and she shrinks back into her cocoon.

Moments later a light flickers. A wall of warmth buttresses her body. Bertrand is speaking in her ear. 'Do not give in to the lickspittle now.'

'I don't think I can move.'

'Then we'll lie here together. Talk if you will. Or sleep.'

'But Sir Maurice?'

'Ymbert attends him.' The knight reshapes the last shreds of Jacquot's vair around her head and shoulders.

'Hark,' she whispers. 'The bells for First Mass.'

'Did you ever hear the "Song of the Blessèd Virgin" ring out from the Chapelle-Haute?'

'Oh, I did, Bertrand, I did.' Wings of a memory carry her back into the presence of a mighty king and a magnificent queen; she's kneeling with Raoul, beneath stained glass sparkling in the light of a hundred chandeliers. *'Gloria, Gloria, in excelsis Deo,'* she sings, *'Gloria, Gloria, in excelsis Deo...'* The next line shrivels in her throat.

The silence ossifies.

She wants to begin again but can't find a mote of energy in her voice.

Then the dark vaults of the saltery are shaken by a rich baritone, '*Et in terra pax hominibus bonae voluntatis. Laudamus te, benedicimus te, adoramus te, glorificamus te…*'

'Ymbert,' Bertrand whispers and begins the Angels' Hymn again, '*Gloria, Gloria, in excelsis Deo…*' His breath is warm on her cheek, like Jacquot's when he used to sing to her. Sir Ymbert joins in, followed by Marguerite and the three voices gather a ringing strength before they disintegrate in the ravening air.

'Is it bad news about Guiard?'

'He prevails. But now there's nobody…'

She feels his limbs stiffen in hesitation. Then he embraces her and holds her to him. 'Dear lady, I have you safe.'

'No one will care to understand, now Godfrey has…'

'Is the Master…?'

She nods weakly.

'My lady, the king has no reason to destroy you. You have no standing army, no gold.'

'But you, Bertrand? Even now the bells ring out for Christ's Nativity and you said by now—'

''Tis but a short delay to our liberation. The hearings resume at Candlemas.'

'And what then?'

'I don't know how our Order will emerge from this. I have to believe we will survive in some manner. But even living in a hovel would be preferable to…' The thought he's unable to complete is the thought she's been dodging ever since Hébert mentioned the name Guillaume de Paris on the track through Lower Mead.

ON THE FEAST of the Holy Innocents, Marguerite is up. She moves cautiously, like one of the grandmothers who've survived many childbeds only to end up begging in the Grande Place. Enveloped in Oshaya's boiled wool, she hobbles into the curing room.

The aromas of winter spice uncoil tendrils of comfort inside her.

Sir Ymbert, standing between the drain chute and the well, combs his fingers through his hoary mane and smooths his tunic with the flat of his palms. 'Blessings of Our Saviour's birth, my lady.' He bows like a seasoned courtier. 'I'm in your debt. On Holy Night my soul was in sore want, and then I heard your voice. Such an abundance of mercy filled me. As you must have heard, we've recommenced our daily prayers.'

'Your devotions this morning performed a miracle. Here I am, raised. And you are most courteous, my lord,' she gestures at Bertrand who has just exited Maurice's pen, 'but it is your Brother who deserves the credit. He brought me through the dark hours of that night.'

Ymbert tips his head to Bertrand and moves surprisingly fast to stand in front of him. 'I have a cousin who is a religious at Abbaye Saint-Germain-des-Prés. He has the ear of his superiors. Even now he works to secure my release. When we're delivered from this…this scandalous disgrace, I intend to share with him your plight.'

She cannot imagine the Benedictine monk will hold any sway with Guillaume de Paris. 'I value your solicitude,' she says. 'However, I'd not have your kinsman implicate himself on my behalf. Already I've one friend on my conscience.'

'You see?' he says to Pons who remains propped on the table, his back to her. 'She has the mark of true nobility.' Ymbert reaches for the alms dish and offers her the spiced fruits. Although her gown is stained, her threadbare coif failing to hold in her tangled mop of hair, she's never felt more a lady in her life. Biting into a fig, the juices shoot painfully to the back of her throat. 'Your supporter,' he says, 'what's his name?'

She works her tongue around her raw gums and swallows hard. 'Guiard. From Cressonessart.'

'Is this Guiard of noble lineage?'

'I believe he is.'

Ymbert glances at Bertrand. 'He must surely be kinsman to the Preceptor of Bellinval. Matthieu de Cressonessart is imprisoned at Crèvecœur.' He makes a sound like a horse dying of the ague. 'They cannot keep members of every highborn family in France incarcerated forever. Philippe le Bel must know it.'

'The king does as he wills,' Bertrand says, 'driven on by the Marignys.'

'And de Nogaret. Loathsome cockroach. Holds no reverence for the Holy See. De Bos said he bullied his way into the Grand Master's hearing, his only aim to disrupt the commission. Will nobody stop them?' Ymbert looks around the basement for the answer none can give.

Marguerite hutches up her boiled wool. 'Where's Oshaya?'

'Gringoire locked him in for the holy season,' Bertrand says.

Taking a handful of fruits she limps to the pen nearest The Birdcage. Pointing a warped finger at Oshaya's iron gate, Sir Pons leaps at her. 'He is a *Jew*. Gringoire says he spat on the likeness of the Virgin.'

'And the king says you Templars regularly spit on the Cross of Christ.'

'Oof.' Bertrand slaps Pons on the back. 'She's got you there, Brother.'

'His kinsman died.' She passes the fruit through the bars of the gate. 'You must surely appreciate, Sir Pons, the importance of carrying out the proper burial rites according to tradition for one's own brother.'

Oshaya's fingers meet hers. 'Peace be with you, my lady.' She presses his icy flesh between her warm hands.

SIR MAURICE'S PEN stinks like the back corner of a smithy. The old knight may look to the mortal eye like a child dressed in men's clothes but his mantle is folded over him, the red cross *pattée* positioned above his heart, and the Angel of Death, when He arrives, will be in no doubt, here lies a Templar warrior.

Marguerite steps into the fug by the brazier where Pons and Ymbert are at loggerheads. 'This is no place for a woman,' Pons spits at her. 'It's a priest we need.'

Ymbert, looking as though he might imminently follow Maurice into the grave, steadies himself against the wall. 'The inquisitor withholds the Rites from him, the most devout of our brothers.'

'Not one of us can remember the prayers,' says Bertrand who is kneeling beside Maurice on the plank-bed.

Pons advances on him. 'And I say, playing priest would guarantee our damnation.'

Bertrand throws Pons a look as if he thinks he's being deliberately stupid. 'I'd call this *in extremis*. Are we not Christian men? Or do you side with Guillaume de Paris?' Maurice lets out a panicky cry and Bertrand cradles his head. 'I'm here, my brother. God's angels gather around you.'

The audacity driving Marguerite to speak makes her chest pump like bellows. 'I know the prayers.'

Pons points one hand at her. 'Hear her blasphemy?'

Momentarily wondering what his other hand is holding beneath his cloak, she walks straight at his rage. 'Is it blasphemy to have mercy on a soul such as Sir Maurice? Do you not think God looks on him even now, His mercy overflowing, with or without the holy words, shriven or unshriven?'

Bertrand speaks urgently. 'Can you do it?' She gives a confident nod and his fingers beckon at Pons. 'Let's have it.'

Pons glares in rebellion at him and glances at his dying brother-in-arms. From under his tunic he brings out a straw-coloured pillar and sets it on the bed. Marguerite stares as if she's never seen an altar candle in her life.

'One moment,' she says and hurries back to her pen. Oshaya is chanting, purposefully. She recognises the psalm and she's reminded of the countless times she witnessed Curé Nicolas perform the Rites on victims of war and the plague that prowled around Valenciennes in its wake. Calm overtakes her.

When she returns with her cruse, she offers it to Bertrand and understanding passes between them. He pushes his thumb into the last smear of oil. Maurice's face is a fragile husk for dead bones but when Bertrand anoints his forehead with the sign of the cross, the skin seems to glow. Marguerite says the prayers as she remembers them, '*Per istam sanctam unctionem…*'

Peace fills the squalid room, a peace holding an invisible substance more real, more solid, more lustrous than gold as Sir Maurice expires.

A man is weeping. As she turns to leave, she sees it's Pons.

AFTER THE GUARDS have carried Maurice's body out, after the cleansing stream of Paternosters has ebbed away, after Marguerite's tears have run dry, footsteps clap across the curing room. Undoubtedly Bertrand, coming to seek comfort. Manifesting in the shadow by her gate is the spectre of Sir Pons.

In defence against another tongue-bashing, she reorders the blanket around herself. The knight stood loitering on her threshold brings her a flash of memory, of the pageboy who came to the solar at Salle-le-Comte; he was so in awe of Marguerite Noire, he'd completely forgotten the message he was to deliver.

'Do you want something, Sir?'

'I come to render you my deepest, deepest apologies.' From behind his body, the crumbling fortress which won't beat off another siege, he produces the altar candle. In his own little ceremony, he lays his offering on her island. 'Pray, accept this to light your way. At Christ's Mass the Friars Minor sent it to us. I pilfered it.' His feet in ragged boots shuffle around on the mud floor. 'I will do penance for my selfish act. I am to serve Oshaya his food and empty his bucket for a week. Might the candle be of use to you?'

The honeyed smell of beeswax? Golden light to write by? 'Of immeasurable use,' she says. 'I am in your debt.'

'The debt, my lady, is all mine.' His yellowing eyes close. 'I'll remember the peace around Maurice's passing as long as I live. Which may be but a short spell. Ha!' He fills out his chest as if summoning a valour he was once well acquainted with and again she is transported back to Salle-le-Comte, forced to watch from the gallery as young lords practised their courtly skills on the noble maidens. 'What you said, earlier…' he begins, 'if Maurice is in Hell right now, do you think God's mercy— I mean, can God's mercy…'

She holds her breath, urging him to find the courage to speak his heart. Come on, Pons. You can say it. But no. He's losing his nerve. He's going into retreat. 'Do I think God's mercy…' she says, '…can reach him there?' His head and shoulders droop. 'Unequivocally, my lord. God is present in every corner of His universe. He is without beginning. He is without end. He is our Father, our Brother and our Loyal Lover who will never abandon us. Such is the Lover of our souls.'

'Amen.' Taking her hand, he presses the fingers wrapped in shreds of Worstead to his cracked lips. 'I bid you good day, my lady.' As he turns, his leg wobbles to one side. Then head held high, Sir Pons strides out.

Sniffing at the beeswax, she can't help but chuckle. Joy overtakes you in the uncanniest of places. When she's had her fill of the aroma, she lights the wick ready to erase Godfrey's story from her tablet. First she wants to spend a few moments with her memories of the great man.

'BISHOPS. ARCHBISHOPS. I've remonstrated with
them. Inventing heresies where none exist.' Godfrey took
my new manuscript from his pile. 'You think your words
have naught to do with statecraft? Well, when you touch
the heart of God, you mayn't avoid it. Our tall fair king
casts a long dark shadow and your *Mirror* exposes the
sins of self-aggrandisement and greed, though they be
well-hidden from the transgressor himself. *Hmph.*' He
stood to survey Rue Saint-Jacques. 'How they venerate
Saint Louis' head. Ha! No brains in it even when he was
alive.' The chanting of pilgrims on their way to Sainte-
Chapelle rose to a crescendo, fading as they passed by. 'I
wonder.' Godfrey tapped his fingers on the table. 'You
know the Italian expired before reaching Salerno?' *Tap,
tap.* 'I wonder. Might we secure an invalidation of his
judgment?' *Tap, tap, bang.*

I MARVELLED at his words. 'Can that happen?'
'Depends on who hears the case. To whom have you
shown this new work?'
'Friar Jehan. He gave me like advice to you. Few should
see it.'
'Good man. Marguerite, there was a beguine, in
Magdeburg. They wanted to burn her writings but the
nuns of Helfta took her under their wing. Now, I'm
acquainted with a scholar at Villers Abbey. Gifted man.
He'll grasp your thinking. If I approach him for aid, will
you, like Mechthild, consider the veil?'
My ribs constricted as if my bodice were being laced
tightly around me, nevertheless I said, 'I'll consider it.
But they'll have to let me write.'
'I pity the one who tries to stop you.' He laughed,
though his hands fidgeted with my treatise.

EPIPHANY 1308 Godfrey's letter arrived.
I rejoice! Your Mirror now reveals what is truly divine living, illuminating a practice which surpasses all human practices. The Soul cannot arrive at the divine life till She arrives at the practice you describe. He reminded me not many should read my treatise lest they set aside the life they are called to, aspiring to one at which they might never arrive.
One could easily be deceived. The book is made from a spirit so strong and ardent, few are like it. Dom Franco, however, has proved by scripture what you write.
For months I dwelt in Peace. Twilights I reminisced with Pascal over a brew. Daybreaks I milked the herd.
Ermengarde knew the truth. Goats have all the character sheep lack. I miss my Chou-Chou playing dead simply to get a hug.
I miss my hovel.

'And I miss my Jacquot.'

∞∞∞∞

EASTER FELL LATE. And Jacquot was late. The stinging blue sky chiselled sharp edges to the elderflowers festooning the hedgerows. The Ointiel winked at me irresistibly. Throwing aside mantle, bag, and hose, I waded in shin deep; I'd forgotten how much the minnows tickled. Gathering a handful of blossoms to my nose, I thanked God for the promise of an abundant summer and prayed that Villers Abbey would have a pretty river nearby.

'Aren't you too big for paddling?'

'Hello, Moody. You sound like you did the first time we fished in the Ointiel. You said I was too *little* then.' I let the elder petals fall on the scurrying waters.

'Papa made me look after you when all I wanted was to be with Amand in the den.'

'And I always thought it was because you envied my bucketful.'

'Beginner's luck. l let you have the best spot on the outcrop.'

'You refused to speak to me for days.' My heart soared. It was like old times. He held out a hand, pulled me up the last yard into the grasses, and scooped me under the arms. I prodded him in the ribs. 'You're thinner.'

'You're fatter. Did you not fast in Lent?' A plopping sound came from the river and cut off his predictable diatribe before it got going. 'Look,' he said, 'the kingfisher is here.' The bird swooped up to the hedgerow, a silver fishtail drooping from her beak. 'And you, the Queen of Fishers, are here.' He dropped me down. 'I've good tidings. I'm to make my profession on Saint Bartholomew.'

'Good tidings indeed.' I flattened the grass and made room for us both on my mantle. Our mantle.

'Margi, I need to say something. Now. About you and me. When we're together I feel…well, ofttimes I feel…'

'Suffocated?' I suggested. The word fitted best the struggle I'd had all my life.

'Aye. Suffocated. But when we're separated, I long for us to be back together.'

'You don't have to explain. Not to me.'

'No wall, no matter how thick or how high could truly separate us. I know that. And I'll see you on the Virgin's Day. Tell you all about it.'

'You'll be *Father* Jacques.'

'At last I can shed this dreadful black stuff.' He flicked away the outer layer of his novice's habit. 'Now, what about you. You're all cock-a-hoop for a woman about to make sixty years.'

'Godfrey wrote to me.' I felt around in my scrip but could only put my hand on the manuscript I'd collected from the illuminator. 'I must have left the letter at home. Anywise, he and Dom Franco enthuse about my new treatise.'

'Treatise? No, Margi.' He hooked his fingers into the serge bunched at his neck and yanked at it. 'For God's sake. Who's Dom Franco? And Master Godfrey—he does know, doesn't he, what Lord Guido said?'

If I'd heeded Godfrey's advice in the first place and not yours, I thought, there'd have been no Guido da Collemezzo. I managed to hold my tongue. 'Dom Franco is finding me a cell at Villers Abbey—'

Jacquot had stopped listening. 'We've heard terrible things.' He massaged his brow with the ball of his hand. 'About Guillaume de Paris, what he's done to the Templars. They're charged with heresy. The *Templars*,

Margi. *Heresy.* Why do you risk so much for so little a thing?'

'So little a—' I let my indignation pass. 'Don't fret, now. It's not the same book. I've added scriptural proofs, made clear statements of doctrine.' I knelt up and kissed his scalp, lingering over the whiff of frankincense in his stubbly hair. 'What I've written stands up to theological scrutiny. My *Mirror* says something important. About God. About Love.'

'Love?' The air vibrated between us, *love…love…love?* 'What do you know about love?'

'I know about your love for Nicolas.'

As if laying his neck bare for the headsman he bowed his head over his knees. 'Oh Margi, I loved Nicolas so much I would have…' Saying Nicolas' name must have opened up a vein; the words bled out of him. 'Nico abandoned me. He chose to confess. Did penance to save his soul. And I tried doing the same. I believed a man can change. Still I was tormented. So I confessed the true source of my torment. That for love of Nico I would have chosen Hell. Margi, I would have chosen him over seeing Maman in the next life. So. Now I'm absolved and the novice master thinks I'm over it all. But in the night, when I return from chapel, when I'm on my knees peering into the dark corners of my cell, I know I still love him. Margi, I can't give him up. I can't.'

His eyes bored into mine and I felt the fissure opening inside of me, as if I were the abyss he might fall into, fall down and down and not stop falling. *Plop.* The kingfisher had plunged into the river. As she resurfaced and darted back to her concealed nest with her second catch, I thought of Nicolas telling us the bawdy joke about the bishop with loose-hanging teeth, making us laugh so much Jacquot snorted wine out of his nose; I thought of Jacquot in peacock blue, at the head of the échevins, raising his arms when the procession snaked around the belfry to show off his undershirt, snowy and unwrinkled as the Virgin's veil, because he knew he'd come into the view of his lover further up the line.

'Margi, I love Nico more than I fear God.'

The stillness of the afternoon stretched out into one of those moments when the confines of my heart melt away and my soul slides into eternity. My mind knows the moment will pass away, never to return. But I don't want the moment to pass away, ever. And I didn't want that moment with Jacquot to pass away. He'd put into words the desire of love which reaches beyond the torments of Hell and at last I knew we two were identical. The only reason I had to break our perfect silence was to tell him he was safe, I wanted him to know his soul was safe, but the priory bell tolled at that exact moment and Jacquot jumped to his feet. The moment passed unmarked, unfulfilled, ungrieved.

He moved away from me and without a thought for the new copy I'd have to scribe for Bishop Jean, I reached into my bag for my manuscript and pushed it into Jacquot's arms. 'Take it.'

As he tried to push it back at me, the golden wings of the phoenix shimmered. Utter bewilderment was the last expression I saw on Jacquot's face. 'See you on the Virgin's Day,' I shouted and ran off as fast as my aging legs would carry me.

The kingfisher hovered beside me as far as the mill yard and when I crossed the threshold of home, I realised my feet were naked.

Susan Shooter

PART 3

The Phoenix Who Is Alone

Speaking of her Lover, the Soul says thus:
He is, and nothing is lacking to Him;
I am not, and therefore nothing is lacking to me.
And so He has given me Peace
and I do not live except by Peace,
which is born from His gifts in my soul,
without thought.
And so I can do nothing unless it is given to me.
He is my All and my Best.
And such being makes me have one love,
and one will, and one work in two natures.

The Mirror of Simple Souls, Chapter 52.

Susan Shooter

24

Paris,
Epiphany to Candlemas 1310

I KNEW he was coming. I'd heard every word he said to the knights. Someone had to pay and the someone was going to be me.

'Stay!' he shouted at his notary and strode in. Icy puddles splashed the back of Brother Guillaume's heels and the air of my animal pen seared into shreds before his raging soul. Thrusting his face into the last drizzle of daylight from the vent, he put me in mind of Jean le Vilain slavering all over me. But this man is no lily-liver; I could taste his intractable will bearing down on me, a will which had torn away flesh with red hot pincers and put out eyes.

'You, Marguerite, called Porete, you are stubborn of will. You think you know better than the men whom God has put in authority over you. Your pride, contumacious *ab initio*, will no longer be tolerated. At the Feast of the Purification, you will be taken from here—'

'I've done no wrong.'

'*Sub judice.*' A cough. Guillaume's face regained its smoothness. I don't know how he does that. 'We will speak again when you've been transferred to…' predictable pause, precisely long enough so I was begging to know my fate, '…the Grand Châtelet.' He disappeared before I'd dug my nails from out of my palms.

The inquisitor's smell lingered, though it wasn't the taste of grease and winter sweat made me want to gag. It wasn't even raw fear of death. How many times have I pushed myself over the threshold of death and found

Love on the other side, welcoming me home? No. It was Guillaume himself terrified me and I lay, immobile, as if an invisible eagle had knocked me on my back and was tearing at my liver.

'Marguerite. Did you hear the good tidings?' Bertrand sounded excited. It took every ounce of my energy to force myself upright. 'What a painful errand it must have been for Smooth Chops. He had to tell us that leaders have been appointed to mount our defence. A co-ordinated effort. Our mass protest of innocence cannot be ignored. Should stop Marigny meddling now.'

'Marigny?'

'Did I not tell you? He became Archbishop of Sens. Our diocese.'

'That all sounds splendid, Bertrand.' Alas, I couldn't keep my voice from trembling.

'My lady?' He groped his way to the platform. 'Do you still mourn?'

'Sir Maurice and Godfrey are grievous losses to me. But the inquisitor paid me a visit also.' Warm light from Pons' candle was what I needed. I rooted it out but my clumsy fingers dropped the tinderbox. Bertrand fished it out of the bedding and as he got the tinder going, I told him of Guillaume's plans for me.

'That explains why he came to us in person. We deemed it odd. And how injurious of me to speak so boldly of the upturn in our own fortunes.'

A talon clawed at my innards but the candle's golden light awakened courage in me. 'I'm delighted for you, Bertrand. Truly.'

'Will your letter be ready by Candlemas?'

'I've a few lines to copy, though I'm afeared my ink will run dry.'

He reached inside his tunic. 'How fortuitous the inquisitor's notary left this behind. Accidentally, of course.' Fitting snugly in his palm was a metal object shaped like a pear. The clasp of the inkpot glistened luxuriously. 'For you, my lady.'

My eyes smarted. How unprepared I still am for Generosity to find me.

IT WAS CONVENIENT for you, wasn't it? That you abandoned me for the monastery and missed my humiliation in the Grande Place. It was as though I'd ceased to exist for you. And when I offered you a copy of my Mirror of Simple Souls, you didn't even want to touch it. You ~~said you~~ had absolutely no desire to read ~~'so little a thing.'~~ it. Night and day I'm tormented by the change in you. What happened between the time I last saw you and the time I last heard you? On the day the royal guards came to arrest me, why was it you were singing so rapturously?
~~I hoped at first, with all my heart, it was the solemn profession of your vows that had lifted your spirit so high. Sadly~~ I ~~now~~ believe ~~you are my betrayer.~~ it must have been the thrill of a brother's betrayal.

KING LOUIS' thread of gold scintillated in the candlelight.

"Tis a thing of beauty.' Bertrand was awestruck. As he leaned over, whiffs of lavender emanated from him. His concave cheeks were well-scrubbed and although he had refused to let me touch his beard, I'm glad he suffered me to trim his hair with my penknife.

Pressing my face into the half-plucked coverlet, I kissed the seraph. Was it for the last time? The cloth drooped over my palm like a bird with a broken wing and as Bertrand's hand descended, I couldn't stop my fingers from curling up over it. 'None other hands but his.' I'd said it so many times in the last few days but the dear man didn't rile up.

'Upon my honour,' he said. As he took the coverlet, I let out a soft moan. Gently he eased it inside his surcoat where it would sit alongside the calfskin wallet I'd manufactured from two folios, tied with an azure braid, and sealed with wax from Pons' candle.

'When we are liberated, I ride north straightway. But dearest Marguerite, I believe you may yet convince Guillaume. You have the words.'

'In which case, I'll be directly on your heels.'

Abruptly, as if the idea had suddenly occurred to him, he took a knee. 'I will stay by you, my lady, and when they come, defend you with my life.'

A ruffle of panic in my breast. Then I felt the gravity of the moment, balancing me. We both knew he could do little against men well-armed and well-fed. Ours was no hero's tale. But we'd swum all our lives in the same waters of ritual and tradition. 'Sir Bertrand, I'm counting on your service. Promise me you will commit no folly, and you will do all in your power to remain safe so as to perform your errand.'

His palm went to his chest. 'God smite me down should I forsake my oath to you, my lady.' Desperately I wanted to raise his unkempt chin to kiss his forehead and reached out my hand.

Love overcame me.

I let my hand fall and bowed my head to the Poor Fellow-Soldier of Christ and of the Temple of Solomon. Bertrand rose and bowed. 'By your leave, my lady.' He disappeared into the darkness with Jacquot's letter and Michel's coverlet and I wondered, how is it possible to lose my heart over and over yet keep on living? The curing room yawned hungrily back at me and upon my desert island I creased in two.

I lay a long while, the monstrous hulk of the Grand Châtelet distending the shape of my mind. A thin little question squeezed itself out into the light. Is there any way back, even at this late hour? I am, exactly as they say, contumaciously stubborn. As a mule. Priests, Preachers, Augustinians, even some beguines say I am mistaken. Why would the Far-Near One choose to reveal Himself to a woman like me? Perhaps there's still time for me to recant, I thought.

Then the dawn prayers of three Templar knights saturated the abysmal void. Once more I was baptised in their overflowing praise and I knew God would, of course, forgive me if I recanted, as He forgives all things. But a question remained I could not answer, and still cannot.

How is it even possible to recant of Love?

MY EYES ARE tight shut. The road to get here has been long and arduous and I don't want to see what has been prepared for me in the Grand Châtelet. My bundle is jabbing into my chest from when the constable propelled me through the doorway and onto the floor.

This morning, a remnant of my old counterpane was enough to wrap around my few belongings. Oshaya's boiled wool was back on his own bent body and my ivory casket was gone, traded for two pails of lamb stew. Yesterday evening was awkward at first, looking at each other around the table in the curing room. Blue eyes, grey eyes, weeping eyes, and Bertrand's eyes which seemed to have taken over his face. We prayed a psalm and broke bread together.

I was tying the hose with the worn-through heel around my bundle when the gate hinges groaned. Boots tramped. A scuffle broke out. Sir Pons was shouting and I held my breath. Then I heard Bertrand's voice. 'My brother, it will go better for Lady Marguerite if we submit.' Relief flooded through me.

There was a hiatus.

Spurs clinked across the tiles. A gen-d'armes strode in and every swollen joint in my body screamed to be left in the putrid familiarity of the old saltery. 'Well, well, well. If it isn't Moreau's little whore.' Hébert dragged me up by the elbow. 'Christ. You're not looking so fresh now.' Trapping me under his armpit, my neck stretched out like a fowl's for wringing, his hand clutched my wizened breast and he marched me out.

The knights shook the bars of Ymbert's pen. They were shouting but I heard only a rumble as if I were underwater. My last view of the basement was of Oshaya, on his poor knees, hands reaching through his gate; I tried but couldn't reach even one outstretched finger. My feet didn't touch the floor of The Birdcage.

The top stair hurtled at me and like some subterranean creature, my eyes closed against the bland February sky. Frosty air bit into my body and released ugly smells. 'Filthy bitch,' Hébert said into my ear as he slung me like an animal carcass on the cart. The sharply chiselled mud on the planks snagged my cheek. He hawked snot into his craw, spat, and splattered the cobbles with livid green. 'Shame the chief's not here. Love to see you in your pretty red dress, he would.' Raucous laughter.

'Is he back from Avignon?' said the guard in the driving seat.

Hébert climbed up beside him. 'Aye. But he went off to Clermont yesterday. Fetching more dirty Sodomites for the hearing.'

My body rattled in the cart like a sackful of gnawed bones.

'Foulques reckons he's gone soft.'

'Saw an old Templar boss he knew at the bishop's palace. Put him in a mood, it did. Reckon he—' The horses clattered onto the Grand Pont and I tried to lift my head but learnt no more about Moreau; my shoulders wouldn't hold me up. I was drifting into darkness until the reek of the slaughterhouses slapped me back into consciousness and immediately the shadow of this place crept over me.

When Hébert pulled me down onto the cold cobbles, the sky turned black. Perhaps death had arrived to bear me away, I thought, and the pain will end. But no, it wasn't death come to bear me away, it was a Goliath of a man. The constable pushed me into the barrel-vaulted passage and we followed the wall of the bailey. 'Be seeing you at the échelle de justice, I will.' Hébert's shriek of delight pursued me to the end.

In the fortress we passed by many doors. The mewls of agony from behind them merged into one pulsating throb inside my skull so that I couldn't separate them out. But the stench? There was one odour I could disentangle from the rest. More intestinal than the slaughterhouse, more sinister than rotting wounds. I first smelt it at Luzarches.

Lying here, I can't expel it from my nostrils. But I have to breathe…

…I haven't tasted air like this since the day Moreau and his men came for me. A barn stacked with winter fodder. I blink away the light stabbing at my eyelids. The chaos in my head is clearing.

The pile of straw is clean. The empty bucket looks newly crafted. And what a shock! A good shock. Up high, a gash of delicious blue, a slug of *eau-de-vie* to my veins, and I'm back on my feet. I'll get to the aperture at the top of the tower room even if I have to crawl.

The slate window ledge may as well be a mile above me as a yard and pounding at the un-plastered stone is getting me nowhere. Is this to be the torment? Beautiful light I cannot reach. I slide to my aching knees.

Along the wall, level with my eyes, spaced equidistantly, is a row of putlog holes. I glance at my toes poking through my dilapidated boots, and now a memory of desperate little me, wanting to sit in the oak bower, Jacquot laughing down at me through gappy teeth. How did he not know refusing to help would only make me try harder? The ledge is like a bough of our tree. One foot in a putlog hole, and yes, I've caught it. Up a little further…if I crook my elbow around the metal bar at the centre…one last effort and my bones settle on the slate.

'Ah!' The sound escaping me is like an arrow has pierced my chest.

Beyond the outer sill is an exquisite image opening up like a painted altar diptych. One side of the diptych is filled with the bustling Grand Pont; the spire of Sainte-Chapelle rises from the pure white walls of the Palais Royal. The other side of the diptych makes a frame around the Jardin du Roi. Underlined with the green ribbon of the Seine, the garden is an enchanted forest; a kestrel hovers above the fruit trees and the charcoal branches are perches on which my famished soul can repose.

'Thank you,' I whisper.

The Generosity of the Far-Near One has found me once more.

25

Grand Châtelet, Lent 1310

DOWN passageways dripping with despair, we skirted remnants of someone's father, brother, son. Down, down, down into a windowless tunnel, and always the suffocating stench of human mercilessness. Constable Goliath shoved me through an iron-barred gate and my foot hit something solid. Unable to save myself from falling, my knees slid into a soft, wet mass.

Now my eyes have adjusted to the light draining through the embrasure, I can make out the pale shape at my knees. A ridge of human vertebrae.

For two months they left me alone. During these lengthening days of spring I've sat on the ledge and watched the Jardin du Roi burgeon into life, weaving together thin threads of hope that all is not lost. In the nights, lying in my straw, the gossamer tissue I've woven is seared away by the sound of Katarine's screams inside my head.

Yesterday, two guards shuffled into my tower room carrying a brazier. The coals hissed and spat for an hour before the Inquisitor of France arrived. Guillaume looked grey in hair and skin and I had to wonder, had someone dangled a threat in front of *his* eyes till he could think of nothing else? A map of the Dominican mission field in Persia perhaps?

I clung to my slate perch.

'Why stand by a book which will condemn you?' he demanded.

'A book cannot condemn. It is men who make and administer the Law.'

'I have witnesses who saw you outside a cathedral, spreading your false teaching.'

'If you've read and understood my teaching, you'd not condemn me by it or call it false.'

'Bishop Guido condemned it.'

'He held no Chair of Theology as Master Godfrey—'

'Not this again. We've only your say-so about the Regent Master's approval.'

How can this wily fox of an inquisitor be such an ass? 'If you disbelieve me on this point—and if I swore your oath I would stand by it—how would you believe anything else I said?'

'Your stubborn refusal,' he said stubbornly, 'to appear in my court makes you *de jure* a heretic.'

Involuntarily my toe grated a smidgen across the ledge.

'There's no place for anarchy in the Kingdom of France. Canon lawyers and theologians from the University of Paris will hear your legal case and decide.'

'So, you're still not convinced of my guilt?'

He disappeared into the fortress.

That was such a confusing exchange. If I am *de jure* a heretic, why has he not already condemned me? And the inquisitor, himself Master of Canon Law, consulting theologians to pronounce on a matter of legality? I couldn't make it make sense.

And today I've been brought to this latrine.

I can't decide whether I want to draw Guiard to me and warm him at my breast, or slap him for being such a damned fool. 'Oh Guiard, Guiard.' I draw him to me. I stroke the blenched spine protruding through the loosened warp and weft of his habit. His head turns upwards to the crepuscular light. The skin of his face resembles a parchment scraped too many times of its content and stretched across an assortment of bird bones.

'You're alive?' he whispers.

The gate groans and our heads jerk round.

The notary hangs back, pressing a sachet to his nose. At arm's length he passes a document to Brother Guillaume who holds it towards the embrasure. '*In nomine Domini*, the decision of the canon lawyers made this third day of April.' He's reading speedily. Wants out of here. 'Guiard de Cressonessart, your defence of Marguerite, called Porete, progressed into vehement, then into violent presumption of heresy. Considering your contumacies, your rebellious and stubborn behaviours, you must be deemed a heretic, condemned as a heretic, and relinquished to secular authority for punishment unless you quickly repent, before or after sentencing. Wherefore, that you do not infect the infirm with your pestiferous doctrine, you will be committed to perpetual imprisonment.'

Guiard curls into a foetal position. '*Dimitte nobis debita nostra sicut et nos dimittimus debitoribus nostris.*'

The inquisitor hurries on. 'Marguerite of Hainault, since suspicion of heresy progressed into vehement and violent presumption of heresy...' I try to listen for a different decision by the canon lawyers but the words are of a monotonous sameness. '...relinquished to the secular arm unless...' He pauses. He knows my imagination is conjuring the executioner's fire, '...unless you quickly repent. Confess your errors, return to the fold, and there will be mercy.'

'Mercy?' My voice is a shriek. 'To die in the filth of the Grand Châtelet?'

As the friar and his notary retrace their steps, the tunnel fills with the cries of dismembered souls. Guiard claws himself onto one arm. '*Vengeance is mine, I will repay, says the Lord.*'

'Vengeance?'

'Want to know about our Inquisitor of Heretical Depravity for the Kingdom of France? Confessor to King Philippe? Or, as we preferred to call him, Guillaume the Shit-licker.'

'You know Guillaume de Paris?'

'Utterly worthless we were. Fourth and fifth sons of minor nobility. But Guillaume, a son of merchantry, more worthless. We were spiteful to the clever little whelp. One day—I forget who threw him into the ditch under the latrines—I offered him my hand, to pull him out but...' Guiard moans like an old wound has caught up with him. 'We were schoolboys. Just children. Every one of us terrified we'd be the next to be singled out.' I thought of Jacquot when he confessed to me the same fear as he had stood by and watched Brother Rémy whip me. Who wants to be chosen for punishment and shame?

'And now, Porete, what are we to do?'

When the Ointiel washed me daily with its rhythms, when I sat on my stone seat and weighed my free, full life in the balance against the agony of my limbs being rendered into tallow, this moment seemed such a long way off. Was the road to get here the true road to the land of willing nothing? If it is God's will that I die, am I capable of relinquishing the desire to live fully which the Far-Near One restored to me in Mormal?

'It seems we have to lie. Or die.'

'Christ forgive me, so many times I've wanted to die. But the fire...' The bones of my wrist grate in the grip of his desperate hand. 'Darkness. Hunger. The cold. Lying in Satan's own filth. None of it broke me. When the doubt ate away at my bowels, I clung to my revelation in the Chapelle-Basse. The moment my life finally made sense. I knew who I was.'

'I remember it. You were all aglow.'

His fingers bite deeper. 'If I swear their oath, tell them of my vision, explain the Angel's message…and that you, Porete, are the Lord's adherent and as such I was compelled to defend you. The clerics, even the Shit-licker himself will understand.'

'They don't care about your visions.' I sound so full of judgment. Aye, I *am* judging him, but just look at him, with his stumps for teeth. 'Guiard, what they want is our absolute surrender. But what they want is not theirs to will or to command.'

'So then.' He's pushing my arm away. 'I see it now. You were jealous of my vocation. You think nobody else but you has anything of worth to say. And I helped you, Marguerite *Porete*. I spread your word. You rebuked me once for seeking martyrdom. But now you would…' The Angel of Philadelphia clasps his arms over his head like two featherless wings.

I want to tell him, 'There exists more than one kind of death, Guiard,' but I can't. All I can do is hold the fallen angel and weep with him.

WHEN YOU CAME to me in this night, your gaze held mine, as it did in the moment before you perished. But what I wanted was for you to look at me with the clear amber eyes which mirrored our perfect world immediately before the deluge. I want to see you now as in the hour I first set eyes on you, laughing like a madwoman, oblivious to all else. I want to see you on the Virgin's Day, when the air in the Grande Place was thick with pork crackling, when the drummers drummed fast and the pipers piped faster and I threw down the challenge, 'Race you to the belfry.'

You nosed in front, but your eye was caught by the duck-apple tub. 'Oooh, I've always wanted a go.' You bobbed your head under the water. You bobbed back up, teeth clenched but empty. 'Get your whole face in,' I said and demonstrated. 'Years of practice,' I crowed.

DOWN, UP, DOWN, UP, you bobbed till your coif dripped and your eyes blinked. Manon said you looked like a frog and giggled. 'Sister Mahaut,' she cheered. A gaggle of children gathered and took up the chant, 'Sister Mahaut,' *clap, clap, clap*. 'Sister Mahaut,' *clap, clap, clap*. Under you went again and nigh on drowned because you couldn't stop laughing. 'Time for a warm ale, Sister.' Jacquot guided you away from the tub. I took your other hand. 'A reel around the bonfire will dry you off.'

And we reeled and we stamped and we whirled under the Harvest Moon in the streets of Valenciennes.

'I've got you,' you said. 'Let go.' And I did let go. You spun me round and round. Heads thrown back, we spun and spun, inebriated by a more intoxicating drink than new wine.

We did not feel the Joy that night. We *were* the Joy.

'GUIARD DE CRESSONESSART has recanted.' Brother Guillaume sits on a stool, his spine in a violent shape, no doubt hammered there by his covetous heart. 'Couldn't shut him up in the end.'

I lay aside my stylus and climb down from the ledge. Lowering myself onto the stale straw, my eyes draw level with his once porcelain fingers which are grasping at his kneecaps. What a marvel. The Inquisitor of Heretical Depravity for the Kingdom of France has chewed his nailbeds till they are whitlows full of pus. What is it Guillaume Humbert desires but fears he cannot have?

'Will *you* not repent, Marguerite?'

'How do I repent of Truth?'

'Truth? Pah. I understand why you would infect simple folk with your "Truth". Beguines. Beghards. Silly noblewomen whose heads are full of fripperies. But answer me this: Why send your treatise to the Bishop of Châlons?'

It's so tragic, comparing the young Lord Jean at Lady Marie's wedding, full of vitality and mischief, with the bent figure lumbering up the Grand Degrés in the palace yard. How dishonour ages a man. 'Once upon a time, Jean de Châteauvillain had a profound capacity for joy. I'd say he's forgotten how to laugh.'

'You make merry of trumpeting your heresy to a prince of Holy Church?'

'My book is not heretical. You must know this.'

'Must I? Well, tomorrow we'll find out.'

'We?' A thrill surges in my chest, like when Jacquot used to dangle me over the Ointiel. Except I trusted my brother would never let me fall.

'The faculty of the university is convened to meet at the Couvent des Mathurins. They will examine your *Mirror*. What do you think the most learned men in Paris, nay in all Christendom, will find there?'

I wonder if rainbow-coloured light will spill from the south window of the Mathurin chapel onto the black robed clerics. Seated in front of *The Wheel of Fortune*, their ghost-white faces poring over my words, their acute minds dissecting my sentences, will they be able to penetrate my thoughts? 'So my book is yet to be condemned by a competent theologian?'

'Have a care,' he growls. 'It lies within my powers, *ex officio*, to revoke clemency. We both know you are in relapse.'

For God's sake, why then do you procrastinate? An extreme weariness drops on me but this is a fresh lifeline. I must test its strength. 'Why do you summon the Doctors of the Church?'

As Guillaume leans forwards, I smell the rotten breath of a stringent faster. 'Why should a body *give unto Nature all that is necessary without remorse of conscience?*'

'Because what Nature requires is perfectly innocent, as a babe naturally requires his mother's milk.'

'Even a new-born is tainted with Adam's sin.'

'It is not our material body, but our will that diverts us from the good.'

'Bodies cannot do as they please. There would be chaos.'

'Without doubt. On this we agree.'

'Now you contradict yourself.'

'Oh, Brother Guillaume, I am full of contradiction.' (Such as how I want to keep silence, yet at the same time I want to dispute with you. Such as how I want Bertrand safe, yet I don't want you forced by humiliation into extreme action when the Templar Order is acquitted.)

'Why, when I have your life in my hands, do you make light of your situation?'

'Why do you summon the Doctors of the Church? Are you worried you've set your wager on the wrong dog?'

He looks surprised rather than antagonised. 'Explain your contradiction.'

The last time I visited Godfrey, he asked me to do the same. He watched me with amused curiosity as I gave my explanation. Let's see if Guillaume grasps it.

'Chaos is created by human will. Our desires run after this, run after that. When we're thwarted, like discomfited children we make war. But if we offer our free will back to God, which was *His* gift to us in the first place, we begin to view ourselves in *His* light. All we once deemed good about ourselves, about our deeds, even our evil deeds, is revealed to be nothing— nothing at all when compared with God's Goodness. Is there any greater than He?'

'None.'

'When our will no longer puts up any obstruction we are fully open to God and He can fill us with *His* will. It follows, therefore, since our deeds proceed from our fullness in God's perfect will, these deeds can only be well-ordered, as God's are well-ordered. *Ergo* no chaos.'

Deep in thought, his rough cuticle plays with the dark skin of his lower lip. 'But you say we must *take leave of the Virtues*. Why do you rob the faithful of their righteous path to God, their road out of Purgatory? They will no longer pursue good works. There would be no penances.'

'Precisely. There would be no need for penances. How marvellous.'

'Everyone must do penance.' He folds his arms and sits back. 'You are *de facto* enemy of the Church.'

'So, Inquisitor, are you saying, someone who does God's will must do penance for it? A man of your education must see the absurdity in that proposition. Doing God's will—God's *perfect* will—cannot possibly be sinful, can it?' The debate is sparking my energy. I'm sitting up on my heels like I used to when Raoul challenged my meanderings. 'Perhaps I've been imprecise. I see it like this: Our good deeds are not the pathway to God. Rather, true acts of Virtue are the *result* of being filled with God's Grace which we must seek in the first place. You have to take your pot to the source in order to draw water for your chores. You do not fill it yourself. You cannot fill it yourself.'

Guillaume remains silent for a long time. His pose reminds me of Bertrand on my last day at Gringoire's. As I worked at his hair, the beloved knight bent forwards on his stool and allowed me to pour myself out like a libation; his silence caught every drop of my darkness so I could examine its nature, its essence, and whence it came.

'I have a question for you.' As if I've woken him from a nap, Guillaume jerks upright. 'Why, Inquisitor, did Guiard speak of forgiving our debtors? Why that particular line from the Our Father?'

The haunted look on his face disturbs me, deeply and terribly. Severe doubt is making its presence known. Not the everyday doubt whether the butter will turn, or the rain will hold off long enough for the hay to be gathered safely in, all those petty anxieties which used to fill my life and seemed huge at the time. But the kind of doubt that festers, an untended and shameful wound we try to shut away in an oubliette. Words Mahaut once said about Hell come back to me. Guillaume has foisted the festering Hell in his heart onto so many. The Grand Châtelet is full of men who know they are abandoned, that no one will come and save them from their agony, and perhaps most devastating, they are themselves helpless to end their own degradation.

A flash of insight!

I know why the inquisitor has come to me—the exact same dread resides in his heart as resided in my own before I cast it away with Sir Bertrand's hair. The dread that God cannot, God will not save a man such as Guillaume de Paris. The Inquisitor of Heretical Depravity for the Kingdom of France lives in terror that he is beyond the reach of Love. What a contradiction in him. He needs my writings proven false so he can win his legal case and earn his reward. But as a man terrified he cannot be loved, he needs them to be true. For if there is no Divine Love as I've described it in my *Mirror*, he will be consigned without hope into the abyss.

So does my *Mirror* reveal the truth? I'm up on my knees.

'Here's a story. Once upon a time there was a clever child whose father was a wealthy merchant. This child caught the eye of a great and noble personage who ensured such a promising intellect would be properly schooled. The highborn children in the benefactor's charge, for their part, ensured life was unbearable for the little upstart who suffered terribly of loneliness and became enclosed in a world of books and words, hostage to a wild imagination. When fully grown, choosing to become a mendicant creature—'

'Stop. Stop. How do you know all this about me?'

'This is *my* story.' I shuffle closer to him. His breathing quickens. 'After many trials came the tossing and turning at night, seeking a purpose for my existence. Merely serving God like everyone else wasn't enough. Because I was chosen. I was special. So I starved my body. I scourged my flesh to make myself feel anything I could interpret as a blessing from the Lord.'

'Yes. Yes.'

'Finally I believed I'd been abandoned in the darkest pit with no loving hand to pull me out. Brother Guillaume, when were you last at peace? When did you stand in the forest, drink in the green light, taste the sap? When did you lose all you had and laugh at your own nakedness?'

I call on the memory of the hermitage, the stag lapping food from my palm. I stand so I am eye to eye with my inquisitor, the man who has the power to annihilate me. Passion blazes inside me and I'm travelling down dark passageways. The voices of the shattered souls in their oubliettes are calling to me. The Templar priest at Luzarches is howling. Guiard is sobbing. But I must offer Brother Guillaume my hand. Passion burns away my conceit that this man's salvation depends on me, it burns away the conceit that my life depends on him. No contradiction remains in me. I am free of all doubt. I no longer question why I'm doing what I am doing. There is no reason for it. The Far-Near One is here, and I am not. It is the Presence Who is reaching out to Guillaume.

On my hand I feel the lightest pressure, a touch of skin, like when I carried Carmelle's boy out of the consuming flames. A thumb slides softly over mine.

'Would you, Guillaume, render your will to the Love of God? Love which is *gratis*?'

Love overcomes me. A surging power. Power not to hurt or to harm or to hate, but to free. Power not my own. Desire for this Love transforms Guillaume's face. If he can let himself fall, just this once, there'll be no going back. I imagine him standing up in the Couvent des Mathurins tomorrow, defending my *Mirror of Simple Souls*. And I picture him now without his Dominican robes, his boyish face, un-tonsured, laughing.

His knee touches the floor, his head is bowed under a tremendous weight. 'I've had men tortured to death… but…they *were* wicked; the king…'

'Raise your eyes, Guillaume, upwards, up to God's eternal Goodness.'

His mouth is open at this marvel, his eyes too. Because I, Marguerite, am witnessing his raw, naked need without judgment and without stepping away in revulsion. I grasp his hand more tightly to pull him to his feet and in the blink of an eye, he's looking down again at the straw. Now he's the isolated, bullied child covered in human detritus and I strengthen my grip on his hand. 'I've got you, Guillaume.'

He snatches his hand away. He glances up, the amazement gone from his face. 'He told you.'

Immediately I know, although I don't know how I know, what the boy Guiard de Cressonessart did. Guiard may not have been the one who threw this son of merchantry into the cesspit, but when he hauled little Guillaume Humbert up out of the mire, he was only pretending to rescue him—Guiard let go of Guillaume's hand and down he went again, down, down, down.

'Don't go back to your prison of shame, Brother Guillaume.' I open wide my arms to him. 'See? I am free.'

He springs to his feet and the stool clatters across the floorboards, coming to rest by the brazier. 'You forget yourself. I am Inquisitor of France. I am Royal Confessor to Philippe le Bel. And you? A beguine. From Valenciennes. A false woman.' He looks me up and down in my bespattered red dress. 'You are *nothing*.'

I take a step towards him. 'I am.'

26

Grand Châtelet,
Sunday after Ascension 1310

MY HAIR is a bird's nest. Flecks of blossom have ensnared themselves in it. To my fingertips my cheeks feel striated like the bark of an ancient apple tree. All afternoon, my eyes remained mulishly dry but lying here, belly down in my mildewed straw, my lids want to close and shut out the world as if coins already weigh them down. Except my body won't have eyes when I'm dead. I'll have no body.

Every inch of my flesh stings, though no one pelted me in the streets. The Parisian mob lapped like a cold, calm sea against the edges of our gaudy little procession. Doubtless tomorrow will be stormier.

After the constable dropped me down in the tower room, he pushed a steaming bowl inside the door. The smell of the rich gravy is making my stomach lurch. *Freed souls have neither shame nor fear for aught that happens to them*—words I once poured out with confidence line up in my muddled head to taunt me. Right on cue, Madame Reason bobs up and carries me away on her raft of 'if onlys'.

If only you'd sworn the oath.

If only you'd let Adélie and Alain hide you.

If only you'd drowned in the hermitage pool instead of tomorrow's—

How long have they been there, at the edge of my bed? Two sandals filled with dusty toes. It strains my neck to see who has come to gloat over the *pseudo-mulier*. The Prior of Couvent Saint-Jacques is staring down on me.

'Some wine.' He places a flagon at my feet. His spotless palms reach out, his face cluttered with anxieties. 'Marguerite, I am so sorry.' His hands scurry back under cover of his scapular. 'Did I not warn you about Brother Guillaume? Father Jacques of Notre-Dame de Macourt—'

'Jacquot?' I'm on my knees, grasping folds of the prior's robes. 'You've seen him? Does he know?' But of course, he can't know. Not yet. It will all be over long before tidings reach Valenciennes. 'What do *you* know of Father Jacques?'

The prior is waiting for me to release his habit. I let go and he takes his place on the inquisitor's stool.

'Brother Guillaume despatched men to the Charterhouse. He suspected they might harbour a copy of your treatise. Mistakenly it seems.'

Jacquot is safe! That's all I needed to know.

'Why did you not confess? Why remain so stubborn and refuse the mercy of Christ's Church?'

Like the reeds beside the Ointiel when the winter northerlies blow, I'm trembling. The prior's temper subsides. Reaching out again, he touches my hand, his flesh so soft, his smell so clean. 'Marguerite, I'm here to save your soul. Put aside your conceit. If only you say the word, I've been given leave to grant you absolution. At this late hour, pray mercy.'

'Mercy?' He can have his hand back. 'You tempt me with the mercy of strangulation?'

'Spare yourself the agony. Not only of the executioner's pyre. Without absolution you will suffer the eternal torments of Hell.'

'Hell?' Fury sluices my brain and like pure lye brings dazzling clarity. 'Holy Church believes the woman who fed me love with her milk is burning in Hell. And my little one, merely a babe, the Doctors cannot even agree. Is he in Hell, or not?'

'Do you not grasp, Marguerite, I'm here to help you? I pray you, confess your errors. *Even murderers will have Paradise should they cry "Mercy".* You wrote that. Now, tell me where copies of your *Mirror* are secreted.'

'Ha! This was always your mission. Weren't you in the Place de Grève this afternoon?' An army of clerics formed up on the gravel square, surely the whole Dominican priory, to witness their triumph. Yet I don't remember Guillot de Saint-Euverce's face amongst them, and I hadn't expected, after the sentence was read out, I could be any more shocked. But then they brought out many more manuscripts than my own pen produced. 'Did you not watch them cast a pile of parchments into the bonfire?

'Contagion must be eradicated before it spreads. More searches will be made. The inquisitor is not satisfied your brother is entirely without guilt.'

Thank God for Bertrand. And thanks to Jacquot, I won't have to pull off a lie about the phoenix copy. I truly do not know where he has hidden it.

'Marguerite, you can be saved. Separate not your soul from God.'

'*Naught can separate us from the love of God.*'

'You quote the Scriptures? At me?'

'If I, wretch that I am, will not abandon the ones I love to Hades, what of God? The apostle said, *Even though I give my body to be burned and have not love…*'

'You think yourself a martyr?' His voice is rising. He's failing to tidy bits of me away into drawers labelled "Saved", "Absolved", "Job Well Done". He pushes back the stool and folds away his hands. 'Holy Church will not be mocked.'

I collapse back on the straw. I can't tell, is the sound coming out of me laughter or keening?

'So be it. You had every opportunity to acknowledge your errors. Of your own free will you will go to eternal damnation.'

A stillness descends on me but my heart is churning. Words come out, smooth and coherent and fresh to myself. 'If it is of my own free will that I go to eternal damnation and you Preachers say it is also God's will that I go to eternal damnation, do you not grasp it? God and I are in full accord. Our will is one.'

The man who refuses to acknowledge he is in error goes away. The solid clarity I had in my head a few seconds ago flips back into confusion.

MY MADDER-RED HEM hangs on by an obstinate thread. On the way back to the Châtelet this afternoon my remaining boot fell away. The climb will be excruciating but a long draft from Prior Guillot's flagon will help.

The last drops of May sun bleed crimson into the sky beyond the western loop of the Seine. Sitting up here, I might be back *à la porée*, the Rose walled into her tower, looking out across Paris from my lonely bedchamber, before I knew the man I would love; before I knew he would not wake each morning of my life on the pillow beside me; before I knew I'd never suckle his child at my breast, never dandle our grandchildren on my knee.

I'd have liked to climb the twin oaks once more with Jacquot and…Ah! Now I know. Without any doubt, Jacquot has tucked the phoenix in amongst the shards of blue ceramic. Oh Jacquot. I'll never look into your beautiful eyes again. Before I break apart, I must thank God for Bertrand;

by now he must have made it to Marlis. How blessed I have been with love.

A fluttering sound disturbs the quiet of evening. A pair of house martins have been nesting in the rafters. The male bird flaps past and in the setting sun his throat shimmers golden like Saint Louis' thread. 'Fly, little bird.' He darts down to the riverbank where it all began, where it will all end. This time tomorrow, not a scrap of me will exist in this place. Although that does not mean I will not exist some place else.

My breaking apart begins.

TO ABANDON YOU was not my will.

Your eyes burned into my soul, demanding I take the child to safety.

It was not my will that you abandon me when I was yet a child myself.

You look at me now, in this moment, and I see myself in the mirror of your calm eyes.

I know why you have come.

27

Paris, 1st June 1310

THE SHADOWS at the bottom of the hermitage pool rippled over the surface of the water. Creatures murmured at the limit of my earshot. If only now it was the tall hornbeams swaying over my head and not the motion of men's limbs reflected in the limewash. Their graveyard babbling is pierced not by the *kars* of a jackdaw but by hoots of anticipation carrying in through the arrow loops.

I want to shrink into my squalid corner of the guardroom, away from the rack holding the kind of implements you'd find in a barn. And from the two gens-d'armes. One of them takes up the double-pronged pitchfork.

A clink of metal and the door opens from the inner baily. The June sun burns my scalp before any fire is lit and the wound the constable made with his shears is weeping.

By now the wax of my tablet will have melted onto the ledge in this blazing heat. No one shall ever read my last words. No matter. My story is written into the fabric of the universe, and She knows my voice as the tree knows the song of the wind.

The constable throws a man onto the flagstones. Cramp rips through my bowels, but there's nothing left inside me to expel. The man sprawling on the ground has a head shorn like mine; his brow is mangled, his beard torn out of his jaw, but I know him. It's… His name drops off the edge of my mind before I can catch hold of it.

The older guard yanks me up by the elbow; doubtless a bird dangling from a poacher's belt feels like this. He addresses the silent man with the bullish neck, the mountain of boiled leather piled onto the stool by the main door. Thévenot.

'All bravado she was,' the guard says, 'till now.'

'The old girl's got spirit, for sure.' Thévenot's voice contains thunder which might be unleashed at any moment.

'Are we walking them or taking the cart?'

Thévenot addresses the constable who is dwarfed by the executioner's presence. 'Did she walk from her cell?'

'Aye,' says the constable. 'No torture. Though she's had a mighty flogging to her scrawny back at some point. You know what they say. Once a miscreant…'

I inch my toes across the rutted stone. Who are you, man crawling towards me on your belly? I must reach you. I know you're my friend. I put out a hand but the daylight is blotted out. Thévenot has risen from his seat. 'Chop, chop. They'll be here in a—' The outer door of the fortress swings open. The clamour of the crowd rushes in.

A cope of red and gold comes swishing across the flags at us. The collar stands up, stiff with carnelians and above it, the soused hog's head of Guillaume de Baufet, Bishop of Paris.

Another dignitary enters. The door bangs shut behind him and my legs crumble. The executioner's armful of hard muscle hooks around my neck, keeping me on my feet, trapping my skin tight across my cheekbones, so my eyes angle upwards and all I can see is the Inquisitor of Heretical Depravity for the Kingdom of France.

Tetchily the bishop says, 'You'll have to keep them both upright out there.'

'Do not fret yourself, my lord. All will go off as it should.'

'I've every confidence in you, Thévenot. What's the formation?'

A throat clears itself. 'Clergy, behind the Cross of course. Followed by you, my lord.'

'Brother Guillaume, your efforts here,' the bishop flourishes a gloved hand at me and my crawling friend, 'are puissant vindication of your reinstatement. Jews, Templars, defiant beguines. You've excelled yourself with every colour of deviant heretic. Son of merchantry or no, I always counted you noteworthy. You must walk alongside me today.'

'My lord.' The inquisitor doesn't look at me. He bows, presenting the bishop with his crozier; the gilded Lamb of God glistens at the head of the shepherd's crook. 'The provost leads off first with the men of the city—'

'Where in God's name is the provost?' bellows the bishop.

A gruff voice answers from the door of the baily, 'Ready, my lord. Shall we be gone?'

Thévenot has released his hold on me. He kneels and while the bishop shrives him of culpability for what he must do to us, the man who is my friend tries to speak with a mouth so broken I can't grasp what he's saying.

The dignitaries exeunt. *Kar, kar. Kar, kar.*

Clenching his fists, Lucas circles around Oshaya. That's it. His name is Oshaya. I must get close to Oshaya. 'Dirty Jew.' Spittle froths on the lad's downy chin. 'Dirty, fucking, Christ-killing Jew.'

A growl from Thévenot. 'Let's keep things calm, shall we?'

'Been too much excitement for the boy,' says the older guard. 'All these burnings.'

'Lucas,' Thévenot says, 'the little woman may need carrying at some point. You keep by her, in case.'

'Me?'

'There'll be an extra gros in it for you.'

The older guard kicks Oshaya. 'What about him?'

'He'll draw the spite,' Thévenot says. 'And there's plenty of it. Paris has had its fill of Christians being roasted alive.'

'The Templars are thieving scum.'

'There's been a lot of mumbling in the tavern,' Thévenot says.

'They're filthy Sodomites. Devil worshippers.'

'People are asking why they didn't confess.'

'Which is why they're burning in Hell right now.' The guard hawks and spits his phlegm onto dear Oshaya. Still my hand can't reach him. 'And this afternoon, these two are gonna be down there with their mates from Gringoire's.'

A roaring noise in my ears. Oshaya's unclosed eye stares at me. 'Bertrand?' I whisper. The eye closes. Oh God, not Bertrand. No. Not Bertrand. 'Pons?' The roaring gets up inside of me, outside of me. I lunge and grab at Oshaya's knobbly fingers, desperate to keep hold of them.

Thévenot pulls me by the chin, away from Oshaya. 'Come, my ladyship. You've to trust in me now.' He cradles my head and puts a vial to my lips. The smell of crushed petals. I'm going to vomit. He forces me to swallow the thick liquor. 'It won't take long. I chose the best wood myself.'

How can my mind do that? I didn't even know I had the memory, yet it's so vivid, of Jacquot crouching by the hearth, knee poking through his hose. *It won't take long.* Jacquot...You were meant to be safe...Bertrand? The world is fading. The bitterness is fading. Pain is fading. The roaring fades and the ripples in the limewash melt into golden light...

FIERCE SUN. Persistent *karring*. I still exist on earth.

A scream. 'Burn the Jew.'

The old guard tugs on the strap in his hand and Oshaya crashes to his poor knees. Pain rushes in. I want to stop the clods of filth from hitting my friend. 'Lord, have mercy,' I cry and a punch in the small of my back knocks black bile out of my mouth. It sits like an oil slick on the pavement.

'Let her be, lad.' Thévenot's breath on my ear. 'Halfway there.' His voice is steady, soothing. My executioner has become as a buttress to me, the only human I can touch; my hand reaches for the strength of his leathern palm.

The gilded Cross of Christ sways before the towers of Notre-Dame.

'Marguerite.' A man's voice calling, 'Marguerite.' Beneath the *échelle de justice*, amongst the seething bodies, a royal guard, his hand drawn high above his shoulder. 'Been looking forward to this, I have.' He hesitates while Thévenot passes by but as Hébert launches his missile, out of nowhere a fist comes smashing into his jaw. Bloody gobbets fly and he flails, he topples, he scatters people like ninepins. All the faces around him are wrecked with grief. I don't want to latch onto the sympathy in their eyes, treacherous sympathy, softening me when I need to be hard like a stone. Stones don't burn, stones can't breathe, but my lungs keep on filling.

The Cross of Christ advances.

'Carry her over the bridge, then she can walk across the Grève.'

Lucas swings me up onto his shoulder. A girlchild is waving and smiling at me as if she would be known to the woman on show to all of Paris.

'That's it, good lad.'

Lucas grunts; a flush across his cheek, beautiful, like parchment stained with red ink and painted over with gold filigree.

The girl has been swallowed up in the crowd.

'*Pater noster, qui es in caelis…*' A thousand voices, two thousand voices, more, chant the Our Father. The words reverberate through the lad's living bones, pressing into my soon-to-be-dead bones.

'*Libera nos a malos…*' The crucifer lifts high the Cross and the '*Amen*' sends a thunderclap around the Place de Grève. The clergy are ascending a timber staircase and the world stops.

A stripped rood has been hammered into the gravel.

Terror.

Peace.

The two indistinguishable.

Untrammelled nothingness.

'*Eloi, Eloi.*' Oshaya was so long silent I thought he was already dead but his cry of desolation has dragged me back into this place and this time.

For Thévenot I am a feather to lift. Over his ox-blood shoulder the clerics ooze around the edges of my vision and I cling to my executioner. My finger-ends slide down the polished hide.

Pungent and resinous in the sunshine the wood hurtles me back into the glades of Mormal, where I pressed my skin against the coarse bark of the black elder, stripped of all things, and I heard the Far-Near One say:

I am the All. What do you want of Me, My Beloved?

And I responded, *I am Pure Nothing, so how can I will any thing?*

And of a sudden, He filled me with Himself.

'People of Paris,' the voice of Brother Guillaume falls from on high, 'hear the judgment against these two heretics.'

The iron links are a cold belt tight across my breast. Oshaya, behind me, is silent again. If I could stretch back, I could touch his hand…just with one finger…yes. The ancient roots.

'Their depravity cannot be permitted to infect God's holy people. For this reason, Oshaya, perfidious Jew, and Marguerite of Valenciennes, false woman, you deserve and shall receive no mercy.'

I petitioned for none. For there is none in your heart, Guillaume de Paris, not even for yourself. Especially not for yourself.

The Dominican, whose will is about to be done, disappears behind the bishop's cope. Lord Guillaume de Baufet stretches out his arms in prayer and for one shimmering moment, he looks like Maman's seraph. He will not save my life. Not today.

All is hushed except my breath, insistent, unaware it has to stop, still pushing in, out, in and out. Barge sails like ivory clouds hang motionless over the green silk ribbon of the Seine, waiting to be filled with the breeze which will propel them to the ocean where all rivers lose their names and become one.

Oshaya screams.

The serpent is at my heel. He injects his venom. I still have a tongue to speak of the Far-Near One. 'You are the Fire. You are Love. You and I are one.'

28

June 1310

LIGHT cutting through the golden foliage stripes the soft forest floor. Where the oaks peter out, Moreau slows Gäelle to a walk. Reining her in, he brushes sweat from his eyelids and focuses on the line where the river divides the meadow, north from south. Above the neat white turrets a dark grey tide is rolling in from the east. Why, in Christ's name, did he agree to this?

He strokes the mare's neck. 'Come on, girl. Let's get it over with.' He's surprised to find grit still in his belly, the capacity he's always had to get the unpleasant job done. Earned him recognition at Girona. Proud days. He touches his scar to his lips.

Generous splashes of rain drip from the palfrey's mane and he wraps his mantle around his saddlebag. They canter between the strips of green barley and by the time the gatehouse opens to them, the cloudburst has rinsed away the dust of the Paris road.

THANK CHRIST the prior let him find his own way to the cloister. The odour of the puddled flagstones made him suddenly aware of the Hellish thirst he's been trying to slake for a week. Slumped heavily against the limewashed wall he loosens the collar of his gambeson. He shoulders his pack and presses on into the quadrangle, across the slippery lawn.

Distracted by the unusual oak, its twin trunks perfectly intertwined, he almost walks into the pillar at the entrance to the covered passageway. Along the inner wall, the sturdy doors are set back under arched frames.

Fourth door down, the prior said. Assuming it won't open easily, he pushes hard. The door gives and he stumbles down a step into a dim corridor. At one end is an arc of light.

Sun slicing through the mullioned window creates a sharp diagonal line across the chamber. Low down in the obscurity, like a sewer rat, Monk-boy is hiding. Slumped over the armrest of his prie-dieu it looks like someone has glued his pate to the parquet floor. The unhealed scabs on Moreau's knuckles itch but as the monk struggles to his feet, his instinct is to go to his aid. He's seen bodies struggle like that, soldiers who've fought a brutal war, but he can't trust himself not to throttle Father Fucking Jacques.

'For God's sake, you've already searched every inch of my cell. What makes you think you'll find what you're looking for this time?' Monk-boy's eyes flit for an instant in the direction of the quadrangle and then he stands, yards of habit hanging off his skeleton.

It takes Moreau a moment to grasp why Father Jacques is glaring at his chest—his gambeson is open, showing the fleur-de-lys on his tunic. His mind rushes through his half-baked plan to ride further north when he's made an end to all this. Take ship. Sell himself to Robert de Brus. Never had himself down as a *routier* and the thought of it makes his guts ache but what else does he know? He drops his saddlebag. 'I'm not here on the king's business.'

The monk glances at the desk. A creased leaf of vellum lies opened out. 'Are you the one who…?' He scrutinises Moreau more intensely. 'Aye. It's you. You're the one who took her to Paris.'

'And I was there, in Paris, to watch her die.' He gets a jab of pleasure, watching Monk-boy crawl on all fours to his pallet. Pulling a small package out of his saddlebag, he throws it on the blanket next to his pathetic face.

Father Jacques snatches up the calfskin wallet and holds it to his nose. He smells it, like a starving man who's about to take his last breath and is thrown a crust of bread. Inspecting the braid, he turns his ridiculously large eyes on Moreau. 'She'd never have tied it so clumsily. You've read it.'

He is judging *me?* Father Jacques, who was holed up in this place the day she— On the day they did *that* to her? When he, Moreau, had to get blind drunk with Alain and next thing he knew, he was waking up in La Tête Noire thinking the roof had fallen in on his head. Like Satan with a hammer, one thought splitting open his brains: *What if I'd been the one who had to carry her?*

Monk-boy already has the bulky knot untied and the folios spread out on the bed. He lets out a groan, 'She calls me "the king's man"?'

All the way from Saint-Denis, Moreau has imagined how much he would enjoy watching this traitorous brother of hers squirm. He wants to punish the bastard. But just look at him, with his gaunt cheeks and his tortured eyes.

'Margi hated me in the end. I don't blame her. But…she was passionate about truth. All she's written here, it's not quite right. It's her hand, I grant you, but it's not…*her*.' Jacques closes his eyes, bracing himself. 'When you last saw her, when she gave you this letter…I imagine she wasn't in her right mind?'

'She didn't give me the letter.'

The unbearable eyes flick open. 'Then how did you come by it?'

Moreau isn't going to confess the part he played in herding five men into the field outside Porte Antoine. It's like a recurring nightmare. He keeps seeing the circle of scorched earth where fifty Templar brothers had perished a few weeks before, the vibrant grass already growing back only to be turned black again. And the tall knight who knew Moreau's name.

'A Templar Brother. Don't know his name. He must have shared a prison cell with your sister.' Moreau glances at his saddlebag. He pictures her hands working at the stitching, the tiny hands which held him when, like a festering wound, he was open to the world. The cloth was on the desk when she gently stroked his hair and he doesn't want to part with it. But there's no going back. He made a vow to a dying man and this time, he's no child. 'The Templar said I should also give you this.'

In the post-storm glare, the thread of gold sparkles. Jacques leaps up. 'Michel's coverlet?'

Michel. The name she breathed into Moreau's ear the night he watched her sleeping so peacefully. Father Jacques grabs the cloth from him and laughs. The filthy whoreson actually throws back his head and laughs. Moreau grabs him by the throat and Monk-boy crumples like a dead cony dropped in a sack. The bastard is still laughing! His right hand clenches and the scabs across his knuckles split.

'Oh Margi. She asked why I was singing. I knew she'd hear me from her little stone seat. I was singing for you, Margi, I was singing for you.' He kisses the seraph. 'And you didn't know. You didn't know your *Mirror* had already saved me.'

The ground shifts beneath Moreau. His legs trample around, trying to get a foothold, like the time when he fell into the Middle Sea and the waters were going to take him and he could no longer struggle against the waves, and he let go. Hervi's strong arm had grasped him and pulled him to safety.

And now, somehow, he doesn't quite know how, but he, Moreau, is the one holding on. He's holding onto Father Jacques and Jacques' hands cling to the padding of his gambeson.

'I was singing for you, Margi, I was singing for you.'

Moreau drags the wreck of a man onto the pallet. He has a strong urge to stroke his hair but he lays his scarred hand on Jacquot's shoulder. 'Tell me about Margi.'

The parchment folios float to the ground. They land with the last page facing upwards.

If we never meet again on God's good earth, know that I choose this path willingly. When you have swum in the Sea of Joy, there is no going back.

THE HIDDEN MIRROR OF LA PORETE

AUTHOR'S NOTE

NOTHING certain is known about the life of Marguerite Porete, only about her death. The records of her trial, and later chronicles which refer to her execution in the Place de Grève on 1st June 1310, fail to mention the name of the 'heretical' book she authored. Yet despite this book being a banned text, historian Robert E. Lerner wrote in 2010, 'it appears as if dozens of copies...were bobbing up continually in the seas of late-medieval western Europe like unsinkable corks.'

It wasn't until 1946 that medievalist Romana Guarnieri made the astonishing discovery that the text Marguerite Porete was condemned for by the Inquisitor of France was none other than the anonymous *Mirror of Simple Souls*. It seems remarkable, then, that two decades before this, Clare Kirchberger's modern English translation of the treatise was published by the Downside monks and given the formal Church approvals.

Engaging with *The Mirror* was the jumping off point for imagining and re-creating Marguerite's life. However, I've kept as close to known historical facts as possible. Although she may have been an itinerant beguine, she was called Marguerite of Hainault and Marguerite of Valenciennes in records, so I placed her home in that city (I've used the old names Ointiel and Marlis for the River Rhônelle and Marly, respectively; and there really was a provost called Jean le Vilain!). The extent of Porete's theological and scriptural knowledge suggests she came from a wealthy family, even perhaps from the minor nobility, books becoming at that time more accessible for women of high social status.

Some of the fictional characters in my novel are inspired by historical events. The characterisation for Jacques, for example, was born from two sources. In 1292, during the war with Count Jan d'Avesnes II, a well-respected man called Jacquemon Seywars gave a rousing speech to the people of Valenciennes who feared standing against their lord. Secondly, *The Mirror* was twice translated into Middle English by Charterhouse monks. In the extant Middle English manuscripts are found the clearest examples of the 'approval' from three theologians, which was to assure the reader of the treatise's soundness. The three were Jehan de Quérénaing, Dom Franco

of Villers Abbey and the much better known, Master Godfrey de Fontaines.
Documents pertaining to Porete's trial, and that of Guiard de
Cressonessart, were found in the collected papers of William de Nogaret
and William of Plaisians—two royal advisers who played a huge role in the
process against the Templars (1307-1314). Scholars agree there must have
been a strong link between these legal cases . Professor Sean Field's analysis
of the political tensions surrounding the Templar affair and the Avignon
papacy in *The Beguine, The Angel and The Inquisitor* (Notre-Dame, 2012) is
compelling. It seems plausible that a high-flying churchman such as
Guillaume Humbert would be desperate to regain his status with the Pope
after being used, even if willingly, by Philippe IV as the fall-guy for his
machinations. Alain Demurger's excellent *La Persécution des Templiers* (Payot
& Rivages, 2015) is a deep dive into the daily practicalities of the relentless
persecution of hundreds of brothers, kept under arrest from October 1307
until the dissolving of the Order in 1312. He supplies details of the
resistance put up by the Templars and informs what I have subjected my
characters to.

Although it may seem Marguerite is a mere footnote to this history, her
impact on the Christian Church in Europe was significant. The Council of
Vienne (1311-1312) was a watershed moment. The main item on the agenda
was to suppress the Templar Order but the Council also cracked down on
the so-called 'heresy of the free spirit'. Although there was no organised
movement of believers, excerpts from Porete's *Mirror*, robbed of their
context, were used to delineate the tenets of what the Church saw as a
'gnostic' heresy. Amongst those who suffered from the Council's 'reforms'
were evangelical women like the beguines who had been living an
unenclosed life, preaching the Gospel, and educating girls.

Porete's message almost certainly influenced mystic and theologian
Meister Eckhart (d.1328) who lived at Couvent Saint-Jacques in Paris in
1311 contemporaneously with Guillaume Humbert. Also, we can see from
the writings of reformer queen Marguerite of Navarre (d.1516) that she
knew of the beguine's fate and the contents of *The Mirror*.

In only two instances have I knowingly taken liberties with the facts:
Philippe de Marigny, Bishop of Cambrai, probably interviewed Marguerite
in 1308—uncertainty over whether this meeting actually happened
presented the opportunity to reduce an already large cast of ecclesiastical
characters. Secondly, the background I gave to the unnamed Jewish man
who accompanied her to the stake rests on evidence that moneylenders
were readmitted to France several years after their expulsion to help royal

officials with debt collection. However, the legislation for this practice is dated 1315 and though it may have happened earlier, we have no record of it.

There are two complete flights of imagination in my story:

Although 'Porete' could well have been a nickname, the suggestion that it derived from wordplay on the name of eleventh century theologian Gilbert de la Porrée and *porée* (meaning leek in Middle French) is pure invention. And as far as I am aware, there was no cult surrounding the relic of Christ's blood at Abbaye Saint-Jean in Valenciennes, though there were of course many such relics in medieval Europe. Valenciennes was, and is to this day, famous for its veneration of *Notre Dame du Saint Cordon*. On September 8th every year, the Blessèd Virgin, holding the holy cord, is borne on a raft around the city.

See www.shooterspen.com for more information.

HISTORICAL CHARACTERS

VALENCIENNES

Marguerite, called Porete, writer, beguine, mystic (d. 1st June 1310)

Saint Elizabeth's beguinage
Cécile de Nimy, Maîtresse of Saint Elizabeth's infirmary
Mahaut, beguine and later Souveraine
Ermengarde d'Aubenton, beguine and later Souveraine
Jeanne de Bavay, beguine and later Souveraine

Salle-le-Comte
Marguerite II, Countess of Flanders & Hainault (1202-1280)
Guy de Dampierre, Count of Flanders, her son (1225-1305)
Robert de Béthune, Guy's son, aka the Lion of Flanders (1249-1322)
Marie de Dampierre, Guy's daughter (d.1297)
Philippine of Luxembourg, Countess of Hainault (1252-1311)
Jan d'Avesnes II, Count of Hainault, her husband (1247-1304)

Clerics
Nicolas de Gerpinnes, Curé of St Elizabeth's (c.1276-1303)
Pierron Douchart, Prior of Notre-Dame de Macourt from 1297
Dom Alard, Abbot of Hasnon from 1301
Guido da Collemezzo, Bishop of Cambrai (1296-1306)

Provosts of Valenciennes
Amand de le Sauch (1279-1283)
Renier Faumin (1289-1292)
Jacques/Jakemon le Père (1293 and 1296)
Simon du Gardin (1304 and 1307)
Jean le Vilain (1305 and 1308)

PARIS

Godfrey de Fontaines, Regent Master of Theology (d.1306 or 1309)
Guiard de Cressonessart, beghard and supporter of Marguerite
Jean de Châteauvillain, Bishop of Châlons (1285 to 1313)
Guillaume Humbert/de Paris, Inquisitor of France, Confessor to Philippe IV (d.1314)
Guillot de Saint-Euverce, Prior of Couvent Saint Jacques (c.1307)
Guillaume de Baufet, Bishop of Paris (1305 to 1319)
Jehan de Quérénaing, Franciscan friar
Oshaya, Jewish prisoner (his real name is absent from the record)

ACKNOWLEDGEMENTS

COMPLETING this novel has been a long journey and there are many people who have helped me along the way: historians and academics who generously shared their knowledge with me; friends and family who have supported me.

I am deeply grateful to Professor Sean Field who answered many emails and supplied me with information on the Templars, Couvent Saint-Jacques, and Marguerite herself. The competent and helpful staff in the *'patrimoine'* section at the public library in Rue Ferrand, Valenciennes were marvellous, allowing me access to medieval documents connected with Saint Elizabeth's beguinage.

Other experts who answered my questions via email or social media: Dr Thomas Hinton of Exeter University on the Old French text of the *Mirror*; Dr Jessica Marin Elliott of Missouri State University on Jewish moneylenders in medieval France; the Fitzwilliam Museum in Cambridge on medieval coinage; Historian Dan Jones on the Templars; and Professor Kelly De Vries of Loyola University Maryland on medieval ranks and military structures. Thanks are also due to Shakespeare & Co in Rue de la Bûcherie who told me about the ancient spaces found during renovations beneath their 16th century cellars.

There are many friends who have read one or more drafts of my manuscript throughout its many incarnations. Thank you, all. I must particularly mention my late friend, Ros Eastman who, with Porete-like passion, encouraged me to soldier on when I was ready to give up; likewise Franki Anderson, drama teacher, who helped me find my 'voice'; Franki and her partner Ray generously allowed me to stay for two fortnight stretches at their unique, sacred space, The Quarry, which overlooks the Atlantic. I'm also grateful to our friends Sue and Peter Twynam who hosted me for a three-week period in Boscombe when I was facing the daunting task of a fundamental redraft of the manuscript.

Bridget Holding of www.wildwords.org was a great encouragement in helping me make the transition from academic writing to fiction. Andrew Noakes at www.thehistoryquill.com guided me through two major redrafts. Thanks also to Jonathan Oliver who copy-edited the text, and my friend Emma White who generously gave of her time to do a final proof-read.

The stunning cover design was created by graphic designer Ken Dawson of www.ccovers.co.uk. And the neat little logo for our imprint *Hurlestone Books* was created by Kayleigh Shooter of www.kdscalligraphy.co.uk who, apart from being my lovely daughter-in-law, is a skilled calligrapher.

My journey with Marguerite Porete began during my PhD research fifteen years ago and I have dedicated this novel to the nine courageous and faithful women who bared their souls to me about surviving awful experiences of abuse. Their stories led me deeper into *The Mirror*. Consequently, there have been some dark moments through which my spiritual director, Canon Gordon Oliver, and my priestly colleague, Rev Dr Adam Carlill, have been solid allies. I can't thank them enough for their companionship.

In the preface to my book *How Survivors of Abuse Relate to God* I wrote that it was my husband who provided me with time and space to think and write: 'Only he knows how costly the research journey has been, because he has shared the storms. Yet he has remained my best friend'—words which bear repeating now and thank you, Ian, that you are still my best friend, the one in this world who understands me most, even when I am a mystery to myself.

Printed in Great Britain
by Amazon

63343401R00153